Dark Iris

Winter 2018

KAREN TAYLOR

Published in the UK in 2023

Copyright Karen Taylor 2023
ISBN 978-1-3999-6912-3

Cover illustration: Janine Wing
Cover layout: Cavan Convery

Karen Taylor has asserted her right to be identified as the author of this Work in accordance with the CPDA 1988.

Printed and bound by Imprint Academic, Devon.

For Yvonne

There is no darkness but ignorance.

Feste to Malvolio, Twelfth Night, act 4, scene 2.
William Shakespeare.

1

Brandon

Stones rained down like a meteor shower, bouncing off the cliff face, glancing Brandon Hammett's face. But he held onto the soggy trainer which squirmed in his hand like a fish, the guy's other foot doing all the damage, kicking sharp pebbles and clumps of turf at him.

Brandon could smell blood, feel it slipping down his cheek where one of the stones had made contact. He clamped his mouth shut, didn't want to lose a tooth – didn't want to lose an eye. Was the bloke ever going to give up?

The nutter was halfway up a cliff, fifty feet from certain death on the rocks below, with a copper hanging off his foot.

Where the hell was Phillips? He was meant to be at the top, taser ready to wave in the bastard's face if it emerged. The guy's free foot kept on kicking, the other shaking and twisting and then jolting in triumph as it pulled free.

Brandon lunged at the bottom of the man's trousers, but the sodden material slipped through his hands. He lunged again, grabbing the ankle beneath, squeezing it hard, making the guy yelp and jerk. The sudden movement threw Brandon off balance and the two of them tumbled onto the wider ledge below.

The guy was on top of him now, one hand forcing his head over the edge. Brandon could see the sharp drop, knew he had to flip him. As Brandon heaved himself over, the man grabbed something. A rock? The lump of turf smashed down on his face, making him loosen his grip just enough for the guy to pull away. Shaking dirt from his eyes, Brandon made a grab for a foot, but it kicked away, and he was left with one filthy trainer. He slipped it in his jacket pocket. Could be the sprat to catch his mackerel if this farce ever came to court.

He wiped his sleeve across his eyes, blinking and straining for vision. In the moonlight it was difficult to gauge the man's age, but he was agile, that's for sure. At thirty-five, Brandon wasn't the fittest cop in town. Winded from the chase, the climb, and the tussle he could only watch as the perp scrambled to the top, levered himself up over the edge and sprung to his feet.

Brandon moved to the edge of the ledge and leaned back for a better view. The guy was legging it now, as lithe as a panther in his black clothes and balaclava. Phillips was nowhere to be seen. Menhenrick was after him though, but too far back – she'd never catch him.

'Leave it, Jo,' he called. But she didn't. He knew she wouldn't. And he watched as she pounded the clifftop, her red hair aflame in the light of the moon.

Brandon steadied himself against the cold rock. His hands were covered in blood, not just from the gash to his head, but also the sharp edges he'd grabbed in his frantic ascent. He was more measured as he felt his way down, taking his time, his feet finding foot holes, his hands reaching for support – a gnarled root, a mossy crevice – jumping the last few feet onto the sandy beach.

Reaching into his pocket, he pulled out his torch and shone it at the sea. He'd seen something floating in the shallows before taking chase. It didn't look like it was going anywhere fast. The sea was calm, the incoming tide edging its sly delivery into the tiny cove. His small hesitation while he clocked the details could have cost him the race across the beach to the cliff face. Or, perhaps, he should get to the gym more.

Someone called his name, and he looked up to see DS Menhenrick and PC Phillips staring at him. He beckoned them down.

Turning to the three plastic barrels bumping against the rocks, he leaned over and pulled one onto the sand. There'd been a tip-off about the drop and what was in the barrels – and it wasn't bottles of rum. He turned the stopper, yanked it out and felt inside, pulling out one neat white packet. Making a small incision with his Swiss Army Knife, he confirmed his suspicions. Cocaine. There had to be fifty packs in the barrel: worth something on the street. Brandon was lugging the other barrels out of the water when he heard the chatter of Jo and Phillips as they dropped down into the cove from the rock steps.

'As expected, Boss?' wheezed the plump PC, coming alongside him.

Brandon gave Phillips a long hard look. 'Where were you? You let our man escape. Although …' He pulled the trainer from his pocket. 'I may give you the chance to find our Cinderella. Make some door-to-door calls. Have you got an evidence bag on you for this?'

Of course, he hadn't.

'I was in the carpark waiting for him to show. There was a transit parked there.'

Jo took the trainer from Brandon and slipped it into a plastic bag.

'But he didn't show, did he? I take it you've got photos of the van? Made a check on ownership?'

'Yes, Boss.'

So not completely useless, then.

'Our man ran off through the fields towards the A30. I put

a call through to the station,' Jo said, sealing the evidence bag. 'Told them to get a patrol car out. We could get lucky.'

'Good work, Jo. Looks like someone else's luck ran out this morning, though.' Brandon looked down at the barrels. 'It would have taken a bit of effort to get this cargo delivered. The loss will sting.'

They picked up a barrel each and started to walk back towards the cliff steps.

'Any idea who the grass is?' Jo was looking at him as if he had all the answers.

'Ideas, yes. But not ones I'm on first-name terms with. A … Nonymous.' Brandon paused. 'Maybe a rival supplier?'

'Why send for us, then?'

'Good question. Perhaps they didn't have the resources to pick this up themselves tonight. Maybe they just wanted to teach someone a lesson. Clear them off their patch.' He stopped walking, readjusted his load. 'Odd that there was just one man – considering there are three barrels. Perhaps someone was tipped off about the tip-off?'

'That would make sense,' Jo said, looking up at him. 'These aren't light.'

Brandon considered the barrel in his arms – maybe it had been dropped at sea and allowed to drift into the cove on the tide. An old smuggler's trick. Or perhaps the boat had been intercepted and the cargo ditched.

He looked up at the sky, saw a few streaks of pink filtering through the black.

'Let's get these tubs back up the steps and into the car.'

* * * * *

Phillips drove them the ten miles back to Penzance. The streets were filling up with workers and delivery trucks heading out of town, rough sleepers rolling up bedding in the bus shelter, a stray sniffing for leftovers in the promenade gardens.

'Wow. They've gone to town this year.' Jo was pointing at a tower of wood on the Quay, the sun rising behind it.

'The Montol bonfire? For the Solstice?' Phillips asked, slowing down to look.

Brandon was impressed. They'd stacked the timber high – fifteen feet or more of it dominated the Quay.

He asked Phillips to pull up beside it, so they could get out for a better look. The wood was piled vertically, leaning inwards, a wigwam of timber. There was no security around it. No barriers. The festival organisers didn't much bother the police – it was a given that people would act responsibly. Brandon smiled – it was what he liked about Penzance, the absence of intrusive health and safety. But he did fear for the day when this trust would be abused.

He flinched at the screech of a gull circling above; thought, for a moment, that it was a siren. But no, too early for that. If their guy had been picked up, the patrol car wouldn't be announcing it at 7am.

'Let's get out of here,' he said. But as the others got back in the car, Brandon turned round for another look at the pyre. He rubbed his eyes. The sunrise was messing with its colours, the wood flesh-pink in places, dark red in others.

He hadn't been to the Montol for a good few years. Tonight looked like it might be the night to revisit an old tradition.

2

Rachel

Shadows were lengthening in St Mary's Churchyard when the bells chimed four. It was the Winter Solstice, the shortest day of the year, and Rachel Matthews was sitting on a bench dedicated to someone who had once enjoyed the sea view. She was enjoying it herself, looking down past the neglected headstones and overgrown grass to the wide flagstone promenade which lined the ocean. Waves glowed red and gold in the setting sun.

She didn't turn when she heard footsteps from behind crunching the frosted grass. St Mary's Churchyard was a popular short cut from Chapel Street to the Penzance promenade.

The light, quick steps stopped by the bench.

'Thought I might catch you here.' It was Sam Trenowden, Julia's husband. He looked down at her through small metal-rimmed glasses, his hands tucked away in the pockets of an expensive-looking coat. There was a pronounced line of intent on the brow below that slicked-back hair.

'You might also have found me at The Hall, Sam,' Rachel replied, glancing up at him and pulling the plastic bag at her side closer.

'Been buying supplies?'

Not waiting for an answer, he sat down beside her.

'I thought this might give us a bit more privacy. A chance to speak openly.'

Rachel turned to look at him. He was sitting rather theatrically with his head down, his shiny-gloved hands pressed together between his legs.

'We both know this isn't going to work,' he said, looking back up at her.

Rachel gave him a quizzical stare.

'Things haven't been right since you came to stay. You must know that? Julia's been jumpy. Her son won't speak to me. You rebuff every attempt Julia makes to accommodate you. She got you the job at the school – covered for you to get it.'

'Covered for me?' Rachel cut in. He was speaking quietly, but she was aware his words could carry on the wind. A couple in Solstice carnival costumes walked past, the woman giving them a look.

'You didn't exactly leave your last job on good terms, did you, Rachel?'

Rachel went to stand, tugging at her coat which was trapped beneath his leg.

'How would you know, Sam? Been reading my messages? Is that why I found you in my room the other night? Snooping?'

'No need to get touchy.' Sam got up to join her. He was barely two inches taller than Rachel and only had to tilt his head to jut a petulant chin in her face.

'We needn't be enemies, Rach,' he said, placing a hand on her arm. 'We could be good friends, you know.'

Rachel shook him off and started to walk down the steps towards the stone arch, heading towards Under Chapel Yard and the Quay.

'Rachel,' she heard him say, 'there's something I need to discuss with you. It's about the gallery.'

What now? She walked faster, conscious of him scurrying to catch her.

The wind had picked up, blowing her hair across her face.

She brushed it aside as Sam moved ahead to block her way. Over his shoulder she could see the waves storming the shore, smashing against the sea wall. Seaweed and froth were being tossed in the air. The scent of the sea mingled with Sam's smell, a musky mix of expensive aftershave and something else, something unpleasant.

'Let's go for a drink. I just want to make a suggestion. That's all,' he said, reaching for his phone as it began to ring. He stretched out an arm and raised his palm to stop Rachel moving off. She looked past him towards St Michael's Mount in the east. The medieval fortress was drenched in blood-red light. An hour earlier it had been dark as a shadow, rising from the water like some mythical seabird. To the west was the hilly fishing town of Newlyn, its white brick houses stacked like cartons of fudge.

'Hi, Julia. In Penzance right now,' Sam was saying. 'Yes, they're getting things ready for the Montol. Perhaps we should eat in Chapel Street tonight? Not at The Hall? Yeah, the wood's all stacked up on the Quay, ready for the bonfire. There was some lowlife hanging around there earlier, looking to thieve some timber, I guess. Nick? He's coming with us? I thought he'd have some friends of his own age to go with? Okay, Julia – but he's not a baby anymore. Okay. I'll text you. B'bye'

'Shall we go to the Fisherman's Catch?' Sam slipped his phone back into his pocket.

Rachel nodded. She was tired after a long week at work and a large glass of red would lessen the load which was Sam. Another suggestion? He was full of them.

Sam couldn't have picked a better venue for a quiet chat. The Fisherman's Catch was an over-rated, over-priced pub, generally avoided by the locals. He steered her to a table in a secluded corner.

'Now, what would you like, young lady?'

Rachel cringed. He was barely a month older than her. She'd known him since she was a young lady, which felt like a long time ago. She was thirty-three now and he was still in her life. More's the pity. Living with Julia meant living with the frenemy too.

'A large glass of Cabernet Sauvignon and a crab sandwich, please.'

'A crab sandwich? But we'll be eating later.' Sam's eyes were on the menu and the £15 tab.

'I didn't have any lunch.' Rachel suppressed a smirk. She knew the expense would gall.

'Yeah, sure.' Sam got to his feet and headed to the bar, still wearing his coat. He returned with a large glass of red and a small white wine, placing a wooden spoon with a number on it between them.

'They'll be over in a while with your *sandwich*,' he said, tapping the table with the spoon. 'They're probably out catching it right now – needs to be fresh at that price.' A clipped laugh.

Rachel forced a smile. 'What did you want to discuss?'

'Ah yes,' Sam said, twisting the spoon in one hand. 'Your dad, Rachel. Your dad's paintings. There's a beauty hanging in the Tate at St Ives. I'd like one in the new gallery. Pride of place.'

'I've told you before, I don't have any paintings. Mum doesn't have any either. Dad sold the lot years ago, long before he died. The ones he didn't sell he gave away or traded at the pub. I would like to help. Just can't.'

Sam's lips tightened and he shook his head lightly. 'Rachel, you can do better than that. You must know someone who would loan us a work for the opening? You are his daughter; the very talented artist daughter of the late, great Lawrence Matthews. O. B. bloody E. Matthews. Come on. What about that heiress he was shagging in the early nineties? I've heard she's got more than a few. Surely, she could loan us one? What about your other artist pals? Work your contacts.'

'Thanks,' Rachel said, as a young Goth with an elaborate nose ring placed a plate before her.

Sam stared at her, his head cocked to one side, the spoon turning in his hand. 'I wouldn't ask, but ...' He picked a cucumber slice off the small, tired salad on her plate.

'I'll try.' Rachel pulled the plate closer and took a bite of her sandwich.

'That's my Rach.' Sam leaned back in his chair, resting his hands behind his head. 'I know Julia doesn't say anything. She's nuts about you – we all are. But things have been tense at home. This would be the best possible gesture at this time. Show we're all pulling together. Are on the ... same canvas.'

Rachel bit into something hard. A piece of shell? As she picked it from her mouth, Sam was back on his feet, walking towards the door, taking a call. She could see him through the window, grinning into his phone, running a gloved hand through his hair. He had his gloves back on. *Pillock.*

'Sorry about that,' he said, plopping back down in his seat, a salacious smile on his face. 'Meghan, from NewlynWave. You know, the small gallery in Newlyn? She came round a few weeks back? Well, she and her bloke Ed are joining us tonight for drinks before the procession.'

Rachel remembered. Meghan was an imposing presence: voluptuous, demonstrative and predatory. If she wasn't actually physically touching you, she'd be sex-raying you from across the room. No wonder Sam was grinning.

His face tightened when his phone buzzed again. Rachel saw a name flick up; someone beginning with B? Sam snapped off the device and put it away.

'No one important,' he said, answering Rachel's look.

Leaning forward, he swiped some more salad from her plate and popped it in his mouth.

'You should eat your greens, Rach. You're looking a bit peaky.'

A piece of dark green lettuce was clinging to one of his teeth like seaweed. His feet were tapping under the table. She watched him pick up the salt cellar and pour a little hill onto the check cloth.

Swirling a finger in the mound, he said. 'I don't know why you took the job at the school. Julia thought it would be a good idea. But, with all that's happened, I'm not so sure.' He turned to face her.

'I could say it pays the rent. But, thanks to you both, I don't have to pay rent. It …'

'Fills a void? Kills time?'

'Yep, I guess so.'

Sam downed the last of his wine and got up.

'We're meeting at The Barn at seven and then drinks at the Benbow. Weird choice of pub. Haven't been there for years.'

Nor had Rachel. It had featured heavily at one stage, sneaking in on a Friday night for underage boozing. Getting pissed on a pint of Doom Bar and heading off to The Venue to see some godawful band. It wasn't often that she dialled back to her school days. She felt Sam looking down at her. When she looked up, he began feeling for his car keys.

She met his eye. 'Going back to The Hall, then?'

'No. Bit of business in town. See you later, Rachel. You'll make that call?'

'Yeah, sure.'

'Sooner rather than later,' he said, flashing a quick, firm smile as he walked away.

Rachel searched for her own car keys. She was enjoying the wine, could probably have had another, but she'd promised her mother she would pop in tonight. It was just down the road. It would kill a few hours before it all kicked off for the Montol. Killing hours again. Sam had a point.

3

Rachel

Rachel had spent more hours at her mother's in the past two months than in the past two years. But it still felt strange to walk down the familiar path to Seabird Cottage, the garden just that little bit more forlorn than the time before.

It was almost pitch black as she waited at the front door. Only a few shy stars peeped out of the night sky. She expected her mother to emerge in her usual haze of benign chaos. Streaks of paint on her face, wild greying hair escaping from some sort of scrunch – the last time a pair of skimpy knickers. She was convinced it was a façade. A mask. What disturbed her most was when it slipped.

The mask was intact when Rachel stepped into the ramshackle cottage holding a fraying length of rope from the front door cowbell. Rachel wasn't the most practical person herself, but she was concerned about the state of the place. It was collapsing around them. She put the piece of rope down on the messy living room table.

'Rachel, darling, you don't know your own strength. You don't yank something as fragile as my darling cowbell. You know it's been in the family since … since Larry and I did Europe. Switzerland – yes, that's where we got it. We were staying at this incredibly beautiful house in the country. Belonged to a charming friend of your father's.' Lizzie Matthews had picked up the rope and was stroking it like a silk scarf.

She'd bought it in a knick-knack shop in Chapel Street back in the nineties, Rachel remembered. One of the many flea market purchases that her mother had made over the years, her daughter tagging behind, repelled by the stale-smelling emporiums, desperate to cut loose.

'Shall I make some tea?' Rachel moved around her to the kitchen. It wasn't so bad, thank God. Lizzie didn't eat much so the mess was restricted to a few crumb-ridden plates and mismatched teacups with various liquids lurking at the bottom.

'Not for me, darling. I had one a little while ago. I just want to get on with a portrait I'm working on. Come and see, darling. Leave that.' Lizzie frowned at the dish cloth in Rachel's hand. 'Come and see.'

But I just want to clean up, make supper and get out of here, thought Rachel. She'd brought two ready meals from the Co-op with her. Her visits never went to plan. On the one hand, it was brilliant that Lizzie was still painting at seventy-five. On the other, she seemed to be developing a penchant for grotesque Francis Bacon-style portraits. Lizzie had always painted delicate landscapes – since Lawrence died, her paintings had morphed into abstract aberrations.

Rachel braced herself as she followed her mother into the studio. This room, at least, hadn't changed one bit since Lawrence ascended to the great garret in the sky. The smell of turps and oils, the half-filled paint pots with their congealed lids, the massive old wooden table which ran the length of the room, covered in smears and spills, was as it should be. As it always was. There was an easel by the window at the far end of the room. The light wasn't great for an artist's studio. Lawrence had talked of, but never organised, building a new one, with massive picture windows and skylights.

'TaRa!' Lizzie said, arranging her arms like a magician's assistant to frame her creation.

Rachel peered into the gloomy corner at the grim canvas. She could feel her mother's eyes on her. Was that Rachel's green woollen scarf, the one her mother had bought her last Christmas? Probably. A streak of green swirled below a pink oval, framed by an arch of yellow. It wasn't exactly a mirror image; her mother was maxing out her artistic license. Two dark green pits, circled with red, glared above a sliver of bone and a black gash of a mouth.

Rachel cracked a smile. 'I think you've caught my likeness, but possibly not my *joie de vivre.*'

'Rachel, darling! You like it … it's a departure, I know. But …'

'I know, Mum. Yes, I know.'

Before she could summon the energy to protest, Rachel had been 'styled' and positioned on a stool in the studio. Her foot was tapping like Sam's. She didn't need this. A *Radio Four* interviewee was emoting on human rights in the Yemen. Lizzie was frowning and clucking in approval as she mixed paints and angled a lamp, so the light shone straight in Rachel's eyes.

'Mum!'

'Sorry, darling.' Lizzie adjusted the lamp a centimetre.

Rachel glanced up at the clock: 6.15pm. The others would be at The Barn in forty-five minutes. Would Sam mention their conversation to Julia? There was no way she was going to find him a painting. Certainly not from *that* woman. She looked at Lizzie's sweet face creased in concentration. Did she know about the heiress? Probably. She hadn't been her father's first or last lover.

'Mum, how long is this going to take?' Rachel fidgeted on the stool, kicking out her legs like a schoolgirl.

'So, you're rushing off to leave me to go to that tacky Montol carnival.' Lizzie was dabbing at the portrait with a brush.

'Don't move your mouth, darling, I'm working on that sardonic smile of yours.'

'I need to move my lips to answer your question, Mum. Move onto my sardonic brow – add a few more lines.'

'Rachel! Where is the sweet young dreamer that Larry and I knew and loved? Moving to London and working in that ghastly ad agency has made you so brittle. You should have continued to do what you do best – paint! You're an artist, not a suit.'

Brittle? Broken, more like. But she didn't want to think about it now. The Montol was the first thing she'd looked forward to since arriving back in Penzance. How long would she be expected to stay in town? It was like being trapped in one of Lizzie's curios emporiums. Your mother's going to need you, Doctor Bryant had said. The dementia will develop.

'Dreaming doesn't pay bills, Mum. Anyway, back to the Montol. Yes, I'm going. Haven't been for years. Are people still raiding the junk shops for tatty toff outfits? Have they introduced rap to the usual medieval drone?'

'You'll be disappointed, darling. Move your head to the right, just a little. It's become a commercial jamboree. Lots of stalls selling tat. About time they came up with something new. Something really … celebratory. Just something different.'

Rachel pulled at the scratchy green wool scarf Lizzie had fixed round her neck. She'd been sitting for over half an hour. Three electric heaters were whirling, throwing out heat. Was her face as pink as her portrait's?

'I thought Market Jew Street looked rather charming as I walked up it earlier. Not commercial at all – lots of pretty stalls selling local produce.'

'But you bought our supper from the Co-op?'

Rachel sighed. 'I don't have time to put a meal together, Mum. This will have to do for tonight. Unless we go to The Barn. Julia is eating there with Sam and Nick. We could join them … if we hurry.'

'No thank you, darling. You go if you like.' Lizzie put down her paint brush and wiped her hands on her apron.

'I'd rather not. I'll stay here with you and then meet them later for a drink.'

'He was round here earlier, you know.'

'Who?' Rachel said, slipping off the stool and following her mother into the kitchen.

'Slimy Sam.'

'Sam? Whatever for?'

'Oh, some pretence or another. But it didn't take him long to get to the point.'

Rachel frowned. She knew what was coming.

'He was after Larry's paintings. He asked if I had any for the new gallery. I said no and he asked if I was sure. Whether your father hadn't stored some in the attic or wherever. He was very persistent, Rachel. And clueless. Calls himself an art dealer! He must be able to source a Lawrence Matthews. Maybe from one of the London galleries?'

'You'd like to think so, wouldn't you? But it would cost him. Sam wants something for nothing as usual. He asked me much the same thing.'

'When?' Lizzie turned away from the sink where she'd been cleaning her palette and brushes.

'This afternoon – he must have left your place and headed straight into Penzance. He found me in St Mary's Church-yard.'

'What were you doing there, Rachel?' Lizzie spoke softly.

'Just having a quiet moment, that's all. It's been a busy

week.'

Lizzie walked across the red-tiled floor and rested a hand on Rachel's arm. 'You go and sit down for a little while, darling. Let me sort supper.'

'I've been sitting down for nearly an hour.'

'But we all know that sitting for an artist is not like sitting, sitting. And it's only ping-ping carbonara. Off you go – there's *Tate Magazine* on the coffee table, I think. They get one of Larry's works for their opening exhibition and I get their free magazine! Larry's *Head of The Titan* is on Page 6. They got it from a German collector, I believe. Now, if Sam had any gumption, he would do the same.'

Rachel found the magazine poking out from under the sofa. It fell open at Page 6. The painting wasn't one of his best, but they'd positioned it well in the light-filled reception. The *Head of The Titan* would make an imposing first impression. As Lawrence Matthews always had. Both charming and frightening people in equal measures, he could as well have been an actor as an artist. His public life was performance art. But beneath the bravado, there was real talent, raw emotion. The best times were in the studio, chatting over the radio, the two of them painting. He put painstaking care and precision into his trademark torrents of colour; standing back, retouching, asking her opinion. There was mutual respect between artist and artist, father and daughter. And love. She sometimes forgot about the love.

Lizzie brought in trays, and they sat eating in front of the TV. Although Lizzie didn't want to go to the Montol, she wanted to see whether it was on the local news.

'Oh, here we go,' Lizzie said, as Penzance popped up on BBC Spotlight. There was footage of the earlier daytime procession, winding its way from the end of Chapel Street, up

Causewayhead to The Princess May Recreation Ground. At the front was a big yellow paper sun effigy, destined for the bonfire. Children were running in and out of the lines of masked revellers and musicians. Dickensian figures in dark cloaks and top hats lined the pavements.

'Bloody racket,' Lizzie said, toying with a strip of tagliatelle. 'And then they do it all again tonight.' She dropped her fork on her plate and pushed it away. 'Got anything to wear? You can't go like that.'

'It will have to do. I haven't got time to go back and change. Besides, I don't have any mock toff. Just mock M&S. Peacocks. And Julia's bringing along some fancy feathered masks.'

Lizzie screwed up her nose. 'I'll find you something. You will be the belle of the ball – not a dreary schoolmarm. How is that job going? I never did have the patience for children … I'll just go and see what I can find in my witchy-poo wardrobe.'

As soon as she was out of the door Rachel looked around for a task. She'd washed the dishes and vacuumed by the time Lizzie returned with satin and velvet garments thrown over one skinny arm. She was wearing a big floppy felt hat.

'You should come too, Mum.' Rachel swooped on the pile of clothes. She remembered them well from Larry and Lizzie's glory days.

'These are perfect – just the right amount of dust and moth holes for Montol authenticity.'

Lizzie smiled indulgently as Rachel sorted through the clothes.

'You should wear the red velvet.' Lizzie caressed the rich fabric, breathed in the scent of yesterday's parties. 'It's Biba.'

'It's beautiful.' Rachel slipped it on. She'd lost weight and the Twiggy-size seventies dress fitted, just about.

'And the hat. You can't go to the Montol without a hat … and scarf.'

Rachel took the purple felt hat and the woollen green scarf, which, although incongruous, suited the crazy dress code. She felt like a little girl trying on her mother's clothes, except these weren't falling off her. They were pretty tight. Lizzie was thin then and thin now. Rachel had inherited her mother's fast metabolism and rangy figure, but she doubted whether she would fit into these clothes at seventy-five.

'You look lovely, darling,' Lizzie said as she stood in the porch to see her off.

'Sure you don't want to come, Mum?'

'No, darling. I've been to enough spooky Solstice celebrations. I prefer to stay at home with my own demons. They're company enough.'

4

Rachel

Two hours later, Rachel was sitting in the Admiral Benbow next to Julia. Sam, Meghan and her boyfriend Ed were squeezed tight on a faded floral sofa to their right. The pub was packed, full of people in mock-formal Montol garb, masks pushed up on their heads as they drank and chatted. Things were getting raucous – it was 10pm and the celebrators were well-watered.

'How is Lizzie?' Julia asked, raising her voice to make herself heard.

'Same old – maybe a little more forgetful.' Rachel omitted the fact that she'd remembered Sam coming round earlier, asking about her dead husband's paintings.

'What's Seabird Cottage like?'

'Bit like the Benbow!' Rachel laughed, looking around at the nautical junk shop décor.

'Clean?'

'Difficult to tell under all the mess. I did get out the vacuum while she was rooting around in her wardrobe for this outfit.'

'It's great, Rachel. Your mum always had style.'

Julia put down her glass: 'She owes you big time, Rachel.'

'Let's not go there, eh. She's elderly and, well … she hasn't got anyone else.'

'I could send round Agata? Once or twice a week – to clean, chat, keep an eye. Sit for her.'

'Agata's far too young and pretty. Lizzie's only interested in the walking wounded right now.'

'Well, I could always go round.'

'Is everything okay? I ran into Sam earlier and I sensed something was up. He asked about dad's paintings for the gallery.'

Julia shook her head. 'We've had this discussion time and time again. I told him you don't have any – end of. Besides, it would look like we were copying the Tate. The whole idea is to showcase new talent.'

'Artistic differences?' Rachel took a sip of Doom Bar. Drinking beer in the Benbow after all these years. It felt good. The old Montol magic was working its charm.

'And the rest.' Julia glanced over at Sam. He was squeezed in close against Meghan, her black lace dress rucked up high. 'You should have come to supper at The Barn. God, we needed you. Nick was closed down, just eating and yawning and itching to get onto his phone. Sam wouldn't let him have it at the table. But, of course, he had his out. Left a couple of times to take calls. Unbelievable.'

Rachel could imagine. He wasn't on it now though. Too noisy to hear and too preoccupied by something else rubbing against his leg. Surely Julia must suspect something? She looked as serene as ever, her cool beauty undiminished. Maybe a smudge of shadow under her clear blue eyes, a reddening on the tip of that perfect aquiline nose? Her boxy blonde bob framed her face like a crash helmet.

She might need a helmet tonight. Things could get wild at the Montol. Rachel remembered that other time, when they'd driven from Falmouth in Jago's van and parked it on the promenade. It had been a stormy night, their pop-up tents billowing and flapping on the beach. They'd piled stones in them, to keep them grounded, but Rachel's had taken off and they'd chased it along the water's edge until it had blown out to sea like a balloon.

'Fancy another drink?' Rachel got up from her chair.

'No. I'll get these.'

Rachel scrunched her face in refusal. 'What would you like?'

'A pint of Doom Bar.'

'What?'

'I've had enough wine.'

'I agree. Can't see Sam mixing the grape with the grain, though.' They looked over at him laughing and flirting, Ed seemingly at ease with the situation.

'Don't bother with Sam. He can get his own round in.' Julia turned away from him. 'Seriously, I wouldn't bother. He seems perfectly happy.'

'Exactly,' Rachel said, going over to their sofa.

She interrupted them mid-chuckles.

'Sam was just telling me about some of the submissions for the gallery,' Meghan said, her wide, open face glowing with mirth. 'Intriguing!' she added, giggling and wriggling like a 1950s starlet. Ed looked on with an air of faint amusement.

'I just wondered if you wanted a drink. Just time for another before we head off.'

'That's very generous of you, Rach,' Sam said, his arm draped along the back of the shabby sofa. She was surprised he wasn't wearing his gloves.

'Small white wine?'

'Let's make it a large one.'

'Meghan?'

'That's very kind of you, Rachel. Pinot, please. A small one. You really must come visit NewlynWave. It's hard to talk right now, but I'd be interested to hear your views on my new artists. Sam says you paint. And that you're amazing.'

'I don't paint anymore.'

'Why ever not?'

'There are enough artists around here already.'

'That's no excuse.' Meghan got to her feet. 'Let me help you get the drinks. The bar is mobbed. Ed?'

Ed looked up from the Montol events brochure he'd been reading for the umpteenth time.

'I'm fine. Just dandy.' He raised his half full pint of beer and tapped the brim of the battered top hat he was wearing. 'Or maybe I'll go join Julia. Your girl's looking lonesome on her own, wouldn't you say, Sam?' Ed looked pretty lonesome himself. Like a pissed off Artful Dodger waiting for Nancy and Bill to finish their business. Consider yourself part of the furniture, Rachel thought.

Sam gave Ed a quick, tight smile and started tapping into his phone. 'Julia's a big girl. I think she'll cope on her own for a few minutes.'

Rachel could hear the faint sound of drumbeats and chanting as she returned with the drinks. The minstrel players were making their way down Chapel Street towards the Benbow.

'Down in one.' Meghan presented Sam's drink with a flourish. He picked it up and clinked his glass with hers.

'That was quick.' Julia put down her phone as Rachel approached.

'Meghan,' Rachel replied. 'The crowd parted.'

'We've got some time. Nick just texted to say the procession will probably be here in around ten minutes.'

People had started spilling out of the pub into Chapel Street, putting on their masks, hats and cloaks. Julia pulled out a couple of masks from her bag.

'Thanks, Julia,' Rachel said, taking a black Venetian creation. 'Is Nick okay, by the way? Is he joining us?'

'Yes. He's with some friends. He'll be here soon.'

Nick arrived at the pub waving a flaming torch. He was flanked by an ensemble of musicians and people in guise – the Solstice queen in a sedan chair and a black-robed man wearing a long-beaked crow mask, who stamped and twirled a percussion stick.

'Careful!' Sam snapped, stepping back as Nick pushed his head through the Benbow door, sparks spraying.

He was with two boys from school.

'Hi, Miss,' said one of the boys, recognising Rachel.

'Hi, Jack. Where'd you get the torches?' They were unwieldy things, like oversized ice cream cornets with scoops of fire.

'Guy down the road. Here, have mine. I'll get another.'

Rachel peered down the street. A man was handing out torches next to a small cauldron of fire. He was resting against the exuberant pillars of the Egyptian House, a giant tropical fruit of nineteenth century architecture plonked in the middle of Chapel Street.

Rachel took Jack's torch and also the one in Nick's hand. 'For your mum,' she said, handing it to Julia.

They walked out into the street, pulling their cloaks around them. It was a clear, crisp night; just a few thin grey clouds draped the slender moon like torn nets. The front of the procession was at the bottom of Chapel Street as they joined the tail end, treading the cobbles to the rhythm of fiddles and drums.

As they reached St Mary's Church, Rachel could hear voices and the rustling of long skirts and coats against grass as people took a short-cut through the churchyard to the promenade. A middle-aged man was slumped outside the stone entrance. She stopped to check on him; he was drunk or stoned –

but warm enough wrapped in a thick great coat. The group of people she'd heard earlier were hurrying through the bottom arch, trailing light from their torches. Julia and the others had moved on with the procession, so she walked into the church-yard and past the church. Her torch cast patterns of light on the tomb stones, picking out names. She paused, listening to the wind rustling bare branches and the soft scratchy sound of a night creature scurrying in the grass and gravel.

On impulse, she turned right to the untended graveyard, where ancient, forgotten stones jutted from the earth. There were no bunches of decaying flowers here. This was the rest-ing place of the long dead, although the grass beneath her feet was trampled. A sudden gust of wind brought with it a musky smell of marijuana. Rachel looked into the shadows. Thought she saw a dark shape shrink away behind the ancient Oak by the far wall. She pulled her cloak around her, was about to retrace her steps, when an explosion of colour lit the sky. The fireworks had begun. Hitching up her long dress, Rachel hurried through the grounds, a group of young masqueraders dashing past like spirits of the night.

'Watch ya step,' said someone behind her, the words ac-companied by a whiff of dope.

Rachel turned to face two teens in dark clothing and masks. 'Sorry?'

'I said watch ya fucking step.'

Rachel made to move, but the one who'd spoken blocked her path. He looked about eighteen, dark hair shaved at the sides in a skin fade. A cheap, plastic Montol mask covered his eyes and forehead; his mouth a grimace.

'It's the bitch that works at the school. Hangs with that wanker,' he said, his lips tightening.

'Right?' said the other one.

'Wanker's bitch, innit. Reckon teacher needs teachin' a lesson,' the guy with the skin fade said, starting to giggle.

'Fuckin lessin, right,' said his mate, trying, but failing, to laugh. He was out of it. Lank, sandy hair fell across his mouth and mask.

Rachel swerved away, but Skin Fade cut across her, barging her with a shoulder, making her stumble and fall.

'Told ya to watch ya step, *Miss*,' he said, as Rachel pulled herself up. The sandy-haired teen shoved her down again. They stood over her, grinning, Skin Fade prodding her with one foot.

She heard someone coming along the gravel path. 'I'm here, guys,' she called out. 'Over here.'

Skin Fade flicked them a look and pulled back. Sandy froze, considering her as if she were a wounded animal. Rachel sprung to her feet as the group approached, Skin Fade tugging at her cloak as she made a dash for it.

'Watch ya step, bitch, and the company ya keep,' she heard him hiss as she darted through the arch and headed for the Quay.

She steadied herself when she arrived at the Quay, her hands shaking as she readjusted her cloak and brushed it down. She was breathing hard, her heart thumping, as she replayed the scene. Two druggies getting their kicks through mindless intimidation. That's all. But they knew she was a teacher. Seemed to recognise her – or the one with the skin fade did. She straightened her dress – the hem had caught in one boot when she fell – flicked lumps of soil off its front. Everything was fine. She wouldn't let two stoned kids spoil her night.

Rachel turned her attention to the bonfire, which was crackling and leaping, spraying sparks into the crowd. People were linking arms, circling the fire, tossing torches into the flames. She joined Julia and Nick at the outer rim of the circle. Meghan was already pushing forward, tugging at Ed, who threw an arm around her. Sam was edging towards Julia, but she kept her eyes fixed ahead, watching as others held hands, bowed heads and moved to the music.

'Want to join them?' Sam said, drawing close.

'In a while,' Julia said.

He shrugged and took Meghan's hand as she and Ed joined a line of dancers.

Julia was holding her torch well away from her body. She was in a mood with Sam, but still sensible enough not to let the wind blow sparks on her coat. Her face looked sullen below her mask before it suddenly lit up.

'Hey, don't we know that guy, standing at the back.' Julia pointed her torch towards a tall man in a cloak over the other side of the fire.

'Don Giovanni? Or is it Ross Poldark?'

'Seriously, Rachel. Someone from Falmouth? The guy that used to hang around the Union Bar and the Arts Common Room. Bit of a loner. The sort you "always found in the kitchen at parties".'

Rachel smiled. 'There were loads of those types at art school. That said, the cloak looks familiar.' *Was he with someone? It wasn't clear.*

'Yes! I think that's what triggered the memory. He used to waft around in a cloak like Percy Shelley, or Byron. Crap at art.'

'He's looking straight at you guys,' Nick said, 'Do you have to be so embarrassing?'

'Oh my God,' Julia said. 'I know who it is. Euan. Euan … Tremayne. He had a thing about you. Remember?'

36

'Julia, it's so long ago. I really don't remember.' But she remembered all right. She remembered the party when he had managed to move out of the kitchen. She'd stumbled over him sitting on the stairs. What had she been thinking at the time? How much had she drunk?

'Well, I think he remembers you, Rachel. Is he coming over?'

'God, I hope not.'

Euan took the route of least resistance; he linked arms with a circling line of dancers and dropped off by them. Rachel instinctively pulled her mask down to cover her face. But he was looking better than she remembered. Much better. Taller, bigger – dark blonde hair swept back under his hat; black mask resting on high cheekbones. Someone had reworked a badly-drawn boy. He must have been around twenty-one when she last saw him.

'You haven't changed a bit,' Euan said, pulling up his own mask. 'Despite the disguise. Neither of you,' he said, turning to Julia.

He was smiling a contained sort of smile, a row of straight white teeth just visible.

'Euan, isn't it?' Julia stepped back as a line of dancers threatened to collide with her.

'It is, indeed, Julia.'

'And this is Nick, my son,' she replied, moving out of the way as the dancers changed direction.

'Nice to meet you, Nick.'

He turned to Rachel; the smile replaced by a look of compassion. 'How are you? Good, I hope. I was so sorry to hear about your son.'

Rachel gave a small nod, glad for the mask. She didn't want to think about it now. She wouldn't think about it now.

'Are you here with your family?' Julia had adopted a crisp small-talk tone.

'No. I'm here with some people I know,' Euan said, his eyes fixed on Rachel.

'Do you live around here now?' Julia kept up the conversation, raising her voice slightly as another rowdy line passed by.

'Yes. I've moved back to Penwith.'

'Still painting?'

'Taking photos. But some art, yes. I'm working on some stuff.'

'Cool.'

Julia gave Rachel a pleading look.

'Shall we dance? If you can't beat them, join them,' Rachel said. 'Nick, come on.'

'Think I'll go find Jack. See you later,' Nick said, making a dash for it.

Euan held out a hand to Julia, reaching out to Rachel with his other, before leading them into the circle of dancers. They looked like they were in some sort of trance. Or elephants moving trunk to tail. Rachel had a flash of the hallucinogenic Pink Elephants scene in *Dumbo*. The booze had gone to her head. And then she had a vision of Oliver; his sweet face watching the screen, laughing at the little drunk mouse. Oliver who would never laugh again. Never get drunk.

Bottles of wine and rum were being passed down the lines; the sky blazed with stars and fireworks. Some revellers were already falling away, tumbling into dark spaces on the Quay and in the walled gardens beyond in bacchanalian fervour.

Like a rogue elephant, Euan broke free of the line and spun Rachel round, coming back towards her his arms behind his back in ceilidh fashion. Bowing, he turned back to Julia and spun her too, before proceeding to weave backwards and forwards between them. A purple plume quivered on his hat as he moved from one to the other. A cock doing a mating dance.

Rachel could feel the heat from the fire on her face; her cheeks were flushed beneath her mask, her body hot against her cloak. She undid its clasp, releasing folds of red velvet.

'Beautiful.'

She turned to Euan.

'You are a work of art. A renaissance vision.' He moved towards her and took her hand. His eyes reflected the fire, yellow as a tiger's.

'I can see you've lost none of your charm.'

'I never had any charm at Falmouth. I was a creep. Like the Radiohead guy. But I've been practising.'

Rachel smiled. 'Maybe a little too hard?'

He was looking at her and, in that moment, seemed sincere. The enigmatic smile wiped off his face.

'I'd like to apologise for how I was last time we met. I acted like a fool, and I've wanted to make it up to you for years.'

Rachel felt tears prick the back of her eyes. It had all meant so little at the time. Or so she'd thought. He reached out a thumb, as if to wipe away a tear, and then drew back.

'We didn't really know each other, did we?' Rachel regained some composure.

'I thought I knew you. Maybe not.'

'Rachel, we need to get out of here. Where's Mum? Something's kicking off over there. Come on.' Nick was at their side, waving an arm at a group of people to their left. There was some sort of commotion. People were shouting.

Rachel was right at the heart of the action, right up against the fire, sparks spraying everywhere.

Euan pulled her back as a man staggered towards them, the

sleeve of his coat in flames. He was patting at it furiously, his face flushed and distorted.

'Help me,' he shouted. 'Help me!'

'Get an ambulance,' someone bellowed. 'We need an ambulance.'

And then, out of nowhere, came a piercing scream. Too anguished, too human to be a gull. People were backing off from the fire, making towards the seafront. Some kids were running. Mothers tugged at others.

Julia had rushed to join them. She grabbed Nick, who was straining to see what was going on.

'What is it?'

There was something on the ground – something blackened, charred. A log that had rolled out from beneath the pyre? The fire was crackling and imploding. Two pieces of burnt timber crashed down, jolting the thing on the ground, sending it rolling towards Rachel. She was still wearing the green scarf her mother had given her. Rachel pulled it up around her face, sucking on the coarse wool, her gaze fixed on what lay below: what looked like two empty hollows and a row of blackened teeth in the remains of a jaw.

5

Rachel

'Just when the night was getting promising … it decided to throw a curved skull,' Euan said, as they watched the emergency services storm the Quay. It was like a war zone; uniforms, fire engines dousing flames, mothers cuddling young children, anguished faces fixed to phones, fingers scrolling.

Sam was pacing a small area, like a caged hyena. 'So, what now? How much longer do we have to wait out here in the f-ing cold?'

'Maybe not so long,' Euan said moving aside as a team of SOCOs approached, allowing them to duck under the crime scene tape.

Rachel turned away and, in that moment, heard the click of a car door opening. It swung open, to reveal a man with a full head of unruly dark hair. His blue overcoat was open, revealing a slight paunch pressing against a crumpled shirt, half in-half out of his trousers. He strode towards them, a young woman with red hair hurrying to his side.

'Good evening, folks. Sorry for the wait.'

'Brandon?' Rachel said, her words a hoarse whisper.

Slow, dark blue eyes moved to her face. 'Rachel Matthews. Long time … I heard you were back in town.'

'Couple of months now,' Rachel said. 'I'm staying at The Hall with Julia … and Sam.'

Brandon glanced at Julia and switched his steady gaze to Sam.

He paused before continuing. 'Rachel, I believe you made

the call to the station? I'll take the statement.' He nodded towards his car, and then addressed the gathering crowd. 'We'll need a few words with the rest of you before you leave. DS Menhenrick and PC Phillips will take your details.'

As the stunned band of people formed ragged queues, Brandon turned to Rachel. 'The station filled me in on what happened. This shouldn't take long. This is some reunion, eh?'

Rachel gave a weak smile and walked with Brandon to his car.

* * * * *

'You warm enough?' he said, one hand on the car roof. 'You want to sit inside?'

'I'm good,' she said, feeling anything but.

Brandon opened the passenger door. 'If you continue to lie to me through chattering teeth, Ms Matthews, I may have to book you.' Brandon waited for her to get in the car before going round to the driver's side, opening the door, tossing a packet of cigarettes onto the back seat and easing himself in.

They sat staring ahead, said nothing for a beat.

'Rachel, how are you? When were you last in Penzance?' He pulled a bottle of water from the glove compartment and offered it to her.

She shook her head lightly. 'A lifetime ago.'

'I heard about Oliver. I'm so sorry. I tried to get in touch.'

Rachel gave him a sideways glance before looking at her hands. 'I was … incommunicado for some time.'

'You needed your space. I understand.'

She turned to look at him. 'Of course, you would. I'm—'

Brandon looked to the side before continuing. 'Hey. I hear you're a schoolteacher now?'

'Yep. I'm working as an LSA, a Learning Support Assistant, at St Piran's.'

'You know my gal, Chelsea?'

'She's in my Year 10 art class. Nice girl. Real character. She has your eyes.'

Brandon edged forward on his seat. 'How does it feel teaching in the school we both went to?'

Rachel was still looking at her hands. 'Odd. At least at first. But it can't be any odder than you working as a copper.'

Brandon threw back his head and laughed. 'The long and winding road, eh, back to Penzance. Via the UT ... University of Texas Police Academy.'

Rachel turned and regarded him closely 'That was some detour.'

He was a few years older than her but had been part of her school set. She remembered when he'd pitched up at school from Alabama. Must have been about fourteen. Same age as Chelsea now. He still had that lazy southern drawl. And then he'd gone back to the States, got married, become a cop.

'What made you come back?'

Brandon bowed his head and then raised it slowly. 'We came back to be with my family ... after Jessica died. Jess didn't really have any family, none close by, anyway.'

'Oh, I'm so sorry. That was insensitive of me. I've been caught up in my own problems and grief.' Rachel's heart lurched and she reached out to touch him. But he turned away, made a thing of rolling down the window.

'Thank you. Yes, it was a difficult time for us. For me and for Chelsea. But my parents have been great. My mom's been brilliant.' His fingers were rapping the open window frame.

'I remember your mum.' Rachel smiled, thinking of the friendly Cornish woman who had dished out cheese on toast when they'd turned up after school – a whole bunch of them

– collapsing in front of her telly to watch cartoons.

His face was still turned away, but she caught the edge of his smile. 'Yes, she's been great and so has Chelsea. So, we're just fine.'

'And your dad?'

'He's cool. Misses Alabama, of course. But the States ain't what it was. Nothing is, really, is it?'

'Not a lot has changed around here,' Rachel said with a wry smile.

'Oh, you'd be surprised.' Brandon relaxed back into his seat. He'd shaken off his discomfort like a wounded bear breaking free of a trap.

'But it was the right decision coming back. Right for everyone.' He turned to her; his gaze unwavering as he felt for a pen in his jacket pocket. 'Anyway, I suppose we best do the biz. You'll be wanting to get home.'

Rachel breathed a sigh of relief. 'Sure. What do you need?'

'Just some contact details for now. And a witness statement tomorrow. Procedural stuff.' He smiled that big old friendly smile she remembered from school and held out a card.

Rachel paused before taking it. 'It's probably nothing,' she said, turning it in her hand.

Brandon raised his eyes to hers. 'Go on.'

'There were some men, teens, in St Mary's Graveyard as I passed through around quarter to eleven. They were stoned and threatening. Seemed to know I was a teacher. Told me to watch my step. Shoved me so I fell. I've only just thought about it again. I brushed it aside because I knew I'd be okay. There were people around. But it was quite scary. Really scary, all the same.'

Brandon twisted round to face her. 'What did they look like?'

44

'They were young, as I said. Late teens. They both wore Montol masks – the cheap ones you can pick up anywhere. Both were skinny – looked like druggies.'

'Any distinguishing features?'

'Not really. They were white. One had a skin fade cut.' She stopped to think.

'Take your time,' Brandon said.

'His hair was dark brown. The other one was less slick, wore his sandy hair long and straggly. They both wore dark clothes – hoodies and black or dark grey jeans. The one with the skin fade wore white trainers. I didn't notice what the other had on his feet. He held back and let his mate do the talking.

'Did you see where they went?' Brandon was looking right at her.

Rachel returned his gaze. 'No. I just rushed away. Quick as I could. The guy with the skin fade made a grab at my cloak. I didn't see them later, though, so they probably didn't go to the Bonfire. I would have noticed.'

'Any weapons?'

'No,' Rachel said, 'At least not that I could see.'

Brandon wrote something on his notepad and picked up his mobile. 'Thanks, Rachel. This could be helpful. You never know. A lot of people were out of it tonight. But I'll circulate the descriptions.' He went to make a call, and then stopped: 'You didn't recognise them? So, they aren't at your school?'

'No. But they were wearing masks and it was dark. And I haven't been at St Piran's long.'

'Anything else? Did they say anything else?' Brandon rested his mobile on the dash.

'The skin fade guy seemed to think I *hung* with someone they knew. He called him a wanker. I assumed he'd mixed me up with someone else. You get reports of mistaken identity in gangs.'

Brandon rocked back in his seat and nodded in agreement. 'You do. But you say they called you a teacher?'

'Teacher and bitch,' Rachel said, rolling her eyes.

'Some night, eh, Rachel?'

Rachel nodded, before adding. 'Their accents. The way they spoke. They weren't from round here –' She turned to Brandon. 'Do you need me to do the statement now, after all?'

Brandon caught her eye. 'No. I can relay this – patrols are out and can stop and question anyone fitting the descriptions.' He leaned towards her and gave a reassuring smile. 'We can formalise your statement in the morning. And register a complaint about their anti-social behaviour.'

Rachel heaved herself up and reached for the door handle. 'Thanks, Brandon. Speak to you tomorrow?'

Brandon got out of the car and hurried round to open the door for her.

'Hey,' he said, as he watched her walk away. 'Nice running into you again, Rachel Matthews. Shame about the circumstances and all. But good to see you back in town.'

6

Brandon

Brandon was about to join the throng when his phoned pinged.

'Social media is going large on what looks like the arms and legs of this investigation, if not the brain.' It was a typical text from DC Stewart (Stew) Bland, a joker new to the force. Brandon gritted his teeth and phoned him, getting out of the car as he did so.

'Details, Stew.'

'Human remains littered in St Anthony's Gardens. A call just came into the station.'

'By whom?'

'Chap called Marcus Raynor. I've told him to stay put, for now.'

'Good. I'll get the SOCOs over.'

Brandon was on the phone to Jo as he strode over to the Crime Scene Investigator crouched on the ground beyond the crime tape. He was examining the skull, his torch lighting the cavities and one gold tooth.

It had to be Al Chapman, one of the best forensics in the West Country. Brandon hadn't had the dubious pleasure to be introduced to him before.

'Mr Chapman?' Brandon said, towering above him.

The CSI was talking into his recorder. 'Human skull, likely male, collapsed cranium suggesting blunt force trauma.'

He clicked off his phone and rose unsteadily to his feet.

'DI Hammett,' he said, turning to face Brandon. 'A pleasure, albeit a compromised one, to meet you.'

With handshakes out of the question, they stood for a moment appraising each other.

'They've found some human remains in the gardens.' Brandon jerked his head towards the small low-walled area that skirted the coastal road.

'Someone's been careless,' Al said, ushering over one of his team to deal with the skull and ducking under the tape to join Brandon.

'Or in a hurry,' countered Brandon. The images of the two guys in the graveyard Rachel had mentioned flashed through his mind. No better place to discard dead body parts. 'Al, could you ask your team to take a look in St Mary's?'

Al cocked his head to the side.

'A witness was assaulted by a couple of teens in the graveyard earlier. Could be a connection.'

'Indeed,' Al said, his eyes twinkling behind his metal-framed glasses. 'Heaven knows what we may stumble upon.'

7

Brandon

Three days later, Brandon was at the morgue. Bits of local fisherman Pat Ryan had been found littered around St Anthony's Gardens on the promenade and at the harbour. The pathology team had pieced him together as best they could, but Ryan wasn't in a good shape. His decapitated, charred skull had been cleaned and placed above his torso. Two dismembered arms rested against it – one with a tattoo of a ship's figurehead. Unusual and easily identifiable. Below was just one leg, giving Ryan the appearance of Long John Silver after a spell in Davy's Jones Locker. Brandon imagined the other leg floating out to sea, never to be found, or being chewed in the jaws of a dog.

At the station, Brandon's team were piecing together the motive behind the murder.

Ryan had his own boat and he had developed a habit of taking it out in the early hours. Drugs smuggling? They were waiting for the DNA report on the trainer Brandon had swiped off the perp in the cove on the morning of the Montol. Could well be Ryan's.

Brandon moved aside as the lab technicians bagged up Ryan's remains, leaving his tattooed arm resting beneath a white cloth. A porter placed the arm on a trolley and Brandon followed it out of the Examination Room and through to the Viewing Room. It was 10am and Ryan's wife would be along in a few minutes to identify the body. She hadn't been required. A missing person report, the tattoo, a discarded empty wallet and clothing were proof enough – but Susan Ryan had insisted. Brandon prepared himself. Commanding a calm, compassionate presence for the bereaved was the hardest part of the job.

The white coats had disappeared, but he expected McKinsey from the Coroner's office to join him when Susan Ryan made her appearance. He hoped so. She wouldn't have to stay long.

Here she comes.

High heels clicked their way down the corridor. Brandon took a deep breath and turned to the door to greet them.

'Jesus.' Susan's knees buckled and she grabbed hold of McKinsey's arm. The world-weary Scot was unfazed – these visits produced a spectrum of reactions.

'Oh my God!' Susan let go of McKinsey and staggered towards Brandon and the bed where Ryan's arm rested.

'Mrs Ryan, thank you for coming. I know how difficult this must be for you. I am so sorry for your loss.' Brandon gave her a sideways glance. She was probably late forties, a small, wiry woman who hadn't worn the years well. Her weathered face was creased with lines, her thin, dull hair scraped back in a small, tight bun. She gave the impression that this was just one of a succession of tragedies she'd had to deal with over the years.

Susan stood perfectly still, swallowing and blinking, her sparrow-like body bracing itself.

'Are you ready, Mrs Ryan?' Brandon said, gesturing to the shape below the sheet.

She blew out, gripped the edge of the bed with both hands and nodded. 'Yes,' she whispered. 'Ready as I'll ever be.'

Brandon pulled back the sheet to reveal part of Ryan's arm, his stiffened hand curled like a claw, a thin band of white still visible where his wedding ring had been.

Susan gasped, her left hand lashing out, her right one making a fist which found its way to her mouth. She sucked on it, her eyes, all the while, on her husband's arm.

'It's him,' she murmured. And then, letting her arms fall to her side, she leant forward as if to make absolutely sure. 'It's him, alright. That's Rosie on his arm. Oh my God, Pat, you fucking bugger. What a fucking mess! Oh my God, Pat.'

They stood for a while, tears trickling down Susan's face, her hand finding Brandon's.

He never knew quite what to expect in these circumstances. But he wasn't one to consult the rule book and squeezed her hand as if it were a child's.

'Is that it?' Susan tilted her small head up at him, letting him go.

'Yes, this part is over. We'll be in touch.'

'About releasing ... Pat?'

'Yes. We'll do our best to.'

'Just find them, Sir. Just find the scum that did this to Pat. Please.' She rubbed her nose and looked away.

'Make no mistake we'll find them, and they'll be brought to justice.'

Susan looked amazed. 'You will?' Her look said it all. She clearly wasn't used to getting her own way, or things working out.

'You hear that, Pat? The copper's gonna find those bastards and make them pay.' She moved back towards the bed, looked over her shoulder at Brandon and mouthed, 'Is it okay?' Brandon nodded, and she bent down, brushing her lips against Pat's fingertips. 'They're gonna get the bastards, Pat, you hear?' she said, turning away wiping her nose on her sleeve.

Brandon agreed. He was confident that this was one crime which could be solved. It looked amateurish and hurried – the haphazard disposal of body parts, pieces of clothing and personal items still on the corpse. It was just a matter of time, he told himself.

'Thank you, Sir,' Susan said, looking up at him. 'If there is anything, anything at all I can help you with, you know where to find me.'

Brandon nodded and smiled lightly escorting Susan out of the room, leaving McKinsey with Pat.

8

Brandon

A short while later Brandon was at the Smugglers Tavern. It was just two days to Christmas but the place was far from jumping. Brandon was sitting at the bar with a pint of Doom Bar, chatting to the landlord Rob Nancarrow. Rob was a saturnine man at the best of times, but today his face was as chewed up as piece of gum.

'How could this happen in a place like Penzance?' Rob had one elbow on the bar, his other arm pulling a pint for a customer. 'And to a man like Pat. A proper Cornishman born and bred. A fisherman. Things are going from bad to worse, round here.' Rob pushed the pint over to a red-haired young man on the stool next to Brandon.

'When did you last see Pat?' Brandon was addressing Rob, but anyone in the small, red-upholstered room could have answered the question. They were all ears. Aware of who was speaking.

'He was in here four nights back,' Rob said. 'He was here most nights – early evening like. He went back to his family.'

'Was he with anyone?' Brandon took a sip of beer, wiped away the froth on his top lip. He felt the bristles and wondered whether to grow a beard again. It was an idle thought, in the circumstances.

'Everyone knows everyone in here. I suppose he was passing the time of day with a few.'

'He was with a woman … Meghan. And her bloke Ed, the electrician,' said the redhead. 'I've seen them in here before, from time to time.'

Rob rubbed his forehead as if it were a genie's lamp and he might conjure up something useful. 'Yes, I believe he was here with Meghan – the pretty lady that runs the gallery in the town. Meghan and … now I don't know his name, but he's been in here a few times with Meghan and Ed, her fella.'

'Did you catch what they were talking about?' Brandon swilled the remaining drop of beer in his glass and thought about ordering another.

'Same again?' Rob said, never missing a trick.

'No. Best not.' He felt in his pocket for his wallet.

'It's on the house, Brandon,' Rob said, waving a dismissive hand.

'No. Take this.' Brandon gave him a fiver. 'And put the change in the Lifeboat box.'

'You are a gentleman. A real gentleman.' Rob stretched his mobile features into a smile.

'If you hear anything, or see anything, give me a call,' Brandon said, getting up from the bar stool. 'If you remember any strange people hanging around or coming in for a pint. And if you remember any of those conversations, likewise. It will help, believe me.'

'I'll give it some thought.' Rob rubbed his head again. 'And I'll ask around. You can be sure that someone will have seen or heard something.'

Brandon nodded a farewell and made for the door.

'Merry Christmas,' the redhead called out.

Christmas Eve tomorrow. And then Chelsea's birthday on the 28th. He needed to fit in some shopping. Whoever invented Christmas must have had time and money on their hands, he thought, pushing the door open and walking out into a fine mist of drizzle.

9

Rachel

Rachel looked across the cliffs, at the meringue-tipped waves, the gulls circling against mountainous grey clouds, the heavenly shafts of sparkling light, the picture-perfect scenery, and vowed she'd never paint it. She'd seen the varying attempts in every gallery from Land's End to Bude and had nothing new to give.

Her head was still fuzzy from the Montol three nights before. She braced herself. *Be vigilant.* The kids were like hyper lemmings.

'Miss, Miss,' Peter Burton shouted, turning his blotchy red face to her. The wind was blowing greasy strands of hair into his eyes. Why must they get so close to the edge? she thought, as the bespectacled thirteen-year-old flapped a hand out to sea. He was like Piggy in *Lord of the Flies*: just needed a conch. 'I've seen a seal. A seal!!'

Rachel forced a look of interest. She was beginning to regret signing up for the Christmas Holiday Club art trip. Sure, the extra money would help. But fifteen teenagers on a clifftop, still pumped up from the Montol murder? She'd earn every penny. The victim was Josh Ryan's uncle, Pat. She taught Josh one-to-one English. The thirteen-year-old boy was her star pupil, his only 'failings' poor confidence and poor spelling. It was all too close for comfort. Pat Ryan was just a regular Joe. Wrong place, wrong time. A devoted family man said his memorial *Facebook* page.

Peter was leaning over the edge, clicking away with his phone.

Peering down into the swell by the rocks, Rachel saw something black bobbing up and down. The seal was pretty scraggy looking. Ribbons of black seaweed gave it a bizarre comb-over.

Mixed media abstracts are big now, she thought, as she spotted a splash of red on the speckled black rock far below. A plastic bag? They were making sculptures out of the waste washed up on the beach – they'd built one in the shape of a whale by St Michael's Mount, she remembered. Clever. But time-consuming.

A buzz on her mobile made her check the time: 14.30. Would it look bad to round up the kids now? Get them back to school a touch early? It would give her more time to re-work that frame for Julia. Could also rain. She looked up. A lumpen grey cloud face was knitting a darkening brow.

'Come on, pack up your sketch books, no dawdling, let's get back before it pours.'

As she spoke a shaft of sunlight struck through, glancing off Peter's specs and dazzling him.

'Miss, it's really sunny now. Can't we stay a few more minutes? Sketch the seal? Please?' he whined, the crooked line of gappy yellow teeth slashing his pink face reminding her of a Lucian Freud portrait.

'Nope. There's plenty more seals in the sea, Peter. Next time.'

'I think it's hurt, Miss," Peter said, his face falling. 'I saw blood.'

'Why don't you help Miss Stevenson with the holdall, Peter?' Rachel suggested, gathering her things together. 'Miss Stevenson, we're making a move, before it pours,' she called over to the young teacher who was fiddling with a pencil, demonstrating perspective to class bad boy Damien Kane.

Last time Rachel checked his work he'd been doodling graffiti tags.

She could see Nick jostling with Jack at the back of the pack. They were taking selfies right on the cliff edge. *For God's sake. What was the matter with them?*

'Come on, Nick, Jack. Put your mobiles away and get over here,' she shouted, her voice cracking. Control your fear, she told herself. Don't transfer it.

'But, Miss,' Jack called back, 'the seagulls are photobombing us!'

'Over here, now!' She dumped her bags on the ground and stomped towards them.

Peter had turned his attention to Miss Stevenson. So much for helping her with the holdall, thought Rachel, as she watched his scrunched-up face pleading with her, his arms waving out to sea.

'Peter's seen a stiff!' shouted one of the boys, who was on tiptoes, inches from a sheer drop.

'It's a seal!' Peter pushed to the front of the crowd, Miss Stevenson in tow.

The kids were swarming all over the clifftop, mobile phones clicking, sketch books dumped in heaps like cow pats. Rachel raced towards Nick who was on his stomach, head and shoulders over the edge, taking photos.

'For Chrissake, Nick, get back.' Her heart was racing, her words shaky. Dropping down beside him, she pulled him back sharply, sending small rocks tumbling and ricocheting down the cliff face.

'Rachel, I mean, Miss,' Nick said, jerking backwards. 'You've made me drop my phone!'

They watched in horror as the phone fell, bouncing off the rock face before landing on a grassy knoll.

'I can get that,' Jack said, coming up beside them. 'I rock climb all the time.'

'Not on my time.' Rachel got to her feet, holding out an arm to bar his way. The wind was getting stronger, her skirt was billowing.

'You could paraglide down, Miss,' Jack smirked.

Nick didn't look amused. He was standing now, but still staring at his phone, Jack capturing his misery on his own.

'Get over it,' Rachel snapped, shepherding the kids away from the edge. 'Everyone get back. Now!' She fixed them with her practised teacher glare. 'Put away your phones, or they'll join Nick's. Pick up your things and get moving. Unless you want to stay behind with me this afternoon and finish those sketches in your own time?'

This was one mantra Rachel had picked up on day one at her new job. Detention threat. Easy to say. Easy to forget, particularly when you were as keen to scarper as the kids.

They walked along the clifftop towards steep, wooden steps which zig-zagged down to the carpark. Rachel strode ahead, Becky Stevenson held back, chatting to a couple of the girls. She didn't look much older than them, with her shiny, pink-cheeked face, invisible braces, and ponytail. Rachel felt far older than her thirty-three-years. She pulled out the minibus keys, couldn't wait to bundle the kids in and get out of there. The trip had been a duff idea.

It'd been two long months since she'd returned to Penzance. Two months cooped up in a school and one of Julia's spare rooms. She'd killed a few hours learning to drive the minibus, just scraping a licence. That was fun and served a purpose, thought Rachel, as she beeped the bus open. Could come in handy if she started up a framing business.

'Shall I do a head count?' Becky said, as Rachel started up

the engine.

'Yes, good idea.' *I should have thought of that.* It was at times like this that Rachel appreciated Julia's role as pillar of the community. Why else would St Piran's have been persuaded to employ her as a Learning Support Assistant? Good old Julia – a word in the right ear, the promise of a fund-raising fete in the gardens of her big old house. And, unlike many others making grandiose gestures, Julia would keep her word. Deck her gardens with white and black Cornish flag bunting. She was a saint. Where would they be without her?

Rachel glanced at the time on the dashboard. 'Seats belts on, everyone.'

'We're all in,' Becky said, as Rachel checked her face in the rear-view mirror. Her shoulder length blonde hair was a wind-whipped mess. Should have tied it back like Becky. Her cheeks were glowing, while Rachel's were wan. Rachel hadn't slept much last night. Her green eyes were red-rimmed, like the ones in Lizzie's painting.

'All in,' she said, reaching over her seat to pull the door shut. Becky gave her a look, as Rachel forced the gear stick into first and then tugged it back into second, propelling them out of the carpark. She switched on the radio to drown out the kid's chatter.

As soon as she parked the bus outside the grey stone schoolhouse, the kids started jostling and pushing their way through the aisle.

'Miss,' said a hesitant voice. 'Miss.'

She turned round to see an ashen-faced Peter Burton. He thrust his phone in front of her – his arms outstretched, his hands shaking, his whole body straining to hold onto the thing.

'You look like you've seen a ghost, mate,' Jack said, as he

pushed past, peering at the phone as he went. 'What the hell!' he yelled, stopping in his tracks.

'That's no seal,' Damien said, coming up behind him.

Peter stood, his eyes fixed on Rachel, the phone ranged on her like a gun. As she took it from him, the screen turned black.

10

Rachel

Nick edged onto the passenger seat of Rachel's battered old Fiat 500, careful not to spill the debris of empty packets and papers onto the floor. Rachel smiled. He was a good kid – had sat patiently with nattering Peter Burton while she gave the police details about the body at the bottom of the cliff. The one Peter had captured on his phone and was glorying in, making the most of his moment. Christ, she'd been a witness to two deaths in three days. Should she be wielding a scythe rather than a paintbrush?

Exhausted after the ordeal, they sat in silence, Rachel driving on auto pilot along the narrow winding roads bordered by high hedgerows which dipped here and there to reveal flashes of sea. It was sunny now, in that bi-polar Cornish weather way. The wind from the ocean was always rushing in, shooing the clouds off somewhere else along the coast. It was a constant struggle between light and dark.

Nick was staring out of the window hugging a lumpy sports bag, rocking slightly.

'Do you reckon the bodies – the deaths – are connected,' Nick said, giving her a quick side eye.

'Maybe,' Rachel said, 'It's too early to say. The body was unrecognisable from the photo.'

'The SOCOs will be down there right now. That one from the Montol. Al Chapman.'

'I don't think it will be as straightforward as identifying … Pat Ryan's body. There was so much littered around belonging to him,' Rachel said.

'Same people could have made the same mistakes. Or perhaps it's their "signature".'

'Signature?' Rachel said, glancing in the rear-view mirror, at a fast-approaching van. 'That van is coming up fast.'

'I guess you don't watch Line of Duty?' Nick said, twisting round to check the van. 'Don't worry, Rachel, it's just DPD. And it's indicating left. We're not being tailed.'

'That's a relief,' Rachel said. She just wanted to get to The Hall, finish the frame she'd promised Julia. She wouldn't ask for money but would reluctantly accept some when Julia offered the third time. Her LSA salary was a pittance. She had huge credit card debts that she wanted to chip away at, if only to help salvage her rating.

She glanced at Nick. He was deep in thought, curling and uncurling his earphones wire around one finger.

As she turned a sharp corner to face a steep slope, Rachel moved the gears down to second and started to pump her foot on the accelerator. It was always a mammoth task getting the old rust bucket up the final mile to The Hall, Julia and Sam's house. It sat at the top of the hill; its sallow stone front as snooty as ever. Julia had inherited the place from her mother's side of the family, just one of their many Cornwall properties. The Trenowdens owned half of the neighbourhood and other choice chunks of Cornish 'cream'.

Hartington Hall had an assured air. It looked down on the town below, with its cobbled streets and cramped fishermen's cottages, many gentrified, but all doffing their slate rooftops at The Hall.

'Shall I get out and push?' Nick grinned, as the Fiat dropped down to 10 miles an hour, its engine shrieking.

Rachel laughed. 'Just lean forward and pray to Saint Piran.'

The row of firs which lined the long drive to the house

swayed in the wind, as the Fiat spluttered onto the forecourt.

Rachel was surprised to see Julia's silver Mercedes parked outside the pillared front door at an erratic diagonal.

'Your mum's home, Nick. I thought she was going through some stuff at the gallery with Sam this afternoon?'

Nick muttered in agreement. 'Thanks for the lift,' he added, stuffing the empty wrappers and rubbish he'd been sitting on into his pockets.

'A pleasure,' Rachel said, noting his thoughtful gesture.

The front door was open, and Rachel could see Julia on the phone in the vast black and white tiled hallway. She was running fingers through her thick, blow-dried hair. She'd had it done that morning before meeting some of the new gallery's investors.

Nick had gone round the back of the house to the kitchen, for food, probably, and to shove the contents of his pockets in the bin. He'd also taken the bag of dirty sports gear. Sam wouldn't want it littering the place.

Julia raised a palm at Rachel to stop her going past and up to her room. She waited in the lobby as Julia nodded and muttered 'yes' in quiet, choking tones.

One of the investors has pulled out, thought Rachel, fiddling impatiently with her phone.

Julia put the receiver down on the pretty French hallstand. She stood before it, her back to Rachel, straight arms at her sides, her head bowed.

Rachel slipped her mobile back into her pocket as Julia turned to her. Her usually flawless complexion was blotchy. She put a shaking hand to her mouth, and with her other reached for Rachel. Rachel grabbed her as she stumbled, Julia's legs giving way beneath her.

The two women looked at each other. Rachel could see the

fear; could feel it. 'What is it?' she said, gripping Julia's arms. She could hear Nick at the door at the far end of the hall, which led into the kitchen.

'Mum, why's there a police car parked out back?'

'Nick, just a minute, please,' Rachel said, brushing away some strands of hair that had fallen across Julia's face.

'What's happened?' Rachel's stomach clenched.

Nick was standing rigid as a sentry waiting for orders.

'It's Sam, Nick.' Julia walked slowly towards him. 'There's been an accident. He's ... he's dead.'

Rachel's reached for the hallstand to steady herself – her eyes on Julia, who had wrapped her arms around her son. Nick remained still, one arm at his side the other tentatively curved around his mother's waist.

'How?' he said.

Rachel strained to hear. Julia's usual confident voice barely audible.

'The police are here. In the living room. They found Sam at the bottom of the cliffs between Sennen Cove and Land's End.' She began to whimper.

Rachel went cold. *Surely not. Not Sam?* She fought an urge to be sick.

'We were there today – this afternoon.' Nick brushed a hand over his mother's bowed head and looked across at Rachel. She looked away – the living room door was ajar, and she could see Brandon sitting on the sofa with the red-headed detective who was taking statements at the Quay. She felt an irrational desire not to keep them waiting. To get it over with.

Instead, she walked over to Julia and hugged her.

'I'm so, so sorry.' Rachel pressed Julia's face hard against her chest, the awkward gesture jolting them apart.

'I was going to make some tea for the detectives and then

the phone rang. It was Sylvia. Sam's mother. Oh God, I wish I'd had time to think through what to say.'

'It's okay. Julia, what could you say? Come here.' Rachel gave her another hug; felt her body tense.

'I'll make the tea,' Nick said, going back into the kitchen. Rachel watched him fill the kettle and turn on the washing machine.

'I guess we'd better go through.' Julia was looking at the living room door and the occupants beyond. 'They'd only just arrived when Sylvia called. I shouldn't have picked up. I … I thought maybe it was Sam. Maybe there'd been a mistake.'

Rachel took her by the arm, and they walked in together, Brandon up on his feet to greet them, his dark brows rising a fraction.

'My son is making tea. Would you like some, Detective Inspector? Detective Sergeant?'

'No, thank you. We'll leave you with your family shortly.'

Brandon stood there, stroking the stubble above his lip. 'Mrs Trenowden, once again, I am so sorry for your loss.'

He felt in the top pocket of his jacket and pulled out a pen and small notepad.

Julia let out a small gasp and pulled at the neck of her dress.

'Come and sit down, Julia.' Rachel steered her to the massive cream sofa opposite Brandon. 'Ah, here comes the cavalry.'

Nick was at the door gripping a heavy tray in trembling hands. Cups, saucers and spoons rattled, and milk sloshed from a china jug as he brought his load down on the coffee table.

'As you've gone to all this trouble, I'll have a cup with you. He looked at Julia, who nodded her ascent. 'DS Menhenrick take the car. I'll see you back at the station.' He threw over the keys.

Julia, poured the tea, raised hers to her lips, lukewarm liquid splashing over the rim and trickling down the arm of her expensive block-colour dress.

'We don't have to go into anything now,' Brandon said, watching her carefully, passing a cup and saucer to Rachel. 'Do you have anything stronger?' He looked at Rachel who went to get up, but Julia touched her arm.

'No. It's fine. I'm fine. Oh my God. Sam. Sam.'

Brandon pushed aside his cup and picked up his pen.

Julia gripped the edge of the sofa. 'I had the most awful feeling something had gone wrong … late morning when I was waiting for Sam at the gallery. Before he set off for his morning jog, he said he had a few things to go over before the meeting. And then nothing. His mobile just rang and rang and we waited at the gallery; waited for what seemed like hours. I made my apologies. To our guests. We were hosting a lunch for our sponsors.' She looked up at Brandon in explanation. 'I went through things with Guy Baxter and the Bowen-Lacys. We had lunch. It was awful. Just awful. Going through the motions not knowing – but somehow knowing, that something had happened.'

Brandon was leaning in, listening intently.

'It didn't make sense him not showing. Not phoning. The new gallery,' she bit her bottom lip, looked at Rachel, 'was his passion.' She studied her hands, a sob escaping. 'The gallery meant everything to him. Could he have got last-minute reservations? Did I miss something?'

Brandon was regarding the two of them. 'It was most probably an accident. You say he was preoccupied? He may have lost his footing. Got too close to the edge.'

Julia started to sob gently. Her body trembling, she stretched an arm out to one of the sofa cushions and pulled it to her.

'I know that this is distressing for you. I won't keep you much longer. But had you noticed Sam acting out of character recently,' Brandon spoke softly, his hands resting on his thighs.

'No. He was tense – but he often is. Was …' Julia bit her bottom lip and looked to the side. 'A lot was riding on the gallery. It was his project.'

'Was there any tension with the sponsors? Financial or creative?'

'No. They were on board. The lunch was intended to cement our relationship.'

Julia looked at him and he held her gaze. 'Did they seem surprised that he hadn't shown up.'

Julia looked down and took her time before replying. 'No. Well, not at first. They were very courteous to me, as they could see that I was embarrassed by his absence.'

'And later?' Brandon said.

Julia looked him straight in the eye. 'They were concerned. We were all concerned. And –' She sighed deeply. 'Rightly so.'

'Indeed. I am so very sorry, Mrs Trenowden. If you could please give me your guests' contact details.'

Julia looked flustered. 'Now?' She went to get up.

'If it's not too much trouble. And then I'll leave you. Give you some time to yourself.'

Julia shook her head lightly. 'Time to myself. Yes, I'll have plenty of that.'

'We found Sam's wallet, Mrs Trenowden. It will be returned, after the forensics have examined it.'

'And phone?' Rachel said. He always had his phone. Never off it.

'No, we didn't find his phone. May have been washed

away. We'll keep looking, though. Is your phone synced to his, Mrs Trenowden?'

'His phone synced to mine? No. No, it's not. Why do you ask?'

'Just to check his last calls. See if he was meeting someone, perhaps?'

Julia clutched at her neck. 'You don't think?'

'No. No. Sam's death is unexplained and it's helpful if we can understand as much as possible about his circumstances. That's all. We can check his calls via his service provider. Just to get a clear picture of events.'

'He didn't have any enemies if that's what you think.' Julia got up from the sofa, pulling at the damp sleeve of her dress.

She stood there in silence, before Nick started clearing the table.

Brandon picked up his coat and got up. 'I'll leave you now. Once again, my sincere sympathies.'

'The contacts. You want the contacts,' Julia said, fumbling for her phone in the bag by her feet. She tapped into it. 'Your number, DI Hammett?'

He gave her the number. 'Thank you,' he said, when his phone pinged. 'I'll be in touch.'

Julia gave a small nod and stood watching him as he made to leave.

'I'll see him out,' Rachel said, getting up and following Brandon into the hallway. When they reached the door, she asked: 'How are you going to get back to the station? I could give you a lift?'

'Don't worry. I could do with the walk down the drive. And I can call for a station car.'

Rachel lowered her voice. 'I was at the station earlier. One of my kids photographed the body. I mean Sam. Of course, we didn't know it was Sam, at the time.' She looked over at Julia, who had sunk back into the sofa. 'Uncanny.'

'I heard,' Brandon said, as he shrugged on his overcoat and walked into the hall. 'Perhaps we can have a chat tomorrow.'

'At the station?'

'Your second home. Not quite as plush as your first.'

Rachel looked back at Julia, but she hadn't heard. Brandon had pitched his voice just right.

He opened the front door. 'When things have begun to sink in, it might be a good time to talk. In the meantime, if anything occurs to you, anything at all. Give me a ring. But you stay here and look after Julia, tonight. She needs a good friend.'

Rachel nodded in agreement.

'What's this?' Brandon had knocked over a package which had been resting against the front door. He stooped to prop it back up. 'It's addressed to you.'

'I wasn't expecting anything. It wasn't here earlier. The doorbell didn't ring. Did it?' She looked at the package. Knew immediately that it was a canvas beneath its wrapping.

She was right. A canvas. A blank one. No note, or receipt.

'Who's it from?' Brandon was stroking his stubble again.

'Doesn't say,' Rachel said, tidying up the paper. 'I didn't order it. Must be a mistake.'

She looked down the drive. Whoever had delivered it must have put it there in the last half an hour. Walked there, otherwise they would have heard the car.

'What's that in the corner?' Brandon had come round to her side.

'Looks like a spot of red paint.'

'Indeed. That's what it looks like. Best get this checked out. I'll send a car round to pick it up.'

11

Brandon

Brandon walked down the drive, hands in his pockets, eyes on the road ahead. Fir trees lined the narrow path, their branches bending inwards. He felt like a sportsman or a musician in a tunnel, senses alive, adrenalin pumping, coming out to perform. His nerves were on edge – something wasn't right. Something was badly wrong. He'd spent half an hour in Julia and Rachel's company and was little the wiser about the circumstances of Sam's death or, indeed, their own situation. Why was Rachel living at The Hall and not with her mother? He had assumed that she was primarily in town to keep an eye on Lizzie Matthews. But were relations so strained after Oliver's death that she couldn't bear to live in the same house as her?

Brandon turned back to look at The Hall. It was an impressive place – somewhere you could hide away in, create your own space in its airy rooms and wings. So, yes, he could see why Rachel would prefer this to living in the claustrophobic confines of Seabird Cottage, with a woman who filled every inch of the place with her presence and memories.

But Sam. It would be hard to live in the company of a man like that, even at The Hall, massive as it was. He hadn't been a welcoming person – quite the opposite. Brandon had observed him, seen him about town, making endless calls on his mobile, turning up in unexpected places, always looking like he was eager to leave. Pubs on the Quay. Meghan's gallery in Newlyn. He was there when he gave Meghan a flyer for his

New Year gig. She was as friendly as ever, but Sam looked shifty, until something clearly clicked and he forced a smile.

That smile had faded fast when he'd asked about Pat Ryan. Ryan had been at the Smugglers Tavern the night before the Montol, according to the landlord. So had Meghan, with a man whose description fitted Sam's. Could there be a connection?

He paused as he approached the end of the drive and looked across the road to the sea tumbling into the cove below. He was enjoying the walk. It was good to get clean air in his lungs, get some oxygen to his brain. He pulled a cigarette out of the packet in his top pocket, the irony of his action making him smile.

He'd give up next year. Make it a resolution, stop Chelsea nagging him. But right now, the cigarettes helped him focus. There had never been a better time to focus, he thought, turning back to look at The Hall, with its regal columns, French shutters, and stone façade.

12

Rachel

A ragged streak of yellow light underlined the grey sky. The waves rolled onto the beach and rolled back like playful toddlers. Rachel assessed the conditions as she stepped into her wet suit, her clothes discarded in a heap on the sand. She leant down and picked up a stone to keep them in place, although there was barely a breeze. Things could change in minutes. It was a lesson learnt and never forgotten.

She had considered going for a morning run along the clifftop. The run Sam had taken every morning until that last one, a week ago now. Somehow it didn't seem right, not with him laid out cold in the morgue. He would hate that, thought Rachel, as she walked towards the water's edge. He would hate the limbo, be impatient for them to get on with it, do the 'fucking autopsy', 'get him out of there'. His feet, once forever tapping and anxious for action, were now bloated, blue blocks.

The water was freezing. Her own feet would turn blue if she stood there much longer. So, she waded in to her waist and dived below the waves, that first immersion winding her, making her gasp as she came up for air. She dived again, kicking hard to the surface and then rolled onto her back and began to swim out to sea – watching the coast shrink to a thin white line. Flipping onto her front Rachel changed direction and started swimming parallel to the shore. *I still have the survival instinct?* In the deep, the sea was calm, the action taking place on the edges; but you never wanted to go too far.

She thought she'd drummed that into her son.

Lift your arm, take a breath, two more strokes, maybe three, four, take another. Simple mechanics for a good, strong swimmer. This was the first time that she'd been back in the water since returning to Penzance. She didn't know whether she'd deliberately shunned the sea. Whether she was still blaming it for Oliver's death. She'd blamed too many things, too many people for that. Herself. Why did she leave him with her parents? They could barely look after themselves. But he was nine. Not a baby. It wasn't their fault, was it? He could swim. She'd taught him to swim. She'd swum with him in these waters, in the warmer waters of a sea under a summer sun. Lizzie dozing in a deck chair on the beach; the one beside her empty apart from a crumpled newspaper, her father having sloped off on some erroneous errand. She'd warned Oliver about rip tides, how you stay calm, float on your back until you drift out of their clutches. How it is futile to fight the primal energy. It is in the sea's power to release you. 'Yes, Mum, I know,' he'd say, a teenager-in-waiting, 'I've seen it on *YouTube*.'

She thought of Lizzie perched on the edge of her deck chair, next to the empty one, that blistering hot August day three years ago. *Was it three years now?* Her bright kaftan, golden flipflops and floppy hat, marking her out like a tropical bird. Oliver would have looked out for her from the sea. When did she start to worry – put down her book? Could she even read a book when her grandson was out there in the sea? There were lots of others out there too. Did this give her a sense of security? Or did it make her uneasy? That cheap red lilo, like so many others, but his legs kicking harder, pushing him out beyond the rest. Rachel turned and began to swim back towards her own landmark, the muddle of clothes on the sand.

In her mind's eye, she could see Lizzie getting up, taking off her sunglasses, fishing in her bag for her spectacles, her hand fretting over all sorts of stuff, all the time looking out for that red lilo. *Where was he? Silly sausage! No spectacles. Where are they?* Then Lizzie charging across the sand to the sea, kicking off one gold flipflop and then the other, her hat flying off, plunging into the shallows, the bottom of her kaftan clinging to her legs, her face strained, looking, looking for that piece of red. That sign of life blood.

Rachel had gone through the scene many times. How she imagined it. How Lizzie had described it. The pain was as real now as it was that day in August when the phone rang in London. She'd wanted to die, wallow in misery, but Lizzie had stolen her grief. Parading it in interviews, blogs, seminars, a campaign for safer swimming. Lizzie was drowning in grief, flailing around, *rescue me, rescue me, rescue me.* So, she'd mostly kept it together; for her mother and for her father, a man once so colourful, so full of life, reduced to an art installation. A pale spectre wailing in the shadows. He was dead by Christmas.

On she swam, her arms cutting through the waves, choppy now, over a patch of seaweed, black as oil, past rocks that lurked on the sea bed like recumbent monsters. She lifted her head to scan the beach. There it was, the muddle of clothes, the rock still holding them down. She was right to place it there. The wind had picked up. *Was that a lifeguard? Penzance didn't have lifeguards in the winter. Silly thought.* But there was someone standing on the rocks behind her clothes looking out to sea. Looking at her. Rachel dipped her head back into the water, swam a few strokes. When she looked back up, they were gone.

13

Rachel

'How was your swim?' Julia was in the kitchen making coffee when Rachel returned, wet hair dripping down her neck onto her t-shirt. She plonked the bag with her wet suit and towel in the corner.

'Cold!'

Julia smiled. 'Want a cup?'

'Please.' Rachel sat at the table, the seat of her jeans still wet. She thought how this would have irked Sam. He'd treated her and Nick like unruly Labradors, bounding in with their mess. Well, he's gone, she thought dispassionately. But all the same, his absence was felt.

Julia placed a cup before her. 'Brandon called.'

'Oh, yes?'

'They've had the post mortem results. Sam died by a massive blow to the head, and chest, in keeping with a fall. Absolutely nothing untoward. No signs of a struggle, deep cuts, or bruising to the arms or face. Nothing suspicious.' Julia reached for her cup. 'And so … arrangements can be made. But not just yet. They want to keep Sam for a little longer. Just …' Julia put down her cup, let her hair fall across her face. 'Just in case.'

Rachel had a sudden vision of Sam on that slab in the morgue. She'd visited him with Julia. A debt of friendship. It was a difficult image to erase. Rest in Peace. Please.

'Thank God, nothing … nothing untoward.' Rachel reached out a hand to Julia.

'Yes, thank God,' Julia replied. 'Oh, and Brandon left a new canvas for you. To replace the one the police picked up. He just wants to keep hold of that one, for now.'

'Cool.' *What did she want with a fucking canvas? New, old or dusted with a fine film of forensic powder. Or whatever they used. She'd give it to Lizzie for her 'art therapy'.*

'Is there anything I can do? Start looking at making arrangements? Make some calls? Let people know? Find out what people do ... in these circumstances?' Rachel knew what the reply would be. Julia wouldn't trust her with anything important.

'No, Rachel, darling, but would you mind sorting out a few things at the gallery? There's a whole stack of paintings which will need to be delivered. Sam has the details on his computer. I just couldn't – face it.'

'Of course. No worries.' Could Rachel face it? All those examples of Sam's idea of art?

'His computer's at the station. The police station,' Julia added. 'It's clean. No evidence. No clues. Just Sam's business dealings. Bless him.'

Nothing dodgy?

'I'll go into town this morning. Drop off the canvas at Lizzie's. Get some food in.' They hadn't shopped since Sam's death. Christmas had come and gone and they'd lived off the Ocado turkey and trimmings for the duration. Julia had lost her appetite, but Nick hadn't. And nor had Rachel. Eating at the dinner table was a much more relaxed affair. As a nod to Sam, Rachel had taken his signature fish stew out of the freezer. *Was that disrespectful?* If it was, Julia chose to see it as the opposite. Through her misty eyes, Sam's stock had risen since his untimely death.

14

Brandon

Photos of Pat Ryan, including his body parts, were plastered on the station's incident board. In many respects they were just decoration, albeit gruesome, designed to focus the minds of Brandon's team. A photo of the trainer which Brandon had swiped off the drugs runner on the morning of the Solstice was an interesting exhibit. Confirming suspicions, Ryan's DNA was all over it. Pat had been their *Crimderella*, but hadn't made it to the Montol bash that evening. At least not in one piece.

Brandon's detective training at the University of Texas Police Academy had helped place him at the centre of the investigations. Also, his local knowledge was seen as a huge advantage by the Major Crime Investigation Team (MCIT) at Newquay. They were happy for him to lead the investigations in Penzance, all the while on call to give practical support.

Brandon addressed his team without turning from the board, his eyes on the trainer. 'Someone got to Ryan between the hours of 6.30am and early evening. Sliced him up and disposed of his body in daylight hours.' Brandon rubbed his chin. 'There is no CCTV on the Quay and, so far, no suspicious sightings. But someone must have seen something. People moving around the bonfire – hauling a heavy load. What have you got?'

He turned to face Jo, who needed no incentive to get on with her job and dig deep. But DC (Stew) Bland was as grindingly slow as ever, forever box-ticking and filling in forms to avoid hard graft.

'Nothing yet, Boss. But, I agree, someone must have seen them. I assume it is them? Pat was a fit bloke – would have taken some strength to take him out,' Jo said, getting up to stand next to him.

Brandon nodded, remembering their wrestle on the cliffs. He'd been a tough cookie and a fighter.

Stew's eyes were glazing over. Brandon guessed he was already worrying about what to eat for lunch and decided to jolt him out of his daydream. 'Stew, what new leads have you got on Nike Boy?' He pointed to a fuzzy CCTV photo of a dark-haired man in his late teens or early twenties, wearing a hoodie with the tick logo. The young man's image had been captured all over Penzance.

Stew shuffled in his seat. 'Well, he came in on the … train … around 9am on …'

'I said any new leads, Stew. Come on. You need to do better than this. We've had the CCTV photos for days now.'

Jo waited a beat then launched in. 'Nike Boy was seen hanging around the Smugglers Tavern on December 15, according to the landlord, Rob. I showed him the photo. He had a coke at the bar. Kept his hood up, but Rob remembered him. Didn't say much but looked like he was waiting for someone to show.'

'Was he seen there on the night of the murder?'

'Rob didn't notice him. The pub was packed that night – with locals and tourists.'

'Any sightings of him coming or going that day?' Brandon was frowning. Things weren't going as well as he thought they would. 'Maybe Nike Boy was on a recce the previous week? Maybe he decided to wear something a little less Logo on his next visit? Maybe he was a decoy and someone else came in on the train on December 21?'

'No more sightings, Boss,' Jo said.

'Okay, guys, we need to do some more digging. Stew, go through the CCTV again – take stills of anyone who looks suspicious over the two-week period. Turning up in odd places, hood up, nosing around. Was Nike Boy definitely alone? Did he hook up with someone else on a different part of the train? Did he come in and check into a hotel, or Airbnb? Phone round. Penzance isn't big. Someone will have spotted something.'

Brandon fixed them with his steady, scrutinising stare. 'Dig. We need to find Pat's killer soon, otherwise Nike Boy will disappear back into the sewer he slithered out of. Jo, see if the MCIT guys in Newquay can name Nike via face recognition software.'

'Will do, Boss. Also, we've had quite a few calls following the media blitz. I've been following them up on the phone and I've got a few marked up for visits.'

'Good. Keep me informed.' Brandon ran a hand through his hair. 'Nike has dark hair, right? But it looked standard length, from the photos we have when his hood isn't up.'

Jo nodded.

'Otherwise, he pretty much fits the description of one of the two teens who threatened Rachel Matthews on the night of the Montol.'

Brandon looked Jo in the eye. 'The dark-haired kid Rachel described had a bleed – shaven sides. Maybe,' he paused, 'Maybe it's the same guy. Perhaps he had a haircut that day. Maybe even in Penzance. Worth checking out.'

Jo held his gaze. 'Absolutely. I'll call round the barbers. Odd that he would hang around after the killing, though. You'd have thought they'd have scarpered.'

Brandon looked down. 'You have a point, Jo. But Rachel

said they were out of it. And not, by all accounts, the brightest boys on the block. Perhaps they had train tickets for later that evening. Or the next day. If they were young mules, they might not have had the cash for new tickets.'

'Even when they could be suspects in a murder case?' Jo moved towards him.

'Perhaps they were getting their kicks from watching it all unfold? Maybe they thought they were invincible – no motives, no evidence. Or just dumb arses. Worth checking out, Jo. And, if they are still lurking, Rachel could be in danger. If they killed once, what's to stop them doing so again?'

15

Brandon

Brandon ambled out from behind the front desk and motioned Rachel to the interview room. A scruffy young guy, sitting in a row of orange chairs, pulled his dog towards him as they passed.

'How's it going?' Brandon said, as they sat opposite each other in the sparse back room.

'Much better since this morning. It was tough, for Julia and for all of us, waiting for the results of the post mortem.'

'Yes,' Brandon said, getting up and walking to a metal cabinet in the corner. He turned a key in the lock of the second drawer and produced Sam's computer.

'Clean as a whistle,' Brandon said, passing it across the table to Rachel.

'As a whistle?' Rachel raised an eyebrow.

'A dog whistle. If there's anything here, it's not making itself heard, at least not to me. A little surprising ... for someone like Sam Trenowden.'

He could see her waiting for him to continue but let the suggestion hang.

'Someone like Sam Trenowden?' she offered.

Brandon leaned forward, a small smile flickering. 'Someone like Sam Trenowden.' He was enjoying this.

'Oh, for Chrissake, Brandon. Let's call a wheeler dealer a sleazy toad when he's staring you in the face.'

Brandon threw back his head and laughed. 'Aha, Rachel Matthews is still there! I thought I might have seen the last of her.'

Her eyes flashed – the lights were on.

'Fat chance. If I try to leave someone, or something, calls me back for an encore. I guess you're stuck with me for a while, Detective Inspector.'

He observed her in silence. Noted the flush of colour reddening her cheeks. 'Good,' he said after a while. 'Good. Look, there isn't too much more to be said about Sam Trenowden right now. Best let him rest a while. But I figure, this might not be the end of it. Just a feeling. He might get an encore too.'

Someone shouted in Reception. The dog yelped and then fell silent.

Rachel waited a beat. 'Hmm?'

'Sam knew a lot of people. The great and the good and the less so.'

Rachel was giving him a wary look. He didn't want to worry her unduly, but best she got wise. The laptop lay on the table between them, her fingers rapping on its lid.

'Why did Julia send you in for the computer?' Brandon fell back in his chair, resting his hands behind his head.

Rachel shook her head, as if clearing it. 'Well, she's pretty cut up. As you can imagine. She can't get her head around the gallery opening. Wants me to sort things – pick up where Sam left off. It's going to take the best part of the weekend just to make a start. And, of course, we're in holiday hiatus.'

'Will you postpone the opening? Could be the best thing in the circumstances.'

Rachel frowned. 'Would be good, but a lot of stuff has already been organised. Caterers, deliveries, the invitations. I think we will just have to push on through. It's distracting, too.'

'In a good way?' Brandon fell back forward.

'Well – I'll find out, soon enough.' Rachel looked at the

laptop. 'But – anything to fill the time, break the limbo.'

She ran a finger over a smudge on the laptop lid.

'Rachel,' Brandon said, cutting through her thoughts. 'Something off topic. Do you do extra tuition?'

'Why?' She cocked her head to the side.

'Chelsea is keen to get onto the A Level art course next year; I thought maybe you could give her some tutoring. I'd pay, of course.'

Rachel looked down and started worrying the laptop smear again. 'Well, I don't know. What about Becky Stevenson? I'm just the LSA.'

'She likes you.'

'Hmm.'

Brandon guessed she probably tidied up Chelsea's work for her. He'd compared the artwork she brought back from school, with the flat doodles of smiley people that littered their home.

'But where? It couldn't be at school,' Rachel said, looking back up at him.

'My place. We have a big old room at the top of the house. It used to be Chelsea's playroom. And, yeah, I practise up there too. The fiddle in case you forgot.' *How could she forget?* He remembered her sitting in the front row of all those small venue gigs he'd played when they were still at school, smiling up at him like an encouraging aunt.

'I've improved,' he said, with a wry smile.

'Well, we'll see.' Rachel got up from the table and slipped the computer under her arm.

'Don't forget the canvas.' Brandon pointed to it as he rose to join her. 'And you'll have to sign for the computer.'

Rachel smiled. 'Of course. Oh, and you keep the canvas. Give it to Chelsea. She could get started on something.'

'Why don't you come round tomorrow? Give it to her yourself? It's her birthday. I'm having a few people over. Nothing big.' It came out in a bit of a rush, but hell, why not.

Brandon stood, his legs parted, arms crossed, watching her getting her stuff together, thinking it through.

She buttoned up her coat and turned to face him. 'I'd love to come, Brandon. Can I bring anything?'

'Just yourself, Rachel. Just yourself.'

16

Rachel

Rachel waited until she heard Lizzie's soft whinnying snores before switching off the TV and sneaking out of the living room and into the studio with Sam's computer. She needed peace and quiet to concentrate. Julia had given her Sam's passwords: *Invincible1* and *Challenger1*. Like something from *Thunderbirds.* She opened the laptop. *Invincible1.* The predictable icons leapt up to greet her. Then Google Mail. *Challenger1.* Rachel expected an avalanche of incoming emails, but there were few. A couple of promotions: invites to private views, some sales spam, all related to art. No Gieves and Hawkes, his bespoke London tailor, nothing personal. How had he vanquished the ubiquitous smorgasbord of spam? The computer really was clean as a whistle. Rachel called up his choice freebie news site: *The Guardian.* She expected to see some targeted adverts. Nothing. It was like Sam's virtual spirit had been exorcised. Had he kept another computer? She'd have a root around at The Hall. Or had he done his main business on his phone? The missing one? Highly likely. But Julia suggested his gallery work was on this computer. She must have seen him tapping away on it, fuming and fretting over late replies or refusals. A little hissed 'Yes', when he got lucky.

Rachel typed Bowen-Lacy, one of the gallery sponsors, into the search. A slew of emails popped up. The last one was confirming the meeting on the day Sam died. The email led her to a folder and Rachel clicked in to see the other sponsors. Another folder revealed a respectable list of exhibitors that she could get working on. Sam had met little resistance getting artists to loan their work. They were hungry for exposure and the gallery – *did they even have a name for it yet?* – was expected to be the biggest thing in the Penwith arts community since the renovation of Tate St Ives. Rachel scrolled through the emails, downloading the images. Some were good. Some were of the moment. Sam had had a knack for tapping into commercial winners. The ones which would generate the most publicity. Julia had already vetted the works and it showed. Rachel relaxed. She wouldn't have to do much after all. Just make the calls and organise the deliveries.

So, all good. Or was it? There was no trace of Newlyn-Wave, Meghan's gallery. She had some good artists. Would he have gone to them direct? Bypassed Meghan?

Rachel shutdown the computer. She could hear Lizzie stirring, emitting a sharp jerky snore. She didn't want to get into any conversations about the gallery. Her mother still counted Sam as Public Enemy No. 1. Death did not become him, in her eyes. Rachel looked at the computer. A metal sphinx. A goody-two-shoes of data. Hmm. It hadn't 'spoken' to Brandon but he wasn't techno savvy. At least she didn't think he was. The station probably didn't have the resources to dig that deep, either. She remembered the meaty-faced PC on the night of the Montol and sensible red-headed Menhenick. The sphinx needed a different, darker mind, perhaps? Someone with hacking skills to prise it open. Damien Kane? The student antichrist. The boy banned from computers because he had hacked into the school network. Who knew the dark web like his backyard. Perhaps she could ask Nick to have a word? No! It would be unethical. Wasn't worth the risk. Was it? No. She remembered Damien's small dark eyes. The eyes of a corpse. Black ink wells: ironic, because at fourteen he still couldn't write legibly. But he could read with the cadence of a Shakespearean actor. And he could use a computer better than anyone. She'd take the obvious route first. Call in on Meghan at NewlynWave.

'Rachel, darling, why did you turn the TV off. *Pointless* is on!'

She was up.

'I didn't think you liked *Pointless* – thought it was boring.'

'It is, darling, but nothing else is on.'

Rachel put the computer into the carrier bag she'd brought it in. The emails could wait. And so could Meghan. But not for long.

17

Rachel

Chelsea opened the door to the small, terraced house in Newlyn, a great big grin on her face. 'Miss Matthews, you made it! You can be my – my artist in residence for the day!'

Rachel could see a gaggle of girls spilling out into the narrow hall behind her.

'Joking! Dad! Miss Matthews is here. Fetch her a drink. A large one!'

'I brought you a canvas. Your dad said you were keen to work on your art. And this.' Rachel produced a book on how to draw superheroes.

'Awesome! Oh, Dad!' She gave him an impish smile as he came alongside her, a glass of punch in his hand. 'I want to get a job at one of the galleries. One of the ones in St Ives. That would be awesome. So, I definitely want a pass.' Her blue eyes shined with optimism behind thick lenses, lenses too hefty for their light lilac frames.

Rachel nodded encouragingly. This could be achievable. Chelsea wasn't a natural talent, but she was the cheeriest and most enthusiastic girl in class. Always offering to set out the paint pots and brushes, clearing them away and washing them up. A wave of affection swept over Rachel. Chelsea's dreams were so small. She felt tears pricking the backs of her eyes again. She'd help her get that pass.

'Come on, Miss, look what Dad bought me. An easel – and all this paper and a huge tin of *Heroes*.'

Rachel followed her into the small living room. A low coffee table was laid out with plates of food. Sandwiches, chocolate fingers, custard creams and a unicorn birthday cake. They had been all the rage a few years ago, Rachel remembered. This one was still in its Tesco's box, a few candles by its side.

'Isn't it lovely! I was just going to get it out of its box and then everyone turned up. I've always wanted a unicorn cake.'

'My mum baked me one for my tenth birthday,' said a pretty girl with intricately braided blond hair. Daisy Beckett from school. She tended to speak in a whisper, her small mouth barely moving. When you leant in to listen it was usually something you didn't want to hear.

Chelsea's face fell, before rallying. 'Well, this is the only unicorn … in Newlyn!'

'That and the other six on the shelves and the ones out back.'

'What is this? A unicorn hunt?' Rachel said. Time to put the spiteful little minx back in her box. 'Besides, Chelsea has an artist in residence. Form an orderly queue and I'll draw each and every one of you. Unicorn horns on request.'

'Miss!' said Chelsea, jumping with glee. 'Dad, Miss Matthews is going to draw us. She's brilliant. Will you draw Dad too, Miss?'

'If he keeps me topped up with punch and cake,' Rachel said, smiling at Brandon.

He shrugged. 'So where would Miss Matthews like to perform – somewhere where there's more light? By the window?'

'Perfect.' This was working out well. Rachel hadn't sketched for a good few years, but it had to be better than discussing the recent deaths with the other parents and family friends. Town talk was of little else. As soon as they found out who she was, it would be the Penzance Inquisition. Did Sam

know Josh Ryan's Uncle Pat? *No. At least she didn't think so.*
Did Sam seem depressed? *Sam sensitive? Hardly!* How come
she hadn't recognised his body at the bottom of the cliffs?
Did they think she had superhero sight? In comparison, she
found it easy to impress her young audience. A deft likeness, a
flattering portrait, the accentuation of a feature – like Daisy's
small mean mouth – had the girls in raptures or fits of gig-
gles. She'd given Chelsea's centre-parting, limp, mousey hair,
a cool makeover. And then the adults joined in.

'You look like you might even be enjoying yourself.' Brandon was studying his portrait, a small smile on his face. Rachel had coloured it with blue and red pastels, twisting his
messy fringe into a unicorn horn quiff.

'It'll cost you.'

'Well, there had to be a catch.'

'A slice of the unicorn horn, please.'

'You drive a hard bargain.'

'And a turkey sandwich. You still have turkey?'

'When there's just the two of you …'

Rachel mimed someone playing a sad song on a violin.

'What are you saying? You want me to play my fiddle?'

'No. Gosh, I forgot. Well, if you like?'

'Nah. Looks like the party's breaking up now anyway. The
girls are going down to the skate plaza. But funny you should
mention my fiddle playing.'

'Well, actually, it was you … but never mind.'

'We're playing at The Acorn Theatre on New Year's Eve.
I could get you in on the guest list. That's if you haven't got
anything else on. We have a surprise guest singer.'

'Oh, yes?' Rachel looked curious. 'And who might that be?'

'Wouldn't be a surprise if I told you, gal. Come and see for
yourself.'

'Let me check with Julia. I couldn't leave her alone on New Year.'

'Of course. Of course. Has she … How is she?'

'It's not easy, not knowing when the body, when Sam, will be released. She seems fine, puts on a brave face and then … every now and then, just starts crying.'

Brandon creased his brow and looked away before continuing. 'I can imagine. It's been tough. For all of you. But at least there was good news with the post mortem, as such.'

Rachel gave him a sharp look. 'Good news?'

'No violence. That's something to be grateful for.'

Brandon didn't look convinced; his eyes were turned down.

'But it's not really satisfying, is it? For any of us. A lot of unanswered questions. Like we are in limbo. Like we're in purgatory.'

Brandon raised his eyes slowly to her face. 'I hope you can make it. Both of you.'

Rachel thought that old friends – really good, dependable ones – were as rare as unicorns.

18

Brandon

The guests had gone, and Chelsea wasn't likely to be back for a good few hours. After they'd finished up at the skate plaza, they'd go on to the ice cream parlour on the promenade. Brandon had given Chelsea enough money to treat her friends to a sundae.

He walked through the living room to the kitchen, ignoring the party debris piled up on the kitchen table and work surfaces. Reaching up to a top cabinet, he searched around for a bottle of bourbon. It was there, at the back, a good third still left over from last Christmas. He splashed some into a paper cup with a pink unicorn on it. Cheers, he said, as he took a sip and snatched a leftover sausage roll off one of the plates.

Sinking back into his worn armchair, he wriggled to get comfy, pulling out the large cushion prodding into his back and tossing it aside. The warmth from the bourbon was just what he needed – that and a moment's reflection. Rachel. She looked better today, but she still had that beaten, haunted look. He'd seen that look many times on many faces over the years. And now she was taking an interest in the investigations. It was to be expected, he thought, taking another sip. She was living at The Hall, and Sam was still very much part of their lives. Pat Ryan less so. Brandon was confident they would find his killer shortly. It had been a brutal, bloody murder and the DNA would out, in the end. It was just a case of going through the CCTV tapes again and following up the appeal leads. Brandon had a hunch it was an outsider, one likely to have come in on the Great Western line. And left on it. There were no further sightings in town. In many respects that was a relief if Nike Boy and the teen with the bleed were one and the same. He was concerned for Rachel. Shady guys had been hanging around the school, peddling drugs. If they took a dislike to her, for whatever reason, things could spiral out of control.

As it was, Nike Boy ticked most of the boxes. Brandon was enjoying the irony of the brand's logo. *Just Do It!* Nail the bastard.

The Jack Daniels was doing the trick. He rolled his neck, let the tension ease away. Rachel had Sam's computer. She wasn't convinced it was as innocent as it looked. But Phillips had sent it off to the techies – they would have spotted anything suspicious. Rachel was, understandably, on edge.

He glanced at his watch and surveyed the sea of cups and glasses, the plates with their half-eaten sandwiches and chunks of drying sponge cake. It could wait until the morning. Levering himself up from his chair he walked back through to the kitchen and refilled his cup. He closed the living room curtains against the night and picked up the fiddle and bow propped up against the wall, behind the kitchen door. Sometimes the only conversation he needed was the vibration of strings against wood. Resting the instrument under his chin, he stroked the bow across the bridge, letting the strains of a slow ballad fill his senses and clear his mind.

19

Rachel

Walking along the promenade to Newlyn was always invigorating, whatever the weather. The sea was calm today: wasn't throwing itself at the promenade in a frothing, tempestuous tantrum, dousing cars and people alike. That was last night's performance and it had left a brown carpet of seaweed. Slimy ribbons squelched beneath Rachel's feet. Today, though, all was good. The tide was out. Frilly doilies of surf fringed the sand and stone. Patterned pebbles in grey, white and black stacked up against the sea wall, pretty as sugar candy. Penzance was on charming form. Rachel wondered what she could charm out of Meghan, just minutes away in Newlyn.

She hadn't planned their meeting other than to check NewlynWave was open. It was. Meghan would be keen to capture any bonus New Year business from walkers and tourists idling in the town's cafes and galleries. So, she'd go in, kiss, kiss, hug and business. She wouldn't stay long. If she could help it. But once in Meghan's company it was hard to get away.

NewlynWave was a small box of a gallery in the epicentre of the town, just off the main junction. Twentieth-century town planners hadn't realised Newlyn's potential. The main street was essentially a busy through-road to Mousehole, St Just and Land's End. But Newlyn's reputation as an artist's enclave had pulling power.

Meghan was smiling brightly at a prospective client when Rachel arrived. A middle-aged man was gazing fondly at a striking painting of a sea nymph in shades of aqua blue and

sea green. A firm breast, dusted lightly in gold, was commanding his attention. Meghan was waving her arms like a siren,
calling him to the cash register. Her face faltered slightly as he
reached for his phone and a second opinion. Meghan caught
Rachel's eye through the window and beckoned her in.

'Rachel. How lovely to see you.' She planted two quick
kisses on Rachel's cheek.

'Rachel is the very talented daughter of Lawrence Matthews, the doyen of Cornish art,' she said, turning a full beam
smile on her prey. The man, as intended, looked interested.
Important people were calling.

Meghan seized the advantage. 'Stephen Myers will be exhibiting at the new gallery that Rachel is involved in. *The Sea
Nymph* is one of three of Stephen's works for the opening. If
you like, we could put a red sales sticker on the piece to ensure it isn't snapped up? The exhibits sell fast.'

So, Sam was going through Newlyn Wave.

The man had a hurried phone conversation. 'Lovely piece.
Included in the first night of the new gallery in Penzance. We
could reserve it?'

'I should imagine the price will increase after the event.
These exhibitions can launch artists. Have launched artists.
Celia Bradshaw, for example.' Meghan added.

He took a few shots on his phone and pinged them off.

'Do you have anything less ... exotic?' he responded, having read the text reply.

Meghan gave a triumphant smile. 'We have *In Deep Trouble*. I was torn between exhibiting this and *The Sea Nymph*.
The good news is you could take it away with you now. It
is such a complex and beautiful piece. A metaphor for our
times.' She gestured towards a painting in the corner of a person in full diving kit surrounded by small fishes and sharks.

Just in view, in the far corner of the canvas, was the nymph, sizing him up.

The man took a photo and pinged it over. Meghan smiled longingly at the deep-sea diver. Could he be her knight in shining armour? Pay this month's rent?

'Yes,' the man was saying on his mobile. 'And,' in hushed whispers, 'Rachel Matthews is here, Lawrence Matthews' daughter. She's exhibiting the works. Could go up in value. But do you like it?' He switched off his phone. 'How much?'

Half an hour later, the painting bubbled-wrapped and paid for, Rachel broached the subject of the gallery.

'It was all verbal agreements,' Meghan said, beaming at Rachel. 'We didn't need to put anything in writing. We were close. Good friends.' Meghan lowered her voice and touched Rachel's arm. 'It's just awful what happened. I still can't believe it.'

Rachel nodded, looked Meghan in the eye, noticing the dark rings below. 'Yes, a real shock. You say you were close. Did he give you any indication that something was up? That he was concerned about anything?'

Meghan's brow crumpled. 'No. He was just Sam. Lively, attentive, fizzing with energy and ideas. Sure, he was preoccupied with the gallery. He wanted the best artists. But he was confident that he had a good catalogue already. It was all good.'

Rachel waited a beat. But Meghan had turned her attention to a small display of artisan jewellery. She was smiling at the pieces, lifting a silver chain with dangling birds up to the light.

'These just flew off the shelf before Christmas. They're still selling. Make excellent last-minute gifts.'

'*The Nymph* – was that one of Sam's?' Rachel was keen to

get on.'

'We may have mentioned it. Sam was interested in a lot of the work here. What do you think, Rachel?'

Rachel thought it was tacky. The gold dusting, the subject matter. *Deep Trouble* was better. But not right for the gallery. 'What else do you have?'

'I'll show you. Sam particularly liked Ben Jordan's seascapes.'

What a saleswoman. Whether Sam liked the pieces or not, they were good.

'I can help you with the launch,' Meghan said. Her smile smaller, more serious. 'It can be a lot of work.'

'Thanks.' Rachel turned to leave. 'For now, could you just email some details: your artists, paintings, prices?'

'Of course,' Meghan said brightly. 'I used Sam's email before.'

So, she has used his address. 'Use mine.' Rachel felt in her bag for a pen and piece of paper and scribbled down her email address for Meghan.

All good? Meghan's words resounded as Rachel made her exit, fumbling with the shop doorknob. Did Meghan's tradesman boyfriend Ed fit this dodgy handle to stall people? With a click to the left and then a hefty pull she was out – right into the path of a man looking at the window. He appeared to be reading a small promotional flyer.

'Rachel.'

It was EuanTremayne. She hadn't seen or heard from him since the Montol.

'Hi.'

'There's a New Year's Eve gig on at The Acorn. Are you going?'

Rachel peered at the flyer. It was Brandon's band, *The*

Deep West.

'Are you?'

'That depends.'

He looked different in the daylight. Paler, his face tense. His eyes hard.

'On what?' Rachel said. *For God's sake. Had life become a quiz show? Pointless?*

Euan looked back at the flyer. 'Is your policeman friend in the band? Is that him in the photo? Looks like a younger version. Slimmer.'

'Yes.'

'So, I assume, you'll be there tomorrow?'

'Probably.'

They stood in silence, cars whipping past them as they navigated the junction.

'I guess that business is keeping the Detective Inspector busy? No new leads, though.'

Was there no other topic of conversation? Rachel checked her phone for the time.

'Are you okay? I heard about Sam Trenowden.'

'I'm fine. It's just a lot to get your head around. But we're coping. How about you?'

He shrugged. 'Same old. Going back to Penzance?' Euan was giving her a meaningful look. Everything he did was drenched in unfathomable meaning. He was trying too hard again.

'That was the plan.'

'Mind if I join you?'

'Be my guest.' She blushed thinking of the Montol dance. Had a vision of the two of them waltzing along the promenade à la *LaLaLand*.

'What are you smiling about?' Euan had a sweet smile on

his own face.

'Yes, what are you smiling about?' Meghan had joined them.

'Oh, nothing. Just a thought,' Rachel said, surprised to see her.

Meghan gave Euan an appraising look.

Rachel got the hint. 'Meghan. Have you met Euan Tremayne?'

'I don't think I've had the pleasure.' Meghan treated him to her warmest, sexiest smile.

'Pleasure's all mine,' Euan replied.

'You were looking at The Deep West flyer,' Meghan said, folding her arms below her breasts, which adjusted them nicely.

Euan fixed her with his cool gaze. 'We're going to see the country copper tomorrow night. Want to join us?'

Rachel's 'hmm' was wasted on them.

'May well do. I'll have a word with Ed …' She hesitated as Euan looked at her for clarification. 'My boyfriend …You're a photographer?' Meghan was referring to the professional-looking camera slung over his shoulder. For some reason Rachel hadn't noticed it. Or it had melded into his being like an extra limb.

'Yes.'

'Nice to know,' Meghan said, moving back from the doorstep to let in a prospective buyer. 'Rachel, maybe see you and Euan tomorrow and, of course, I'll be in touch about the gallery.'

'That Sea Nymph in the window is attracting a lot of traffic,' Euan said as they walked away, turning left towards the seafront.

'Is that what lured you?'

'No.'

'*The Deep West?*'

Euan gave her a scornful look. 'Terrible name. Let's hope the music's better.'

They walked in silence. Rachel didn't feel inclined to break it and Euan was unlikely to. But it wasn't awkward.

And then Euan did what he did best and made an unexpected move. Motioning to a bench, he said: 'Shall we sit a while? I want to take some photos of the promenade.'

'I've really got to get back.'

'Just a while, please. I'd like your opinion on some of my work.'

Rachel sighed and gave him a wary look. He looked confident standing there, light blue shirt tucked into cream chinos. Slim, fresh-faced and … handsome, with his fine features and grey-blue eyes, the colour of his shirt, the colour of the sky.

'Sure, why not?'

'Thanks.' He sat down on the bench, brushed off some seaweed, and beckoned her to join him, moving along so she wouldn't get the wet spot. She thought he was going to show her photos on his camera – but he passed her his phone.

'I've started building montages … of all the photos I've taken around here. These snaps are just for quick reference.'

There was a quality about them. Rachel could recognise that. The photos of people at work, doing touristy things, just sitting or standing by the sea, told a story. Colour washes gave some of the montages a stained-glass window effect, others were like surreal tapestries. They had something. Euan's eyes were boring into her, gauging her reaction.

'They are good.' Rachel gave him a sideways glance and handed him back his phone.

'Thanks. Can I take a photo of you here? With the sea

behind you?'

'I'd rather you didn't.' Rachel got up.

'Fine.' He took the cap off his camera and trained it on the sea. 'Fine. The light's not so good right now anyway. I've got some better ones; Sennen Cove at sunrise. No-one around. Well, hardly anyone.'

'What are you working on, apart from these?' Rachel said as they started to stroll.

'The usual, weddings, events, birthday parties. But this is my ... This is what I want to do.'

'Well, like I said, they are good. Have you tried any of the galleries?'

'Not yet.'

Euan stopped to take a shot of the beach – small dogs splashing in the shallows, chasing across the sand and rocks, careering back to their owners. In the near distance, Rachel could see the steeple of St Mary's – a watchful matron peering over the hotchpotch of Georgian townhouses and seafront B&Bs.

'Do you have a photographer for the gallery opening? You'll need some publicity shots.' Euan had turned back to her.

'Well, no, actually. I hadn't thought about it. Not sure if Sam had sorted this out. Or spoken to Julia.'

'If you need a photographer, give me a call. I'll do it for free. It would be good PR for me.'

'Oh, I'm sure the gallery will pay. We wouldn't want you to be out of pocket. I'll mention it.'

'Thanks,' he said, striding out. 'What's your number? I'll text mine.'

They'd reached the Jubilee Pool lido, where Rachel had parked her car. She felt in her bag for her keys.

'I'll send you a text about tomorrow night?'

Tomorrow night? Of course, The Deep West.

'I'll text you,' Rachel said, after they'd exchanged numbers. 'Let you know if we're going. Not sure if Julia will be up for it. But I'll have a word – about the gig and, also, about the photography.'

'Okay. Here, let me take a photo of you. In this light, by the pool, it would make a great publicity shot. Stunning.'

Rachel could imagine. It was some backdrop. The white-walled art deco pool resplendent as a 1920s liner, anchored to the shore. The sea caressed its curves; a battleship, beyond, patrolled its waters.

'I'm not looking to promote myself. Just the gallery.'

He ranged his camera on her for a few seconds, before letting it swing from its strap against his side.

Rachel heard his camera snapping as she put the key in her car door. As she turned on the ignition and pulled away from the kerb she saw him taking pictures of the sea, the people on the promenade, the empty pool, the forgotten Montol bunting blowing in the wind.

20

Rachel

'They really are rather good.'

Julia was sitting next to Euan at one of the tables closest to the stage at The Acorn Theatre, flicking through his montages. The support band had just cleared off and *The Deep West* were setting out their stall: a fiddle, banjo, double bass, guitar, drum kit and two mics. There was a reasonable crowd in the small, black-walled auditorium – all the tables were taken, and people were crowding in at the back and on the balcony.

Julia returned Euan's phone.

'Perhaps you'd like to see them?' he said, putting the phone back in his pocket. 'It will give you a better idea of their scale. They're big. In fact, they've taken over my place. Need to find myself a studio, probably.'

'Maybe we could arrange something, end of January? What do you think, Rachel?'

'Why not?' Rachel's mind was wandering. Julia had been locked in conversation with Euan for the past fifteen minutes. Exchanging little snippets of chat during the support band, passing their phones between them. She was quite animated for a grieving woman. Rachel suppressed a wry smile. Who would have thought? Julia had loved the idea of going to the gig and sizing up Euan as a photographer for the opening. Maybe even as an exhibitor. She'd taken a renewed interest in the gallery, saw it as a way of 'taking her mind off things'. And here she was, looking radiant, her foot tapping under the table to a string of country ballads. *What possessed her?*

Rachel was scrolling through her emails for the umpteenth time when Ed turned up at their table, a big grin on his face.

'You made it!' Rachel cried, springing to her feet and hugging him like a long-lost brother. Or, as things stood that night, a kindred spirit.

'Meghan's at the bar,' he said, breaking away, the grin still on his face. 'May I?'

'Please do.' Rachel budged her chair along to give him room to join them.

Julia leant over and gave him a gracious smile. 'Lovely that you and Meghan could make it.'

Meghan was winding her way through the tables towards them, a bottle in one hand, two glasses in the other. She plonked her wares on the table and leant in for a circuit of kisses, before squeezing in next to Rachel.

'Let me top you up,' she said, pouring some Sauvignon Blanc into her glass.

Rachel didn't object. She felt surprisingly flat. Counting the minutes until Brandon came on stage and gave her an easy, welcome distraction. Chelsea had popped her head around the stage door just a few minutes earlier, pulling funny faces at Rachel and mouthing 'Shouldn't be long'.

'Did you get my email?' Meghan said. 'I've given you quite a choice. I'm more than happy to organise the deliveries and stuff, give you and Julia some time.'

'Thanks, Meghan. I did get it. Just need to run through the images with Julia. But if you could deal with the artists and deliveries, that would be perfect.'

Meghan squeezed her leg. 'Leave it to me.'

Rachel was happy to. But would Julia be? Or had she already airbrushed out Meghan's relationship with Sam in her new, sanitised version of their relationship? She seemed happy

104

to forgive and forget tonight, moving in to listen to something Euan was whispering as the band came onto the stage. Julia gave a girlish giggle as Brandon strolled on, fiddle in hand, languid smile on his face. Rachel gave her a sharp look, which Julia most certainly missed as the lights dimmed dramatically. Someone had switched on the glitter ball, which was hanging over the stage, throwing out jewels of light. Two sculpted white angels, suspended from the ceiling, were stretching out to clutch it. Nice effect, if not a little *Mamma Mia*, thought Rachel. *Stop it!* The urge to laugh was infectious – she could feel Julia's shoulders shuddering and gave her a quick pinch. Biting her tongue, Rachel turned her attention to the backdrop – a gaudy neon Vegas street, red mountains in the background, the glitter ball lights dancing off it.

'Good to see y'all this evening. Really appreciate y'all coming out tonight.' Brandon was addressing the audience. The darkened stage wrapped around him like a cloak to mask his nerves. They didn't show ... much, thought Rachel.

'Thought we'd take a walk on the wild side tonight. Y'all ready to come walk on the wild side?'

'Woo!' shouted Chelsea's party of friends to the left.

Julia gave a little reciprocal: 'Woo!' *What was she on?*

'Let's kick 2018 out the gate! Bolt it fast so it ain't ever coming back.'

What had he got against 2018? Sure, the local crime rate had spiked. But compared to 2017 it was just fine, thought Rachel. And then pushed the thought right out of the gate and bolted it fast.

'I said we are going to have a wild night, t'night.' Brandon was labouring the preamble audience chat. Rachel was beginning to squirm on his behalf. Euan was whispering in Julia's ear again and she dipped her head, as if to conceal great mirth.

Rachel was starting to feel hot, squeezed between Meghan and Julia, the theatre lights overhead, one of them beaming a spot on the stage. Brandon turned to it, bringing his hands together as a fifth member of the band leapt into the spotlight.

'Let's give a big Cornish welcome to The Wildman of Penwith,' Brandon announced.

Benedict Arscott-Rowe needed no other introduction. Meghan and Julia sat up to attention, Euan momentarily forgotten. Rachel couldn't read Euan's face in the darkened room, but the atmosphere had changed, become charged.

Benedict hadn't changed much. He still looked as thin and debauched as a sixties rock star. A roll-up rested between the yellowed fingers of one hand. In the other dangled a mic. He flipped it upright.

'Good evening, ladies and gentlemen.' His eyes were on their table, a knowing smile on his face.

The band exchanged looks and launched into *Ring of Fire*.

It was strange to see him again. He couldn't sing that well, Rachel conceded, but his presence set the stage alight. He'd burned through her teens and early twenties, living a celebrity lifestyle on his family money. As a lecturer at Falmouth, he'd slept with an endless stream of female colleagues and students. Including Rachel. She'd gone out with him, if that's what you could call it, for a year. Her last year at Falmouth when she'd crashed out with a third and something a bit more tangible. A son. Had she loved Benedict? Maybe. Everyone had. Women. Men. He was Benedict. Benedict who had the power to set your world on fire and, if you didn't get too close, you didn't get scorched. Rachel reckoned she'd sustained third degree burns – *how appropriate* – but no lasting damage.

Julia was staring at Benedict. Had she slept with him? Possibly. Although Julia had always tended to play it a little safe – settling for second-best. Sam. How could she have settled for Sam? And Jago before him, Nick's feckless dad. But men were afraid of Julia: her manner, her cool beauty, her money. Perhaps she'd had no choice? It took jumped up arses like Sam and Jago to try their luck.

The Deep West went on to play a string of their own country tunes. The rhythms were old and familiar, like the blues, like the soundtracks of favourite films.

Rachel watched Benedict with detached interest. She was reminded of a hologram at a museum performing an old act.

'Going to change the tempo slightly,' he was saying in his confident, baritone voice. He wore his privilege lightly, but it was always there. 'I filched this little tune from Canadian Bluegrass band *Dead South*. Canada, who'd have thought it, they look and sound straight out of *No Country for Old Men*. Your neck of the woods, Brandon.'

Brandon smiled.

'This number – *In Hell I'll Be In Good Company* – is for departed friends,' Benedict announced.

Julia jolted. The man always knew how to get a reaction. Euan leaned forward and caught Rachel's eye. He looked amused.

The tune suited Brandon's fiddle-playing. It was good and even Julia's foot was tentatively tapping again after a few beats.

'Now, is there a female singer in the house?' Benedict was looking out into the auditorium. 'Country or Karaoke, I'm not fussed. Anyone fancy doing a duet with me? Save Brandon the indignity?'

Chelsea leapt up from her seat but slunk back fast when she saw her dad's disapproving look.

Benedict's eyes had travelled the room and landed on their table.

'What's the song?' Meghan said, smiling up at him.

'*Jackson.* Do you know it?'

'You big talkin' man? Go comb your hair?'

'That's the one. Give this charming lady a round of applause.'

Meghan protested for a nanosecond and then bounded onto the stage. *Could the night get any more weird?* She was good, raising the temperature and smiles all round.

Rachel gave Meghan a hearty clap before getting up to go to the Ladies.

'Can I get you a drink?' Euan was waiting by the stairs to the Cabaret Bar when she came out. 'I'm buying a round,' he added.

'Thanks, I'll have a glass of white, please.'

'Sauvignon?'

'Aha. Yep.'

'Strange seeing Benedict again. He's been away for some time,' Euan said as Rachel made to move away.

'Europe, I believe.'

'Letching? I mean Lecturing?'

'Business, I think. He doesn't really keep in touch these days.'

As she spoke Benedict burst through the door, a glass of wine in his hand, the contents slopping over the side. 'Hi! God, Rachel, hi. I didn't know you were back in Penzance. Last time we met up was at The Groucho, wasn't it?'

He gave her a massive hug and three kisses. It was like being enveloped in an electric blanket – warm and tingly.

Euan stood there, no apparent urgency to get to the bar.

'Benedict,' Rachel said, disentangling herself, but letting

him circle her waist with the arm not attached to the wine glass. 'This is Euan Tremayne. You must remember him from Falmouth?'

'Of course,' he said, looking him up and down and letting go of Rachel for a brief second to shake his hand. 'How's it going? You were into mosaics, right?'

'I was, yes. I'm surprised you remember. You were hardly ever at those classes.'

Benedict smiled and took a glug of wine. 'Mosaics. Indeed. Anyways, best get myself a refill before the next sess. Catch up with you afterwards, Rachel.' And he was gone – straight into the warm embrace of another old friend.

The Deep West were playing an instrumental – a duelling banjos type number – when Euan arrived back at the table. Julia moved her bag so he could sit down. They'd played three more tunes before Benedict returned.

He looked out into the audience, said nothing for a good few moments, and then, in a soft country voice, said: 'You've painted up your lips and washed and brushed your dark blonde hair. Rachel, are you contemplating going anywhere?'

Rachel returned Benedict's smile. *Always the charmer.*

The band launched right in, playing *Ruby, Don't Take Your Love To Town* at a fast clip. Chelsea was on her feet with her party. Was that Damien Kane with them and, heaven forbid, Peter Burton? Peter's popularity had risen a bit since the 'Seal' incident. Damien remained seated, but Peter was up and jigging around with Chelsea and her friends.

'Move back the tables. Give yourself some space,' someone shouted from the back.

'*Don't take your love to Newlyn*,' Benedict was belting out. Meghan was up and shimmying.

'Come on,' she said, grabbing hold of Ed and Rachel.

'Come on.'

'As you can see I'm not the man I used to be,' Benedict sang.

'But ladies, I still need some company.'

'It's tough to love a bloke, whose oft legless and paralysed.'

'And the wants and needs of women your age, ladies I realise.'

As Rachel got up, she heard a creaking sound, just audible above the music. Then a loud crack. She swung around.

Damien Kane? Had he got a firecracker? A gun! She wouldn't put it past him. He was standing on his table now, swigging from a bottle, grinning at his own audacity.

The creaking sound was getting louder. *He'd break that table.* There was another massive crack.

'What the fuck!' someone hollered.

'The bastard's coming down.'

'Clear the area – back everyone. Back.' A man in a waistcoat was pushing through the tables, pointing at the ceiling.

Rachel looked up and saw the glitter ball, jerking down from one chain, clunking onto another and then another.

'Chelsea, Damien, Tilly, get back. Now!' Rachel yelled.

Peter was already aware of the danger and filming it on his phone.

A woman dragged him away, shouting at the band to stop playing.

The ball was swinging from one broken chain, like a camp wrecking ball. Its lights still blazed, casting great splashes of colour on the stage and front row. Euan was sitting there, drenched in green light, the ball swinging feet from his head.

Rachel called out to him, and he dashed to her side.

Someone screamed, but the band played on.

'It won't be long they say until I'm not around.

Oh lay … dies, don't take your love to Wherrytown.'

Benedict was in the spotlight – centre stage.

'Benedict, for God's sake, shut up and get off the stage!' Rachel screamed. *Couldn't he hear her?* It was so loud in there. She waved a hand at the ball. Everybody was aware of it now. But he carried on singing. *Must be pissed.*

The band had stopped playing and Brandon lunged to grab Benedict as the glitter ball swung its last, pulling away from the clutches of the plaster angels, sending them tumbling down with it.

The ball, some lights still burning, others faulting, bounced off the stage, scraping Benedict's foot and shattering into pieces. An angel, like Lucifer falling from Heaven, smashed down, knocking Benedict to the ground. The other hung by a jagged piece of wire over his prostrate body. Brandon was just inches from him.

Fragments of white plaster fell onto the tables and people at the front. Julia wiped a film of dust from her brow. Meghan's auburn hair was streaked white. Chelsea huddled up against Rachel, her friends rallying round, speaking in soft whispers. There was a barrage of noise as people tried to make sense of it all. Others stared speechless at the stage, while Brandon tended to Benedict, feeling his pulse, putting his head to his heart.

'Hey, that's enough of all that.' Benedict raised his head and then an arm, brushing giant flakes of plaster off himself.

'Rumours of my demise have been greatly exaggerated,' he said, coughing and wiping powder from his mouth. 'At least I hope so. Don't want my body mangled like Ruby's old man's. Could someone kindly call an ambulance?'

21

Brandon

The wrecking glitter ball had made its mark – the tables at the front taking the full impact, two turned on their side, all covered in plaster dust. The heavy, swinging ball had pulled at its mount, ripping a star-shaped patch out of the ceiling, revealing the rafters above. Broken glass was everywhere and Jon, the manager, was scratching his head, assessing the damage. He'd rang the emergency services and evacuated the place on Brandon's advice. If there were questions to be asked, Brandon reckoned, they could wait until morning. They had the names and numbers.

Brandon sat down on the side of the stage next to Benedict and lit up two cigarettes, passing one to his friend. Benedict had refused to lie on his back, against the general medical advice.

'For fuck's sake,' he'd said, as Brandon attempted to do the correct thing, 'I've been in a worse state on a Saturday night.'

They sat smoking and surveying the wreckage.

Jon came over with a couple of whiskies, as the firefighters made their entrance.

'Just what the doctor ordered,' Benedict said, taking his gratefully.

Brandon took his and put it to one side. His attention was on the glitter ball – or, more particularly, the chain. He slipped down from the stage and went over to it, bending down to take a good look. The metal links in the chain were massive, about 10cm thick. And the chain wasn't old. And yet two of the links had snapped in two, causing the ball to pull away and come tumbling down. Brandon took out his phone and took a few snaps.

'Anything suspicious?' Jon said, coming over.

'Not sure.' Brandon crouched down again. 'How long have you had this ball?'

'A few years now. Why?'

'You wouldn't expect it to break then?'

'Well, no. It had been checked out, too – just yesterday.'

'Oh yeah,' Brandon said, turning to him. 'Who by?'

Jon looked concerned. 'Look, Brandon, I'm not here all day, you know that. I'll need to check with one of the women that run the front desk.'

'Let me know as soon as you can.' Brandon gave him a reassuring smile and patted him on the shoulder. 'Thanks for the whisky. Can't say I don't appreciate it.'

'Well, yeah. Quite a night, eh? You were shit hot too, before it all came crashing down.'

Brandon smiled and turned back to Benedict as the bellowing sound of a siren broke the silence. 'That sounds like your ride, Benedict.'

'Not before time.' Benedict downed his whisky.

Brandon moved aside as two paramedics rushed to Benedict's side.

As they sorted him out, Brandon returned to the glitter ball. Two firefighters were cordoning it off for examination. Others were checking the roof for structural damage. Brandon would ask for a full report on the findings. Although this wasn't a classic crime scene, something didn't add up.

One of the firefighters moved aside a table at the front and dislodged a piece of A5 paper stuck to its leg.

'Just a minute,' Brandon said, as the guy stepped back onto

it. 'You've got something stuck to your boot. I'd like to take a look at it.'

The firefighter reached down and peeled it from his heel. 'It's just a flyer,' he said.

Brandon held out his hand. 'Thanks,' he said as the man handed it over.

It was one of his band's flyers – but it had been doctored. Someone had drawn a noose around Brandon's neck and speech bubbles had been inserted in the Acorn angels' mouths. 'See You In Hell, copper,' read one. 'Bring along that Arse of a mate of yours!' read the other.

'Not very polite,' Benedict said, peering over.

'No,' Brandon agreed. 'You been rubbing anyone up the wrong way recently?'

'Par for the course,' Benedict said, stretching out an arm to have his blood pressure taken. 'And you?'

Brandon brushed a hand across his mouth. 'Evidently.'

22

Rachel

Rachel was waiting outside with Julia and Euan when Benedict was stretchered out, his head wedged between the plastic blocks of an immobilizer. He gave them a cheeky wink as he passed.

'Taxi's coming,' Julia said wearily, looking at her phone.

'Great.' Rachel glanced at her own mobile, which had just beeped. It was Lizzie. Scrolling down she could see that she'd been trying to get hold of her for hours.

A text, timed 18.45, read: 'He's here. Rachel, he's here. Sam's here. Asking about the paintings. You've got to come and tell him to go. Rachel, come now!'

Rachel went cold. Was this the first sign of Lizzie's demise? The final descent into senile dementia. Into madness?

Julia was hailing a cab. It glided to a halt by the kerb of narrow Parade Street.

'Are you coming?' Julia stood by the open car door.

'Mum's been in touch. Seems troubled. I'll go there tonight.'

'It's late … are you sure?'

'Yes. I'll see you tomorrow. Happy New Year.'

'Happy New Year, darling. Happy New Year, Euan. I'll be in touch about the montages,' Julia said, as the cab pulled away from The Acorn.

'I'll walk with you if you like.'

Rachel had forgotten about Euan as she flicked through Lizzie's increasingly paranoid texts. As he spoke, she was listening to a voice message; could hear the rising hysteria in Lizzie's voice. 'Go away. Go away. Nasty man. Rachel's com-

115

ing. My daughter will sort you out. Go away.' Timed 19.20. Rachel and Julia had just arrived at The Acorn – were having their names checked on the guest list.

Euan was watching her. 'Let me come with you. It's late.'

'Okay,' Rachel said in a distracted way. But some innate sense did want him there. Wanted someone with her to face Lizzie. Face this other side of her mother. The one cowering below the surface.

It had started to rain. Big drops – slow at first, then hard and fast.

Euan ran to the top of the parade and flagged down a passing cab. He called over to Rachel and they bundled in for the short drive to Seabird Cottage. All the lights were blazing when they arrived.

'I think it's best if I go in alone,' Rachel said, as the taxi drove away. Euan had taken a card from the driver, for the lift home.

'I'll wait out here. I'll be here if it gets ugly. You've got my number. Just text me if you want me.'

It was pouring, wind lashing the branches of Lizzie's maple tree, shedding what leaves were left.

Euan read her concern. 'I'll find somewhere to shelter. Don't worry about me.'

* * * * *

'Hi, Mum,' Rachel said as Lizzie opened the door, her eyes wide, mouth trembling.

'He was here, Rachel, Sam was here. He may be still here – hiding.'

'I'll go see, shall I?' Rachel walked through the living room to the kitchen and then into the studio. She'd read online that you should be non-confrontational with dementia sufferers.

116

Not question their 'reality'. But she couldn't resist a small dose of sanity.

'Mum, Sam's dead, you know. He won't – he can't – bother you anymore.'

'He was here, Rachel! Standing right where you are now. Grinning, demanding, taunting me. He knows you will think I'm mad – because he's dead. What a con man; dies so he can sneak in here and bother me. Steal from me. Steal your father's paintings!'

'He won't come any more, Mum. I'll make sure of that. I'll have a word with Julia.'

'He'll be back. I know he will. He's not afraid of you. Not afraid of Julia ... look how he treated her. Look what he did to your portrait.'

Rachel turned to the easel in the corner by the window. She was surprised that her portrait was still there. *Hadn't Lizzie finished it yet?* A brilliant flash of lightning lit it up and, in that instance, Rachel could see it had been tampered with. The rain was hammering the window, shaking the rotten pane as she approached the painting, waiting in its dark corner. There rested her alter ego, with the grim, reproachful mouth, sad, tired eyes, a violent slash of red from the brow to the coarse, choking scarf around her neck.

'Not exactly Ziggy Stardust, is it?' Rachel said, trying to lighten the mood. Lighten the mood despite feeling sick with fear and trepidation. There would be more of this. This wasn't going to vanish in the light of day.

'It's not a laughing matter, Rachel. Why must you always mock me? You're as bad as him.'

'He's gone, Mum.'

'You might as well go too.' Lizzie looked calmer. Her mood had switched from deranged to disgruntled. She pulled at her misshapen cardigan and tossed back her hair.

'I can stay.'

'You may as well go. He won't be back tonight. And if he dares to show his face around here again, I'll tell him where to go!'

'Are you sure?'

'Yes. I'm too tired to make up a bed. Just go, darling. I'll be fine. Really. Just go.'

'Happy New Year, Mum,' Rachel said at the door. The rain beyond the porch was horizontal. She could feel it pressing hard against her back. Lightning zig-zagged the sky, trees waved frantically. 'Go,' wailed the wind. 'Go!'

Lizzie was oblivious. 'Happy New Year, darling.'

Rachel turned to wave, as she always did, at the end of the path. As she did so, she thought she heard Lizzie say, 'thank you.'

The rain was torrential as she turned left onto the lane. Her shoes were sliding in mud. She was stumbling and skidding, battling to stay upright. Perhaps she should go back to the cottage? Insist. How was she going to get to Penzance in this? The promenade would be flooded. Tears coursed down her face, saltwater mingling with rain.

'Rachel.' His voice was light, ethereal, like the wind.

'You're still here?'

'Of course.'

Euan was soaking. His clothes plastered to his body, rain streaming down his hair, his face, his shirt, his trousers. He wasn't wearing a coat. Where was his coat?

'Here,' he said, handing it to her. 'Put this on. It's better than nothing.'

'But.'

'Here.' He took her arms, dressed her like a child, pulled

her to him. 'Here.'

Here, the wind seemed to say, as his arms encircled her, one hand stroking her hair, the other on the small of her back, pressing her to him, his lips planting small kisses on her brow, moving down. Soft at first, then harder.

Rachel pulled back. 'I …'

Euan relented, but was still close, the down on his face gentle against her cheek. 'Why do you always pull away?'

'I don't know.' And she didn't. Not then, a storm raging around her, not before.

His head was bowed, touching, almost imperceptibly, her brow.

'I thought tonight you liked Julia, not me.' The words escaped.

He caught her hand, twisted her fingers between his own. 'Why would you think that? How could you ever think that? I just want … you know what I want. To be near you. With you. I'll do what it takes.'

They looked at each other. Rachel's arms limp at her side, one hand still in his. With his free hand Euan stroked her face and, as she raised it to his, kissed her lightly on the lips.

'I'll call the cab,' he said, as they broke away from each other.

'Do you think he'll come back in this weather?' Rachel struggled to find her voice. She lowered her eyes, unable to meet his.

'Yes, I do. With the right persuasion.'

Within minutes the welcoming headlights were there at the end of the lane. As Rachel went to open the cab door she let go of Euan's hand, their connection lost as they sat at opposite sides of the back seat, each staring out of their respective windows into a bleak New Year.

23

Rachel

Tyres squealed on sodden gravel as the cab did a tight turn and headed back down the long drive from The Hall. Through the front door stained-glass, Rachel could see a faint light in the kitchen. Was Julia still up? She turned the key slowly in the lock, cursing the stones that were rattling in her rain-soaked shoes. She took them off and placed them in the porch to be dealt with tomorrow. Tomorrow, that would be January 2 – how time flew when you weren't having fun. But it had been fun in parts. It was just that the annoying, worrying, confusing parts had been that much bigger. That much more pressing. A near-death incident at The Acorn Theatre. Was nowhere safe?

'Rachel.' Julia was at the kitchen door, a tumbler of whisky in her hand. 'You came back after all. Was that Euan in the cab?'

Too much to explain at this hour, but Rachel saw that it would be impossible to hit the sack without some explanation.

'Yes, Euan sorted a cab. It all became a bit ...' *What was Euan's word?* 'Ugly. Lizzie wasn't herself tonight. I've never seen her like that before.'

'Let me get you a drink. Whisky? I think you need a whisky, or brandy.'

'Whatever.' Rachel walked into the living room and sunk into a sofa. Thank God it was still the Christmas holidays. But what the hell was going on? It felt like Halloween. She'd phone Brandon tomorrow, get some info.

She took the tumbler from Julia's outstretched hand and took a welcome sip. And then another.

'How, in this day of stringent health and safety, did that glitter ball come crashing down? Benedict was lucky to have survived relatively unscathed – as were we all, right there at the front.'

'Awful. Truly awful. I spoke to Benedict in the interval. He seemed quite distracted, even before the accident,' Julia replied.

Rachel looked surprised. 'He was just a bit drunk, wasn't he? Seemed much the same to me.'

Julia smiled. 'Well, you know him better than most, but he seemed distressed about Sam. He was so kind about him. Had me welling up.'

Rachel looked at her friend. She'd known Julia for more years than she could remember. Many more than she'd known Benedict. But did she really know her? There was always that veneer. Like the film of powder that coated her brow at The Acorn. There were things she thought she knew about Julia. About her relationship with Sam. About her feelings now he was dead. But it was all unspoken. Never confirmed. Julia kept her own counsel.

'Quite a night.' Rachel reached for the bottle Julia had placed on the coffee table and refilled her glass. *Probably a bad idea. Most certainly a bad idea. But sometimes needs must.* Julia sat on the matching cream sofa opposite, swilling the contents of her glass. Rachel wasn't going to divulge her conversation with Lizzie. At some point – yes, maybe. But not tonight. Not with Sam still in the morgue, not with feelings so raw.

'I think we should view Euan's work as soon as possible.'

Julia had fast-forwarded to her topic of interest. 'If we are going to include it. The works are huge. It could be a logistical nightmare getting them from Gulval.' *So, she knew where he lived?*

'We haven't even seen them yet – just thumb prints. Besides, I have the school minibus.'

Julia took a tiny sip of whisky. 'All the same. Look, I have some time tomorrow. It doesn't need both of us. I'll drive over and, if I think they're worth considering, then we can go back together. I've already told him that he can do the photography at the opening.'

'Wouldn't that be a bit weird? Dilute his brand, as they say? Exciting new artist is also jobbing photographer?'

Julia scrunched up her face and reached over for the bottle. 'No. He could even do a montage of the event. It would be a great introduction for him. Working the room, taking shots, an artist in action. And he has that air, doesn't he?'

She had a point. Had probably thought this through while Rachel was out fighting demons, including Julia's late unlamented husband. Was already positioning the massive photo montages in the gallery, beside the huge picture windows where the light would be best. Best not to mention the kiss in the rain. *How could she have let it happen?* Regardless, she felt a warmth, a forgotten glow, just thinking of it.

Rachel drained her glass. 'Julia. That sounds like a good idea. Very sixties. Do you know that old arthouse film *Blow-Up,* with the rampant, sex-crazed photographer?'

Julia nodded. 'Exactly. And so … Penzance. Why don't you go to bed, darling? Like you said, you've had quite a day. I think I'll just wait up a while. I don't feel sleepy.'

That was obvious. That new energy was still there, and it would take more than another tot of whisky to subdue it. *Sex-crazed photographer?* Rachel touched her lips. *What was that all about tonight? The come-on in the pouring rain? The illogical end to an illogical evening.* And yet she had felt something. No matter how she tried to trivialise it. No matter how pressing events had been, were, would be. She had felt something. A kiss in a perfect storm had stirred some dormant desire.

'Maybe I'll join you for another, Julia. I don't feel too sleepy myself.'

They sat in silence a while, probably considering similar things.

Or maybe not.

'Rachel, what do you think of Benedict as a speaker at Sam's funeral? I know we don't have a date – yet. But when we do. What do you think?'

Rachel put down her glass. 'What?'

'Would it be so bad? He is such an eloquent speaker … and they were friends.'

Friends? Maybe in Sam's small coterie of companions he could be classed as a friend.

'I mean, who else have we got?' Julia said, her brow creased in concentration.

'True,' Rachel agreed. They could hardly ask Meghan and Ed barely opened his mouth other than to grin. 'But perhaps, James Bowen-Lacy?'

'Too corporate.' Julia edged forward, cupped her face with her hands. 'Although maybe a short speech – about his support for the arts.'

'Family? His mother, an uncle?

'Goes without saying.' Julia waved a dismissive hand. Poured herself another drink.

'I want this to be a celebration. Benedict would be perfect.

I'll ask him to rein it in, of course.'

'Of course.' Rachel remembered Benedict's quip at The Acorn. *Good Company in Hell.* Could he be relied upon to be suitably sombre? Or sober? Did he even know Sam that well?

It was as if Julia had read her mind. 'You know, Sam and Benedict were quite close.'

Rachel shifted on the sofa.

Julia took a breath, stared at some unspecified object over Rachel's head. 'They spoke on the phone a lot.'

'Really?'

'Yes. I was surprised myself. They barely knew each other at Falmouth. Sam wasn't really in our set. Then.'

Rachel sat rigid, as if the briefest movement would throw Julia off track.

'I'm still not sure what they had in common. But they had regular chats. I picked up his mobile once and it was Benedict calling from somewhere in Europe. After that I … I became aware of the calls.'

Julia ran her palms down her thighs, straightening the creases in her dress. 'I checked Sam's phone and saw there were lots of 'caller unknowns'. That would figure if Benedict was calling from France, or wherever.'

Rachel shook her head. Put down her glass. 'Julia, what the hell do you think they were talking about? What did they have in common?'

Julia gave her a sharp look. 'Art. Sam would have contacted him about the gallery and, of course, Benedict is so well-connected. He told me last night he was sourcing artwork in Europe.'

'Of course,' Rachel said. Sam had bled his contacts dry.

'So, a good idea?'

'Inspired. I think I'm going to turn in now.' Rachel got up

from the sofa.

'Rachel.'

'Yes?'

Julia was looking down, one hand gripping her tumbler. 'Things hadn't been good between Sam and me for some time.'

Rachel sat back down.

'I don't know if it was me. Maybe I shouldn't have rushed into the relationship. Was it an act of desperation? We weren't really suited.'

'But you seemed fine. At least at the start.'

'Yes. We both tried then. I wanted a father figure for Nick and Sam wanted, I'm not even sure what he wanted, but it worked for a while. The new gallery was, I guess, our last chance to make it work. Our baby. Our own baby didn't happen, did it?'

Julia looked at Rachel, tears in her eyes. 'Perhaps for the best. And then this awful thing happens – I feel guilty that I didn't, couldn't, make him happy.'

Rachel got up to go over to her. 'You couldn't have done any more. You gave him your beautiful self – and all this.' She stretched wide her arms. 'Don't ever blame yourself. Sam just wasn't right for you. That's all –'

Bang!

Julia flinched. 'What's that?'

Another bang.

Julia jumped to her feet. 'It came from out back. Or the kitchen.'

'The kitchen door? Could it have slammed shut?' Rachel bent forward, craning to hear, her feet refusing to budge.

'I thought I'd locked up.' Julia looked at Rachel. Grabbed hold of her as the door slammed again, and then again, like it was swinging on its hinges.

Rachel's heart was hammering, her mouth dry, a precursor of the morning hangover. She picked up a small bronze nude from a side table.

'Good idea.' Julia grabbed its companion piece.

'Ready?' Rachel said, leading the way out of the living room. As they entered the kitchen, the door slammed again. Rachel raced to it, opened it, straining to see something or someone in the dark and driving rain. The wind forced her back as she stepped barefoot onto the wet gravel. Julia was behind her flashing the torch light on her phone.

'There's no one there,' Julia said after a beat. 'The security lights would have come on. I must have left the door ajar when I went out for a ...'

'Cigarette?'

Julia looked sheepish. 'Yes. Foolish, I know. But since Sam's death–'

'Understandable.' Rachel took one last look around and stepped inside, closing and locking the door behind them. Then something, or the absence of it, caught her eye.

'The security isn't on.'

Julia glanced up at the box. No pulsing green light. 'I didn't turn it off.' Julia looked at her phone. 'Maybe I did by mistake, these phones are so intuitive.'

'Surely it would have asked you to confirm if you wanted to turn off the security?'

Julia knitted her brow. 'Yes, of course. You're right. That's a failsafe feature.'

They looked at each other.

'And, before you ask, unless I'm going mad myself – sorry, Rachel, no offence meant to Lizzie. Unless I'm drunk – which I don't think I am – I didn't climb onto the table and switch it off manually. I never do that. Ever.'

'A systems fault?'

'Unlikely. Sam had just had the security serviced and upgraded. He'd made it like Fort Knox round here. I thought it was a little excessive, myself, but he said crime rates were rising and we shouldn't take any chances.'

Rachel felt a chill, as if brushed by Sam's ghost.

'Sam's phone?' Rachel said, her voice faltering as she contemplated the awful possibility that someone could have it and was using it right now.

'Maybe someone found it on the beach, or it shorted, or something.' Julia looked far from convinced. A damaged phone smart enough to operate high-level security systems without a password or face recognition?

'Best change the passwords first thing, just in case. But how the hell would someone have Sam's password?'

'He tended to use the same ones,' Julia replied.

'It's not something you'd broadcast, though. There must be another reason. I'll mention it all to Brandon. I was going to call him anyway.'

Julia looked pained but resigned. That earlier energy sapped. 'Yes, please do, Rachel. I'll call security now. They're 24/7.'

As Julia tapped into her phone, Rachel pulled out one of the chairs from beneath the kitchen table and wedged it under the backdoor handle.

24

Brandon

'Do you take sugar? Milk?'

'No sugar, just a little milk,' Rachel said as Brandon made coffee in his compact cottage kitchen. Chelsea's colourful pictures of cheerful-looking girls decorated the fridge. One fluttered to the ground as Brandon opened the door. He knelt to pick it up and placed it on his cluttered work surface.

'Benedict's okay, by the way,' Brandon said, as he placed two mugs of coffee on the kitchen table and sat opposite her. 'He's lucky it was just the plaster angel and not that massive wrecking ball that floored him.'

'Yes.' Rachel took a sip of coffee. 'Do you know how it came to fall down?'

'Yes,' Brandon said, fixing her with his calm gaze.

'Would you like to tell me?'

'You'll get me slung out of the force.'

Rachel smiled. 'You know I wouldn't breathe a word to anyone. I just want to find out what on earth is going on around here. I feel, somehow, that I'm involved in all this. It's touched my life.'

That was true, Brandon thought. Rachel was far from Prime Suspect, but she was connected. Pat Ryan – she was at the scene when his head was discovered. She teaches his nephew Josh. Sam – her best friend's husband – dead. Her pupil, Peter Burton, took the photo of Sam's body. It was a small town, granted, but Rachel was at the epicentre of all this. And he trusted her. He always had. When she walked back into his life two weeks ago, it was as if she'd never left.

Brandon sighed and ran a hand across his mouth. 'The chain was tampered with. Sawed at. It was only a matter of time before the weight from the ball, with all the vibrations and activity of an evening of such intense excitement, brought it down.' He smiled to downplay the seriousness of the act.

'Silly question, but do you know who sawed through the chain?'

'Serious answer. No. There is no CCTV at The Acorn.'

'Surely someone would have spotted a guy with a chainsaw on a step ladder sawing away?'

'You would like to think so.' Brandon pulled a packet of cigarettes from his top pocket. 'Do you mind?'

Rachel shook her head.

'The place relies on a lot of volunteers. People come and go all the time. They have a few local electricians that sort out the lighting, but not everyone knows who they are. Someone could have slipped through. We'll be interviewing people over the next few days as part of our investigations.'

Brandon lit his cigarette and took a drag.

'In danger of asking another silly question, why would anyone want to do it? A vendetta against you? Benedict? The Acorn? A bad review, perhaps? A connection with the recent *unexplained* deaths?'

'Fancy giving up that job at the school and joining the force, Rachel?'

'I wouldn't last a week. But seriously, something is up. And you know it, Brandon.'

Brandon let out a long stream of smoke. 'I didn't want to get you involved. You have enough on your plate. But … yes, you're right. There is a lot going on around here and I'm struggling to get to the bottom of it. But I will.'

'Does it involve Sam's death?' Rachel leaned in, resting her elbows on the table.

'I wouldn't rule that out.' They'd hit a wall with Sam. But, he felt, just one loose brick and the whole edifice would come tumbling down.

Rachel stretched her lips into a firm line. 'I've got something to tell you. But after you.'

Brandon lit another cigarette from the tip of his first. 'We found some interesting CCTV footage – Sam talking to a man, or what looked like a man, in the *Pets At Home* carpark.'

'What?'

Brandon puffed out a small cloud of smoke, like a pensive dragon. 'Drug dealers tend to use these edge-of-town retail parks to do business. *Pets At Home* is a new one, granted. Anyway, Sam looked agitated, pacing around, clearly looking for and waiting for someone. And goods were exchanged.'

'What time was all this going on?'

'Early. 6am. The dark made it hard to identify Sam's "friend" … but we recognised Sam's jogging jacket and leggings. We're pretty sure it's him.'

'No idea who the other person is?'

'No. Looked too well-built to be one of the young drugs mules.'

'Jesus,' Rachel said, slowly. 'Sam? I had no idea. But it makes sense. It absolutely makes sense.'

'Why?' Brandon stubbed out his cigarette.

'He acted like a cokehead. Jumpy. Agitated. It clearly wasn't just the Colombian coffee he drank by the gallon.'

Brandon thought he'd acquaint Rachel with some details. 'Sam kept some interesting company – but not around here. Mainly the clubs in Newquay. He kept his *entertainment*, his other business, out of town.'

His words hit the mark. 'Bloody hell! Who'd have thought it? This could make an interesting footnote to a funeral eulogy.'

'We don't have anything incriminating yet. He was known around the clubs, yes, but Sam could well have been just another well-heeled social user. After all, Julia was unaware, wasn't she?'

'She never let on if she did know.'

'Well, if you do remember anything, Rachel, just let me know.'

'Want another coffee?' He reached over to the cafetiere.

'Yeah, sure. Thanks. There is something else. Something I came here to tell you, and which seems even more relevant now.'

Rachel went over to the fridge and got out the bottle of milk. Attaching Chelsea's discarded picture to the door with a *Minions* fridge magnet, she said: 'I think someone has Sam's phone and is using it.' She turned to Brandon, handing him the bottle.

'Who?'

'No idea. But they may have used it to shut down security at The Hall last night. Security which Sam had recently upgraded.'

Brandon blew into his coffee. 'The user would have needed Sam's password. I hope you've sorted the security, by the way?'

'Yes. The phone, what shall we do about the phone?'

'Well, it's far from certain it's the phone.' *It most certainly wasn't. This was elementary stuff for security firms – the password would have been encrypted.*

Rachel's face fell. He could see she'd staked some time on the theory.

'We did contact his network provider after the incident,' Brandon said. 'There'd been no calls since. I told them to keep the contract ongoing – for now.'

'You had an inkling? You think the phone could be … with someone?' She'd perked up again.

'I like to keep all options open. I'm glad I did. We'll check and see if there's been any recent usage and they can locate it.' *Surely that was the end of it?*

'Brandon.' Rachel looked at him across the kitchen table. 'Has this become a murder investigation?'

Woah. Brandon looked down and then back up, running a hand through his hair. 'Unexplained, Rachel.'

'And the funeral?'

'We're going to have to keep Sam on ice for now. We did a full autopsy. No illegal drugs in his system. He was nothing, if not, the control freak – a time and a place for everything. Pleasure was in another compartment – in another town. It was all about business that morning. The gallery, clearly. Maybe some side-line deal too.' He didn't want to put a finer point on it.

'I see. But you'll contact Julia?'

'Yes. We'll need to ask a few more questions.'

'I'd better go. Leave you to it.' Rachel got up from the table and swung her rucksack over her shoulder.

'Okay. Thanks for coming round, Rachel. I really appreciate it.'

'I had to. Hang on. I forgot to say that someone was at The Hall last night. I'm sure of it. The back door swung open – that's how we noticed the security failure. I'm worried, Brandon. Is Julia, are we, in danger?' She paused, as if recollecting something. 'Those young druggies – the ones in the graveyard on the night of The Montol. The ones that told me to watch

my step. Who knew I was a teacher. They thought I was …
with a wanker. If Sam was involved in drugs. Maybe they
meant him?'

The idea had also crossed Brandon's mind. Particularly as
Nike Boy was flashing on his radar.

Brandon reached for his cigarettes. Lit up another. 'It's a
possibility. Although no one, fitting the descriptions you gave,
has been sighted. But I'll speak to Julia asap. I'll make sure
The Hall is secure. Don't worry.' She should have told him
sooner. He'd go there immediately, check the security, alert
Julia. He wasn't particularly happy with them being up there
on their own. Sam may have had other reasons for upgrading
the security, but he was glad he had.

Brandon rested his cigarette in a saucer, got up from the
table and walked her to the front door. He always seemed to
be saying goodbye.

'Did you enjoy the gig, by the way?' The one chance he'd
had to impress, to change the mood, and it had been ballsed
up.

'The gig? Oh God, yes, your gig. It seems like a lifetime
ago now.'

'Well, it was last year.' Brandon smiled as he lounged
against the doorframe.

'You were great, Brandon. You brought the house down,
remember.'

Brandon burst out laughing. 'I don't think I can take full
credit for that.' He could hear Chelsea moving around upstairs. It gave him an idea. 'By the way, any time this week for
some extra-curricular?' He looked at her through the shield
of his fringe. 'Just an hour, perhaps? Maybe work through
some of the sketches in that book you bought her?'

'Morning, Dad! Who you chatting to?' Chelsea was up,

bellowing down from the landing.

Rachel looked at her phone. 'It's ten now. How about to-day?'

'Sure. If that works for you?'

'Yes. Just need to check in on my mum.'

Brandon frowned. 'How is she?'

'It's probably nothing – she wasn't feeling too well yesterday. But I could come back early afternoon?'

'Thanks, Rachel, really appreciated. And, also, for you coming round. Your input has been invaluable.'

'Not really. Still so many murky details and unanswered questions.'

'It's the nature of the beast. But things tend to emerge, if left a while. We'll solve this.' He didn't feel as confident as he sounded. Sometimes he felt like he was working on his own in a vacuum and wished there was more of the 'we'.

'I hope so, Brandon. Sam, for all his faults, deserves justice. And, if he was murdered.' She'd said the M word. 'Who's to say the killer won't strike again?'

Brandon put a finger to his mouth as Chelsea wandered into the hallway. He wrapped an arm around his sleepy daughter and opened the door for Rachel.

'See you later, Miss Matthews,' he said.

25

Rachel

The first thing Rachel noticed after she'd entered Seabird Cottage was that her portrait had been moved. It usually glared at her through the open door to the studio. Not today. Someone else had taken up residence.

'You're working on a new piece?' Rachel chose her words carefully. Lizzie still seemed fragile after last night.

'Yes.' Lizzie gave a curt answer. 'Tea?'

'That would be nice.' Never too much caffeine after a night like the last one. She followed Lizzie into the kitchen. There was a pile of sodden leaves near the back door which fanned out into the room, blown in by the wind or stuck to Lizzie's mules.

'So, who are you painting now?' Rachel took the cup from Lizzie, noticed her trembling hand.

'No one of interest.'

'That's not like you, Mum. And where's my portrait?'

'I put it in Larry's storeroom.' Lizzie, her back to Rachel, was fussing with a sugar bowl and packet of biscuits. She ripped open the packaging and plonked the lot on a chipped dinner plate. 'Here, have some sugar. You must need some after all that boozing last night.'

Nice. Rachel took a couple, bit back the insult and bit into one of Tesco's Finest Belgian chocolate biscuits. Lizzie looked pleased, took one herself and, after a hesitant nibble, left it on the work surface.

'Come and see if you recognise him.' Lizzie couldn't resist

it. Her body was simmering with excitement.

Rachel picked up another biscuit and followed her into the studio. Lizzie had clearly been working on the painting for a while – either through the night or since early morning. Other than looking like a man, the figure was unrecognisable.

'Well?'

Rachel studied the painting. Slicked back hair, a certain arrogance about the flick of a mouth, cold blue eyes which bore into her as she scrutinised them. Sam? It would make sense. He was her obsession.

'Sam?'

'*Voila*! So, I've captured him well?'

'Well, I recognised him, although he has – had – brown eyes.'

'Definitely blue. I should know.'

Rachel bit into her biscuit. So, Sam hadn't gone away? Lizzie's nightmare would be ongoing.

'You know, darling – maybe I was a little harsh on Sam.'

What?

'When he visited yesterday afternoon, he gave me some very good advice. I was freaked out at the time. Darling, who wouldn't be! But … well …' Lizzie draped one of her thin arms around Rachel's shoulder, moving her away from the portrait. She whispered in her ear conspiratorially. 'Sometimes those on the *other side* have access to information that we don't.'

Rachel shuddered; Lizzie's fingers were caressing her spine in an absentminded manner.

'Sam said he'd spoken to Larry. About the paintings.'

Rachel pulled away. She was going too far.

'Hear me out. I know you think I'm bonkers. I have material evidence – is that what your policeman friend would say?

Oh yes, I know you've been seeing Brandon again. Sam told me. He said he was useless. Only went into the force because he couldn't get another job. Couldn't make it as a musician. He said I should tell you to drop him.'

For Chrissake! Now Brandon was the object of her derision.

'We are, and always have been, just friends. He's heading the investigation into your *friend's* murder.' She'd let that slip! But Lizzie didn't pick up on it.

'Sam told me where Larry used to keep some of his later works. The ones he wasn't so sure about.'

'Hmm?'

'They're in the storeroom – where I put your portrait. It still has the red slash on it, darling. Sorry. I will remove it. It's just that I wanted to work on this.'

Lizzie had turned back to smile lovingly at her portrait of Sam – her new muse.

'So, where are the paintings? Dad's paintings?' Rachel was curious. Lizzie seemed calm. Maybe there was a rational explanation.

'They're still in the storeroom. Too heavy for me to get them all out. But I did manage to bring out one. Just to show you. Just to show that I'm not ready to be carted off to the care home just yet!'

'Mum, you know I wouldn't do that.'

Lizzie gave her a mock annoyed look and a little 'humph' and walked over to pull the cloth off a canvas which was propped up against the back wall. In the dull winter light, it looked like just another abstract. Could be a Lawrence Matthews, could be any number of works with great smudges of colour and pallet-edged texture. Rachel walked towards it, cocked her head, and knelt to examine it thoroughly. It didn't smell of new paint. Which was reassuring. And it did look like one of her father's works. Like Picasso, he could churn paintings out in no time. Yet they were 'his' – the spontaneity of those brush strokes, tamed, reworked, made good. This wasn't one of her father's best. The browns were muddy and discordant. Probably why he had stored it away to be worked on. *He had stored it away? Was she so readily convinced that it was a Lawrence Matthews?* In the corner was his trademark signature in black biro. It looked quite fresh – but no real surprise, the painting hadn't been exposed to light for a long time.

'Well?' Lizzie was standing beside her, arms crossed, looking triumphant. 'Well?' She was daring Rachel to disagree.

'Quite a find. And you say there are more?'

'Yes.'

'How many?'

'Oh, I don't know, I'm not a storekeeper. I haven't counted them!'

'Well let's go and –'

'Rachel, not this morning. I have a splitting headache. I don't think I can take much more excitement.'

'Oh, okay.' Rachel was disappointed. This was something, surely? How they'd been spirited up was another matter. But she was itching to see the collection, if only because they were her father's. It was like finding a diary, or an album of old photographs. Ones that she never knew existed. Rachel's own head was throbbing, not with pain but with a sense of wonder and bewilderment. She looked at her phone. One o'clock. At least it was still early, and she'd avoided lunch with Lizzie, always a fraught affair. Poor food, poor conversation, her stomach struggling to digest it all.

Rachel picked up her bag and walked to the front door. 'I'll give you a ring tomorrow. Make sure you call me if you need me. If you get any more – visitors.'

'Will do.' Lizzie practically slammed the door in her face. It was as if she had a secret lover waiting in a secret place, whom she couldn't wait to rush back to.

26

Rachel

Chelsea was sitting at her desk in the attic room, concentrating on her shading. She was pressing her pencil down so hard on her sketchpad that she risked tearing into the paper.

'Go easy, Chelsea. A light touch first and then you can add more, if needed,' Rachel said.

'Yes, Miss. Have you got a sharpener?'

Rachel glanced around the room, spotted a box of writing material, and fished out a sharpener and rubber. 'Here you are,' she said, walking over to Chelsea and giving her work a quick appraisal. 'Not bad. Let's see if you can finish Wonder Woman this afternoon for your dad.'

Chelsea turned her head and smiled up at her. Then, the tip of her tongue protruding in concentration, got back to work.

The room ran the full length of the house, and despite the sloping eaves it felt spacious. There was little clutter: just a few boxes in one corner, a battered leather armchair, a music stand and a table bearing Brandon's collection of fiddles. Rachel walked over to the far side of the room and looked out of the Velux window. It gave more than the sea glimpse often touted by estate agents. She watched as the waves rolled in and out, gulls gliding and swooping above them, scouting for pickings.

She thought of her father's painting, the one Lizzie had discovered and knew it would be swooped upon, if the art world got a sighting. Part of her yearned to go back to the cottage, to give it another close look before Lizzie did something impulsive. She'd have to wait, though. Go back tomorrow, when the excitement had died down a little. Lizzie had complained about too much excitement. Tell me about it, thought Rachel, still staring out of the window, events ticker-taping through her mind.

'Miss?'

Rachel turned to Chelsea, whose head was still bowed in concentration, one hand rubbing out or blending her pencil work.

'Did Oliver like to draw?'

The words, so unexpected, made Rachel reel.

Chelsea continued to work on her drawing, her eyes, very much like her father's, turned down, seemingly intent on the task in hand.

'Yes. Yes, he did,' Rachel replied, the words catching in her throat.

'You must miss him so much?'

Rachel gripped the top of the armchair. The attic shrunk around her.

'Was he good at drawing, like you, Miss? Like you and your mum and dad?'

'He preferred football.' Rachel remembered the times she'd dragged him, complaining, around art galleries.

'Football. Typical boy!' Chelsea got up from her desk and walked over to Rachel. 'Here. What do you think?'

Rachel took the piece of paper from her. It was Wonder Woman but with a heavily shaded face, like hair and make-up had caked on the slap. 'It's, umm, moving in the right direction.'

'It's rubbish. I did one of you yesterday, though. I thought you'd like it. Make you smile.'

Chelsea produced a portrait, very similar to all her others, but now with her trademark dark shading. She'd got her colouring right, though – the blonde hair, the green eyes, a pretty, red-lipped smile. In the sky was a cloud with the face of a child. Looked like the *Teletubbies* baby that came on at the start of the shows. How many times had she watched those in the early years?

'It's Oliver, Miss. I saw him once. Years ago, at the school fete. He was beautiful. Like an angel.'

Rachel felt her throat constrict. She turned away, didn't want Chelsea to see her grief. 'He could be a little devil when he wanted to be.' *Why did she say that? No need to say that. He had been an angel.*

'Miss. He wouldn't want you to be upset. Don't you see that? It must be awful for him, up there, looking down, seeing you unhappy.'

'Chelsea, I think it might be an idea if we call it a day.' The tears were falling now. She couldn't stop them. 'You know, he told me once … that if he died and I didn't get on with life he would rain on me from above, like he was my own little cloud, until I bucked up. Fancy that. Fancy him saying that.'

'He's right, Miss. He wouldn't want to see you sad. It will make him sad. He's probably waiting for you to – get better. So, he can move on. Come back as a – footballer, or a snow leopard, or a vampire.'

'Vampire!' Rachel laughed, despite herself.

'Yes! How cool would that be! A handsome, dreamy, vampire.'

'You kids.'

'We ain't so bad. Do you like the picture?'

'Yes, I do. Very much.'

'Awesome.' Chelsea gave Rachel an uncharacteristically shy look, before bouncing back to her desk. 'I'll sign it for you.'

'My mum tried to teach me how to draw, but I was useless,' Chelsea said, pulling a blue pencil out of its box. She scribbled on a blank page, softening its tip.

It was the first time Rachel had heard her mention her mum. Brandon hadn't mentioned her either, apart from on the night of the Montol.

She walked over to Chelsea. 'I wasn't much cop myself, at first. My dad taught me how to draw. Art, like anything, is about building blocks. Learn the basics and you can take flight from there.'

Chelsea rubbed her nose and shuffled in her chair. 'Sometimes it's hard to get a likeness of someone you're close to. It's like you know them so well, that you don't really see them at all.'

Chelsea was looking down, her hair falling across her face. 'I've tried so hard to draw my mum, but it just keeps coming out wrong. My pictures don't look anything like her.' She paused. 'Sometimes I wonder if I'll ever remember what she really looked like. What she was really like.'

Rachel put a hand on her shoulder. Could feel it shuddering beneath her palm. 'You never forget, Chelsea. You think you have, or you will, but you won't.'

'Thanks, Miss.'

'Do you have photos of your mum, Chelsea? You could work with those.' Rachel hadn't seen any around.

'I've got a few on my phone.' Chelsea wiped her nose on a piece of kitchen roll and flipped open her phone wallet. 'Here, look. It's a bit fuzzy – I took it years ago, before Mum passed.'

Rachel looked at the screen and the photo of a confident, smiling, auburn-haired woman standing beside a tree in an orchard.

'Here's another.' The same woman, with the same smile, in a hospital bed with a baby in her arms. 'It's me – the squinty little thing in her arms is me. They didn't know, at that point, that I was practically blind. Mum spent so much time at the hospital afterwards sorting out my eyes.'

'Time well spent,' Rachel said, smiling at her.

'Yeah,' Chelsea said, 'I feel bad, though, that she had to spend so much time at the hospital, when she had so little left and a lot of that … was in hospital.'

'Chelsea.' Rachel gave her a hug, could feel the desperate sadness stashed away behind those ready smiles.

There were footsteps on the stairs. When Brandon came in, she was looking over Chelsea's shoulder at her sketch. *He needn't know.*

Brandon came round to the other side and took a look. 'That's pretty good. Who is it? Catwoman?'

'Wonder Woman, duh!' Chelsea gave him a mock contemptuous look, before grinning up at him.

He ruffled her hair. 'Very good.'

'Have you found out who killed Josh Ryan's uncle yet?'

'Chelsea!'

'Well, if you need some leads, people are talking about his house being a cuckoo's nest.'

Rachel looked at Brandon for explanation.

'They call it cuckooing when a county lines mule uses a local addict's house as a base for operations. Not that I want to discuss police matters during an art class with my daughter. But thought I should clear that up. How do you know about cuckooing, young lady?'

'Damien Kane. He knows everything. They tried to use his house. His mum's a druggie.'

'Perhaps you should stop seeing Damien Kane.'

Chelsea shrugged. 'He's not so bad. I think he's been suspended again, anyway. Or excluded.'

Excluded, probably, which usually meant isolation at school. Time with Rachel's department. She'd find out Monday when term started. She'd take Sam's computer along with her – just in case an opportunity arose. Rachel felt she had the measure of Damien Kane. The first time she'd been assigned him, also her first day at the school, he'd told her to keep her distance. She couldn't believe her ears. He repeated the command in his quiet, firm voice. Affronted, she'd replied: 'No one tells me what to do. Least of all a student.' But she'd soon learnt to back off and monitor him from a suitable space. He had his reasons; suggestions of a difficult childhood. They had come to an unspoken understanding.

'Back to school, Monday.' Rachel was gathering her things, making ready to go.

Chelsea's face brightened. She loved school. Rachel was looking forward to it as well. A return to some sort of structure. A diversion. Or, possibly, a breakthrough. Brandon's investigations were grindingly slow. She wanted to get hold of one of his fiddles, shove it under his chin and make him liven the tempo. Perhaps she could make some headway herself? Finding out how Josh Ryan's uncle Pat died would be a start. And then Sam. Was there a connection?

Chelsea and Brandon were hovering by the door, waiting for her to move.

'Can I just have a word, Brandon?'

Brandon gave Chelsea a little prod.

'I know when I'm not wanted,' she said. 'But, here, Miss. Here's a fridge magnet for you. For your portrait.' She squeezed it into Rachel's hand. 'It's Mom out of *The Incredibles*.'

Rachel smiled. 'Thanks, Chelsea. Perhaps you could draw her next?'

'I'm on it,' she said, walking out of the room.

Brandon stood, his hands in his pockets, listening to Chelsea's retreating footsteps. The door to the kitchen creaked on its hinges.

'So, what did you want to talk to me about?'

Rachel walked over to the armchair and sat down. 'I just wondered how the Montol investigations are going?'

'Ah, yes. Chelsea's little outburst about Pat Ryan. Did it capture your imagination?' Brandon dragged the wooden chair from under the desk, placed it by Rachel, and sat opposite her. Rachel noticed a few buttons were missing at the bottom of his shirt.

She smiled. 'Of course.'

'I spoke to Jodi Kane, Damien's mother. She wasn't too helpful at first. They rarely are. Eventually, she indicated that Pat Ryan wasn't "one of theirs". He was a clean skin.'

'Working for someone else, you mean?' Rachel leaned in.

Brandon mirrored her, moving close, as if the eaves had ears. 'That's what she thinks. Not one of her dealers and not one of the county line mules. That Facebook page that said he was a family guy, just a regular Joe – well, that's what he appears to have been. No criminal record. Pat was a fisherman. Like his dad and his dad before him. A Cornishman born and bred.'

'Shouldn't say it, but that makes it worse somehow.'

'Yep.' Brandon lounged back in his chair. 'One of us. And yet … He may have been diversifying.'

'Indeed. He didn't end up on that bonfire for nothing, Brandon. There has to be a reason.'

'Of course.'

A shaft of light from the window cut the air between them like a sabre. Flecks of dust and fruit flies danced in its beam.

Rachel got up to go. 'I like this room, you know.'

'Would you like to come here and paint? Use it as a studio?'

'Brandon, I have The Hall. There's a massive studio there.'

'You haven't answered my question. Would you like to come here and paint?'

'I might. I might well. In just a while.'

'It's here. When you're ready.'

Brandon fumbled in his pocket and produced his wallet. 'Thirty pounds cover the class?'

Rachel scrunched her face. 'No, I couldn't take any money. Chelsea is a joy to work with.'

'Come on, take it. Otherwise, I can't lean on you to come again.' He pulled some notes out of his wallet.

'You could bring me in for questioning?'

Brandon smiled, still brandishing the notes. 'Seems that you do most of the questioning.'

Rachel moved past him to the door.

'How about dinner next week? If you won't take the cash?'

She stood, her back to him. 'There's the gallery opening next week. It'll take up a lot of time. Getting things ready. And I'm back at school.'

'You knock off school at 3.30. Come on. A girl's got to eat, doesn't she? Especially a busy one. How about The Mermaid on Thursday? Night after the opening. Give you a chance to chill. You don't work Fridays, after all.'

'How do you know I don't work Fridays?' She was looking at him now, smiling.

'I'm a DI, remember.'

'Easy to forget, sometimes.'

Brandon laughed. 'I'm coming to the opening, by the way.'

'Business or pleasure?'

'Both. See you then.'

'See you then.'

'And The Mermaid? Thursday?'

'Sounds good,' Rachel said, her eyes flicking past him to the desk. 'I forgot something.' She walked over and picked up Chelsea's portrait of her. Held it between two fingers, so it wouldn't get creased.

Brandon smiled. 'Here, let me show you out.'

27

Brandon

'You okay, honey?' Brandon watched as Chelsea sat at the kitchen table stirring a spoon in her mug.

She pulled it out and licked off some hot chocolate froth. 'Yes, why?'

He walked over and crouched down by her side. 'Your eyes are red.'

Chelsea took off her glasses and rubbed her eyes. 'My eyes are often red, Dad. They're not the greatest.'

'You've got your daddy's blue eyes. They'll break some hearts, that's for sure.'

'Yeah, right,' Chelsea said, smiling weakly.

'Do you need to get them checked again?'

'No. Grandma took me a month back. Prescription's the same. Thank God! I won't need another pane of double glazing.'

Brandon stood back up and ruffled her hair. 'We'll see if we can't get that sorted. Maybe when you're a little older.'

Chelsea grunted and looked back down at her mug.

'Did they set you any homework for over the break?'

Chelsea waved a hand at her rucksack in the corner. 'A bit.'

'Need any help with it?'

'Why all the questions, Dad?' She got up, dumped her mug in the sink and stomped over to the bureau in the living room.

Brandon ran a hand through his hair as he watched her going through the drawers, searching through each one and slamming them shut.

'What are you looking for? A pen? I've got a pen.' He picked one up from on top of the microwave.

Chelsea slapped her thighs and turned to him in exasperation. 'What have you done with the photos of Mum?'

She stared at him, eyes blazing.

'I haven't done anything with them. Let me look.' Brandon pushed past her and felt in the top drawer, fishing around at the back. 'Here, stuck between the drawers.' He pulled out a crumpled photo. 'Let's see if there's more.'

He pulled out the three drawers, photos and papers which had been wedged between them spilling out onto the bottom of the bureau and floor.

'They're all here. They just got a little lost, that's all – among all the junk we store in there.'

Chelsea rushed to him and gave him a hug. 'I'm sorry, Dad. I should have known. I'm sorry.'

'No need to be sorry.' He stroked her hair, could feel her tears seeping through the fabric of his shirt. 'Why don't you choose a few photos and go into town tomorrow, buy some nice frames?' He reached for his wallet on the work surface and took out twenty-five pounds.

Chelsea pulled away. 'Thanks, Dad,' she sniffed. 'I'll nip out in a while.'

Brandon gave her a look. 'You know it's New Year's Day? There won't be any shops open.'

'Duh!' Chelsea swung her head around. 'Sainsbury's will be open. I can get a ton of frames with twenty-five pounds from there.'

'Well bring back the change, girl. Don't want you spending it on *Desperados*.'

'Do I look old enough to buy alcohol!'

Standing there with that defiant, confident smile on her

face, she did, he thought. She looked a lot like her mom. Christ, he hadn't realised just how much she missed her mom. Jess had left a gaping hole in their lives. He should have got those photos out sooner – instead of pretending that it was all in the past and that hiding Jess from view would help them heal. Help them forget. He watched Chelsea going through the photos, putting them in piles, taking more time over some than others.

'And if you just happen to run into that Damien Kane on your travels, tell him your Daddy wouldn't mind a word with him.'

'Dad!'

Brandon winked, but he hoped he'd got the message across. The boy was a concern. He didn't want his tender-hearted daughter getting caught up with him.

28

Rachel

It was January 3, the first day of term, and *I Don't Like Mondays* was playing on the radio as Rachel drove the Fiat out of the drive and onto the road to school. She hoped the song about a school massacre wasn't an omen, particularly as she was likely to be cooped up with Damien Kane. She always seemed to be given the nut jobs. 'You're so good with the kids', was the usual refrain when she was allocated a child excluded for some major incident. The last time it had been with a boy who gloried in sketching guns and going wacko in the classroom.

Damien wasn't so bad, really. Not when he was on his own. He'd opened up about the recent death of his dad. 'No need to be sorry, Miss. I didn't really know him.'

She hoped the traffic wouldn't be too heavy getting into Penzance. It was getting colder, and she'd lost time scraping ice off her windscreen.

What a week. She wouldn't argue with this Monday, that's for sure. It was a joy to get out of The Hall, out of Seabird Cottage and away from the gallery. Julia had been hyper. She'd loved Euan's photo montages – of course. And so, Rachel was going to use the school minibus to pick them up that afternoon. The school were fine about it. The headmistress was a friend of Julia's and The Arthouse, as it was now named, *was* a not-for-profit community project.

Rachel hadn't seen Euan since New Year's Eve. *What a night*. She crashed the gears into third just thinking of it.

And then there was Lizzie. And two more 'finds'. Rachel had scrutinised them, brought out a magnifying glass, checked against the one Lawrence Matthews they had which hung in the living room. They seemed good. But it was all too good to be true.

'Darling, these are gifts from heaven!' Lizzie had exclaimed. If anything, she was more hyper than Julia, insisting *Browned Off*, as she called it, should grace the gallery's first night.

'Don't you think we should get it authenticated by an expert first?' Rachel had argued.

'Meghan's been round,' Lizzie replied in her breezy way. 'She's Cornish. We don't need a London toff to tell us what we already know.'

The only person seemingly not infected with this mania was Brandon. There were still no new leads on the Montol murder, Sam's clandestine meeting, or the sabotaged glitter ball. Rachel put her foot on the gas as she took the final approach to the school. Let's see if I can't make a little headway, she thought, as she squeezed the car into the last available parking spot. She checked the time. Two minutes to the bell. Rachel had got to the front door before she remembered the computer. She ran back to the car, grabbed Sam's computer – hidden away in a sports bag – and headed back.

There was a tangible air of relief when she flung open the Special Needs Room door. The team were huddled around the centre tables, discussing special assignments. A small group of students was already settling down for some literacy work. Janet Price, the literacy co-ordinator, was typing on her computer, preparing a white board lesson. The boys were smirking and chatting. She'd have her work cut out, as always, getting them to pay any sort of attention.

'Rachel, do you mind dropping out of Y7 art today to do

some one-to-one with Damien Kane?' Jaqueline Kelly, the Special Educational Needs Coordinator, collared her before she'd had a chance to hang up her coat.

It was a rhetorical question. Damien was already sitting in the 'cell' at the far end of the main room. He looked pissed off. He always did unless he was playing some prank or other.

'Of course. Has he been excluded?'

Jaqueline lowered her voice. 'Yes. Stabbed Arek Thompson with a compass. Damien denies it, of course. But Arek filled out *another* form of complaint and his parents have been on.'

Jaqueline handed Rachel a plastic folder containing some papers. 'Gregg Peters has set him some English. If you could try and get him to do some, that would be good.'

Rachel nodded. She usually managed to get a bit of work out of them. *Boy, did it take some effort.*

Damien didn't look up when she entered the room. His small, skinny body was hunched over the rucksack on his desk. The dark lank hair, which framed his fine-featured face, gave him the air of the Knave of Spades. She left the door slightly ajar – even though windows lined the cell, you couldn't be left alone with a pupil. This was ostensibly for their protection, but also for the teachers. They'd evolved into a cautious breed.

'Happy holidays?' Rachel said, sitting down next to Damien. He seemed fine with the distance she'd given him.

'No. But thanks for not ratting on me about The Acorn,' he said, giving her a furtive glance.

Rachel remained silent. He knew he owed her.

'Today we're going to read and discuss one of Shakespeare's greatest soliloquys. Macbeth. Act 5, Scene 5. Do you know what a soliloquy is?'

'Soliloquy? A speech of some sort?'

'Yes, it's a speech. But it's more than that. It's when a character relates their thoughts and feelings out loud. It's a dramatic device, so the audience can get inside a character's head. Well done for pronouncing soliloquy, too. Greater people than you and I have stumbled over that word.'

'You mean Miss O'Leary?'

Rachel gave him a stern look. 'Damien, if you'd like to read the soliloquy.' She faltered over the word.

A small smile flickered on his lips. 'One *soliloquy* coming up.

… Out, out, brief candle!
Life's but a walking shadow, a poor player,
That struts and frets his hour upon the stage,
And then is heard no more. It is a tale
Told by an idiot, full of sound and fury,
Signifying nothing.

'What do you make of that? What do you think Macbeth meant?'

'That life ain't worth a toss? That people think they're important but they ain't.'

His black eyes were fixed on the desk as he spoke.

'It reminded me, also, of that old guy that got knocked down at The Acorn.'

Rachel bristled. 'Only because of the stage. There are no other similarities.'

'Danger, Miss. Like Macbeth, there was danger. Who do you think wrecked the glitter ball?'

'You?'

Damien sniggered. 'No. I was up on the table trying to stop it crashing down.'

'You were up on the table swigging from a bottle of vodka, Damien. But let's not dwell on that now.'

Damien fiddled with his pen, took out the ink tube in the middle and then reinserted it. 'The police – the DI playing in the band – have been questioning people about what happened. It was sabotage, Miss.'

'Is that what you've heard?'

Rachel looked out of the cell window to see if anyone was listening. But no. The boys were keeping Janet Price busy.

'They've interviewed all the handymen and electricians that work at The Acorn. It seems there was a hippy guy who came in. Nobody knew him. But he signed in on the day before the gig. Said he knew Ben. Said he was checking the ball, making it safe.'

'How do you know all this?'

'I hear things.' Damien was looking down again, dismantling his pen.

'Have you spoken to DI Hammett?

'No.'

'Then I strongly advise you do. You can't withhold this sort of information, Damien.'

'He'll know already.' Damien rocked back on his chair.

'That may be the case, but you should, must, pay him a visit.'

Damien shrugged. 'I see and hear a lot of things.'

'Listen to me, Damien. You need to speak to the police. I'll come with you if you like.'

'No. I'll do it. He's spoken to my mum. But she don't know the half of it.'

There was a burst of laughter in the main room. Janet was raising her sing-song voice, but control was slipping away. She caught Rachel's eye through the glass.

'Damien, can I rely on you to report what you've heard and what you've just told me?'

'Yes.'

He presented his pale face to her like a death mask. She believed he would speak to the police. But she'd prime Brandon regardless.

'Time's getting on, Damien. I'd like you to write your own poem. One that you think expresses Macbeth's words and feelings.'

He didn't complain. She'd found children liked to write poetry. It was a quick fix way of expressing themselves without having to worry too much about grammar.

His pen was moving slowly over the page of his exercise book as Rachel pulled the computer out of her bag. Damien gave a quick look and then returned to his work.

They had their heads down in the main room too. Janet was walking around the desks, trying to police them. Every few seconds one would make a wise crack or steal another's pen or paper and she would reprimand them in her dull voice. She was coming towards the cell, as if her radar had picked up on something. Rachel slipped the computer under her chair and leaned towards Damien to check his work. She caught Janet's eye when she looked up.

'Tosser!' shouted one of the boys outside, prompting Janet to swizzle round and return to the group.

Rachel pulled out the computer and fired it up.

'I've finished, Miss.' The computer was a magnet for Damien.

'Already?' Rachel said, keying in Sam's password.

'Yes – take a look.'

Rachel put the computer back on the floor, let it do its start-up business, and picked up Damien's exercise book. She always recoiled when she saw his scribbling. It usually made no sense at all. Sometimes he just scratched one long line across the page. But he'd tried here. Had formed words. Poorly spelt and poorly presented. But words all the same.

'Read it to me, Damien.'

He took the book and started reading his poem in perfect cadence. *Where did he get that voice?*

The King Thing
His life was torture
We could see that, my mum and me
The way he walked
Talked
But did we care
Hell No
He strutted like he was King
Took what he wanted from who he wanted
Our thing
Cursed us. Dragged us down into the dark
Cold flesh, pressing on bones, into the black. Into hell
But he paid the price
We saw him fall
His tragedy?
That he was born at all.

Wow. 'That is something, Damien. Well done. It really has power. I'll give you a Merit for this.'

He looked pleased. Couldn't help himself. 'What did you expect from an angst-ridden teen?'

Rachel smiled and glanced down at the computer. It was ready.

'What have you got there, Miss?'

They both peered up out of the window to ensure Janet Price was still fully engaged. She was bringing up something on *YouTube* – a cartoon. The last resort of a teacher at the end of her tether.

'A friend's computer. A lot of his work has gone missing. I wanted to check for him.'

'Do you know anything about computers, Miss?'

'A bit.'

'Let me have a look.'

Damien was banned from using computers and iPads at school, following his hacking escapade. They both scanned the main room. Homer Simpson was being fast-forwarded on the white board. Janet Price was saying something about finding the right clip.

'Okay, quickly, Damien.' Rachel slipped the laptop to him. He pulled it down onto his lap, ran his small, smooth fingers over it like a safe cracker and started to tap the keyboard.

The cartoon, a *Simpsons* Special on a tenuously linked educational theme, was playing.

'It's been wiped, Miss.'

'What do you mean, wiped?'

'There's a link to a folder, but the folder's not there.' Damien ran a search which came up empty. 'See, Miss, there's a link to a folder called *Frida Kahlo* but there's no folder with that name and Deleted Items is empty. Hang on.'

Damien launched a spreadsheet programme, checked recent items there, did another search. 'Yeah, see – that folder had spreadsheets in it called *Diego, Botero, Lam* – but they're not there either. Must have been deleted.'

'Can you get them back?'

'The hard disk hasn't been formatted, so someone with the right software should be able to recover the files.'

'Do you have the right software?'

Damien shifted in his seat, looked out of the window, checking on Janet Price.

'Not here, Miss.'

Damien handed back the computer and started playing with his pen. 'But I'll see what I can do.'

Rachel put the laptop back in the sports bag just as Janet started to walk towards them.

Janet popped her head around the door. 'Would Damien like to join the others and watch the cartoon?'

'I'm in solitary confinement,' Damien said, not bothering to look at her.

'Oh, I'm sure we could make an allowance.'

'I'm writing poetry. Shall I read you my poem, Miss Price?' He was giving her his death stare.

In the background the boys were restless, cuffing each other and messing around.

'Poetry. Well, Mr Peters will be pleased,' she said, turning to leave. 'Ah, there goes the bell.'

'Have I got you after break?' Damien said as Rachel made a move.

'No. Miss McCall will take over. Thanks for looking at the computer. You will go to see DI Hammett?'

'I said I would, didn't I?'

'Yes, you did. Good.'

'Miss?'

Rachel turned back, moving close so she could hear him. His voice was quiet at the best of times, but now it was a whisper.

'Pat Ryan. The guy who got done in. He was involved in stuff.'

'He was a fisherman, wasn't he?'

'Yes. He had a boat. Sometimes I'd see him coming in late. Turning off the engine and cruising into Prussia Cove.'

'What were you doing there?'

'Nothing better to do. I take my bike out. I like to know

what's going on.'

'What is going on?'

Damien picked up his pen, dragged the nib across a clean page of his book.

'Stuff. Don't know what, but the regulars didn't like it. You don't mess with those guys.'

'Hello, Damien.' Suzy McCall poked her head around the door. 'See you after break.'

Rachel gave him a long hard look. 'I'll get you that Merit. I reckon you deserve it.'

29

Rachel

'He said the computer's been wiped.' Rachel was sitting in the minibus outside The Hall talking to Brandon on the mobile. 'You've had it checked? Maybe a second opinion? Okay – forget I mentioned it. He said Pat Ryan was into *stuff*. No, he didn't say what. Damien said he'd come in and see you. Probably with his mum. Okay. See you.'

'Who was that?' Julia had climbed into the minibus and was strapping herself into the passenger seat. Nick and Jack, earphones in, were in the back.

'Brandon. Just picked up a few details on Pat Ryan which might be useful. He had a habit of going out in his boat late at night.'

Julia didn't look interested. 'The sea doesn't shut up shop at 6pm. Hardly a revelation.'

'Damien Kane said he was turning off his engine and cruising into Prussia Cove. Seems a bit suspect.' Rachel reversed the minibus and straightened it to take them out of the drive.

'And you believe him? Old fisherman tales. Sam said the pubs in Newlyn and Penzance harbour are full of them.'

'Oh, yes?'

'He sometimes went to the Smugglers Tavern for a drink, after visiting some of the Newlyn artists.'

Including Meghan.

Rachel glanced at Julia. She looked calm – quite happy to share snippets about Sam's life, as if he still had one. In a few weeks' time they would be travelling out of the same drive in a funeral car, tailing a hearse carrying his dead body. Today, she was preoccupied with another journey, and another body – this one very much alive.

Euan was waiting for them as Rachel manoeuvred the mini-bus into the small side road where he lived in Gulval village. He'd put out some sandbags so they had a parking space. It was still tight, though, and Rachel felt sweat on her brow as she backed the bus in.

'Hi,' he said, when she got out. He was smiling at her, holding her gaze.

'Hi.' Rachel averted her eyes and looked beyond him to the open door of his Victorian cottage. His creations lined the front room – twilight played on the glass, casting shadows and sparkles of colour.

Julia gave Euan a quick kiss on his cheek. 'Well, shall we get to work?'

They filed into his cottage. Rachel hadn't seen the montages in situ – just on the phone. They were giants – the four in the living room – crowding out the sparse furniture.

'I did warn you,' he said, catching Rachel's expression. 'Can I get you a coffee? A drink?'

'I'm fine.' Over his shoulder, Rachel scrutinised the small kitchen. He kept it tidy. She could see a few gadgets on the work surfaces, but it was mostly clutter-free. There was no TV in the living room. Just a small grey sofa. No cushions. No shelves. No books or family photos. It didn't feel like a home. More like a pod.

'That's very kind of you, Euan.' Julia was standing in front of one of the montages admiring it as if it was a window in a cathedral. 'But we should get on. Nick and Jack have home-work'

'Thanks for coming, guys,' Euan said, addressing the boys.

Nick smiled at him. 'These are awesome. How many are we taking, Mum?'

'The lot.'

Rachel was struck by a photo in one of the montages. She moved to get a better look.

'Hey, is that me?'

Euan peered at it and smiled. 'I think you might be right.'

It was a photo of her getting into her car, the Jubilee pool behind her.

He was close behind her now. She could feel heat from his body. Smell the shampoo he'd probably used that day. It was both intoxicating and intimidating.

'Well, you can take it out!'

Julia winced. 'Don't be so precious, Rachel, he can't remove it now.'

'Yes, he can.'

Euan was smiling. 'What religion do you practise, Rachel? Do you think I have captured a tiny piece of your soul? A tiny piece of your heart?'

'Just a small piece of my patience, Euan. I'm sure you can find a seagull or two to fill the void.'

He laughed. 'Okay, consider it done. Let's get them all in the bus and I can work on the offending piece at the gallery.'

* * * * *

Rachel sat up abruptly in bed, the last vestiges of her dream panning away like the end sequence in a film. Her duvet lay in a heap on the floor. She must have kicked it aside in her sleep. Kicked it off as she'd tried to escape the nightmare. She was breathing hard, her heart slamming her chest.

The dream had been so vivid – she'd climbed into one of

Euan's montages like *Alice through the Looking Glass* and the world she'd entered was as bizarre and disturbing. Black waves crashed against rocks in secret coves. A fisherman's boat lay marooned on the sand, its cargo drifting back out to sea on the receding tide. A gull circled and screeched above. And in harbour-side taverns, the lights were dim and folk huddled and talked in the shadows.

'He's coming,' said an old man, two yellow teeth glinting in the hollow of his mouth.

'Who?' she'd asked. 'Who?'

'He's coming. He's coming.'

A drum beat a solemn rhythm in the street outside. Through a boxed window she could see torches flickering – the light, like the beat, getting stronger. A cloaked figure led a procession that was making its way along the sea path. The Don Giovanni of both dreams and nightmares. Others fell in line behind him – one man bound in chains, pulled by another. The mournful tune of a lone flautist was barely audible, a wisp of wind above the hard beat of the drum.

Rachel thought she saw someone at the back of the procession. Someone in white. The figure moved away from the rest and darted into the gardens on the promenade.

Rachel gave chase. 'Hey, wait. Wait for me. I'm coming.'

The figure moved on. She saw it slip into one of the narrow alleys behind the sea front terraces. When Rachel reached the passage, he was standing motionless at the far end, his back to her.

'No need to run away. No need to be afraid. I'm here now.'

The boy turned slowly, raising sad, shy eyes to her face.

'Oliver.' Rachel walked towards him, tears streaming down her face. He looked uncertain, as if his very presence was causing her pain. As if he had no place in her world anymore.

'Oliver.' She reached out to touch him and draw him close. To make everything good, again. And he smiled. A beautiful smile. Pure and full of love.

As she went to hold him, she hit against something. The montage – the moonlight playing with its captive images, making them dance, like the revellers at the Montol. Oliver was splintering into a mosaic of images. Tiny fragments, like atoms, and then just one child slipping away. Rachel beat her hands against the glass. Pummelled it with her fists until it shattered and tore into her skin. She pushed her arms through the jagged portal, reached out and grabbed hold of his hand. As she drew Oliver close, the shards turned to ice and then snow as he melted into her arms.

30

Rachel

Rachel slipped on the t-shirt she'd dropped on the floor by her bed the night before, pulled on some joggers and went downstairs. She didn't turn on the light, for fear of waking Julia, and tiptoed past her door on the wood-panelled landing, using her phone as a torch.

The stairs creaked as she made her way down to the kitchen. Nick slept soundly, but Julia was a light sleeper, particularly now.

No light in the kitchen. Good. She needed time alone. It was 4am; that would give her a few hours before the house started to break into life. The security box on the wall was pulsing green. Which was a relief.

It was too early for tea, so she reached into the fridge and pulled out a carton of juice. Pouring a glass, she sat down in the armchair in the corner of the kitchen.

Drawing her knees to her chest, she sat there staring into the dark, aware of the chill. Should she turn on the heating? Or would that disturb Julia and Nick? Instead, she unravelled a throw kept in the wicker basket by her side and snuggled up in the chair. She wouldn't go back to sleep. But she wasn't ready to face the day yet.

The dream – and all the events of the day which had inspired it – played out in her head. Oliver. It was heart-breaking to see him. To see and feel their separation and his sadness and concern. But they'd broken through. He would always be a part of her. She hadn't lost him.

Euan. Euan was making as big an impression on their lives, as his massive montages in his cramped cottage. Who would have thought the reserved young man she knew at Falmouth would return on such a scale? He had been charming for the rest of the afternoon; organising Nick and Jack, getting the works in and out of the minibus and up the stairs of The Arthouse. He had advised where they might look the best but wasn't looking to bag the prime positions. He didn't really need to. They'd knock the other exhibits out of the room. Maybe it was his newfound confidence that was so compelling? So why was she holding back? He'd made himself perfectly clear on New Year's Eve.

She remembered that time twelve years ago in Falmouth. Benedict had something else on that evening. Had left her with little more than a smile and a shrug to go to the Summer Ball alone. Julia was with Jago – they were close at that stage. She was fixated on him, with his art, his arrogance. Rachel had found herself pretty much alone that night; drinking too much just to get through it. She'd spied Euan sitting on the stairs. She hadn't sought him out, but she knew he would welcome her. Even back then he made no effort to disguise his devotion. *Was it any port in a storm? A revenge fuck? Or something else? Something beyond curiosity and desperation?*

He hadn't looked surprised when she went to sit by him on the stairs. She'd caught his eye a few times. He'd been watching her. Back then a lot of people did. It was like she was part of a theatrical troupe and her whole time at Falmouth was a performance. She was Lawrence Matthews' daughter. One of the *Bright Young Things*. Euan was one of the audience. He would have seen her moving aimlessly from circle to circle, knocking back the booze. What a state she must have been. She'd just wanted to rest, sit down and watch, rather than do.

Rather than be Rachel Matthews, daughter of Lawrence, the next big thing.

He budged up when she sat down – but still others had to step over them to make their way to the upstairs loos.

'Let's get out of here,' he said, taking her hand, and she'd followed him into the college grounds. There were plenty of people outside – dressed in fancy clothes, black tie, ball gowns, quaffing from bottles. So, they walked through the gardens to the gravestones embedded in the grass – the stepping stones to the sea path. Euan let go of her hand and started playing hopscotch on the stones.

Rachel hitched up the lilac satin dress her mother had loaned her and joined him. He was better than her – probably less drunk – and she stumbled on the stones, falling and gashing her knee. Euan swooped down to her side, poured alcohol from the bottle he was carrying onto the sleeve of his shirt and wiped the blood from the scrape. His head was bowed, his hands gentle as he tended her wound.

'Thanks,' she said, as he looked back up.

'You okay? Do you want me to get a bandage? A plaster?'

'I'm fine, Doc. Can't see there's anything more to be done here.' She was more concerned about the rip in Lizzie's dress and the blood on it than her grazed knee.

'Well, let's go down to the sea. Rub some salt in that wound!'

'Race you there,' Rachel said, sprinting off and leaving him sitting on the stones.

'You'll fall again. This time I'll be there to catch you.'

'Wanna bet?' Rachel was running ahead, clutching her ruched-up dress, her hair flying back like ribbons. The night air was cool on her face, and she could have run forever, chasing along the clifftop, skipping over daisies in the wild grass. The gulls were asleep and all she could hear was her own breath, and the sound of music in the far distance. She couldn't hear Euan. *Was he that slow? Was she that fast?* She slowed her pace. The gate to the beach was only yards away now. She could hear the waves, see the moon reflected on the silver surface of the sea. She turned round to look for him.

'Hi,' he said.

'What the hell!' She swung round to see him on the other side of the gate.

'You mean you don't know the short cut?' He was grinning at her. 'I won the bet. What's the prize?'

'An artist's masterclass with Rachel Matthews?'

'Hmm. Anything more ... Anything less, arty? Come on, Rachel, that would be a busman's holiday, wouldn't it? How much art can a man take? We are surrounded by art. Look at this beautiful setting. Look at this beautiful ...' He looked serious all of a sudden.

'I feel like a fucking maiden in a fucking fairy tale.'

'I don't think princesses swear, Rachel.'

'They don't do much, do they?' Rachel looked him in the eye. 'I guess they kiss. I seem to remember reading that. They kiss frogs, I think.'

Euan burst out laughing. Reached out a hand to brush away a strand of hair which had blown across her face. 'They do. Often with sensational, transformational results. Shall we settle on a kiss? It could be a win-win situation.'

'I have a prince, Euan.' Rachel gave him a steady, appraising look.

'No, you don't, Rachel. He's an ogre. He's entrapped you in his ivory tower.'

Rachel smiled. *He had a point. And was Benedict ever faithful? He said he was. But was he?*

Euan was standing waiting for his answer. For his prize.

'I'm a little drunk, Euan.'

'Just a little? Here, have some more.' He passed her the bottle of wine.

She took a sip, brushed a hand across her moist lips, tilted her head towards him. 'Just the one, mind.'

Euan leaned forward and planted a kiss on her lips. 'Just the one?'

'Oh, go on, have another one then. I'm feeling generous!' Rachel was laughing, but Euan looked deadly serious. He drew her to him, kissed her again, this time with passion.

A couple passed them; others were coming down to the beach from the gardens. Euan held her in his arms, his body pressed close, so close she could feel his heart beating hard and fast.

'Let's go back to my room. Let's go back now.'

Rachel nestled her head against his chest. At that point she wanted to go with him, more than anything.

Her phone woke her in the morning. It was a text. She turned her groggy head to one side, looking for it. Euan was laying by her side. He flung an arm around her, started kissing her back, his fingers trailing her spine, working downwards. Rachel felt a rush of heat. And then her phone beeped again.

'I better get that,' she said, disentangling herself. She picked up her phone and sat on the edge of the bed to read it. Euan wasn't giving up. He wrapped his arms around her, kissing her neck, pulling her back.

Benedict: 'Where the hell were you, Rach? I got back to college round 11 and they said you'd gone off with some bloke. I looked all over for you. Come over now. I missed you last night. London tonight. Remember? The Grayson Perry party? Bx'

Euan took the phone from her hand and put it on the bed. 'Don't go. Don't go to him. He doesn't deserve you. He doesn't love you.'

Rachel started to gather her clothes together. Lifting the satin dress, she slipped it over her head. Rolling up her discarded tights into a ball, she stuffed them in her clutch bag.

'He does love me, in his own way.' Rachel bent down and fumbled under the bed for her shoes.

'It's a crap way, Rachel. You deserve better than that.'

'I don't, you know.'

'Yes, you do.' He walked round to face her, knelt and circled his arms around her waist.

'Euan, I've got to go.'

Slipping on her velvet pumps, she headed for the door.

He was behind her in seconds. 'Rachel. Your dress is undone. Let me fix it.'

She had her hand on the door handle but stopped for him. Felt his fingers shaking as he worked the zip up, felt the heat from his body, his breath on the nape of her neck, his lips as they glanced her skin. And then she was gone. Not to see him again as she ambled through the last days of her time at Falmouth.

31

Brandon

Brandon snapped his notepad shut. Damien and Jodi Kane's visit was a disappointment – they had nothing to say which he didn't know already. All the same, they'd risen in his estimation. They'd made the effort to come in. Many in their circumstances wouldn't. Now it was time to get down to some real business. The prime suspect in the Ryan case had been identified.

He texted Jo: 'Why don't you bring in a couple of coffees and some of those leftover mince pies?'

Within minutes, Jo was bumping the door open with a full tray and placing it on the incident room table.

'And so, we have him.' Brandon reached across the table and shook Jo by the hand. 'Brilliant work. We now need to catch Nike Boy before he slips away.'

'He really did like that hoodie, didn't he, Boss,' Jo said, glowing with pride as she collected some print-out papers together.

'Too much for his own good.' Brandon glanced up at the wall display of photos, Nike Boy a sinister, shadowy presence among them. They now had to find out who ordered the kill and who helped execute it. It would have taken some guile and effort for the skinny young man to bring down Ryan on his own, let alone chop up and dispose of his body.

Jo had gathered eight witness sightings of the suspect around the time of the Montol – one just yards from the unlit bonfire about eleven am. There were also CCTV images of him on the 7.55 Great Western from Bristol that day and arriving at Penzance Station. To crown it all, she had one good image of him with another young man. Brandon had sent that over to the Newquay and Bristol teams – as well as doing his own checks. He wasn't a familiar face, but CCTV footage showed the same sandy-headed youth on a Penzance bus with the suspect and, earlier, tailing him at Bristol Station. They hadn't named him yet, but Nike Boy was known. Both fitted the descriptions given by Rachel of the thugs in the graveyard. At some point Nike had fitted in a shave. He hadn't shown up at any of the local barbers, so he must have got out his razor. Administered a feeble DIY disguise.

'The toe rag's a violent offender – goes by the name of Conor Robson. Newquay MCIT identified him via recognition software.'

'The DNA matches could put him behind bars – all your work,' Jo said, smiling up at him. 'He left a lot on Ryan's clothing.'

'Well, that's the easy part,' he acknowledged.

'We're going in tomorrow.' Brandon lowered his voice, even though there were just the two of them in the room. 'Keep this to yourself. The fewer people that know, the better. Bristol have been tailing him and a few of the boys are going to pay him a visit tomorrow morning. Firearms employed. I'm going along to ask Robson a few additional questions, about Ryan, his time in Penzance and what sort of company he keeps.'

'Want me to come?'

'Sure do. We'll leave Stew in charge of the shop. Robson's DNA didn't show up on Sam Trenowden by the way.'

Jo grimaced. 'That would have been too sweet. I'll keep on Trenowden's case. See if I can't get some more leads. Sam was seen around the bonfire earlier that day too, you know.'

Brandon knitted his brow. 'Yes. There could be a connection. It would tally with Rachel's graveyard story. But it's looking unlikely Robson killed him. That won't stop me from posing the possibility during our little chat tomorrow, though.'

32

Brandon

It was three am on a cold winter's morning and Brandon and Jo were sitting in the back of a cop car nursing takeaway coffees. There were three other police vehicles in and around the terraced street in the student quarters of Bristol. A van at one end of the road and a BMW at the other, with another in the street at the back of the Victorian terrace they were about to raid. A precaution. Usually, the early call caught suspects unawares – if they were in the drugs trade, they were even more likely to be bad in the mornings.

Brandon's Bristol equivalent, DI James Rickman, was sitting in the passenger seat looking at his phone. 'We're going in,' he said, opening the car door and striding across the road. Five police rushed to join him from the van and another two from the car. Brandon let them past – this was essentially Bristol's operation.

Two police rushed the door with a battering ram, bashing it open for the firearms team, who stormed into the hallway and up the stairs.

Brandon followed in their wake, nearly tripping on a bike which had been knocked over in the rush. The place smelt of fast food and fags – the stair carpet reeked of piss, probably an animal's. He looked around – the last thing he wanted to encounter was a snarling Pitbull.

Brandon arrived at the bedroom door, as one of the Bristol team nudged Robson awake with his pistol. Just as Robson was raising his sleepy head. His tattooed arm draped over a grubby white duvet reminded Brandon of Pat Ryan's at the morgue, when he'd pulled back the sheet. He struggled to control his anger and contempt, as he saw Robson realise what was happening – what had disturbed his *beauty* sleep. Brandon noticed the little shit had taken the trouble to hang up his Nike hoodie, which swung from a hanger on the door.

Robson's hand shot out to the bedside cabinet – but was stopped by an officer, handcuffs dangling from one hand, a gun in the other.

'Conor Robson, you are under arrest on suspicion of the murder of Pat Ryan. You do not have to say anything, but it may harm your defence if you do not mention when questioned something which you later rely on in court. Anything you do say may be given as evidence,' Brandon said, watching Robson, all the while, for the tell-tale signs of guilt.

* * * * *

As it happens, Robson was a chatty fellow – who didn't heed the advice of the pious, pinched-face legal aid solicitor at his side in the Bristol station. But whatever lubricated his tongue could well have been snake oil.

'I didn't do it,' Robson said, perched forward on his chair. 'I was there, sure. But I didn't do it. The brief was to rough 'im up. We'd already given 'im a beating the week before. But Ryan weren't listening – so we paid 'im another visit.'

Jo, who was sitting with Brandon across the table from Robson, gave her boss a quick look. She wasn't falling for the smart-arse patter either. Brandon got up and walked to the back of the room. 'Your DNA on the victim and his clothes would suggest differently.'

'My client doesn't need to respond to your suggestions,'

said the solicitor. In her thin, shiny grey suit she looked as sharp as a scalpel.

'Indeed. But your client's DNA on the victim is scientific evidence, not a suggestion.'

'I advise Mr Robson to remain silent until he has had time to consider the charges.'

Until you've had time to consider how to play it, thought Brandon. It was often like this – the lawyer shutting down any initial investigation and moving it on to backroom bartering between the Defence and Prosecution teams. But the police were on solid ground here. The DNA matches and CCTV footage, although not conclusive in themselves, would be hard to defend. Maybe Robson understood this? Or maybe he had good reason to justify his actions? If he wanted to talk, Brandon wasn't going to stop him.

'I didn't kill 'im. I helped get rid of the body. But I didn't kill 'im.'

Brandon returned to the table and sat opposite Robson. 'Who did then?'

'My client is under no ...'

Robson glared at her before continuing. 'He was already at the place – a warehouse, down by the docks, when we arrived. We were given the address. He weren't dead – but he was in a real bad way. Tied to a chair and cut up. He was dead meat.' Robson paused and looked down at the floor between his legs. 'I said we should leave 'im. But my mate said, no. He could survive and he'd seen us. We couldn't take the chance.'

'Really, who's this mate giving you all the good advice?'

Robson looked back up at Brandon who was leaning on the table, his eyes fixed on him.

'My client,' said Thin Grey Suit.

Robson ignored her. 'Tyler Flynn. It was Tyler who finished 'im off.' He looked away. 'With a machete. There was a machete in the room. It already had blood on it.'

'Why didn't you leave the body at the warehouse? Your DNA wasn't on the machete. That would be someone else's – if we are to believe you.'

'Tyler was high on meth – he just kept cutting away at 'im. Just cutting and hacking.' Robson paused and wiped his mouth and then his eyes. 'He had this idea that we got rid of the evidence. He'd seen the bonfire all made up on the Quay and thought we'd just burn 'im. No body – no nothing. So, we ...'

'Go on.' Jo had moved in close. 'So, you what?'

The lawyer had given up trying to gag her client – she was as transfixed as the others.

'So, we got some bin liners and stuffed the body in them and went down to the Quay.'

'First your mate gives you a lesson in butchery and then wraps it all up nicely for you. Just happened to have those bin liners on him, did he? Maybe you just happened to anticipate this outcome.' Brandon thumped his fist on the table. 'Your story is getting more and more far-fetched. You better start telling the truth, I'm getting impatient here.' Brandon got up from the table and walked to the back of the room.

'You gotta believe me. I went to the Co-op, got the bin liners. Ain't far. And there were people all dressed up weird and carrying stuff, so we didn't stand out much until ...'

'Go on,' said Jo. 'What happened next?'

His lawyer tried to cut in, but Robson turned to Jo. 'We got the head out first – smallest part. I tucked it in under the wood, nice and neat. Tyler was just about to toss in a leg – maybe an arm – and then we saw someone coming, walking down from the church towards the Yacht Inn. So, we legged it. We were going to throw the rest of the body in the sea, but someone shouted out, so we dumped the body and ran.'

Grey Suit looked at her watch. 'I would like to advise my client to make no further comment.'

'Just a minute.' Brandon gave her a quick look and then walked back over to Robson, dragged out a chair and sat down hard. He leant across the table, his hands just inches from Robson. 'I don't believe you. I don't believe you found Ryan all trussed up nice and neat. I think you accosted him down by the docks when he'd just come in from the sea. From doing a morning's work. I don't suppose he was particularly pleased to see you – not after your last meet-up. So, things got ugly. He was ready for you this time, wasn't he, Robson?'

Robson fell back in his chair, shaking his head, a look of disbelief on his face.

'Wasn't he!' Brandon thumped his fists on the table again, making Robson jerk forward to face him. 'But this time you had your mate Tyler with you – so you got cocky. You dragged him into one of the empty warehouses and butchered him.'

'I didn't – I tell you he was in there, already.' He was sweating now. His head pivoted, following Brandon as he got up and walked to his side. Brandon crouched down beside him; his lips close to his ear.

'I want you to tell the truth now, Conor. I'd advise that very strongly. We have your mate's name now, so we can do a check on his DNA. But this 'mystery man', the one that you say dragged a full-grown man into a warehouse, tied him to a chair and butchered him – well, am I led to believe we'll find his DNA on the victim too? Because if we don't, that just about rules out your phantom butcher.'

Robson was crying now. 'It was Tyler – I didn't want to kill 'im. There was no reason to kill 'im. But Tyler can get real nasty on meth. Real nasty.'

'And you weren't on meth?' Jo said. 'Because if you were, that could be why you acted out of character. You didn't want to kill Pat Ryan, but you weren't thinking straight. You weren't in your right mind?'

'My client.' Grey Suit was looking increasingly uncomfortable.

'Did Tyler give you the meth?' Brandon had returned to his seat.

'Yes, yes he did. Fuck, can I have a fag? I'm dying for a smoke.'

Brandon took his packet from his pocket and pushed it across the table, with a disposable lighter.

Robson lit up, pondered the glowing tip, and then took a long drag.

'So, you and Flynn were out of your heads on meth?

'Yes.'

'And things got out of hand?'

Robson gave a small nod.

'I'm sorry, son, I didn't hear you. Are you saying you and Tyler killed Pat Ryan?'

Robson looked down at the table, took another drag from his cigarette. 'Yes.'

'Yes?' Brandon was on his feet, looking down at Robson.

'Yes. We didn't mean to do it.'

Brandon gave Jo a look and turned to the solicitor.

'Just one more thing, Robson. Where do we find the accomplice to this murder? Where do we find Tyler Flynn?'

'I ...'

Brandon leaned in close. 'The more helpful you are right now, the better for you. I want that address, boy.'

Robson looked over at Grey Suit, who nodded assent. He wrote it down on a sheet of paper – he could write at least. Brandon gave it a quick read. 17a Banford Avenue. It looked like another student lodging.

He took a photograph of it and airdropped it to DI Rickman who was in the observation room.

Brandon gathered his things together and went to get up. 'Sam Trenowden? Heard of him, Conor?'

There was a flicker of recognition. 'Can't say I 'ave.'

Grey Suit stiffened and opened her mouth, but Brandon waved a hand. 'I'm just asking. Not some *wanker* who was treading on your turf? Needed teaching a lesson?'

'Nah.'

'You don't read the papers, then?'

'Not unless I'm likely to be in 'em.'

'Well, if you remember anything, it could be useful. The man died in unexplained circumstances around the same time as Pat Ryan.'

'That so?'

'Aha. You will have some time for reflection. It will pay you to be as helpful as possible. Assist with our enquiries and it will be considered.'

Brandon wrapped up the interview and made to move from the table. Robson had his eyes on his pack of cigarettes. 'This is a No Smoking Zone,' he said, swooping them up and dropping them in the bin with the lighter. They were soiled goods as far as Brandon was concerned.

Brandon and Jo joined the Bristol detectives outside.

DI Rickman was grinning. 'I can't see Robson giving us too much trouble now on the drugs charges – his admission of murder must be foremost in his mind. Good work, guys. A team's on its way to Flynn's. I take it you're both staying for the second half of this shit-show?'

Brandon smiled. 'Wouldn't miss it for the world, eh, Jo?'

'It would be nice to wrap this up in one inglorious performance, Boss.'

'You reckon you'll be able to bring in their handlers?' Brandon said, turning to Rickman.

'Could well do.' Rickman tilted his head, while looking Brandon straight in the eye. 'We've got some leverage with this admission. I'd certainly like to nail the bastards who are shipping this fucked-up freight. Both the drugs and the kids. And, I reckon, we will.'

33

Rachel

It was just a line of wrapped canvases propped up against the wall. But one, Rachel noticed, was poking out from its cocoon of bubble wrap and brown paper. It made her start. There was something about the tip of the frame, the chipped ornate gilt, which filled her with dread. It looked out of place in the neat row of box-framed abstracts, all uniform and bland like a Turner Prize exhibit. The last-minute paintings Lizzie had loaned The Arthouse for the opening.

Rachel walked over to the painting in small careful steps, as if scared to disturb it. Holding her breath, she peeled back the corner of the outer wrapping, to reveal bubble wrap and the canvas within. The fine brush strokes were familiar, the autumnal colours unmistakable; the burnished orange of a setting sun, strands of straw spun into gold. Her hands shook as she tore away the rest of the packaging. It was Lizzie's portrait of Oliver. The one she'd done shortly after his death. A blend of abstract and old school portraiture. *Why hadn't she told her? Why was it here?* She hadn't seen it since she'd asked Lizzie to pack it away.

'Rachel! Darling, Rachel! I didn't include this. I would never have included this portrait. You must know that. I'm so, so sorry. I don't know how it got mixed up with the other works … I'll speak to the men, I'll …' Rachel heard Lizzie saying from somewhere in the room. Words muffled at first, as if wrapped in bubble wrap themselves, and then loud, bouncing off the walls.

'Rachel, let me get the men to take it downstairs. They're still here,' Lizzie said, coming forward, touching her arm.

'It's okay. I'm fine. It was just a shock. That's all. I'd forgotten how beautifully you paint.'

'He was beautiful, Rachel,' Lizzie said, tears in her eyes.

'Yes. But you captured something else. His essence. His soul, really,' Rachel rubbed her nose, collecting herself.

'If you want, it could be part of the exhibition,' Lizzie said, carefully. 'I really didn't tell the men to wrap it and deliver it. You must believe me. But, if you like, we could include it. If it's not too much?'

Rachel looked into Oliver's clear blue eyes.

'Yes. Let's show him off. He's too beautiful to hide away.'

'Oh, that's lovely, darling. I'm so pleased. He will ... would have been pleased. I'll have a word with Julia. I think Oliver should be placed next to Larry's paintings. It will be like the family are back together again!'

Rachel had to smile. 'I'll leave you to it. I've got to go back to school now.' It was 1pm – she'd better hurry. She wasn't meant to sneak out at lunchbreak.

* * * * *

There were disapproving looks when she pushed open the Special Needs Room door. The troops had all gone about their business and it was just Janet Price and Jaqueline Kelly inside, talking over a small group of pupils.

Josh Ryan was standing to attention by his desk, waiting for Rachel, his head of clean-cut, chestnut hair turned downwards. No other student did this and Rachel was always touched when she saw him standing there. He was thirteen, on the brink of GCSEs, and wanted to improve his English so he could get into some regiment or other in the army. Rachel could never remember which.

'Good afternoon, Josh.'

'Good afternoon, Miss Matthews,' he replied, giving her a quick, shy look.

'Let's see what we can work on this afternoon.' Rachel ordinarily did a bit of preparation for their lessons, but she was winging it today. They did much the same thing each week; usually taking an issue or news story from an online newspaper for students and using it for discussion and exercises. She brought up the web page and skimmed through the stories. She tended to give him a few topics to choose from. There were three that caught her attention. Well, one really. *The social fall-out from county lines drugs dealing. But would it be insensitive to even suggest this? It would be interesting to get Josh's take on it, though.*

'Well, Josh. What do you fancy? *The relevance and the role of the young Royals? Russia and its use of fake news to sow discord in the West? The social fall-out from county lines drugs dealing?*'

'County lines drugs dealing.' There was no hesitation.

'Are you sure, Josh?'

'Yes.' He continued to look down at his desk. 'I know a bit about it. You know my uncle?'

Rachel went to touch his shoulder but pulled back. You weren't allowed to touch the kids. 'Yes. I was so sorry to hear.'

'Thanks, Miss.'

'Okay, if you're sure. Let's read the piece together.'

They went through their regular routine – Rachel reading first and then Josh. He was getting better at reading. He didn't have the confidence and ability of Damien Kane, but he was improving. Rachel read with expression and encouraged him to do similar. She stopped him on certain words, either when he stumbled over them, or she thought an explanation was necessary.

'Cuckooing? Do you know what that is?'

'Yes, Miss. It's when a drugs dealer goes and lives with a local. A local druggie. Uncle Pat wasn't involved with the out-of-town guys.' Josh kept his eyes on the screen; his cheeks were reddening.

'Are you sure?' Rachel gave the room a quick scan to check on Janet Price. She was playing a cards game with her group.

'Yes,' Josh said. 'Just the week before he was cut up rough by one of them.'

'Did you see him?'

'No. But my dad did. Saw him at the Smugglers Tavern. He had a black eye and swollen lip.'

'Did he say who had done this and why?' Rachel could hear Janet's voice rising. She glanced over and caught her eye. Janet registered any change in the room's atmosphere. It was her gift. One of her only ones.

Rachel read the next paragraph of the article.

'He wasn't from around here,' Josh said, when she'd finished. 'The guy that roughed up Uncle Pat. Dad thinks he mixed him up with someone else. Uncle Pat didn't do drugs. He was dead against them. Shall I read the next paragraph, Miss?'

'Yes,' Rachel said, distractedly. 'You finish reading the piece, Josh.' *Does Brandon know all this? He would have questioned Josh's mum.*

When he'd finished, Josh gave her a quick look, prompting her to set him a task.

'So, what do you think the social consequences of county lines dealing are? And how do you think the government should tackle the problem?'

Josh sat silent for a while. He always gave thoughtful, considered answers. 'They've got to get tough. They've got to crack down on the bosses, longer prison sentences, take their cash. And the foot soldiers, the dealers, need to be hit hard too. They have to learn it ain't worth dealing.'

'Some people would argue that when you get rid of one dealer, another will take their place. Like a hydra. Do you know what a hydra is, Josh?'

'Not sure, Miss.'

'It's a multi-headed serpent from Greek Mythology – when you cut off one of its heads, two grow in its place.'

'These guys are evil – they need to be cut down wherever they spring up. No matter how many of them. We can't let them win. There's no room in Cornwall for this scum.' His voice was quiet but full of emotion. He gave her a quick look, and she caught the glint of anger in his eyes.

'I'd like you to write a short story about a county lines dealer. Or someone caught up in the operations.'

He scooted backwards to his desk on his swivel chair, opened his exercise book, wrote the date at the top, and started writing. He wouldn't stop for the next forty minutes. Such obedience and concentration. *He'd make a great soldier.* Rachel went over to join the other group for want of something to do.

With five minutes to the bell, she returned to Josh. He'd finished his story and was sitting to attention. His handwriting was neat, and she would easily be able to work on the piece for him – tighten it and get him to practise his spellings. She might learn something herself.

A few sentences jumped out at her. *You didn't go down to the harbour after closing time if you had any sense. And the townie scumbag had none of that.*

'I'll have this marked for next week. Good work, Josh. You can go now.'

'Thank you, Miss Matthews,' he said as he tidied up his desk. Swinging his rucksack over his shoulder, he left the room.

34

Rachel

'Fancy a drink?' It was a text from Benedict. Rachel hadn't heard a word from him since he was ambulanced off on New Year's Eve.

'Love to.'

'See you at The Turks Head at 4pm.'

'Bit early?'

'FFS, Rachel. I know you work at St Piran's but didn't think you'd been canonized! See you there. Mine, as ever, is a large one. Bx.'

He'd already got the drinks in when Rachel turned up at just past four; he was three quarters of the way through his large glass of red and looked ready to order another.

'Rachel. Lovely to see you, as always,' Benedict said, edging along the bench he was sitting on and getting up to plant two wet kisses on her cheeks. He reeked of alcohol and fags.

'While we're up, why don't we get in another round?'

Rachel glanced at the glass of red he'd evidently bought her.

'You wouldn't want to drink alone, now, would you?' Benedict was attempting to be charming, but the usual twinkle in his eye had dulled.

'Here's the thing,' he continued. 'Left my sodding wallet at home. Could only just scrape together the pennies for this round. Would you be so kind?'

'Yes, of course.' Rachel saw his look of desperation morph to one of mild embarrassment.

'You are the best, Rachel. The best. How did I let you get away?'

She watched him sit back down and take a sip of his wine. He'd nurse that last drop until she returned with a refill.

'Why not get a bottle, Rachel? We've got a lot of catching up to do, haven't we? Been too long. Far too long.'

When Rachel returned to the table the glass of red he'd bought her looked less. He didn't relax until she'd refilled his glass.

'Thanks,' he said, avoiding her eye as he took a gulp.

Rachel took a sip from her own glass. 'So, how's things?'

'Could be better.' One of Benedict's finer points had always been frankness.

'Oh?'

'Yes, oh.'

'Want to talk about it?'

'Rachel, I can't think of anything I'd like to talk about less. I'd much rather hear about your exciting adventures as an *educator*. How are you keeping the little bastards in check?'

'A sharp tongue and a sharp stick.'

'Haha! Thought they'd banned the tried and tested!'

Rachel smiled. He was thawing. 'This is Penzance.'

'So, what's been bugging you, Mr Arscott-Rowe?' Rachel said, when he'd finished regaling her with a story about his own reprobate school days.

He paused to top them both up. 'What isn't?' He was putting undue concentration into sharing out the remaining wine. 'Business partners. Women.'

'You usually have a knack for easing your way out of *situations*.'

'Yes,' he said, taking a gulp of wine. 'But ...' He looked past her, through the window to Chapel Street. 'Maybe I've met my match. Maybe this is a game I can't win.' He started to feel in his pocket as his phone buzzed.

'Rachel,' he said, getting to his feet. 'You *are* a saint. You've never demanded. Never been anything but a real friend. Even after ...'

He came round to her side of the table. 'Don't get up, love,' he said, putting a hand on her shoulder. 'Enjoy the rest of the wine that I, ahem, have left you. I'm sorry, Rachel. So sorry.'

'What for?' she rose to face him.

'For being an arsehole. Take care. I'm not the only arsehole out there you know. This town has its fair share.' He looked her in the eye, before reaching for the coat he'd draped on the back of her chair.

'You're off already?'

'Take care. Seriously,' he said, struggling with his coat and walking away.

'See you at the Opening?' Rachel called after him as he pushed open the door. It wasn't clear if he'd heard. He was striding down Chapel Street, one arm still out of its coat sleeve, a hand clutching his mobile. Rachel moved to the window to watch him. Saw him stop at the corner, lean against the wall and thrust back his head, his arms hanging by his side. A minute later he was walking again, mobile clamped to his ear, in no clear direction.

35

Rachel

Snow was falling thick and fast four days later. It had been threatening all day and had decided to make its dramatic debut just hours before the guests were due to arrive for the gala evening at The Arthouse. The sky had darkened, and the snow came in over the sea like an invading force. St Michael's Mount was a pale ghost, barely visible across the bay. It hadn't snowed in Penzance for ten years and the weather was upstaging the opening.

Julia and Rachel were greeting people as they came in. Each time the door opened a blast of snow blew in.

'Nippy out there,' Benedict said, brushing the snow off the sleeve of his Crombie as he entered. Rachel was reminded of a similar action at The Acorn. He gave her two quick kisses, as cold as ice.

Benedict was one of the last to show. The place was already buzzing. People were cruising the rooms, flute glasses in hands, perusing the artwork. The Lawrence Matthews' were attracting a lot of attention. As were Euan's montages. The artist himself had turned his camera – a Polaroid – on the audience. He was snapping people and then ripping out the photos and attaching them to a board by the entrance. It was instant pop art – a mini montage for the guests to look at and take pictures of as they left.

But the night was still young. Julia was preparing to give a welcome speech. She looked beautiful. A snow queen in a long white satin dress, she could have been giving an address at the Oscars.

'Thank you so much, everybody, for coming out tonight. And for braving the elements!'

There was a ripple of polite laughter.

'I am so proud of what we have achieved here at The Arthouse. This was Sam's idea. His passion.' There was no need to explain to the guests who Sam was; barely a day passed when someone didn't express a theory about his demise.

'To Sam.' Julia raised the flute in her hand.

'To Sam.' Benedict led the chorus of voices.

'He would have been so proud of the artwork on display here. Of course, he was responsible for sourcing most of these wonderful creations. But, also, he would have been delighted by the late additions. You may have noticed the three Lawrence Matthews?'

This was met by a roar of approval.

'We have our very own Lizzie Matthews to thank for them. She discovered these lost paintings. They reveal another exciting period in the master's work. I am delighted that The Arthouse is the first gallery to showcase them. Thank you, Lizzie!' Julia extended an arm towards her. Lizzie smiled back.

A hand went up in the audience. 'Will they go to auction?'

Julia smiled. 'Lizzie?'

Lizzie mounted the small podium, taking the microphone from Julia: 'We will be releasing details soon. It's all most exciting.'

A murmur accompanied Lizzie as she returned to the audience.

'And,' Julia continued, 'As well as these tremendous new works from an old master, we have some stunning artwork from new talent too. Many of our wonderful artists are here tonight, including Euan Tremayne, who is producing a mini montage of our inaugural event. Now has anyone failed to notice his slightly bigger montages?' Julia was looking ironic and drew a burst of laughter from the guests.

Euan smiled at her from the back of the room and took a photo. He was wearing a white shirt and pale trousers – camouflage, in the current conditions. It allowed him to blend with the frosted picture window he was standing against.

'Last, and most certainly not least, I would like to thank my darling friend, Rachel. Rachel Matthews. She has been my rock and helped me pick up from where Sam left off. I wouldn't have been able to do this without her. Rachel, come here, girl.'

Rachel hated the attention, but Julia was beckoning her to the podium, and she just had to support her.

Rachel wasn't in Oscar attire. But she'd forked out for a dress on eBay. The delivery driver had dropped it off that morning, just as the first snowflakes had begun to fall. She doubted whether he would be able to make a similar call tonight, or in the next few days. Banks of snow were stacking up against the windows.

Rachel stepped onto the podium and Julia gave her a big hug. She was crying and Rachel, worried she might set her off, quickly took the mic.

'Well, from one rock to another, the pleasure was all mine working on the exhibition. What a fantastic collection of art and artists we have here in Penwith. It's a privilege to be amongst this community – one that my parents, Lawrence and Lizzie Matthews, were … are so much a part of. And many thanks, also, to Meghan Bacall of NewlynWave who has provided practical help and artistic guidance. Thanks also to St Piran's school for the use of their minibus!'

'And the driver,' someone called out from the audience. She figured it was probably Euan. He was taking a photo of her right then.

'And so,' Julia said, her arm around Rachel, 'please enjoy the rest of the evening. Help yourself to refreshments and, of course, feel free to buy the art! It is all local and will support our arts community. Everything is for sale, apart from the Lawrence Matthews'.'

'Did that go okay?' Julia said as they stepped down. 'I didn't like to mention transport home!'

'Indeed. Best put that thought to one side and enjoy the moment.'

Rachel swiped a flute of fizz and started to stroll around the exhibition. It had turned out well. The montages, although imposing, were suitably spaced and didn't encroach on the rest of the art. Her father's paintings were in pride of place in the room immediately after the entrance. They were well lit and *Browned Off* and its companion pieces *The Blues* and *Mellow Yellow* commanded attention. Next to them, like a guardian angel, was Lizzie's portrait of Oliver. It already had a red sold sticker on it. *Who'd bought it?* She'd have to find out. She couldn't let it go.

She wandered through to the first of Euan's montages. It looked majestic – the images mesmerising behind the stained-glass effect. It also had a red sales sticker on it. And it was listed at £5,000.

'They've all sold.' Euan was standing beside her. 'I'm a rich man.' He gave her an ironic smile.

'So, you are. Blimey. I need to learn your technique.'

'I could give you a masterclass. Or would that be too arty?'

She looked down and raised her eyes back up to him.

Euan met her gaze. 'I made you something special for to-night.'

'Aha?'

'Come on, I'll show you.'

'Haven't you got a job to do? Like taking photos?'

'All done. I'll show you as we go out. The board is very small.'

'Go out?' *Was he mad?*

He grabbed their coats from the rail in the entrance. 'Come on.'

They paused at his mini montage, which was on an easel by the front door. He had finished it. It was covered in photos. Hilarious photos. Each one as unflattering as could be. Even the one of Rachel had her scowling, probably checking Euan out as he took the shot. Benedict looked pissed as a fart. Lizzie looked as startled as a spiked owl. Sponsor Guy Baxter looked like he was going to collapse with boredom as he was assailed by a woman with purple-tipped hair waving a prawn tempura.

'They'll hate these.'

'They'll love them. I'll be their new *enfant terrible*. Come on. Let's get away from these bores. I've got someone I want you to meet.'

They walked carefully down the snow-covered steps and out onto the pavement which skirted the promenade gardens. He took hold of Rachel's hand and led her in. She wondered, momentarily, if this was the garden where they'd found Pat Ryan's torso.

Euan threw a snowball at her.

'Hey!' Rachel bent down and scooped up a ball of snow.

He'd pelted her with another snowball before she'd had a chance to retaliate. Rachel moulded the snow and pelted him back, before running to the other side of the garden wall. Using it as a barricade, she tossed snowballs over at him.

'Great strategy, Rachel! But there's plenty more ammunition.' He looked up at the sky, the snow still falling like it would never stop. It was glorious. They pelted each other until they resembled yeti.

'I surrender.' Euan walked towards the wall, his hands above his head, shaking off clumps of snow.

'No hidden weapons?'

'No.' Euan shrugged and looked over his shoulder. 'But I do have some back-up.'

'I bet you do,' Rachel said, pulling herself up from her crouched position.

'Here he is.' Euan pointed to a blob of snow on the ground.

At closer inspection, Rachel could see Euan had shaped the snow into a creature of some sort. A squat creature with a wide mouth and big eyes.

How embarrassing. Rachel gave him a bashful smile. Was squirming at the thought. *Froggy goes a wooing*. But Euan looked so pleased with himself and then a little uncertain, that her heart went out to him. If there was magic in the air that night it had transformed them both into twenty-year-olds again, with all the awkwardness that entailed.

Rachel took a snap of the snow frog on her phone – to be kind and to break the silence. You could have cut that silence with an ice pick. Euan was staring at her, looking like he was going to make a move.

'What are you two up to?' Rachel turned to see Julia walking towards them, a scarlet cloak draped over her evening dress. 'Rachel, give me a hand with Lizzie, please. She's being swamped by people keen to get their hands on a new Lawrence Matthews.'

Rachel shrugged. 'Sure. Okay.'

'No rest for the wicked,' she said, looking at Euan.

'I think I'll stay out here a while. Take some more photos. Keep the frog company.' He pulled out his Polaroid and took a photo of them as they turned to go back in.

Rachel and Julia walked in silence back to The Arthouse. Her snow sojourn clearly hadn't gone down well with the hostess.

Inside, Lizzie was in her element, promising paintings left right and centre. Rachel sipped her wine and tried to temper the enthusiasm.

'I'll take over here,' Meghan whispered in her ear, sidling up to Lizzie. 'It's wonderful, isn't it, that we have these new Matthews masterpieces.' As usual she was commanding attention. 'But if I could just contain everyone's excitement – we do have some preliminary work to do before we can release them to auction. Please take my card.'

They made a great double act, Rachel thought, as she watched Meghan dealing out cards like a croupier, Lizzie deferring to the professionalism of her new agent. Rachel moved off and left them to it – thought she'd take another look at the paintings which were proving such a hit.

They were good, of course. But something was missing. Lizzie's portrait of Oliver had vanished. The Arthouse wasn't a commercial gallery, you didn't walk out with your purchase until the end of the exhibition. She tried to catch Meghan's eye, but she was locked in conversation. As was Julia. Stolen? Surely not. And why take the portrait rather than *Browned*

Off or *Mellow Yellow,* which would be worth something?

'Don't worry,' Meghan said, when Rachel finally prised her away from a potential customer. 'The buyer hasn't done a runner – just wanted to try the painting at home before committing.'

'We didn't want to sell it. And it's part of the exhibition. Who bought it?' Rachel looked pained.

'I'll get it back. Don't fret.'

'Is Lizzie okay with this?'

'Of course. No worries.' Meghan beamed a smile and returned to the fray.

Rachel was concerned. She tried to shake off her unease by circling the room until she was dizzy and desperate to slip away. See what Euan was up to. The crowd was thinning and dividing into diehard clumps. She wouldn't be missed. Benedict had gone too, by the looks of it. They'd barely spoken a word all night – which was rare for them. But he wasn't himself right now. That was obvious.

Shrugging on her coat she pushed open the front door, cursing the squeaky hinges – they'd have to fix those – and stepped out into the night. Conditions were no better, the snow tumbling down, ankle deep in places.

It was hard to see anything or anyone – like she was looking through a shaken snow globe. She glanced around, spotted someone dashing through the gardens towards the harbour, and then something moving at the bottom of the stairs. It appeared to be on all fours, like a dog or fox. But it was bigger than that. She stepped towards it, heard its grunts of pain or exertion, saw a moat of blood circling the bottom step.

'Rachel?' Euan rose before her, his hands dripping blood, the front of his coat covered in it.

'What the hell!' Rachel reached out to him, but he drew back.

'Rachel, look away. Rachel ...'

It was too late. She recognised the inert form at his feet – the body of a man, blood seeping from a massive gash to the chest. And then she screamed, a terrifying sound tearing through the snowy silence, echoed in the startled cry of a gull, its beating wings shaking snow as it soared into the sky.

36

Brandon

Brandon was with them in moments. He'd heard the scream, pushed past a couple getting their coats on to find Rachel on the steps, the artist by her side, Benedict slumped on the ground.

Not waiting for explanations, he crouched and placed two fingers to Benedict's neck.

'Everybody back. Back inside, please,' he said, flicking a look at the couple who'd followed him out.

'Brandon?' Julia was at the top of the steps. A hand flew to her cheek as she took in the situation. 'Shall I call an ambulance?'

'Julia, please go back inside, settle people down. I'll join you in a bit.'

Benedict was dead. It would have to be confirmed by a pathologist, but he wouldn't be needing medical attention. Brandon got to his feet and phoned the station, organising a lockdown, and putting out an alert to MCIT in Newquay. They were going to send backup right away.

'Who found him?' Brandon said, putting away his phone and looking at Rachel and Euan.

Euan looked at his blood-covered hands. He was keeping them well away from his body. 'I did.'

Brandon moved them both away from the steps. He didn't want to disturb the body. He felt his throat constrict and struggled to get the words out.

'When?'

'Two minutes – maybe three minutes ago. I saw him …

Benedict ... at the bottom of the steps, blood gushing from his chest, his hand clutching at the wound. But it fell limp.' Euan stopped for a moment, took a breath. 'I tried to stem the blood.' He held out his hands. 'Pumped his chest. Did all those things they tell you ... too late. Then Rachel came out and then you.'

Brandon gave him an appraising look. He was good actor if he was lying. 'Did you see anyone else out here? Anyone acting suspiciously?'

'There were a few people leaving as I walked back over. I took a few photos.' He gestured to the pocket of his coat, still reluctant to touch anything.

Brandon grimaced. 'The SOCOs will be here soon. They'll take a sample of the blood, and then you can wash up.'

Euan nodded and looked towards the sound of sirens.

The noise jolted Rachel out of her reverie. She'd been standing there, still as an ice sculpture. 'I saw someone, Brandon. Someone darting through the gardens towards the harbour.'

Brandon followed her gaze, caught the glint of something as he did so. He took a few steps towards it.

'Looks like they may have dropped something,' He knelt and examined the knife, which was already partially covered in snow. 'Rachel, could you see if there's a crate or a lid in the kitchen? Anything that could cover this?'

Brandon spread open his coat to protect the knife as best he could, as Rachel disappeared into the gallery.

'You didn't see the weapon?' he said, watching for Euan's reaction.

'No. I was focused on Benedict. I thought I could save him.'

'Of course.' Brandon leant over the knife to shelter it from a blast of snow.

Rachel came back with a plastic recycling box just as a police car pulled up, two officers and two SOCOs getting out to join them. Brandon covered the weapon and set about briefing the officers. The SOCOs surrounded Benedict immediately, using a sheet of polythene to give him some protection. These forerunners were the first of many; the place would be swarming with police within the half hour.

'Come inside. I'm going to make an announcement.' Brandon beckoned to Rachel and Euan, leading the way back up the steps.

The guests turned from their respective clusters. A second of anticipatory silence, then all hell broke loose with a barrage of questions.

Brandon raised a hand to ward them off, hung up his coat and made for the podium. A few stubborn snowflakes glistened in his hair as he fiddled with the mic.

'If I could just have your attention.' He needn't have asked. The sirens and commotion outside had done the job for him.

A lot of guests had already left – worried about transport home. By the looks on their faces, the guests in the room had their own concerns.

Julia walked towards Rachel, tears in her eyes, her arms outstretched. 'Oh God, Rachel. Oh God. Benedict? What's happening?'

Rachel fell into her embrace, Julia shaking with emotion, tears falling, her face flushed and distorted. Rachel looked cold, as if all the life had been sucked out of her.

Brandon tapped the mic. 'I'm sorry to have to tell you that there's been an incident here tonight.'

There was a gasp from the audience.

'I thought so,' said someone.

'Good God. What's going on?' said the woman with purple-dipped hair.

'If I could just ask everyone to be calm. And, please, stay where you are.'

A murmur rippled through the room.

'Why?' said a man with white bouffant hair. 'If we don't go now we'll be here all night.' He gestured to the window. The snow gave no impression of stopping.

'We'll ensure you're comfortable. There is food and drink. I'm a police inspector, as you may or may not be aware. I would like to ask you each a few questions before you leave.'

'Why?' said Bouffant.

'Has someone died?' said a mature woman in an elaborate kaftan and statement earrings.

Brandon looked down and then back up, before replying. 'The matter is under investigation. Now if you would kindly be patient, we will go through the formalities as quickly as possible, so you can all get home.'

It was two hours before the guests had been questioned by Brandon and the MCIT detectives and allowed to leave. Outside the snow had made the task near impossible for the small SOCO team. They'd looked like North Pole explorers as they'd struggled to erect the tent, their yellow tape flapping and sagging in the snowy breeze. Eventually an ambulance battled its way through, and Benedict was taken to the local hospital morgue to join Sam.

An unmarked police car pulled up outside the gallery. It had got through, thank God. Brandon wanted to get Rachel and Julia home.

'Brandon?' Rachel turned to him as they stood by The Arthouse steps. Julia had given him the keys to lock up when the murder team had finished for the night. Apart from the SOCOs, there were just the four of them outside – including Euan. He was done questioning him. For now.

'How else were you going to get home tonight?' Brandon dropped his cigarette butt in the snow and opened the car door for them.

'Is it okay if I cadge a lift as far as The Hall?' Euan said.

The guy was a limpet. He'd seemed okay during the interview. Had volunteered the photos he'd taken of people outside The Arthouse. Had willingly given swabs for DNA analysis. Had answers for everything and was far from rattled. All the same. He wasn't happy with him sharing the car – he'd have to ask the driver to take him home, wherever that was.

'Stay over. You won't get through to Gulval in this weather,' Julia said.

For Chrissake!

'Well, if you're sure?' Euan got in the front, with the driver. 'Okay with you, Brandon?' Brandon was standing by the car with his hand on the roof. He gave a curt nod.

'And you, Brandon?' Rachel said.

'It'll be a while before we wrap up here. I'll walk,' he said, leaning in through the open car door.

The Newquay team were still going through things inside. It would be some time before he got home, had a chance to write up his notes and think things through. He ran a hand through his hair and blinked hard. Benedict. The arts community had taken a major blow tonight. As had he.

'Get some sleep, eh?' He pulled out a cigarette, struggling to light up in the driving snow.

'You too. Catch up with you tomorrow?' Rachel said.

'Yes. Yes, of course. I'll call you in the morning.' *The Mermaid. She still wanted to go?* The thought brightened him briefly. But their conversation was likely to take a different direction, he suspected, as he shut the car door and watched them drive away.

37

Brandon

It was snowing hard when Brandon handed The Arthouse keys to the night shift officers an hour later. Why would anyone want to kill Benedict? Brandon turned the question over in his mind as he stared at the murder scene.

He walked through the gardens, stopping at the lump of snow he'd seen in Euan's Polaroid snaps. He kicked it hard, sending clumps of ice and snow flying. How long had the murderer been lurking – waiting for his chance? Waiting for Benedict to come out for his obligatory fag break. Who would want to kill a washed-up aristo whose health was fast fading?

Benedict's wallet was missing, so it could have been a simple case of theft. But even if that was the most likely reason, he didn't think so. The sabotaged glitter ball at The Acorn? The threatening flyer inviting them both to go to hell. They both nearly did die on that stage. But what was the motive? You made enemies in the force, of course. And Benedict wasn't exactly a saint. He walked on. Although it was almost whiteout conditions, Brandon could make out the shapes of people in the shelter on the promenade – severe weather conditions attracted spectators. But at this hour? The sea certainly looked stunning, frosted Christmas cake waves rippled below the snowy sky. The thirty-something couple in the shelter were chatting and taking photos as he approached, a picture of innocence. They exchanged looks when he stopped in front of them and showed his badge.

'How long have you been out here taking photos?'

'Some time, I guess.' The guy stiffened, his expression surly. 'Why?'

'Seen anyone else out here? Anyone acting suspiciously? In a hurry to get somewhere?'

The woman came forward and tucked her hand under the arm of her companion. 'There's been a few people – people like us, just looking and taking snaps. And earlier some kids messing around, tobogganing on their skateboards. Why?'

'There was an attack back there, near the Jubilee Pool.' Brandon gestured towards the lido; he figured they wouldn't know about the new gallery.

The woman threw a hand to her mouth. 'How awful! Are they alright? Are they okay?'

Brandon shook his head. 'Do you mind if I look at your photos?'

The man stepped forward. 'Well, they're just shots of the sea. Nothing really, just the sea.'

Brandon reached out his hand. 'If you don't mind. You may have caught something on camera?'

'Is anyone dead?' said the woman, as she handed over her own phone.

Brandon grimaced. He didn't like to say it. Or think it. 'There's been a major incident, which is now under investigation. I suggest you call it a night and get home.'

There was nothing on the phones. Just snow – the snow that they were standing in and under and which covered the land as far as the eye could see.

'Thanks,' he said, handing them back, along with his card. 'If you see anyone, or anything suspicious, call me.'

Why would you take fifty-odd photos of nothing? They were like the blank canvas that had pitched up outside The Hall on the day Sam died. They weren't dissimilar in theme to the new Lawrence Matthews – Lizzie could have called these the White Out series.

His shoulders began to shake with laughter and then something else, a leaden, choking grief which rose within, threatening to bring him down. So, he walked on, through the swirling snow, crunching the hardening layer underfoot, heading for home, grateful Chelsea was at his mom's.

A comforting blast of heat hit him when he opened his front door. Chelsea had left the heating on and a light in the kitchen. Good girl – it would have been intentional. Her small considerations always touched him. The bottle of bourbon which he'd brought out on her birthday was still on the work surface. He reached over and poured himself a large one and knocked it back, standing at the work surface in his coat and snow-caked shoes. He poured himself another, sipping it this time, his back to the room, his arms splayed, hands gripping the edge of the granite.

His phone beeped a text. *Rachel? Had they got back all right?* He pulled his phone from his pocket and walked over to his armchair. It was Jo. She'd heard about Benedict. Wanted to know if he could give her a heads-up on things. God, she was keen. Stew was probably fast asleep, dreaming of Nandos.

He keyed his reply: 'Let's talk first thing.' And reached for his Jack Daniels, his mind racing. He hoped he might have a better idea of what to talk about in the morning.

38

Rachel

'I've found the software.' Damien appeared at her side, just as the bell rang and the kids were heading back into their classrooms. Rachel was on playground duty – the snow had stopped but it was still freezing cold. She'd hoped for a snow day to give her some time alone to grieve Benedict. As it stood, she was operating on autopilot.

'Miss, I've got the software.'

'How much?'

He looked like a vagabond out of *A Christmas Carol*, with his tatty black anorak and worn shoes. He could do with some cash.

'Twenty.'

'20p?'

'Haha, Miss.'

He'd picked the right time to negotiate. They would soon be the only ones left in the playground. 'Okay. Twenty pounds. But I need it asap.'

'This afternoon. After school?

'Yes,' Rachel said, starting to walk towards the Science Block. She had double biology with a fifteen-year-old boy who preferred her to maintain the discreet visibility of a VIP bodyguard. 'See you at The Morrab Library at 3.40pm, sharp.'

* * * * *

She kept Sam's computer in the boot of her car. It seemed as safe a place as any. Safer than The Hall since the security failure. They still hadn't got to the bottom of that, and she continued to wedge a chair under the back door every night.

Rachel parked the car in the small Morrab Library members' carpark. They only had twenty minutes, as it closed at 4pm. Where was he? She walked out of the carpark into the sub-tropical Morrab Gardens, which resembled a petrified forest with their snow-laden palms and trees. The pond was frozen and, just beyond it, the sparkling white bandstand looked magical. A stage for the sugar plum fairy, not a hunched cyclist in a hoodie, doing a wheelie around its perimeter. Damien was making his entrance. He sped to her side, using his spindly legs as brakes. Rachel looked around. She was taking an almighty risk seeing Damien after school. Seeing any child out of school hours was forbidden, unless for reasons of tutoring, but she wanted to search the computer. Brandon had said it had already been sent off to a technology expert by one of the station PCs – so that check had been made. But Rachel wasn't convinced Sam's computer was squeaky clean. It just didn't make sense. How the hell had he covered his digital tracks?

'Keep your hood up,' Rachel said as they wiped their feet on the door mat and entered the library. Unlike the public library, The Morrab was housed in a Victorian mansion and was more like a members' club. There was a wealth of rare and obscure books in the specialist rooms.

Rachel gave a cursory smile and remark about the weather to the woman on the front desk, quickly adding: 'Is it okay if my student does a bit of research for his history project?'

The woman smiled a yes, and, before she had time to change her mind, Rachel had whisked Damien past and up the stairs.

'Now, let's see what we can find out about Napoleon,' Rachel said in a clumsy attempt to disguise her real intent. There was an impressive section dedicated to the French Emperor in one of the first-floor rooms. She pulled out a few books and set them alongside her computer. Damien started fingering the books with his inky hands. He'd been playing with his pen again. She pushed the books aside and passed him the laptop.

'The software? We haven't got much time.'

'I have a code,' Damien said, with ill-disguised superiority.

She left him to it. The Morrab was a peaceful place. Unlike the Special Needs Room, she had no fear of being monitored. She flicked through a book on Napoleon's time in St Helena, barely registering the details.

There were footsteps on the stairs. One of the volunteers would be doing the rounds, turning off lights and checking the rooms. *Come on, Damien.*

'How's it going, Damien?'

'Just bringing up a folder now.'

Rachel looked over his shoulder.

'Was your *friend* interested in South American art?' Damien sneered as he clicked on the folder.

'Yes, very much so.' A list of files popped up, all with South American artists' names.

'You'll save these for me, right?'

Damien sighed and gave her a withering look. 'Yes.'

'Okay. How many more folders?'

'Got to be thirty, at least.'

'Well, bring them up and save them.'

'I'm –'

There was a knock on the door and the pleasant woman who had been on the front desk entered.

'We won't be long. Just finishing up here,' Rachel said, smiling.

'If you could turn the lights off when you leave, please. We will be closing in five minutes.'

'Yes, of course.'

Damien's fingers were flying over the keyboard, dredging up folders. She picked up the books and placed them back on the shelf, keeping her back to him. She didn't want to disturb his concentration. His fingers beat a rhythm, like the ticking of a death watch beetle. From the window, she could see the lights on the promenade and the dark swell of the sea. She thought of Benedict. She'd thought of little else all night. All day.

The ticking stopped.

Rachel swallowed hard and ran a finger under her bottom lashes.

'Is that the lot?' Rachel turned to face Damien. She could hear people talking downstairs, fussing about the weather, saying their goodbyes.

'Yes,' he said, and she thought she saw something other than darkness in his eyes.

He looked away and then back to his screen. 'Your friend has a lot of business in South America?'

'Yes, Damien, more than likely. You've saved it all?

'You've got your money's worth.'

The librarian was waiting downstairs by the front door as they approached. 'Hope you got your work done? Did you want to take out any of the books?' she asked, smiling.

'We were just doing a little research, thank you.'

The woman followed them to the door and bolted it behind them.

Rachel waited until they'd left the carpark before turning to Damien. 'Here,' she said, handing him twenty pounds. 'Thanks for your help.'

'That's okay. I heard about Benedict Arscott-Rowe. Did you know him, Miss?'

Rachel looked over his head at the frozen palms, their fronds stretching skywards. 'Yes, I did.'

'Sorry. Things aren't right round here, are they?'

'Have you been to see the police yet, Damien?'

'Yeah. The DI seemed to know it all already. Told you. But he's cool.'

'I'm sure it helped, if only to confirm a few things.' Rachel was keen to get back to The Hall. She wanted to look at the files before seeing Brandon.

'I hope you find what you're looking for in those files, Miss.'

'That would be good.'

'If I find out anything, I'll let you know.'

Rachel looked him in the eye. 'Find out anything?'

'I'll let you know,' he said, walking over to his bike. He put a key in its lock and bumped it away from the lamppost. 'It'll be easier to get about when the snow thaws,' he added, cycling away through the gardens.

39

Rachel

Rachel could barely open the door to The Hall – a line of industrial-sized bin liners blocked the entrance, forcing her to move them out of the way.

'Julia, what's all this?' Rachel edged her way around them to Julia who was standing talking to someone in the kitchen. 'Have you opened up a waste disposal unit?'

'What – oh, Rachel. Haha! Artist's materials.' Julia gestured to Euan who was standing on the far side of the kitchen island, chopping an onion. 'I've invited Euan to use the studio for a new project he's working on. It's epic, of course.'

'Rachel, hi. Bit of a mess, granted, but I'm going to start shipping the stuff upstairs to the studio. Thought I'd start on supper first.'

Rachel looked on, amazed. *So, she fancies him.*

'Euan insisted on cooking for us tonight – a stroganoff. They take forever, apparently.'

'Oh – I'm out tonight.' *Clearly won't be missed.*

Euan cast her a quick look. 'I thought after last night, you guys might want to stay in with some comfort food.'

Rachel felt the need for something stronger than a stew but tempered her reply. 'It's something long arranged. But can you leave me some for tomorrow?' She didn't want to give details. 'See you later – just need to work on something before I go.'

Euan glanced at the sports bag in her hand as she exited the kitchen, stepping over a bin liner to get to the first step of the stairs.

When she reached her room, some instinct made her lock the door. It wasn't that she didn't trust them – of course she trusted Julia – but she needed to concentrate. She'd managed to hide her suspicions as best she could from Damien, but not from herself. Thirty-five files on South American art and not one item exhibited at The Arthouse. Hmm. She couldn't wait to discuss it with Brandon who, she sometimes felt, indulged her, but had little time for her theories. This might prick up his ears.

She felt her heart rate increase as she accessed the first file, *Frida Kahlo*. An image caught her attention – and it wasn't of a woman with a mono brow and a parrot on her shoulder. Standing there, doing a smiley selfie, was Benedict, against a backdrop of stacked white blocks.

A second image was more specific – Benedict was still centre stage but joined by a mound of white powder on an upturned fruit crate.

Another file, with a spreadsheet called *Diego*, gave weights and purities, while *Lam* detailed timings for deliveries into St Malo.

Benedict! She didn't put it past him to turn a dodgy buck, but he'd clearly got out of his depth. Her head was spinning with possibilities when she heard a gentle knock on the door.

'Yes?' *Damn. Not now.*

'Rachel. Can I have a quick word?' It was Euan.

She slipped the computer under her bed.

'Coming,' she said, unlocking the door. Euan presented her with a concerned expression. His eyes flicked to the floor by the bed. Rachel stopped herself turning to see if the computer was poking out.

'I just wanted to check with you that it's okay me coming here to work?'

Rachel ran a hand through her hair. 'Well, it's not really my place to say, is it? If Julia has invited you then … I guess that's good enough.'

'That's why I wanted to ask you. I won't come here if you don't want me to. I can find some excuse. I don't want to make you feel uncomfortable.'

She looked at him. He did make her feel uncomfortable but, if she was honest, in a good way. 'No, it's fine – Christ, you wouldn't get half that stuff in your cottage. What the hell is it?'

'Plastics and recycling materials. I'm going to use it to sculpt some pieces.'

'Not a whale. That's been done.'

He smiled and rested one hand on the doorframe. 'No. I'm going to work on some other mammals.'

'Intriguing. When are you starting work?'

'Tonight.'

'Tonight?'

'Yes. I want to keep going while interest is high.'

'Your montage sales?'

'Yes. But I've run out of photos and have other ideas.' He was leaning against the doorframe now, looking at her in that uncomfortable, but good, way. 'I got you something out of my earnings.'

Rachel felt herself blushing. 'Oh, you shouldn't have. Really.'

'I wouldn't have made those sales without you.' He paused and then looked down at something to his left. *Not another frog? Please!* 'You introduced me – to Julia and the gallery. And so …' He moved out of sight behind the landing wall and then reappeared with a gilt framed canvas – turning it to reveal Lizzie's portrait of Oliver.

'I figured you wouldn't want someone else to buy it – so I did.'

Rachel was lost for words. She'd almost forgotten about the sold portrait in all the commotion and distress of the past twenty-four hours. Tears were threatening, so she blinked hard before looking back at him. 'I don't know what to say. Words can't express my … gratitude. But thank you. Thank you so much. I would have hated … the portrait to have been lost again.'

She turned away and when she looked back Euan was smiling softly at her. She didn't know whether to kiss him or shake his hand. Instead, she stared at the small holdall on the floor by his feet – he'd moved it into view when he'd reappeared with Oliver's portrait.

He noticed her interest. 'Oh yes, Julia said I could stay over for a few nights to sort the material and to get started. I've been given the room just down the hall – the one next to the studio.'

That was a development and a half. Julia didn't hang around when she was interested in someone. He seemed to be getting closer and closer – from a speck in her peripheral vision to someone bursting into her space. *The Euan in Black.* She hoped Julia's rash decision wouldn't come back to haunt them.

She could hear Julia's feet on the stairs. She was talking to someone on the phone. 'I'll hand you over. Catch up soon. It's Brandon,' she said passing Rachel her mobile. 'It was ringing in your coat pocket.'

They watched as she took the call. 'I'll drive over to you. Probably best to give The Mermaid a miss tonight?' There was a pause. 'Okay, see you in a bit.'

'You're seeing Brandon tonight?' Julia was pressing the

point.

'Yes.' *Was that so very weird? As weird as inviting a virtual stranger into your house with the town's refuge.*

'Don't forget to put the security on when you get back if we've gone to bed.' Julia gave Rachel a knowing smile. *For Chrissake.*

'I have to say, it's quite reassuring to have a man in the house after the other night.' Julia paused. 'I told Euan about the open kitchen door and the security failure.'

'Maybe he should leave that obstacle course in the hallway to deter any intruders looking to murder us in our beds?'

Julia winced, but Euan got the joke and smiled.

'Have a good night. I'll put a plate of stroganoff in the fridge for you,' he said, reaching down for his holdall.

'Thanks. And thanks for the portrait.'

Julia noticed it for the first time. 'Gosh. Oliver's portrait. So, you were the anonymous buyer?' She gave Euan a searching look.

'Yes.' He returned it with his enigmatic smile.

'Meghan said the buyer was someone local, who didn't want to be named. I was going to press her on it when she came back to me with the total sales figures. Well, well. You must be so pleased, Rachel. It really is a beautiful painting. Shall we put it in the entrance hall, for now? Replace the Munnings? And then find the right place for your lovely boy?'

'Thanks, Julia. That's perfect …' The words tailed off – couldn't compete with the well of sorrow bubbling beneath.

Julia touched her arm. 'We'll leave you now. I'll show Euan his room.'

Rachel looked at her slender son, his shoulders turned towards her as if she'd stopped him in his tracks; his expression questioning, but untroubled. She could almost hear him saying. 'Yes, Mum? Whatever.'

It was an uncanny resemblance. It was like having him in the house with her and she felt an immense calm and comfort.

40

Brandon

Benedict's smiling face was staring out of the computer screen at Brandon. Rachel had plonked Sam's laptop on his kitchen table and fired it up the moment she walked in the door. Her expression was a mixture of triumph and concern. The computer images and evidence she'd uncovered had opened a Pandora's Box of incriminating details. At the same time, it answered a lot of questions and would help investigations no end. But Benedict? His old friend. He was no saint, but a drugs smuggler? There had to be more to this, he reasoned. He hoped. And how the hell hadn't the techies noticed the computer had been wiped, if a fourteen-year-old had? This was a major failing.

'Well,' Brandon said facing down. 'Well.' He shook his head, without raising it. 'I'm gobsmacked.'

They sat in silence, Rachel fiddling with the laptop lead, seemingly lost for words. She spoke at last. 'Where do we go from here?'

'The pub?' Brandon gave a wry smile.

'A drink would be good.'

Brandon rose from his chair and walked over to the kitchen cabinets, stretching above them to the wine rack. 'Red or white?'

'Red, please.'

He turned a few bottles, looking at labels. 'Merlot, Cabernet Sauvignon?'

'I'm not fussed.'

He twisted the screw top off the Cabernet Sauvignon and poured them both large ones.

'To Benedict,' Rachel said, raising her glass and smiling weakly.

'What made you question the computer, Rachel?' Brandon wasn't smiling.

'A hunch? Come on, Brandon. When you handed it to me at the station before Christmas you didn't sound convinced yourself. You got me thinking.'

'And tinkering.' He gave her a steady look. 'Why didn't you just ask me to get the computer checked again through our channels?'

'Would you have?'

Brandon rested his forearms on the table and looked at her.

'Well, would you?' Rachel returned his gaze.

He bit his top lip. 'Maybe not at that time. Sam's death was looking like a suicide. Nothing suspicious.'

Rachel rested back in her chair.

'But I would have had it checked again, based on our on-going inquiries. I just wouldn't have fast-tracked it to a teenage hacker.'

'Sorry.' Rachel raised an eyebrow. 'Just trying to help. Damien has no idea what this is all about, by the way. I was the model of discretion. But I'm sorry if I've messed with procedure. I'm not a cop.'

Brandon gave a grudging smile. 'No, you're not. Maybe just as well.'

'I'll run things past you in future,' Rachel said, pouring him some more wine.

'That is reassuring to hear, gal, if there is ever another time.' Brandon picked up his glass and clinked hers.

Rachel took a sip of wine. 'Any idea why Benedict would

get involved in the drugs trade? It seems so out of character. Sure, he smoked dope, did some lines, but smuggling?' Rachel posed the obvious question.

Brandon looked into his glass. 'Debt? An opportunity on his travels? An adventure?'

Rachel gave a small grunt of agreement. 'He loved *Breaking Bad*. I remember him regaling me with some scenes when we last met up in London. Like I hadn't seen it myself, five years ago!'

'Penzance's own Walter White?' Brandon took a sip of wine, looking at her with barely suppressed amusement.

Rachel looked serious. 'I saw him the day before the Opening. Before ... He looked terrible. Tired, troubled. He cadged a bottle of wine off me and then left abruptly when his phone buzzed. Complained of business and women. He told me to take care. Suggested there were bad people around. In town.'

'Did he give details?'

'No. Not Benedict's style. He was still trying, but failing, to be cool.'

Brandon frowned. 'I can imagine. Interesting hint, though; looks like the drugs business was a start-up operation. Barely got off the ground and into the water. Maybe he realised it was a duff – and dangerous – venture and wanted out?'

He paused, thinking of the barrels that beached in Prussia Cove the day of the Montol. They must have been his. But who else was working with him? Benedict was no sailor. And he was no drugs baron, either.

Brandon and Rachel had gone through the files – all thirty-five of them. Just two shipments into Prussia Cove over six weeks. A third was planned for Thursday.

'Do you reckon the planned delivery will take place?'

Rachel asked, draining her glass.

Brandon got the bottle and topped them both up. 'I doubt it. Sure looks like there's another delivery out there – but it's unlikely to come via the same route. I'll ensure the coastguard's on it.' He might get a better idea going through Benedict's stuff. That had to be the priority now.

Rachel raised her eyes to his. 'You can talk freely about this to me, Brandon. Really. I'm not going to spill any beans or interfere with your investigations. I'm not the third party in all this. I'm just trying to help.'

Brandon sighed. 'Rachel, Rachel, Rachel. It's unethical – it's unprofessional. You'll get me –'

'Slung out of the force? You're repeating yourself, Detective Inspector Hammett.'

He wanted to take hold of her hand, the one that wasn't twisting the laptop lead around her fingers. Instead, he smiled, his eyes fixed on that hand. It was good to have her there. He could so easily have cancelled, spent the night turning things over in his head, but she'd brought more than a box of revelations with her. Important as they were. She'd brought company – company other than Chelsea and Jo and the band and the job he was wedded to. She'd brought something he hadn't even realised was missing.

'I did get you the computer evidence.' She was twisting him around her finger like that computer lead.

'True. Okay. This is what I think. Or, rather, what I don't think. I don't think Benedict – or Sam for that matter – was killed by some stoked drug's baron. Whoever supplied the goodies would probably have been happy with a little additional business. This is a grain of sand in the grand scheme of things. I'll need to check the local clubs, but, I'd say, the purity of the coke in those barrels was heading for high-end users. Not school kids and teenagers.'

Rachel interrupted him. 'Or is that just wishful thinking? You not wanting to believe Benedict would supply kids? I mean, I don't want to believe it either. But …'

Brandon wiped a hand across his mouth. 'There's an element of that, possibly. But the purity of the Prussia Cove gear – if I'm not mistaken – is beyond the realms of pocket money.' He reached for his glass. 'And I've seen the crap they're pushing in the playground. Highly lethal concoctions, contaminated with god knows what – could be plaster from that fallen angel.'

Rachel gasped.

'Sorry. Bad image. It just came to me, that's all. But not only do I not want to believe that Benedict was capable of corrupting and endangering kids, I don't think he was pedalling their gear.'

Rachel nodded. 'Benedict would never have hurt anyone – intentionally. He would have gone for the crème de la crème of cocaine and sold it to people much like himself – in Cornwall and London. So – who wanted Benedict out of the way? If it's the county lines guys – would they care if Benedict and Sam were serving a different market?'

'Lines get blurred. The county lines guys would have their better gear, which they'd be pushing elsewhere and, also, to some of the wealthier kids.'

He could almost see a thought bubble appearing over Rachel's head.

'Like Nick?'

'Not Nick. But boys like Nick with rich parents.' Brandon turned his attention back to the computer. He clicked on the image of Benedict with the upturned fruit box and zoomed in. 'Look,' he said, turning the computer round to Rachel. 'There are canvases against that wall. All wrapped and ready to go. Looks like he was shipping some art too.'

Rachel narrowed her eyes, used her thumb and forefinger to enlarge the image. 'Interesting. He was doing some bona fide trade too?'

Brandon raised an eyebrow. 'Possibly. I'd like to find out where those canvases pitched up.'

Rachel peered over the screen at him. 'Do you think he might have inserted, I don't know, drugs in the paintings? In the backs?'

Brandon frowned. 'Maybe. But there are quite a few possibilities. I need to go through the computer thoroughly. The lists – they have artist code names. Perhaps some of the code names refer to actual art? The drugs could be incidental – a diversification.'

'So, he was dealing in art – like he told Julia on New Year's Eve.'

'Would appear so. But it didn't turn up at The Arthouse the other night, did it?'

'No. Maybe he had a collector? Or he was buying for a gallery?'

'Yep. Maybe.'

Brandon shared the final drops of the bottle between them. They'd finished it without noticing. 'Let's go out. Or get a takeaway.'

Rachel gave a small laugh. 'We could go to The Hall – Euan's made a stroganoff. Enough to feed us all – including Nick.'

Brandon sat up straight. 'What? Is that guy still hanging around? Cooking a frigging stroganoff.'

'Yes.' Rachel had a broad smile on her face. 'I shouldn't imagine it's laced with amphetamines, though.'

'I couldn't give a toss if it's laced with Russian Black or Tesco's garlic.' He got up and snatched his keys off the work surface.

'I'm taking you to The Mermaid. No argument, Rachel. And I'll get you a cab back.'

'I have the car.'

'You'll be over the limit. Let's walk.'

She smiled and he felt his mood lighten again. 'I'll keep the computer.'

'That's fine with me. It's been a weight around my neck. Talking of weights – the PC who had the computer checked? Does he need checking out?'

Brandon gave her a half-smile. 'Stop looking so smug. Phillips will pay for this. But no need to voice my concerns just yet.'

Rachel went to speak, but Brandon put a finger to her lips, lifted the coat from her chair and helped her on with it. 'It's all under control.'

'I –'

Brandon pulled her coat around her and did up the first button. 'I may need you, certainly Julia, for some media interviews. Nothing has come in so far about the stabbing – we're still waiting on the forensic evidence and the snow hasn't helped. But tomorrow – now that I have some more *background* – I'll hit the screens and radio with appeals.'

'Where's Chelsea, by the way?' Rachel was feeling in her bag for something.

'At her Grandma's'

'Again?' She produced her phone and checked it.

'Yep. I guess my company can get a little boring.'

Rachel pulled a comical face. 'Maybe for a teenage girl who likes reality TV shows. Your mum's a fan of them too.'

'Howdya know, DI Matthews?'

'Us girls like to talk; you may have noticed?'

'I've noticed,' he said, opening the door for her.

41

Rachel

Oliver was there to greet her as she opened the door. The house was in darkness apart from a small light over his portrait. He had that non-judgmental expression on his face – as if to say: 'After midnight, Mum? Whatever.' She brushed her fingertips with a kiss and stood on tiptoes to plant it on his lips. 'Nighty-night,' she said, hanging up her coat and walking towards the stairs.

It had been a good night. It always was with Brandon. He was so easy to be around – so kind, accompanying her in the taxi, waiting for her to wave from the door before moving away. She yawned, thinking of the bed she wanted to snuggle down into. And then she checked her phone – Lizzie was being conspicuously quiet at the moment. It was tempting to think no news was good news, but she knew her mother too well. She wouldn't be sitting at home watching *Cash In the Attic*, she'd be rooting around in her own one, conjuring up another Matthews masterpiece. Tomorrow was Rachel's day off – she'd pop in unannounced, see what was up.

Bang! *What the hell?* Something large had hit the floor. Sounded close – the studio? She could see a light below the door. *Euan?* There was a rustling too, like he was unwrapping giant sheets of cellophane. He'd have to keep the noise down if he was working through the night.

The studio door opened abruptly. *Oh, for God's sake!*

'Sorry, I didn't mean to startle you.' His shirt and chinos were covered in grit and dust. *What the hell was he making in there?*

'Don't worry. No more bangs tonight. I dropped something.'

Rachel had her hand on her door handle. It reminded her of that other time. He was looking at her in much the same way too. Things were happening way too fast – it was almost as if she was being pulled by currents. An emotional rip-tide.

'How was the stroganoff?' The words came out shaky. Her heart was hammering.

'It was good. Plenty for tomorrow too. Or the freezer.'

'How's your creation? Taking form?' She was babbling now.

'Just need the nuts and bolts to fix the head on.' He was smiling at her in his teasing way. 'Actually, I haven't really started yet. I just lugged the last of the stuff up here. Nick helped, until he went out. Julia's gone to bed. Got bored with me.'

'Nick's out? It's school tomorrow.'

'Well, I think it was Nick going out. He said he had something on, and I heard the door click shut when I was finishing up in the hall around half an hour ago.'

The security was off when she came in. She'd forgotten to turn it back on.

Rachel tapped Nick's number on her mobile. He really shouldn't be out at this time.

'Yeah?' came the reply after a few rings. 'I'm in bed, Rachel. You woke me up.'

Rachel looked at Euan. 'He's in bed.'

'Maybe I imagined it. I thought I heard the door go. He might have just popped outside for something. Do you need me to put on the security?'

'You know how?'

'Yes. Julia showed me.'

'Okay. Yes, please do. I was just going to bed.'

'Night, then.'

'Night.' Rachel turned back to her door.

'Rachel.'

He was behind her, his shadow on the door, eclipsed hers.

'Can you do some modelling for me? Not now, obviously. But in the next few days – I'd like to sculpt you.'

'Out of plastic?'

'Pink plastic.' *Did he think she was Barbie?*

She turned and rested against the door.

'No scratchy green scarf for your neck.' He was referring to Lizzie's painting. *Had she even mentioned it to him? Maybe Julia had?* She thought of Oliver's painting in the hallway. His sanguine expression.

'Whatever.'

'Good ... Good. Thanks, Rachel. It will be my *pièce de résistance*,' he said in a mock French accent, waving a hand. 'Sweet dreams.'

She sincerely hoped so.

42

Brandon

'So, if anyone has any information which could be of interest to our investigations, then contact the number below.' Brandon clicked off his mic and walked away from the camera towards the side of The Arthouse. Julia had already put out an emotional appeal for people to come forward with information about Sam on the day of his death. The person he was talking to in the Pets At Home carpark was central to the investigation. The hazy CCTV image was the backdrop on the screen. It was everywhere else too. In the local media, print and online, and in shop windows, including Pets At Home.

'The calls are coming in already, Boss.' Jo strolled over from the promenade gardens to join him. 'You look good on the screen, by the way.'

Brandon turned round slowly to face her. *Odd thing to say?*

She looked away, flustered. 'Gravitas. You said it all, with minimum fuss.'

Brandon grunted. 'There isn't a lot to say at the moment.'

'I got you a coffee ... and muffin.'

Brandon smiled and gestured for them to sit down on The Arthouse steps. The interviews had taken place there. The tape was still around the murder scene, but the tent had been dismantled. It was two days since the stabbing and The Arthouse was closed for business. Julia hadn't said anything – how could she in the circumstances. But although the place was getting great publicity, no one would argue it was the best kind.

Brandon bit into his muffin. 'Blueberry, eh.'

Jo smiled. 'Figured you might appreciate a taste of home. It's been a tough few weeks.'

'Yep. We're getting there, though. Robson and Flynn's trials are set for June in Bristol Crown Court. Done and dusted.'

'Still refuting any involvement in Sam Trenowden's death?'

'Yeah. And I believe them. My gut says it's the same guy that killed Benedict. Someone local. Someone who knew them. The murders were both swift and clean. No evidence, no signs of a struggle, no messy disposal. Both men were taken by surprise, going about their day-to-day. Benedict at an art gallery opening – taking a fag break. Someone was watching him. Just waiting for him to push open that door.' He flicked a hand at the one behind them. 'Even in the snow. And the snow – that made it so much easier for our killer.'

'Fewer people around – easier to slip away. Apologies!'

Brandon didn't laugh but smiled kindly. 'Indeed. And Sam, just a regular guy out on his morning run. How easy could it be for someone to just stop him for a brief chat and then, so long.'

Brandon pictured him at the bottom of the cliffs. A body broken on the bones of the earth, licked by the blood of the sea. He took a sip of coffee and looked across the gardens to the ocean. 'Think we need to get on,' he said, getting up.

'You reckon Sam knew his killer?'

'Yes. I don't think he would have stopped to give someone directions. He didn't go out of his way to accommodate people. Someone he knew stopped him in his tracks. Maybe there was an altercation. Maybe it was pre-meditated. Let's see if the appeals trigger any memories. A lot of people walk the cliffs. The killer may have timed his strike to perfection, but someone could recall a person walking away fast. Running even. Excuse me, Jo.'

An elegant, white-haired woman in her late seventies was finishing up a conversation with the TV crew by the gallery's massive picture window. Brandon walked towards her. 'Mrs Arscott-Rowe. I am so very sorry.'

'As we all are, Brandon. It's reassuring to see that you are handling the investigations.'

Brandon sucked in a breath, wondered how much she knew about her son's business affairs. He wasn't exactly the black sheep of the family, but neither was he the golden boy.

She started to fuss with the Hermès scarf at her neck. 'Is there anything we – I – can do to help you?'

'You've already given a statement to DS Menhenrick. You said you can't see any reason why Benedict would be attacked. We have your account of his last movements ... as far as you know.'

She started to fiddle with her scarf again. 'Yes. Although he could be ... erratic.'

Brandon gave her a steady look.

'You know what he was like. He'd disappear for days – sometimes weeks – and was vague about his whereabouts.

'You said he travelled to Bordeaux a week ago. Do you know who he was seeing? Family? Friends? Business Associates.'

'Is this relevant? My son was killed in Penzance. His wallet stolen. Shouldn't you be checking on the local homeless?'

'As I said, we are looking at all possibilities. I'm going over to Benedict's place now to carry out further checks. Including looking at his computer and mobile. Any idea what his passwords are?'

Lucinda Arscott-Rowe plunged a manicured hand, bejewelled with old gold, into the bag on her arm. He watched her fish around. 'Here,' she said after a moment, her face ashen. 'Benedict gave me a notebook with passwords and financial information. Said he might pop his clogs before me and wanted to make things easy for me. How prescient of him.' She passed him a tatty little book.

'Thank you,' Brandon said.

She touched him briefly with a shaky hand. 'I hope you find what you're looking for.' Her eyes held an imploring quality. But also, a kind of terror. Brandon shared her unease. Whatever he found wasn't likely to enhance the family reputation.

* * * * *

Brandon pushed open the door to Benedict's apartment – the bottom half of a small terrace house in Penzance's Bread Street. There was a scattering of flyers, letters, and free newspapers on the floor, by three piles of other post. The place looked like it'd been empty for weeks. Brandon knew this wasn't the case. He'd been there all right, but, clearly, not in his right mind. It would take some time to sift through it all. But sift he would. Stew had been in briefly and tagged things, making his job easier. He'd asked him to leave things in situ until he'd had a chance to get a feel for Benedict's situation.

He walked through to the kitchen – days of unwashed crockery, coated with dried leftovers, littered the work surfaces. He opened the cupboard below the sink – stacks of congealing cleaning sprays and leaking dishwasher tablets.

He moved into the small, spartan living area – just one scruffy sofa, an ancient music system and an extendable oak table, one flap down. Benedict's computer and a mobile were on the table. They had his other mobile – the one that was on him the night he was murdered – at the station. So, he kept two. It figured. This one was a burner. He opened the notepad Lucinda had given him. He had the same password for everything. Typical Benedict. He needn't have asked his mom. Benedict had let slip to Brandon a while back that he used the band name.

Brandon keyed *TheDeepWest!* and scrolled through his contacts. All incognito. *Warhol. Pollock, O'Keeffe, Hopper, Rothko.* The battery was low. He'd make some calls later.

He turned his attention to a shallow pile of A4 papers beneath an overflowing crystal ashtray. Brandon slipped on a pair of thin plastic gloves and carefully removed the ashtray. FUCK THE HELL OUT! TOSSER, THIS GONNA GET REAL NASTY. LEAVE THE GEAR AND GO! DEAD MEAT, MAN. The notes had the same threatening tone and block capitals as the messages on the band flyer found at The Acorn. Someone had put the frighteners on him. And they hadn't hung around before delivering the final blow. Unless, of course, they weren't one and the same?

Brandon picked up the phone, plugged it into the charger hanging from the wall socket and went through to the bedroom. It looked like he'd had company – a woman's dress draped on a metal chair in the corner, a pair of kitten heels on the floor by the bed, an empty bottle of wine poking out beneath. Even in his poor state, Benedict was still pulling. There was a wad of notes and some change on the bedside table beside a white sachet. Quite a party. He was glad Benedict had gone out in some sort of style, sordid as it was. Now it was over to the forensics to try and find out whose dress that was. Who'd left those heels.

Brandon went back into the living room and picked up the phone, pressing the first name on the list. *Warhol.* No answer.

Pollock – the long whine of a dead connection.

O'Keeffe – no answer.

Hopper – straight to answer machine.

Rothko. The phone rang four times before someone picked up. 'Fuck off, Columbo.' The line went dead.

Brandon took a step back. This was some clever bastard. He'd either guessed who was on the line or he was watching him. Had seen him enter the house. The killer was close, he could almost smell his scent, and it didn't reek of fear. Quite the opposite.

43

Rachel

'We can always take them to someone else, if you can't take my word, my agent's word, for their authenticity.' Lizzie was standing at the open door of Seabird Cottage, arms crossed, face cross and glaring at a middle-aged man in a suit.

Meghan came up behind her and rested a hand on her shoulder. 'I don't think that will be necessary. I can understand your slight reservations, Alistair, but I am sure we can come to some sort of arrangement.' Her eyes met Rachel's, who had just come up the garden path.

'Well, that may be, but it is our policy to have accreditation from a leading expert. With all due respect, Meghan, Lawrence Matthews was not one of your artists nor one of your areas of expertise.'

'With all due respect, Alistair, you are standing before the widow of Lawrence Matthews – Lizzie is the world's greatest authority on her husband's work. And, of course, as a custodian of Cornish artists, I know more than most about our Penzance doyen too. Wouldn't you say so, Rachel? Alistair, this is Rachel Matthews, Lizzie's daughter.'

Rachel stepped forward and shook his hand.

'Alistair Simmonds-Blake, pleasure to meet you, Miss Matthews.' He stood his ground. Looked like he'd experienced similar situations.

'Rachel, could you please talk sense to Mr Simmonds-Blake. He wants to send your father's paintings off to London. Having just found them, I have no intention of letting them leave the house.' Lizzie's lips were trembling, her eyes watering.

'Well, if that's the case, I am sure we can find someone local to have a look,' Rachel said. 'There will be someone at Tate St Ives, or one of the galleries in Truro. They could come here? Would that suit everyone?' Rachel glanced around, hoping to get a consensus.

'Well, I don't know if I'd want anyone at the house. Any strangers.' Lizzie's arms were crossed again.

'I could be here. It wouldn't be a problem. We could set out Dad's materials – his old paints, so they could be matched, if need be. Arrange lighting – allow time for a thorough examination.'

Rachel looked at Meghan expectantly, hoping she might have some blag to pull them through. But she remained quiet.

'This sounds like an admirable idea,' Alistair said, rubbing his hands together and looking from Rachel to Lizzie. 'One I am sure we could all accommodate?'

Lizzie gave a small humph. 'Well, if you want to go to all the bother and expense, then fine. You know where to find me.'

'I am sure it will be well worth it.' Alistair picked up his briefcase and lent over to shake Lizzie's hand. Lizzie hesitated, before uncrossing her arms and extending a palm covered in specks of red paint.

'Mind if I hitch a lift back to Newlyn, Alistair?' Meghan was coming out of the door, putting on her coat. She winked at Rachel. *Aha, so she thinks she might work some magic with her charms of persuasion.* Rachel wasn't so sure – he looked like a dry old stick. But worth a try. She followed Lizzie back into the house. What a state. She wondered how much Alistair Simmonds-Blake had seen. The studio door was ajar. Looked like she'd been working in there today.

'What an awful man. What an awful, bloody morning!'

Lizzie had collapsed into her armchair and was resting a palm against her forehead like a Victorian matriarch having a fit of the vapours.

'Would you like some tea?'

'Is that the best you can offer! You've landed us in it now with your bright suggestions.' *What?* 'Don't look the picture of innocence. You've invited the bloody Tate committee to my door! Will you offer them tea too! Or the Lawrence Matthews off my very wall.'

Rachel looked at the blank space over the fireplace where her father's painting had hung. It was still at The Arthouse – only Oliver's portrait had managed to escape the crime scene.

'It will all work out fine, don't worry, Mum. Alistair is in Meghan's capable hands now. I'm sure we will smooth all this over. She has her contacts. Probably knows exactly the right person to do the job.'

'If you say so. Are you staying for lunch?'

'No. I've got a few things on, but I've brought you some food.' Rachel produced a white cake box. 'A cream slice.' Lizzie had a sweet tooth. 'And some delicious stroganoff! Freshly cooked. Remember when Dad took us to the Hermitage in St Petersburg? It was an incredible trip.'

Lizzie's face lit up. 'Oh yes, darling, wasn't it! We rode through the city in a horse and carriage, tucked up under furs, like Royal exiles.' *Did we? Ah well if Lizzie was enjoying the fantasy.* 'The food was godawful though.'

'Well, this isn't. Our new artist-in-residence cooked it last night.'

'Really.' Lizzie sat up in her chair. 'And who, pray, is your new lodger? Julia is all heart. Takes in all manner of waifs and strays.' *Ouch.*

'Well, this isn't a waif or a stray, it's the artist who created a bit of a stir at The Arthouse opening.'

'Oh. Which one?'

'Euan Tremayne. Who produced the montages.'

'I remember him. Quite charming and very handsome.'

'You think so?'

'Don't tell me you haven't noticed? Julia clearly has. Good girl. Doesn't hang about.'

'Mum!'

Lizzie was chuckling now, her mood transformed. 'Put the stroganoff in the fridge, darling. I'll have it later. And thank you. Now ...' She levered herself up out of her chair. 'Leave the cake, darling, I'll have that for lunch,' she said as Rachel went to take away the cream slice too. 'And now ... let me show you another new work.'

Lizzie was on her feet and heading towards the studio. Rachel hurried after her – the stew could wait. She was unlikely to eat it any way.

On the easel by the window was an abstract – strong swirls of blue and green circled an oblong of red. At its very centre a sunburst of gold glowed in a shaft of light. It was biblical in its intensity and symbolism.

'Yours?'

Lizzie nodded. 'Yes. It's ...'

'Yes, I know. I can see.'

'It just came to me. I only finished it this morning. That's why I was so ... bloody furious when that auctioneer turned up with Meghan. I was inspired!'

Lizzie pointed to another canvas propped up against the wall. 'This, I found in the storeroom.' It was another find. This time a red one. Not the same red as in Lizzie's painting, but red all the same.

'I think Larry must have been channelling Rothko when he

did this. It's better, of course, has more texture and expression.'

Rachel moved closer. Was it one of her father's? It looked rushed. Maybe he had bashed it out and then discarded it. The experts were going to have their work cut out authorising this little collection.

The other painting was a better composition. Lizzie's new style was electrifying – it was a cathartic creation, combining the desperate passion of Van Gogh's *Starry Night* and John Martin's dramatic seascapes.

'What's it called, Mum?'

'What, the Lawrence Matthews? – Red Letter Day.'

Rachel bit her lip. 'No, the other one? The one with the ...' She stopped herself from shouting. The one with the red lilo. The one with the drowning child. My child. She was shaking with sorrow. Grief. Or was it anger? *Red-blooded rage.*

'It's called Porthchapel Cove. August 12, 2015.'

'Of course, it is!' Rachel shouted, Lizzie reeling back from the force of her words.

'Oh dear, oh dear,' Lizzie whimpered.

But she couldn't stop now. *Why should she stop now?* 'How incredibly ... therapeutic for you!' She looked around, grabbed her rucksack. 'I've got to go. I really need to go. Right now. I left the stroganoff on the table.'

Blood pounded in her ears, blocking out Lizzie, blocking out that voice in her own head. The nagging voice of reason and compassion.

She bumped into the coffee table as she stormed past, bashing her shin, sending the stroganoff crashing to the floor.

'Oh.' She heard Lizzie say. 'Oh. Not even staying for tea.'

Rachel rushed out of the door, still wearing her coat – hadn't even taken it off.

Instinctively, she turned back at the end of the lane and gave a wave. Her mum was waiting there as always. Even now. *Even now?* She thought she recognised a look of concern on her face. Or was it despair? At that very moment she didn't care. As soon as she was out of sight, Rachel began to run, rushing over the cold earth, bits of spidery snow still clinging to branches and gate posts. The wind was getting up, pressing against her as she charged forward, whipping her bobble hat off her head and over a hedge. She ran on, her hair all over the place, in her eyes, in her mouth.

'Watch it!' said the man in the car swerving to avoid her as she dashed across the road to the sea. Her shoulders heaving with effort and sobs, she crashed down on a bench, not bothering to look at the sea.

See what it had done.

44

Rachel

'What's the matter, Miss?'

Damien plonked his bike against the end of the bench.

'Nothing.'

'Then why are you crying?'

'I'm not.'

Damien shrugged and sat down beside her.

'Keep your distance.'

'Haha, Miss.'

'You don't have a monopoly on angst, you know.'

'Who said I did? Here.' He handed her a screwed-up paper tissue, covered in ink splotches.

Rachel shook her head. 'Why aren't you at school?'

'Suspended.'

'Why?'

'I took a swing at some cretin. Look. This one's fresh.' He passed her his last tissue in its little plastic container. He was always having nose bleeds, Rachel remembered. She'd suspected self-harm – that damn pen he was constantly fiddling with. Probably jabbed it up his nose. She took his tissue and blew her nose.

'I've got some news that might cheer you up.'

'Oh yeah?'

Damien got out his phone.

'Look.' Damien clicked on a video of a man unloading boxes from a speed boat in Newlyn harbour.

'So?' Rachel wished he'd go away. If ever there was a time

not to indulge a child's nonsense theories, it was now.

'Look.' He clicked on another video: a man of similar build offloading boxes from a fishing boat. And then he uploaded another – in the full moon light the man's face was visible as he handed down the boxes to the other.

'Your point, Damien? Newlyn is a working harbour. People offload cargo an awful lot. It's called work.'

'At two in the morning?' He was looking out to sea. For once the nonchalant death mask had slipped.

'You really need to get some sleep, Damien. All this night roaming isn't good you know. I should report you.'

'Sure, why not. What have I got to lose? Another suspension?'

'You could get expelled.'

He got up. 'Okay, if you're not interested. I just thought, seeing that the guy on the boat was Pat Ryan, you might be.'

'What?'

'Interested now?'

'Yes. Yes, I am.'

Damien sat back down. 'Ryan's boat hasn't been out since he was killed. It's still in the harbour.'

'That's why the other man was using a speed boat?'

'I guess.'

'Jeez. I think you may have something here. Do you know who the other chap is?'

'No. He always keeps himself covered. Ryan didn't.'

'I guess he didn't need to – it was his boat, fishermen trawl in the early hours.'

'Shall I airdrop you these, Miss?'

'Absolutely. I'll take them to DI Hammett right away – I think you should come with me. The detective will want a word.'

'I've told you all I know.'

'You may not even know what you know, you know.'

'Haha, Miss! Okay. I get yer. As long as he doesn't use thumb screws.'

Rachel burst out laughing. 'I can't vouch for that!'

45

Brandon

'Thank you for coming in, son.' Brandon had got up from the table and was showing Damien to the door. Rachel was in the main room reading her phone.

'All done?' she said as the two of them came over, Damien with a small smile on his face.

'Yep. This has been very helpful. I'll catch up with you later,' Brandon said, dismissing Rachel.

As soon as they were out of the door, he called Jo into the incident room.

'This has got to be our man, don't you think?'

Jo was as impressed as Brandon with the footage.

'I'd say so. But we can't jump to conclusions. He's a shady guy – not much to go on in the video. It's dark and he's wearing a balaclava.' Brandon stroked his chin as he considered the image, squinting to get a better idea.

'Let's see if I can't lighten the image – get an idea of his clothing.' Jo started to work on the video, brightening and enlarging it. 'He seems to be wearing a grey, nylon parka and jeans.'

'Any logo?'

Jo zoomed in. 'Timberland, right in the bottom corner of the parka,'

'Bit posh for your average druggie?'

'Yes. But those boxes – the way they're carrying them. So careful. They don't strike me as boxes of coke.'

'No – and the size of them too. Check the image against

the CCTV frame at Pets At Home. I have a hunch it could be the same guy.'

Jo pulled the CCTV image off the incident board and laid it beside a still of the video image. 'It looks very much like the same person – same build and type of clothing. The light's better here.'

'And look – the Timberland logo on the bottom left. It's him.'

They looked at each other.

'Okay,' Brandon said. 'He wasn't wearing that jacket when he tampered with The Acorn glitter ball. Dressed as a hippy then. But, otherwise, his description fits. Similar slim build, about five ten, thirty-something. The hippy carried a trades-man's tool kit. Of course, he could well have nicked the gear. But it might be worth looking through Checkatrade, see if any of the local electricians or handymen fit the description.'

PC Phillips popped his head round the door. 'You guys fancy a coffee?'

Brandon looked at Jo. 'I'm good. But Phil, while you're here, perhaps you'd like to come in for a chat.'

'Am I needed?' Jo asked.

'Not at the moment. See what you can find out, eh?'

Jo gave him a questioning look and then ran her eyes over Phil as she went out the door.

46

Rachel

Rachel pulled up alongside Julia's Merc in The Hall forecourt. She was in – hardly surprising with The Arthouse still closed. Rachel always felt a slight unease when she faced Hartington Hall's austere facade. She was more comfortable at The Morrab Library, in many respects. But Oliver's portrait added a wonderfully warm touch – she smiled a hello to her son as she entered the hallway. It was so good of Euan to buy the painting. She could hear moving furniture and conversation upstairs in the studio. He was at work already. Was that Julia with him? Figured. He was her protégé after all.

Rachel went straight up to her room – wanted to change her clothes – but thought she should pop her head around the studio door first, to be polite.

'Hi, how's it go ... ing.' The words died on her lips. Words refused to make any attempt on Julia's. Her friend was sitting – like Helen of Troy on a makeshift throne – completely naked, apart from a flimsy drape. Euan was standing a few feet away, working on some sort of structure. No one said a word for several long seconds.

'I ...' Rachel managed, before turning to the door.

'Julia's sitting for my sculpture, Brexitannia.' Euan had taken charge of the situation.

'And it requires an element of nudity?'

'Well, that was Julia's idea. But I think it works, don't you?'

Julia gave him a cool stare, before the words tumbled forth. 'Of course, it works. This is a life study. You can't sculpt the female form in trackie bottoms and sweatshirt.'

'It's my day off.' Rachel tossed back her hair and pulled at the over-long sleeves of her baggy sweatshirt. She felt, for the briefest of moments, her mother's daughter. 'Anyway, glad you've got a head – or should I say body – start on your sculpting. I'll be off, then.'

'We were just going to break for tea. Do you want a cup?' Euan had stepped away from Brexitannia and followed Rachel to the door.

'No, I'm alright.'

'I'll bring you one up. Milk, no sugar?' He seemed completely unfazed. Maybe she had overreacted?

Rachel had changed into a dress by the time she heard the gentle knock on her door. Usually, it was the other way round – she changed out of formal wear into leisure, when at home. But the remark about the trackie bottoms and sweatshirt had stung.

She didn't bother to answer his knock, just went to the door and opened it a few inches.

'Are you going out again?' Euan said, noticing the dress.

She thought about lying. Or taking out the car and pretending she had somewhere better to go. Someone better to see. But just said. 'No.'

'Oh, dressing for tea, then. Should I have brought scones?'

Rachel couldn't help smiling and he seized the encouragement to push open the door with his tray. There were two cups and saucers on it and a plate of biscuits. 'Julia's taking hers downstairs,' he said, placing the tray on the dressing table, watching her all the while in the mirror. She caught his eye as she sat down on the bed. Stretching out a hand she took the cup and saucer, taking a sip before placing it on her bedside table.

'Do you mind if I join you?' Euan was standing before her, his cup and saucer in his hand. She noticed it was trembling. Was this going to turn out like some Mad Hatter's Tea Party? Would the Queen rush the stairs any moment and demand 'Off! Off that bed'?

Euan sat down beside her, resting his cup on the floor. 'I'm sorry if that scene in the studio upset you.'

He was looking forward, addressing Rachel's face in the dressing table mirror.

'I wouldn't go as far as to say I was upset. Just a little shocked.' Rachel paused, looked down and then back up at his reflection. 'I've never seen Julia naked before!'

'Nor have I.' Euan reached for his cup. His hand steady now.

'It's not so much …' Rachel reached for her own.

'Go on?'

'It's not so much seeing Julia naked, it's …'

'Who she was naked in front of? Julia is an artist. This is a life study. It –'

'I don't buy it.' Rachel clanked her cup down. 'Or maybe, maybe, I'm just a bit pissed off today.'

'Oh yeah?'

'Yeah. But I won't bore you with it. Anyway. Will I have to strip naked for my sculpture, too?' She gave him a sideways glance.

'If you like. But it isn't necessary. I feel I know you well enough.'

Rachel got up, but Euan took her hands and pulled her back down.

This time she didn't resist when he took her in his arms, turned her so they lay face to face on the bed. One hand stroked her cheek, the other moved to her back, pulling her to him, ruching up her dress.

'Julia could come up any moment,' Rachel said, his mouth touching hers.

'I don't care,' he replied, turning her onto her back, edging her dress upwards, as he moved on top. 'Do you?'

* * * * *

It was an hour before they heard the click of the front door and the sound of the Merc starting up.

Euan was resting on his side, watching her. 'The coast is clear,' he said smiling and kissing her lightly on the nose. 'Although I was rather enjoying being holed up in here with you.'

'I gathered,' Rachel replied, twisting away from him and hopping off the bed.

'Hey, leaving me already? Come back here.'

'Just stretching my legs.'

'Again?'

Rachel spun round and gave him an indignant look.

'Look, you're restless. Why don't we go in the studio? Everything's set up. I'd really like to get to work on my Plastic Princess. I have a reporter coming round tomorrow to do a profile on me. I need to produce some work. And it would save you getting dressed.'

Rachel leant over, grabbed a pillow from the bed and swung it at him.

He grabbed it from her. 'Come on. Let's make a start.'

'So, what's the costume – more drapes? A ball gown?'

'This.' He leant over and picked up his discarded shirt from the bedside chair. 'I'd like you to wear this.'

'It's hardly princess material, Euan. Honestly.'

'It is to me. I can't think of anything I'd rather see you

wear.' He shook out the sleeves and helped her on with it.

'It's too big.'

'It's just right,' Euan said, pulling on his trousers.

'Quick then, Nick will be back from school soon.'

Euan snatched up the plate of biscuits and opened the door for her with a flourish. 'Your Princessness.'

After fussing around with the 'throne', he gestured for Rachel to perch on it.

'This could get uncomfortable.'

'You'll get comfort breaks. Has to be better than sitting for Lizzie.'

'How would you know?'

'I have my sources.'

'So, if Julia is Brexitannia, what sort of *woman of agency* do you have in mind for me?'

'Let's see. A cross between The Little Mermaid and Neptune's Daughter?'

'I'm not so keen on the sea these days. I've lost my sea legs.'

'Like the Little Mermaid? The one who came onto dry land to win her prince, but every step she took was like … like stepping on glass. Or was it knives. Sharp knives?'

'Hmm. I think I would prefer to be the *Splash* film mermaid or Keira Knightley in *Pirates of the Caribbean*. If I remember rightly that Hans Christian Andersen tale didn't end well. For the mermaid.'

Euan smiled at her and walked over.

'What are you doing?'

'Just adjusting your costume,' he said, fiddling with her shirt collar and kissing her neck. 'I would walk on sharp knives for you, you know that.'

Rachel smiled up at him. 'I wouldn't put it past you.'

She sat for half an hour or so, chatting and laughing, moving from one position to the other to fend off cramp.

'Come and have a look,' he said, stroking his chin and moving back to look himself. He'd concealed the sculpture behind a screen, so she had no idea how it was developing.

'Okay.' Rachel stepped down, fearing the worst. But she was pleasantly surprised. It was quite charming. He'd already worked on the plastic to make it malleable. The head was formed of what looked like giant elastic bands, all bound together to form an oval. Shredded cellophane cascaded from its crown onto the body below – sculpted, curvaceous recycling bins.

'That's inspired. How did you mould the boxes?'

'I melted and manipulated them. I haven't finished yet, though. I'm just getting started.' He moved behind her, his arms circling her waist below the shirt. She felt that rush of heat and he responded. 'I'll be working on it tonight. I was preparing it last night ... that's why, it's more ... fully-formed than you would think.'

She was barely taking in the details. He didn't seem to be either. *Blast.* She heard the front door open and the sound of a rucksack hitting the tiled floor. Nick was home.

'Euan,' Rachel said, moving away.

'Rachel,' he replied, spinning her round and kissing her hard on the lips.

Nick was running up the stairs, two at a time. 'Mum! Rachel! What's for dinner?'

'Stroganoff!' shouted Euan, undoing her shirt.

'Again?'

'Yes!' shouted Rachel. 'It's delicious.'

'Delicious.' Euan tilted her chin and kissed her.

'I'd better go.'

'I'll see you tonight?'

'In the studio?'

'I'll come to you. I'll keep working on this. And I'll come to you.'

'Cool,' Rachel said, looking into his eyes as she broke away.

'Anything but.' He pulled her back, his hands beneath her shirt. 'Keep it on for now,' he whispered, breathing in her scent on the collar.

47

Brandon

'What can I help you with, Boss?'

Brandon gave Phillips a steady look and then pointed to the CCTV photo of Sam and the Timberland jacket guy and then the still of Pat Ryan and Timberland at the harbour.

'Recognise him?' Brandon watched Phil lean in for close inspection and then shake his head.

'Can't say he looks familiar. The light's bad and he's well-covered.'

'He is indeed. Take a look at the video. You may recognise his movements, his gait.'

'Well ...' Phil inhaled and then blew out as if the task was way beyond his job spec. 'Nope. He's just a regular guy, walking on a jetty. Nothing to mark him out at all.'

'Apart from the Timberland logo on his jacket, at this point.'

'Yes. Can't argue with that.' Phil stood there as if time were money – his money. 'Anything else, Boss?'

'That computer you sent off to be checked.'

Phil scratched his head, before configuring a bland look. 'What one?'

'You get requests on a regular basis to have computers checked, do you? You know damn well which one.' Brandon shot him a dagger look.

'Trenowden's?'

'Aha.'

Brandon went to the metal cabinet at the back of the room,

turned a key and retrieved Sam's computer. 'This one. Where did you send it for the check?'

'I, I can't remember, right now. 'erm …'

Brandon watched his face redden. 'I think you better remember. And quickly.'

Phil's flabby face was wobbling. He ran a hand through his drab brown hair. 'I got the number off Chloe in the office. I'll go check with her. Won't be a sec.'

'Don't bother yourself. I've already asked her. She has no receipt for the job. If you are ever in the position to call on technical support again, which I doubt very much, the agency is CrimeTechSolutions. We use it all the time. I'm surprised you don't know that. You've been at the station longer than me. But you did send off another computer to a company called TechFix. You logged the job as Sam Trenowden's laptop, although it's a different serial number. Doesn't your brother Ted run TechFix? Did Ted take a look at Sam's computer too? Give it a *clean*?'

Phil was looking at his feet. When he looked back up Brandon noticed a stream of sweat running down the side of his face.

'You may be interested to hear, we have retrieved the wiped files on Trenowden's computer. Would you like to have a look at them?'

Phil's eyes shot to Brandon's face. 'I, I, I can't see the merit in that. I mean, what would I possibly know that you and the murder team wouldn't already? I didn't know Sam Trenowden, any more than you did. In fact, I was going to follow up a lead on him. Someone said they saw him at the Smuggler's Tavern on the night before the Montol.'

'Old news, Phil. Know anything about art?'

'Can't say I do, Boss.'

'Well, not so sure I know much myself. But, you see, I have this phone. It has a lot of famous artists' names on it. Ones even I recognise.' Brandon went back over to the cabinet and produced Benedict's burner phone. Phil glanced at it and then at the door. 'This,' Brandon said, turning it in his hands and then looking Phil in the eye, 'Belonged to a friend of mine. Someone you will know.'

'I ... I...' Phil was stepping from foot to foot. He looked up at the wall clock; a jerky tick registered the start of a new hour.

'Benedict Arscott-Rowe. Now, don't tell me you haven't heard of him? You were at the New Year gig, I believe.'

'Yes, of course, I know, knew Benedict.' Phil tore his eyes away from the clock and turned them to meet Brandon's.

'Well, this is his phone. I just wondered if you would make a call on it for me. To a person pertaining to be *Rothko*.'

Phil scratched at his neck and then looked back up at the clock. 'Right now?'

'Right now. Listen carefully – no slip ups. As soon as *Rothko* picks up, you say, this is Phil. I've got something important to tell you. When he asks you what, you say you need to see him in person. You insist. You arrange to meet at The Fisherman's Catch tonight at 7pm. You will be wearing a listening device. I will brief you on what to say.'

Phil had adopted his bland expression. 'Why me? Why not Stew or Jo?'

'Because you know him, Phil.'

'I ...'

'It will be so much easier for you if you just do as you're told. You face a tonne of shit for your extra-curricular activity already. Wiping an important piece of evidence, withholding evidence in a murder investigation – let's not add protecting

258

a murder suspect.'

'Woah! That's out of order, Brandon. I'm not protecting anyone.'

'If you want to protect your own lardy arse, then you start working for the people who employ you. The Police. Don't dig yourself any deeper, Phil. You are up to your neck in filth already.'

Phil ran his hands through his hair, which was sticking to his head now. He wiped his hands on his trousers, blew out and reached for the phone. 'Okay. Whatever you say.'

'No cheap tricks. Act like you're Dominic West.'

'Eh?'

'Dominic West – from *The Wire*. Oh, forget it. Just act like you're a bent copper. Okay?'

'Okay. He may not pick up.'

'We'll cross that bridge when we get to it. When he picks up, speak straight away. Let him recognise your voice. I don't want him hanging up. You understand?'

Phil nodded and started shaking his hands like a 100 metre runner in the blocks.

Brandon clicked on *Rothko* and handed him the phone.

'Hi, it's Tony.'

Pause.

'Tony Phillips.'

Pause.

'No, I'm not shitting you. I found the phone at the station. I've been trying to get hold of you on your other mobile. Well, why don't you answer then?'

Phil gave Brandon a thumbs up, as if they were on the same team. Brandon looked at his nails to mask his contempt. They were bitten down.

'I need to speak to you about something important. Something very important.'

Phil held out the phone so Brandon could hear him pro-testing. 'It has to be in person. I have something for you too. Something you'll like.'

Phil brought together his thumb and forefinger in a crass gesture of solidarity. Brandon twirled his own finger, telling him to wrap it up.

'The Fisherman's Catch. 7pm tonight. Yep, that's right. By the tables outside. I'll be waiting for you.'

He returned the phone to Brandon. 'Okay?'

'Yeah. Keep up the good work. You've got a few hours to rehearse your lines. Let's start on them now. Just one question before we begin.'

Phil returned Brandon's gaze. 'Ed Nicholls,' he said. 'The electrician.'

48

Brandon

'Here comes Ed.' Brandon was sitting in an unmarked police car on the Quay as the suspect approached Phil outside the Fisherman's Catch.

'Okay,' Jo said, adjusting her earphones. She switched the recording mechanism on as she watched the two enter the pub. 'I can't say I recognise him. Although ... something familiar.'

'He was at the New Year gig – front row. Meghan Bacall's man. Hopefully Phil will get him chatting about *business*. He's been briefed to.' Brandon sighed and raised an eyebrow.

'They're at the bar now.' Jo passed Brandon a set of earphones and settled down to listen.

'For God's sake.' Brandon ripped the phones out of his ears. Phil was speaking through a mouthful of crisps. 'He's either unbelievably stupid, or this is his way of fucking us over.'

Jo was squinting, straining to hear. 'He called him Ed.'

Brandon put his earphones back in. 'It's a start.'

A slow one. Ten minutes later Phil had made little headway. Ed was monosyllabic.

'He must know.' Brandon slumped back in his seat. 'He's batting back every question Phil asks him.'

'You don't think Phil primed him? Or has passed him a note?'

'More than likely. But it won't do either of them any good. Ed picked up the call. And it won't be too hard to identify him from the phone videos, CCTV and, if we get lucky, DNA.'

I wager, we have a better line in chat than Phil. Let's move in.'

They got out of the car and strode towards the pub, Brandon first, Jo bringing up the rear.

'Stay at the door. Just in case he tries to do a runner,' Brandon said, entering the pub and heading straight to Phil and Ed, who were sitting at a table with a harbour view. Ed looked from Brandon to Phil and was out of his chair in seconds. He threw it at Brandon, leapt on the table, pushed open the window and jumped out.

Brandon sprung up from the floor and yelled at Ed to stop. By the time Brandon was at the pub door, Ed was way ahead, running down the sea road towards the harbour. He was a fast runner – but so was Jo and she raced past Brandon.

'Stop. Police,' she shouted as Ed barged into a family with a buggy, before vaulting the harbour wall and disappearing.

'Where is he?' Brandon was at Jo's side, scanning the harbour.

'There.' She pointed to a figure darting between the sailing boats.

'Looks like he's heading for that speed boat – *The Big Picture*. The one in the video. Must have the keys.'

They scrambled over the harbour wall and down to the boats, Brandon panting with the exertion. Ed was in the cockpit of *The Big Picture*. He cast them a look over his shoulder as he started up the engine.

'Shit,' Jo said, as the boat started to move out of the harbour, bumping its way through the rows of small yachts and dinghies.

'Call out a patrol car. And a boat, if you can get one,' Brandon said, sprinting to the gangway and jumping onto the first of the yachts. His legs were long – they'd served him well at school athletics. As he came to the last yacht, he took a running leap at the speed boat's retreating stern. He missed, but his hands found the metal ladder at the rear and he pulled himself up. Ed picked up a fender and tossed it at him, all the while steering the boat out of the harbour. As Brandon rushed the cockpit, Ed tugged the throttle back hard, lurching the boat forward into the open sea.

The sudden movement knocked Brandon over, but he stumbled to his feet and staggered towards Ed, who went for the throttle again. Brandon anticipated him and gripped the side of the boat as it slapped over the waves. Ed swung his head round and then the steering wheel, spinning the boat as if it were a fairground Waltzer. Brandon fell to the deck and started to slide backwards as the boat accelerated. Darting from the controls, Ed grabbed hold of the anchor coiled on the deck and took a swing at Brandon. The boat leapt a wave and, as it smashed down, Brandon grabbed the anchor, yanking Ed off his feet. Dropping the chain, Ed scrambled back on his feet, only to come crashing down again as Brandon lunged at his legs.

Ed was a small bloke, a good few kilos lighter than the copper pinning him to the deck with one knee, a hand yanking his arm behind his back. With his other hand, Brandon took the links from his pocket and cuffed him. Wiping the sweat from his brow, he turned the key in the control panel and let the engine idle.

He sat, breathing hard, one foot on Ed's back. It was as if he'd landed a Great White rather than a pasty-faced electrician. But it was all relative, he thought, getting his breath back – breath now in rhythm with the gentle sway of the boat.

He had a shedload of questions to ask the guy face down on the deck: a guy so intent on avoiding them, he would endanger himself, a police officer and anyone else who got in his way. But the first question Brandon wanted to ask wasn't so hard. 'How do you drive this frigging thing?'

49

Rachel

'What was your inspiration for The Average-Size Merperson?' reporter Zara Crisp asked Euan. *The Cornishperson* interview taking place in The Hall studio was drawing to a close.

'My friend over there, Rachel Matthews.' Euan gestured towards Rachel who had just slipped into the studio to grab hold of some material.

'Cool,' Zara said, turning to acknowledge Rachel. 'And Brexitannia?'

'My friend and patron, Julia Trenowden. She's not around right now, otherwise I'd introduce you.'

'Yes, of course, Julia Trenowden is well-known for her patronage of the arts.'

Zara glanced at her notes. 'And your montages, the ones that sold a storm at The Arthouse opening. What inspired those?'

'People, places, animals, nature … just about everything. I have spent a lot of time observing life. Not enough time living it. The montages were a way of packaging the past.'

'Interesting.' Zara edged forward on her chair and thrust her recording device at him, checking the red light was still on.

'You were saying?' Zara was nodding her head gently and had adopted an intense look, as if Euan was about to explain the meaning of life, rather than a work of art.

'That's it, really.'

Zara looked disappointed, before knitting her brows and

edging closer. 'There is an intensity about the montages, through your use of coloured and opaque glass and acrylic washes. It's as if the people you present are pressing up against the glass. Are imprisoned by it.'

'That's a good one.' Euan looked over Zara's head at Rachel. 'Print that.'

Zara tried a different tack as she sought to wrap up. 'I've heard you've finished the series. That the Montol Montage is your last.'

'I should have charged more then,' Euan said in a deadpan voice, his enigmatic smile slow to emerge.

Zara smiled back, clicked off her recorder and put it in her bag. 'Euan, thank you so much for letting me have the first interview. I think we may be hearing a lot more of you. These sculptures are just wonderful. And so current. Using recycled materials and the plastics washed up on the beach. Awesome.'

'Thank you. I think I did do a reasonable job of clearing some of the coves.'

Zara got up from her chair. 'Can we expect more sculptures in a similar fashion?'

'Let's see how these go down first.' Euan walked to the door and held it open for her. 'When will the interview go out?'

'I'll write it up today and get it online straight away. It will be in the print version of *The Cornishperson* on Monday.'

'Do you think it went well?' Euan said as he came back into the studio after seeing Zara out.

'I didn't have my ear pressed to the door. But you aced those last questions. I mean what could you say? "I was snooping around the place, taking photos and thought I'd best find a good reason"?'

Euan burst out laughing. 'Thanks for pricking my bubble.'

Rachel gave him a hug. 'Just teasing. You did great. Although, Average-Size Merperson?'

'Well, that's the working title.'

They were in each other's arms when Julia came through the door with a bottle of champagne and three glasses. Rachel jumped back like a scalded cat.

'Rachel! It's okay. I'm not your mother. Let's have a drink and celebrate Euan's new-found fame. And love.'

Rachel's cheeks were burning. Never had she been so pleased to see a bottle of booze in Julia's hands.

'We're just –'

'Yes, yes, yes,' Julia said, popping the cork and pouring them all a glass. 'Cheers! God, it's good to be celebrating something for a change.'

'Too right.' Rachel clinked her glass and touched her arm. 'Thanks, Julia. None of this would have been possible without you, you know that.'

Julia turned her face away as if to compose it. 'Ditto. Where would I be without my – family of friends? And now, thanks to Mr Tremayne, I've been immortalised. The sculptures are magnificent, Euan. They really are.'

He looked down and then back up at Julia. 'Thank you – your support means a lot. I'll do one of Nick next, if you like?'

'That would be marvellous, Euan. Thank you.'

'But not naked.' He had a small smile on his face as he gauged her reaction.

'No,' Julia said with a nervous laugh.

50

Brandon

'You haven't got a leg to stand on, Nicholls.'

It had been two hours since Ed Nicholls had been brought in for questioning and he was being far from co-operative. He'd demanded a solicitor, which had taken a good hour. Now Jimmy Moyle, the legal aid lawyer, was sitting there in crumpled trousers and shirt, Ed was keeping schtum.

Brandon had already got a confession from Phillips about his involvement in Sam Trenowden's smuggling sideline and his attempts to destroy evidence through wiping his computer. Phil had at least acknowledged the leg which he didn't have to stand on. But Ed was refusing to play ball.

Brandon walked over to the interview room table, splayed out his arms and leaned in. His intimidating bear stance quite often did the trick – but Ed didn't blink. He remained monosyllabic. As if programmed to displease.

'I have a written confession from your friendly neighbourhood copper in the other room which rather puts you in the frame for some criminal activity, Mr Nicholls. I have phone video footage of you handling goods in Newlyn harbour in the early hours of the morning, on your own and with Pat Ryan. Your telephone number was in the possession of another murdered man, one Benedict Arscott-Rowe. You were seen on CCTV with Mr Arscott-Rowe's associate Sam Trenowden just hours before he died on December 23. I recognise your voice from the call I made to *Rothko* on Mr Arscott-Rowe's phone.' Brandon lied about the last bit. He couldn't be sure it was Ed who told 'Colombo' to fuck off, when he'd made that call. But he wasn't averse to a bit of poetic licence if it moved things along.

'I think you need to start explaining yourself, sharpish. Because you aren't going anywhere until we get some answers.'

Ed's face remained blank.

Brandon looked at Jimmy lounging in the chair opposite. His eyes were glazing over, as were Brandon's.

'I'm going to invite DS Menhenrick to take over questioning,' Brandon said, getting up and walking out of the door. 'In the meantime, Mr Nicholls can return to the cells.'

*****

A uniform came in and escorted Ed out – a look of studied nonchalance on his face. Jimmy Moyle tailed them, but carried straight out of the main door, presumably for a cigarette break. It was going to be a long day. If not a long week. Brandon went into the incident room and found Jo, going through some blood DNA results taken from Sam Trenowden's clothing.

Brandon dragged out a chair and sat down beside her.

'Not going well,' Jo said, looking up.

'I've had more fun at the Morgue. This zombie is giving me the screaming abdabs.' Brandon rocked back in his chair.

'It looks like he's either been watching too many True Crime shows on TV where the suspect fossilises in the interview room, or someone has put the frighteners on him. Has told him to shut it, at all costs … Jo, I'm going to ask you to use your charm on him.'

Jo gave him a sideways look. 'I'll try, Boss. But something tells me Ed is immune to any charm apart from Meghan's.'

Brandon gave her a quick look and got up from table. 'I agree. That's why I'm going to pay her a visit. But if you can try and get him past base one. Ask him what he was doing offloading cargo at 2am in the morning on 17 and 19 December. His solicitor has the video footage. Where he's storing the product. What his relationship was with Pat Ryan and why he was he meeting Sam Trenowden in the Pets At Home carpark on the morning he died ... then we may well make some progress.'

'Okay, Boss,' Jo said.

Brandon nodded and left the room, headed out the front door, glimpsing sight of Moyle, mobile in one hand, cigarette in the other. He clicked off his phone when he noticed Brandon.

'You off?' Jimmy said, stating the frigging obvious.

'Going to have a word with Ed's gal.'

Jimmy looked puzzled.

'Meghan Bacall.'

Jimmy offered Brandon a cigarette and he took it, cupping a hand round the flame from his lighter.

Brandon took a drag. 'I'm on a hiding to nothing here. I need some answers before we can even consider bail. Otherwise, we'll have to let him stew in the cells.'

His back to the station wall, Brandon tapped ash from his cigarette onto the ground. 'He'll be wanting to make a call home.'

Jimmy turned to him. 'He's being wanting to call home since he got here.'

'I bet he has. But he'll have to wait. As we are being kept waiting. I'll leave you with DS Menhenrick and see you later.'

Jimmy sighed, dropped his cigarette, and stamped on it.

'I don't know what you've got to complain about – you get

paid by the hour. Or is it the minute?'

Jimmy shrugged. 'I was hoping to get this wrapped up quickly – I was in the middle of something when the call came in.'

Brandon glanced at his crumpled clothing – could guess what the something probably was. 'Let's see what Ed's gal has to say. She's usually forthcoming enough.'

* * * * *

Meghan was sitting at the cash register typing on her computer when Brandon entered the gallery. She switched off the screen and got up to greet him with a beaming smile.

'Brandon, lovely to see you!'

She was wasted on Ed, he thought. But, then again, maybe he had his uses.

'Is everything okay?' Meghan was knitting her brow. He admired her expressive features. She would have made a good silent movie star.

'You might want to sit back down,' he said, 'Is there anywhere out back we could have a private chat?'

'Goodness! This sounds serious. No – just a storeroom. I could bring out a chair for you, though. And lock the door. Or maybe we could go out for a coffee?'

'Just a chair will do. Let me help you.'

'It's really no bother.'

Brandon waved away her protestations and followed her into the small storeroom. There were some canvases propped up against one wall and a big roll of bubble wrap, as well as other packaging materials. He noticed one box on the floor. He'd ask to explore it later.

'It's a bit dusty,' Meghan said, dragging out a wooden

chair. 'Let me wipe it down.' She got up on the chair and reached for a duster from the shelf above, her skirt rising to reveal stocking-topped legs. Turning to Brandon, she held out a hand so he could help her back down and then bent over the chair, rubbing the cloth slowly over its surface, her bottom jutting out, Brandon just inches behind.

'Phew,' she breathed, turning back round, her body so close he could feel her heat, feel her breath. 'It gets hot in here.'

'Yes,' Brandon agreed. Their eyes locked, each appraising the other.

'Can I get you anything?' Meghan said as Brandon moved to pick up the chair. 'Some sort of refreshment?'

'I'm good,' he said, not feeling it.

'Tea? Coffee?'

'No, thank you.'

She stood her ground as he moved around her, the chair back tucked under his arm, and then followed him into the main shop.

He set the chair by her workstation and sat down. 'Shall we begin?' He noticed a slight reddening of her décollete.

She swallowed and touched her neck. 'Yes, please. Gosh, you *are* making me nervous.' She gave him a coquettish look from under her eyelashes.

He paused before replying. 'Ed's at the station. He's been brought in for questioning.'

Meghan's mouth fell open and a hand flew to it. 'Oh my God!' She looked down and shook her head, before looking back at him. 'Why? What's happened?'

'Are you all right? Would you like a glass of water?'

'Thank you.' Meghan touched Brandon's hand. 'Thank you. I will get us both one,' she said, getting up and walking back to the storeroom.

It seemed to be taking her some time. Brandon glanced at his watch. After about five minutes she returned with two glasses of fizzy water, clinking with ice cubes, and furnished with slices of lemon. She smiled, her lips replenished with a slick of red.

'I was tempted to add a measure of gin,' she said, sitting down next to him, her thigh brushing his leg.

'That would have been nice. But I'm on duty. To cut to the quick, Ed's in some trouble.'

Meghan looked stern, and she gave a flutter of nods. 'Trouble?'

'Yes. He resisted arrest in an aggressive manner and is refusing to answer questions related to possible criminal activity.'

'Criminal activity!' Meghan's mouth made an astonished circle. 'Ed! He's as good as gold. My little treasure!'

'He was keeping unsavoury company. How well did he know Sam Trenowden?'

'Sam? Of course, he knew Sam. Sam was our friend.'

'But he was more your friend, is that right?'

Meghan bristled. 'If you're suggesting ...' She looked at Brandon, who remained silent. 'If you're suggesting we had a thing going on. Well, he liked me, of course. But –'

'Were you having an affair with Sam?'

'No!' Meghan opened her eyes wide. 'Why do you ask? Because he came to my gallery to discuss business? Because we shared a drink in the pub? Because he flirted with me a little? Men flirt with me all the time.' She raised her eyes to his and held them there.

'And Benedict Arscott-Rowe. How well did he know him?'

'As well as lots of people in the arts community. Benedict was a social animal. Our paths crossed.'

'Benedict had Ed's number on an untraceable mobile. Have you heard of the artist Rothko?'

Meghan gave a teasing smile. 'Of course. Not that you would find any of his work in NewlynWave.' She squeezed his thigh, some way above the knee, leaving her hand there.

'Rothko was a code name. We have reason to believe Ed was involved in illegal trade with Benedict and Sam.' Brandon allowed himself a small sigh when her hand flew from his leg to her mouth.

'Never! Ed is as honest as the day is long. Under-charged for his services if anything.'

'That may be, but he was associating with people who took a different view on enterprise. Were less *righteous*, shall we say. And those two people are now dead.'

Meghan took a sip of water. 'How serious is this?'

'Very. I'll need to search these premises and your apartment.'

'You will need a warrant.'

'I've got one. Ms Bacall, if you are holding anything back – possibly to protect Ed – then you need to know that this will be held against you. The more open you are now, the better for you both. You understand?'

She stood up. Faced him full-on with her towering presence. She was both alluring and formidable, her eyes daring him to cross her.

'I understand,' Meghan said, showing him to the door. 'I hope the next time we meet will be in more pleasant circumstances.' She leaned in, grazing the side of his cheek with a kiss, barely missing his mouth, her breasts brushing his chest.

Brandon felt his cheeks flush and was glad for the chill wind as he stepped out of the gallery. He was hot and bothered and none the wiser. She was, if anything, more inscrutable than

Ed. Maybe they were a good match after all? He pulled out his phone and called Jo. 'Get together a team to search Ed's apartment and the NewlynWave Gallery. I want it done now.'

51

Rachel

'Can I have a word?' Jaqueline Kelly collared Rachel as she walked through the door of the Special Needs Room on Monday morning.

'Sure.' Rachel hung up her coat and followed Jaqueline into her office. Jaqueline shut the door and told her to pull up a seat.

Rachel sat there with a smile on her face, thinking they could throw any delinquent at her this fine morning, and it would be like water off a merperson's tail.

'Rachel.'

'Yes?' *Concentrate.*

'I'm sorry to have to tell you but there's been a major complaint concerning your behaviour.'

'Oh!' The smile drained from her lips.

Jacqueline gave her a sympathetic look and passed over a manila file. It contained photos of her and Damien Kane outside the Morrab Library. One of them showed her handing him money.

'It doesn't look good, granted,' Rachel said. 'But I can explain.' *Who took these?*

Jacqueline shook her head lightly. 'I am sure there is an innocent explanation. But, Rachel, and this is the thing, no matter how *innocent* the encounter – and I'm sure it was – it is a serious breach of school policy.'

'What if I'd bumped into him in the street? Penzance is hardly a large town?'

Jacqueline's face hardened. 'But this wasn't a chance meeting, was it?'

'No,' Rachel admitted, 'But it was a meeting made with good intentions. Very good intentions.'

'That may well be. But, Rachel, you cannot take the law into your own hands. You have already been warned about slipping out of school at lunch break. Your time keeping has also been remarked upon.'

'I've never missed a day of work. Or been late for a lesson.'

Jacqueline pursed her lips. 'But you nearly have. And that has put pressure on the group. We have to work as a team here. It's vital to the smooth running of the department.'

Jacqueline paused, giving Rachel a chance to respond. But she remained silent, concentrating on stilling the lone tear in her eye.

Jacqueline cleared her throat. 'I am sorry to have to inform you, Rachel, I will have to suspend you herewith until your *indiscretion* has been investigated fully.' She passed her a letter. 'It's from HR. Please gather your things and leave now. I am sorry, Rachel. I really am. Hopefully this matter can be resolved.'

Rachel got up and went to take the file, but Jacqueline put a firm hand on it.

'Who sent the photos in?' As she looked into Jacqueline's sensible schoolteacher eyes, she didn't expect an answer.

'I'm not at liberty to say. I'm sorry, Rachel. I really am. I sincerely hope we can sort this unpleasant business out.'

Rachel's cheeks were burning as she made the walk of shame through the SENs room, the children gawking at her, Janet Price giving her a sly, superior smirk over her shoulder. When she was out of the door, she remembered her coat. She'd have to go back in and get it. The embarrassment. She stood with her back to the wall, summoning up the courage.

And then the door opened quietly.

'Your coat, Rachel.' It was Janet Price – observant right to the last.

But she was grateful for this small act of compassion. 'Thank you,' she said, taking the coat and watching Janet slip back into the room, her sing-song voice immediately back in play, issuing its passive orders.

She fought back the tears until she was sitting slumped in the Fiat, her key in the ignition, thinking things through.

Rachel was jolted from her thoughts by a tapping sound. She swiftly wiped her eyes before turning to the window.

'Miss.' Josh Ryan was looking straight at her – a first for him. 'Miss?'

She rolled down the window. It was heart-breaking to see him there, wearing that concerned expression. He seemed to know, on some level, that this was goodbye.

'Why are you leaving?'

'I can't really say, Josh.'

'You won't be teaching me this afternoon?'

'No.'

'Are you leaving for good?'

Rachel nodded, her eyes on his Blazer pocket crest.

'Why? Teachers don't leave mid-term.'

Rachel bit her lip. 'I would have liked to stay. It's just not possible.'

He looked to the side, focusing on a couple of teachers walking past.

'Josh. I've got something for you.' She leant over to the passenger seat, looked in her work satchel and handed him his corrected work from last week. 'This is so good. Full of fire and adventure. You'll get your GCSE English, and you'll make a great soldier.'

He glanced at his exercise book, before looking down. 'We got them, didn't we? The … men who killed Uncle Pat.'

'We certainly did.'

'Thank your friend, the detective. Thank him from me and my mum and dad, Aunty Susan and all the Ryans.'

'I will. You helped too; you know. Some of the passages in that story – they helped build a picture.' The skirmishes down by the docks, the strangers coming into town on the make, the local resentment and fear. Nothing you could use as evidence, nothing Brandon didn't know already, nothing to stand up in court, but they illustrated community pressures.

He gave her a quick look. 'Do you like chocolate?'

'Yes, I do.' She watched him search his rucksack.

'Thank you, Miss Matthews.' He handed her a bar of *Galaxy Smooth*, the wrapping worn around the edges.

'Thank you, Josh. Good bye. And good luck.'

He gave her a small, shy smile, before zipping up his rucksack and slipping it back on his shoulder. She watched him walk away. A couple of boys on their way to a lesson joined him as he left the carpark, one of them cuffing him playfully on the ear. He laughed and shoved him aside. He didn't look back.

Rachel turned the key in the ignition and steered the car out of the school gates.

* * * * *

It was six o'clock before she arrived back at The Hall. She had visited Lizzie – stayed for lunch this time – done some shopping, with the little money she had left in her account and had taken a long walk along the cliffs. By the time she opened the front door, to be greeted by Oliver's loving face, she was feeling a lot better.

Rachel headed straight for the kitchen and opened the bottle of red she'd bought. She took three glasses out of the kitchen cabinet and poured some into one. Sitting at the table she sipped her wine, taking some time for herself, before seeing what the others were up to.

'Rachel?' Julia had come into the kitchen.

'Hi. Would you like a glass? I was just going to bring one through.'

'Thanks.'

Rachel poured her one and was about to pour another.

'Euan's popped out. He needed to pick up some things from his cottage.'

'Cool.' This, in many respects, would make it easier. She'd get the big reveal out of the way with Julia.

As they took their glasses through to the living room, Rachel could hear Nick on his Xbox upstairs. *Good.*

'So how was your day?' Julia said, sitting down opposite her.

'Different.' Rachel took a glug of wine.

'Oh?' Julia raised an eyebrow.

'I've been sacked.'

'What!' Julia slammed down her glass.

'Well, not sacked – yet. But suspended under investigation.' Rachel took another glug.

'For crying out loud. Why?'

'I don't know if I told you, but I saw a kid out of school hours. He helped restore some files on Sam's computer.' *Could this get any more awkward?*

'Sam's computer?'

'Yes. It was just too … clean. Brandon had had it checked,

but, I'm sorry, Julia, it just didn't seem right.'

'So, you got a kid to check it out?'

'Yes.' Rachel reached over to the bottle and topped them both up.

'Rachel! Are you an idiot?'

'Possibly. But – hear me out. Damien did find some interesting files and Brandon now has something to go on.'

'Damien? Not that weirdo Damien Kane?'

'He's not a complete weirdo. He's been very helpful.'

Julia narrowed her eyes. 'First things first. How did the school find out that you'd been with Damien?'

'Photos – someone took photos of us and sent them in.'

'Who?'

'They didn't say. I'm not sure they have to. Anyway, that was enough to suspend me.'

'Rachel! Well, probably for the good. You weren't – aren't – really cut out to be a teacher.'

'I guess not. But I liked working with the kids. I felt I was some use to some of them.'

Julia waved a dismissive hand. 'Hand in your notice before they can sack you. You can take over at The Arthouse.' She took a sip of wine. 'Just don't pour a bottle of wine over a VIP, like you did in London!'

They both burst out laughing.

'He was a dork,' Rachel said, remembering the client that had groped her at an Awards Dinner. 'He'd had it coming for months.'

'Cost you your job, though.'

Rachel got up from the sofa. 'Let's open another bottle.'

'Let's talk about Sam's computer. Let's talk about Sam.' Julia drained the last of her glass.

'I best get that other bottle.'

The two empty wine bottles on the coffee table were like eavesdroppers to a sensational piece of gossip. Julia was looking decidedly dishevelled – she reached out for a bottle, turned it upside down and shook it to get the last drop into her glass.

'Rachel, get another one.'

'There isn't any more.'

'The cellar. Let's raid that dead bastard's cellar!'

Rachel got up. 'Okay. I guess I don't have school tomorrow morning.'

Julia shrieked with laughter. 'To think I was going to call the gallery Sam's Place. Thank God you stopped me.'

'Sam's Disgrace?' Rachel said.

Julia howled with laughter again.

'Get the Petrus Pomerol. If he wasn't dead already I'd pour it all over him, after boiling it first!'

Rachel was convulsing with laughter. 'I'll get that bottle. Make a change from Co-op House!'

Rachel came back from the cellar, a bottle of Napa Valley *Screaming Eagle* in one hand a corkscrew in the other. 'Couldn't find the poncey French merlot.'

She struggled with the corkscrew. 'Can you help me, Julia? I'm used to screw tops.'

'Give it here. I'm used to screw tops too, though. He wouldn't let me near his precious collection. Creep! To think your lovely Euan called himself a creep. Remember that? Remember the night of the Montol?'

'How could I ever forget? It seems like ages ago now. But just a few weeks.'

Julia pulled out the cork with gusto and poured them both

a glass. 'Here's to our two, two-timing, criminal bastard exes. So funny to think of them in twin shelves at The Morgue. What was it that Benedict said at The Acorn – "In Hell I'll Be In Good Company"?' Julia snatched at her glass, spilling some wine over the edge onto the sleeve of her white blouse. 'Whoopsie!' She started to laugh and then held her arm out in front of her and started to examine it. 'It looks like blood. Blood. Rachel – who's next?'

She wasn't laughing now. She looked demonic. Like Sissy Spacek in the film *Carrie*, after being doused in pig's blood. It was as if she'd flicked a switch and seen the light.

Rachel put down her glass. 'We haven't done anything wrong. Why would anyone want to kill us?'

'Because they're cold-blooded killers, that's why. They don't give a shit. They could kill us for the hell of it!' She poured herself another glass of wine. Went to pour Rachel one, but she waved her away.

'We must be careful. Sure. But Brandon's working on some good leads. And …' She smiled, 'And … we have Euan here to look after us. He could impale any intruder on the Merperson's pointy tail!'

Julia grunted. 'Yes. Euan. But he's yours.'

'I don't think that would come into it if –'

'No. He is very gallant. You are lucky, Rachel.'

There was no answer to that. She wasn't sure how much luck had to do with it, though.

'You are so bloody lucky, Rachel. To walk in the studio right at that moment. The way he was looking at me I was sure …'

Rachel felt sick. That familiar kick in the guts. 'Sure of what?'

'Oh, come on. You must have noticed our – chemistry? He

was so attentive. So eager to please. He moved in for God's sake!'

'But I thought you invited him?'

'Well, yes. But he was hinting about his place being so small. Oh, anyway, well done. You won.'

'I didn't know it was a competition.' Rachel spat the words out. 'It just happened. Nothing was planned. I had no idea that you liked him.'

'What? How long have you known me?' She turned to face Rachel, her eyes small blue flames.

'Okay. Yes, I did think you fancied him a little. But I thought you knew our history?'

'What? He fancied you at Falmouth? That was a long time ago, Rachel. You aren't the same girl.'

Rachel took a breath. 'No, I'm not the same person.' She paused. 'Julia, there are some things I should probably have told you. I don't know why I didn't. Maybe I didn't want to cause a fuss. I don't know.'

'What are you going on about?' Julia poured herself some more wine. 'What are you going on about?' Her voice was getting louder.

'New Year's Eve when Euan went to Seabird Cottage with me. He … we kissed. He said some things which made me think he still liked me. A lot.'

'Like what?' Julia was sitting back, watching her.

'I can't remember exactly. "Do anything for me. Just wanted to be with me." Or some such romantic drivel.'

'Lines – men are full of them.' Julia took a sip of wine, pushed back her hair.

'Possibly. Probably.' Rachel looked at Julia, could see she was drunk. She hadn't seen her like that in years – probably not since their Falmouth days. Julia's head rolled from one side to the other. She looked ten years older. Things were taking their toll – on both of them.

'Julia?'

She jerked her head up. 'Yes,' she slurred.

'There is something else. I haven't told anyone else.'

Was this the best time to tell Julia, when she was drunk and less likely to remember in the morning?

'Yes!' Julia hiccupped the word and reached for the bottle. 'Out with it! Something's bugging you. I can see that, even in my condition.'

Rachel poured herself a little wine, took a sip. 'I am pretty sure Oliver was Euan's child.'

'What?' Julia raised her head to look at her.

'Benedict couldn't have children – as far as I'm aware. It couldn't be pure luck and condoms which left him childless. And he did a DNA test – Benedict insisted. He wanted to support Oliver. To his credit, he did support him a little, even though he wasn't the father.'

'But Euan?' Julia was sitting up straight now.

'There wasn't anyone else – at that time. We had a one-night stand – neither of us used contraceptives. We were very young.'

Rachel was looking down, not daring to catch Julia's eye.

'Rachel. Why didn't you say? Why didn't you tell him?'

'It was a one-night stand. I didn't want to load him with all that responsibility. I didn't know him. I would probably not have had the baby if I'd discovered I was pregnant earlier. I was around four months when I realised. I never regretted it. Oliver was, is, my joy.'

Julia nodded, tears dampening those flaming blue eyes. 'I remember so well. I think I noticed the bump before you.' She got up to walk towards Rachel, stumbled and reached for the coffee table to steady herself.

'Will you tell him now?' she said, sitting down next to Rachel.

'I've thought about it. And I don't know. It would hurt him so much.'

'You don't think he might have guessed, already?'

'I've thought about that too. I really don't know what to do. I feel terrible about it. So guilty.'

'Come to think of it – Euan does look a little like Oliver. The light blue eyes. The slim physique.' She looked towards the door, and, for a moment, Rachel thought she was going to go to the portrait and scrutinise it for similarities. 'What a mess, eh?'

'Yes.'

'You know, I didn't see you with Euan. That's why I went for him. I wouldn't have if I'd known. I'm sorry. I didn't know you had this past. This thing. I thought you liked Brandon.'

'Brandon?' Rachel crinkled her brow.

'Yes. He likes you and I thought you were – suited.'

'I'm a recovering artist. He's a copper, Julia.'

'A damn fine one, if you ask me!'

Rachel turned to her. 'You don't fancy him as well, do you?'

'Snog, marry, push off a cliff? Whoopsie, sorry, Sam!' Julia was smiling again. 'I might snog Brandon. But no, I tend to go for bad boys, as you may have noticed.'

'Yes,' Rachel said, throwing an arm around her. 'Not everything escapes my notice. But Euan's not bad – he's a softy.' Rachel's face was melting into slush.

'I'm not so sure. I think he played me. And that's not being soft.'

'Some people would say he was just being charming. Lizzie found him charming. Attractive people can't always help at-

286

tracting people, even inadvertently.'

'Spare me the rose-tinted crap.' Julia wagged a finger at her. 'You'll be telling me he's a victim of his own charisma next. I can see you're smitten. Well, just be careful he doesn't hurt you. That's all. Treat it as a fun thing and keep love in the box.'

A car door slammed outside and then came the sound of someone dragging something heavy across gravel.

'Talk of the devil,' Julia said, pulling herself together.

52

Brandon

'Would you believe it?' Brandon put down the phone and turned his attention to Jo. 'Would you Adam and Eve it?'

'What? And what's with the Cockney rhyming slang, Colombo!' Jo was sitting at the incident room table going through some papers. 'Why are you smiling?'

'Am I smiling? Well, allow me some *schadenfreude*, but someone has given me a very interesting witness sighting. A local woman recognised that … shifty *artist* Tremayne from a *profile* in the local rag. Says she remembers seeing him on the cliffs over-looking Sennen Cove on the morning Sam Trenowden was murdered.'

'Bloody Hell! Brandon, didn't you say he'd moved into The Hall?'

'Yes. I always thought there was something odd about him. Check him out, Jo. See if he has any previous. Make it a priority. Rachel and Julia could be in danger.'

'Will do. But let's not rush to any conclusions. He's a photographer, right? I read that profile. He's been all over Penwith taking photos – coves, cliffs, people.'

'Dead bodies? Make it a priority. If we can rule him out, all well and good. But let's find out.'

'I hear you, Boss.'

* * * * *

'There is something, Brandon.' Jo came through to the incident room ten minutes later with a print-out in her hand.

'Let's have a look.' Brandon took the paper from her, put it on the table and read it slowly. His arms encircled it, as if it might try to escape. 'So, he has previous. A restraining order.'

Jo sat down beside him. 'He was eighteen, Brandon. A kid. It was his ex-girlfriend.'

'Why are you so *understanding*? You don't fancy him as well?'

Jo snorted. 'I hardly know him, although you have mentioned him a few times – in passing.'

'Have I? Well, only because he's always hanging around. And now we have proof that this is his *modus operandi*. He likes to hang around women.'

'He won't be the first to do that. Come on. Men have been chasing women since they clubbed them on the head and dragged them into caves. Since Adam and Eve, if you'd only believe it.' She smiled at him. 'He was just a teenager in love.'

'And now he's a grown man of …' Brandon looked at the notes. 'Thirty-three and he's still stalking.'

'Brandon, you can't say he's stalking. Julia invited him to stay. He was a huge success at The Arthouse opening. The local luvvies adore him.'

'That may be. But, unless it has escaped your notice, people started dying the day he pitched up in town. He was seen on the cliffs the very morning Sam Trenowden fell to his death. He was at The Montol when Pat's skull rolled out of the bonfire. Landed at his feet, I believe.' He paused. 'He was outside The Arthouse in a snowstorm when Benedict was stabbed. Was first at the scene.'

Jo narrowed her eyes. 'Well, yes. But he was, if I remember rightly, outside playing snowballs with Rachel Matthews not long before.'

Brandon shot Jo a look before turning back to stare at

the paperwork. 'Probably thought he was eighteen again ... Rachel found him stooped over Benedict's dead body, hands dripping blood. His coat covered in it.' He shook his head, without raising it.

Sure, they hadn't found any incriminating evidence to charge Tremayne. No DNA on the knife. But ... and it was a big But. 'Bring him in for questioning. We can't let this slip through our fingers. Something isn't right here.'

Brandon got up from the table, taking the piece of paper with him. 'The sooner the better, Jo. Don't put the frighteners on him. Let him think it will be you asking informal questions.'

He walked towards the door and then turned round. 'Any news on Ed Nicholls? Have the DNA results come in from Trenowden's clothing?'

'Not yet. I'll let you know asap. We can't hold him much longer without charge.'

'No.' Brandon stroked his chin. 'The boys didn't find anything at his place or NewlynWave, either. He's a clever operator.'

'And Meghan Bacall? You think she didn't know what her partner was up to?'

'I didn't say that, Jo. I keep an open mind. But, as you know, Julia knew nothing about Sam's involvement. So, possibly, this was a *gentleman's club*.'

'And, in the meantime, you plan to grill Euan Tremayne?'

'Absolutely. No stone unturned.'

53

Rachel

Euan and Rachel were in the studio when they heard a car pull up on the forecourt.

'Julia back already?' Rachel said, setting aside the canvas she was working on.

The doorbell rang.

'It's not Julia then?' Euan gave her a puzzled look.

'Let's leave it. Probably a salesperson.'

The bell rang again.

'I'll go see. The postman always rings twice, as they say.' Rachel went out of the studio and crossed the landing to one of the front bedrooms. Peering out of the window, she could see Jo Menhenrick standing by the front door.

'It's the fuzz,' Rachel said, popping her head back around the studio door.

'Brandon?' Euan put down the chisel he was wielding.

'No. It's Jo. DS Menhenrick from the station. I'll find out what she wants. It could be something important.'

'Miss Matthews,' Jo said as Rachel opened the door.

'Hi. Everything okay?'

'Is Mr Tremayne at home?'

'Euan? Why do you ask?'

'Is he around?'

Rachel's mind was racing. 'I'll just go up to the studio and see.'

Euan was standing as still as one of his sculptures when Rachel opened the studio door.

'What does she want?'

'Well, it's not your autograph. She had a very serious look on her face and just asked if you were around – twice. What have you been up to? Stealing council recycling bins?'

Euan grimaced. 'I can't deal with this now, Rachel. Can you get rid of her? Please? Just say I'm out. She'll be back if it's anything important. Or she can call The Hall, or my mobile.'

Rachel gave him a long, concerned look. 'Okay. I'm sure Jo can get back to us later. Can get back to you.'

Rachel went downstairs.

'He's out, Jo.' Rachel hated lying. She was sure her face was flashing *Liar, Liar.*

Jo took some time to respond. 'Oh. Is that his Mini Cooper?'

'Yes.'

'He can't have gone far then?'

'Probably not. I'll let him know you called.'

'Do you have his mobile number?'

Rachel gave it and watched Jo get in her car and drive away.

Euan was standing outside his bedroom door with his holdall in one hand when Rachel went back upstairs.

'You're leaving?'

He sighed. 'I just need to think things through.'

'The police want to speak to you, Euan. You can't just …'

'I can't speak to them.'

'Why? What have you done?'

'Nothing. But nothing can seem so much like something.'

'I gave Jo your mobile number.'

'Okay. I may have to switch it off for a while then.'

Rachel turned away.

'Just a while,' he said, stretching out a hand to stroke her cheek. 'Just a while. Don't you go anywhere. Promise?'

'I can't promise anything.' Rachel went to walk away, but he put down his bag and took her in his arms.

'You're wearing the shirt,' she said, breathing in the familiar scent. 'From that first time.'

'Not the first time. But a better time, perhaps.' He pulled back slightly and smiled. 'But yes, it is that shirt. I thought your scent might put off the bloodhounds.'

'Worth a try.' Rachel smiled back up at him. 'Are you a murderer?'

'Do I look like a murderer?'

'Do I?'

'I best go,' he said, 'I don't want you to cover for me. Or lie for me again. I'll be in touch.' He kissed her tenderly. 'Goodbye, for now, my little merperson.'

She saw his anguished profile as he walked away, watched him move swiftly along the landing and down the stairs. When she heard the quiet click as he pulled the kitchen door shut, she felt an emotional door slam. Felt the same unease as when he'd reappeared at the Montol with his practised charm, and affectations. Even now he was often watchful, on his guard, one step ahead. What was he hiding? Did she even know him? He never talked about himself, his past, his family. She thought of that time in the storm when she'd questioned him about Julia. He was all over her friend at The Acorn and yet he'd dismissed Rachel's concerns. 'You know what I want,' he'd said. 'To be with you. I'll do what it takes.' Julia thought he'd played her – used her to get into their circle. If Sam had been around, he wouldn't have got a foot in the door. But Sam wasn't around. He was dead. Like Benedict. She remembered Euan's blood-stained hands and gripped the banister, all the while listening for the sound of his car to start up. But there was nothing. He'd slipped away. And she'd let him.

54

Brandon

'He wasn't there and he's not picking up his phone.' Jo caught Brandon as he walked through the station door. 'Rachel said he must have popped out. She didn't seem sure, at first. Had to go inside to check. She gave me his mobile number.'

'You reckon he's done a runner?' Brandon carried on walking, peeling off his coat as he headed for the incident room. 'Stew, get us both a coffee, please,' he said to the DC on the front desk.

'Well, it's only been a short while. He didn't take his car – it was parked outside The Hall. I waited for around twenty minutes at the bottom of the drive. It was still there when I headed back to the station.'

Brandon sat down at the table. 'Doesn't look good, does it? For him.'

'Let's give it a few minutes before letting the dogs out!'

Brandon gave a wry smile. 'I'll call Rachel. He's usually welded to her side.'

'Rachel, how're things?' Brandon nodded a thank you to Stew as he placed a mug of coffee in front of him.

'I'm fine. And you?' Rachel said, her tone cool.

'Good, thanks. Jo said Euan had gone out when she called earlier. Any idea where?'

He blew on the surface of his coffee to cool it. Reckoned Stew had boiled cold coffee in the microwave – an old Phil trick.

'No idea.' Rachel sounded defensive.

'He's not answering his phone, Rachel. If he calls you, tell him to get in touch with the station. It's urgent. We need to eliminate him from our inquiries.'

Brandon took a hesitant sip of coffee, paused to let her vent her indignation.

'It's probably nothing. But we need to speak to him, Rachel. It's in his best interests to contact us as soon as possible. You okay?' He glanced at Jo, who picked up her mug, took it to the back of the room and looked out of the window, pretending to admire the drizzle.

'Call me if you need me. He might show. And he might be in a desperate mood. Do you want to come and stay with me? All of you. You can bunk in the attic like scouts. Hey, do you remember when we were sea scouts?' He heard her smile and returned it. 'Okay, but change the security codes. Yes, I know you like him, but you never know. Take care. Make sure you keep your phone on.'

Brandon got up from his chair and grabbed his coat.

'You going out again, Boss?'

'Yes. I can't sit around here waiting for that guy not to ring. I'm going to my office to do some filing.'

'Filing!'

He grimaced. 'Keep in touch, Jo, in case he just happens to have a change of heart and turns himself in.'

He stopped as he got to the door. 'Check the car rental companies – see if anyone fitting Tremayne's description has rented a car today. And pull some photos of him off the *Cornishperson* profile. We'll be needing them.'

55

Rachel

Rachel lay on her back staring up at the sky, letting the waves rock her. The sea was calmer after last night's storm, but she could feel tension brewing in the depths. She stretched out her arms and legs and did some star fish moves to keep her blood flowing – the wet suit only gave so much protection from the cold.

A rogue wave hit her in the face, and she spat it out. A little slap of spite, to counter the small wave of happiness she'd shared just days ago.

She kicked her feet and watched the clouds change shape. Slivers of blue divided them – but the storm would return. Tonight, tomorrow, soon.

In the distance Porthchapel Cove looked as small as a child's cuticle – if she drifted any further it would disappear altogether. She turned onto her front and launched into front crawl, swimming against the tide. The cove wasn't getting any closer, so she started to swim diagonally, cutting through the waves, dragging herself towards the shore.

She thought about all the miserable concerns that awaited her. The manhunt, the murder investigations – still unresolved, but promising. Highly promising, according to Brandon. And now Nick, Chelsea and Damien – going all *teenage-y* just when she was abandoning school. She'd caught Nick as he'd crept up the stairs in the early hours of the morning and he'd told her about his new girlfriend. He'd forgotten to turn the security back on that fateful New Year night. One mystery solved. Brandon was onto the others. He was a rock. Could have been carved out of the Cornish cliffs. She had names for some of the extraordinary character rocks that lined the cliffs between Sennen Cove and Land's End. Rocky was one with a certain macho swagger. But she hadn't come across a Brandon yet. Maybe one day someone would sculpt his face in stone for services to Penwith.

Lifting her head, she looked around to get her bearings. Not far now. The wind was strengthening, the waves building, and she harnessed their power to deliver her to the shallows, surfing the last few metres amongst tangles of seaweed and stones.

Getting to her feet, she crossed the wet sand, avoiding the pools of water with their tiny ecosystems.

It wasn't a surprise to see him there, sitting by the rock where she'd left her things. He rose as she went to join him, holding out her towel.

'You must be freezing?'

'No, not really. I had quite a workout swimming back against the current.' Rachel unzipped her wetsuit and stepped out of it, letting Euan wrap her in the towel and rub her dry.

'I thought you would be long gone,' she said, her teeth chattering, her chin against his chest.

He took a corner of the towel to dry her hair. 'I didn't go far. I just needed to think things through, that's all.'

Rachel gave a weak smile and stepped back, shaking off the sand from her shins and between her toes, and pulling on her clothes.

'Here,' he said, giving her his jumper. She put it on and they sat down against the rocks, his arm around her shoulders, staring out at a sea as unsettled as themselves.

'So, what did your thoughts tell you to do?' Rachel said

after a bit.

'To go to the station. No point running from the past.'

Rachel turned to him. 'The past?'

'Yes. I assume Brandon has uncovered a few things. I had a restraining order put on me when I was eighteen. I was turning up at my ex's place. She didn't like it. Got the police involved.'

'I wasn't your first love then?'

'No.' He squeezed her shoulder. 'I had previous.'

Rachel slipped her arm around him. 'Thank God for that. The burden of being your first, last and everything would have tipped me over the edge.'

Euan laughed. 'Said by a true romantic.'

He felt in his rucksack and pulled out a flask. 'Fancy some coffee?'

'Wouldn't say no.'

'And a tot of rum?'

'Would say yes.'

Euan poured her a small cup of coffee and added a tiny tot of rum. 'You're driving.'

'When did you get so puritanical?'

He added some to his own cup.

She waited until he had taken a few sips. 'Euan?'

'Yes?'

'I've got a confession to make too.' She paused. 'Can I have just a bit more rum?'

'Sure. I can give you a lift back, if you like. I've got a bike.'

'A bike?'

'A Triumph Bonneville – I keep it at the cottage. It's been very useful the past few days.'

'Okay. I don't know how to tell you this. I really don't.'

Was this the right time? Would there ever be a right time?

He poured the rum.

'Have you ever wondered?'

Euan fidgeted and she felt him edge away.

'Yes. I have wondered.'

Rachel looked down at the sand, trailed a finger in it. 'It was here, you know. Where Oliver drowned.'

Euan got up abruptly. 'I read about it in the papers.'

He sat back down and took her hand, gazing at the waves stroking the shore. 'There was something else I wondered about.'

Rachel sighed. 'I am so sorry. I really am. I didn't know what to do at the time. And I wasn't sure. When I was pretty much sure – later – I didn't know what to say. I didn't know you.'

He turned to look at her and she couldn't read him. It was like a small part of him had closed off to her.

'What's done is done.'

She was crying now, and he drew her close. 'Nobody could have foreseen what would happen,' he said, stroking her arm.

'If Oliver had had a dad, a proper family, then it might never have happened.'

'You can't say that, Rachel. Grandparents look after kids all the time. I might have been a crap dad. Or just a dad happy to have the in-laws look after the kid for a weekend.'

'But my parents!'

'There are much worse. He was nine, Rachel.'

'You know that?'

'Yes.'

'I miss him.'

'So do I.'

She looked at him closely. 'When did you suspect?'

'Benedict wasn't really involved with him, was he? And Oliver looked nothing like him – I saw the photos on Facebook. Saw him grow up over the years. But I didn't know if there was anyone else. And I didn't hear anything from you.'

'There wasn't anyone else – at that time.'

'Why didn't you contact me?' He gave her a hard, questioning look.

'We only had that one night. I didn't want to burden you. And, I suppose, I was proud. Thought I could go it alone.'

'You were great.' His features had relaxed. 'Must have been hard. You taught him to swim – he was in a swimming club. I read Lizzie's blog. Quite recently she let slip that he never knew his father. This makes me sound stalkerish, probably. But I felt he was my child too.'

'Benedict did a DNA test – he wasn't the father. There was no one else.' She steadied herself. 'I feel awful not telling you. But the longer I left it … I had no idea what you were doing. You could have been in a relationship – had kids. I–'

'I should have contacted you. I wish I'd contacted you. What stops us taking those small, simple steps?'

'Fear? Fear of rejection. Of getting the wrong idea.'

'But I'm here now.'

'Why? What made you come to Penzance?'

He sighed. 'This is turning out to be some confessional.'

'Yep.' She squeezed his hand.

'I wasn't so far away – Truro – and I heard you were back. Word gets around. I wanted to see whether we could make a go of something. If that chemistry was still there. The chemistry which created your beautiful boy. Our beautiful son.'

She turned to him, tears in her eyes.

He pulled her close, traced a finger along a trail of sand on her cheek.

'Is that rum having an effect?'

'Yeah. The anti-freeze is doing the trick.'

They huddled together, watching the tide ebb under gathering clouds.

'I want to take you somewhere,' Rachel said after a while. They packed away their things and started to walk across the small beach to the cliff steps. All was quiet, apart from the stream trickling down the cliff from the Holy Well of St Levans at the top. Up they climbed, pausing to rest at the ruins of an ancient chapel, the sea below a seething cauldron. Euan curled his arm around Rachel's head, bringing it to rest against his chest. She could feel his heart beating below his shirt – not from passion, or fear, but grief. She could feel his terrible sadness and loss; the loss of something he never had, never knew. And it rocked her.

'Shall we continue?' Rachel looked up at him.

'Yes,' he said, looking past her. 'Yes.'

The next fifty steps were the hardest. A pale sun shone through a mesh of cloud like a headlight in fog; the wind was absent, as if holding its breath. Rachel stopped by the well when they reached the top and dipped in a cupped hand.

She took a sip and offered the water to Euan, as it seeped through her fingers. Taking the top off her water bottle she filled it. 'For St Levan,' she said, looking across the road to the small granite church.

There was no traffic, and no vehicles in the small carpark, apart from her Fiat and Euan's *Triumph*, his helmet hanging off the handlebars.

'Come on then.' Rachel reached for Euan's hand, and they crossed the road to the ancient wooden gate. It was unlocked as always, the remote clifftop setting not inviting trouble. Unlike the churchyard at St Mary's, St Levan's small graveyard was crammed with head stones. Ancient ones, old ones, rela-

301

tively new ones and some so new the salty sea air had barely brushed them.

The newer ones were on a ridge to the south, dating from 2007 to the present day. A fresh grave rested below a cushion of soft earth. Next to it was a white stone, marbled with veins of pink, its words whispering their sad story. Rachel let go of Euan's hand to search in her rucksack. The small bouquet of flowers she'd brought with her was intact. Pulling back the wrapping, she passed Euan the posy of red camellias.

'I haven't been here for a while,' she said as she watched him kneel to place the flowers on Oliver's grave. Opening the bottle, she drizzled the holy water on them and the surrounding earth.

'I don't like to come, you know. I don't need to be here to feel Oliver's presence. And if I come, it's like I'm dragging him back with me.'

Euan squeezed her hand and spoke softly. 'Oliver Lawrence Matthews. 31 July 2006-12 August 2015. Your short life blessed all those who had the joy of experiencing it. Moments of love last forever.' He paused. 'That's beautiful.'

'Do you want to take a photo?' He was staring so hard at the stone; it was like he was making a visual imprint.

'No.'

Rachel stepped the few feet to her father's grave. It was marked by the same white marble, the exact same size for all the life he'd lived. Dotted around the graveyard were other Matthews, their own life stories summarised in stone, but her father and son lay shoulder to shoulder. She knelt to place a posy of camellias and mistletoe on her father's grave. He would have liked the composition. Oliver would have cringed at the mistletoe. She smiled thinking of the two them, so different but equally strong-willed.

The light was fading, a shadow of a moon just visible above the church tower before Euan slipped his arm through hers.

'Rest in peace,' he said, looking down.

'Rest in peace,' Rachel repeated.

And they started to walk away, Rachel pausing briefly to rearrange the flowers on Oliver's grave.

56

Brandon

Ed Nicholls was looking as grey as his prison-issue suit when Brandon swung into the chair beside him. His face said the game was up, even if his lips refused to acknowledge it.

Nicholls had been moping in the station cells for four days now. They'd got a court custody extension, but the clock was ticking. If they didn't get a conclusive bit of evidence soon, Nicholls would walk. Brandon was holding some revealing DNA data in his hands found on Benedict's Crombie – but it still wasn't enough to book him.

'See this piece of paper? It holds the key to your future.'

Ed swallowed but otherwise remained motionless, as if the merest movement would incriminate him. He was setting his stall out.

'You don't seem interested. I'm surprised – you don't strike me as being the most acquiescent of people. You've been demanding your rights and liberty since I wrestled you off that boat. Well, just so we don't waste any more of each other's time, let me fill you in, Ed. Your DNA matches samples taken from the bodies of both Sam Trenowden and Benedict Arscott-Rowe. Together with CCTV and phone video footage, we have scientific and visual evidence that you were in contact with them both on the days they died. Have you got anything to say for yourself, or do you want to save that for your court appearance?'

Brandon was sick and tired of Nicholls. Judging by the look on his lawyer's face, so was Jimmy.

But it was worth a few more jabs. There were a lot of things which didn't add up. Like why did he kill them? Benedict and Sam's drugs business was small – just two deliveries, the second one intercepted. There had to be more than that. Those canvases stacked in the St Malo warehouse. Where were they?

Ed shook his head. 'Sam was a friend of mine – we rubbed along together. Plenty of chances to exchange DNA.'

So, he does have a tongue.

'You didn't look too friendly in that CCTV carpark footage taken the morning he fell off a cliff. And he was wearing jogging gear. Not casual wear that you might rub up against in a crowded club.'

Brandon stood up. 'Those boxes you were offloading in the harbour – where are they? They're not at your place or NewlynWave. Where have you put them?'

'Just canned fish products from France – they sell well over here, particularly at festival time. All gone.'

'Oh yeah. Who sold you the goods? Name? Number?'

'I don't have them on me.'

'No – and yet you went to all that trouble to ship the *cans* over. You sure they weren't *can ...vases?*'

Brandon saw him flinch, just a little. He'd touched a nerve. His hunch could well be right. *Art theft.* There were huge sums to be made there. And Benedict had connections.

'Your DNA was on Benedict's clothing. On his coat – fatal mistake. Didn't you think to wear gloves? Or a hat to keep those incriminating hairs from shedding?'

Brandon moved round to the other side of the table until they were face-to-face. 'We have a witness sighting of you too. One of the agency waiters saw someone who fits your description hanging around by The Yacht Inn – a great vantage point for a quick excursion to The Arthouse. Just a few quick steps. Did you say hello, before stabbing Benedict in the chest?'

Ed looked at Jimmy. 'Do I have to answer any of this garbage?'

'No,' said Jimmy, stifling a yawn.

'Oh, but you will, Ed. At some point you will. You have no alibi for the evening of January 10 between seven and midnight. Your girlfriend, Meghan Bacall, was at the opening. You weren't. That, in itself, is surprising. You're usually her plus one. Why not at one of the swankiest arts nights of the year?'

'I had a headache,' Ed said blandly.

'I suggest you use that head of yours to come up with something more credible.' Brandon nodded at Jimmy. 'I'm done here for now. DS Menhenrick, any additional questions?'

Jo put down the notepad she'd been writing in. 'I'll just wait here for Ed to remember who the Fish Can guy is.'

Brandon grimaced. 'Reckon you'll be waiting a while, Jo. This interview is terminated, ten thirty am.'

He paused as Jo sealed the tapes.

'Let's have a word outside,' he said, giving her a quick look. They went out into the main station and sat on two of the chairs at the back. 'Why don't you go and have a chat with Meghan? Ask her about this supposed canned fish supplier. See how she responds.'

'I guess this lets Euan Tremayne off the hook?' Jo said, giving him a sideways glance.

'Pretty much so.' Brandon had his hands together, his elbows on his thighs as he stared ahead. 'Got that wrong, didn't I?'

'You were just keeping an open mind, remember.'

He gave a short, mirthless laugh and shook his head. 'I was

a little hasty, possibly, with my *open-minded* assumptions.'
He lounged back in his chair. 'He called in about an hour ago.
Said he was happy to answer any questions I might have.'

Their conversation was interrupted by the sound of a motorbike pulling up outside.

Jo gave Brandon a glance as the biker pushed open the
door and approached them.

'Yes?' Brandon said.

Euan took off his helmet. 'I believe you wanted to have a
chat with me.'

57

Rachel

'Mum, what's in these other boxes?' Rachel was FaceTiming Lizzie from the storeroom at Seabird Cottage. She was getting the new Lawrence Matthews paintings out for the expert Meghan had organised. Piers Jardine had known Lawrence back in the '70s and '80s, when they were both knocking about in Chelsea. His King's Road gallery was a magnet for the 'lions' of the day, including Peter Blake.

'What other boxes, darling?' Lizzie was in her bedroom getting ready for Piers. She'd already applied some wonky eye liner and bright pink lipstick.

Piers had been quite the charmer in his day. Rachel remembered him turning up at their place in a scarlet silk tie and electric blue suit, sweeping her off her feet and waltzing around the living room with her mother. Meghan couldn't have sourced a better expert. The champagne was already on ice awaiting his expected accreditation.

'Oh, don't bother, Mum. I'll open them up and look.'

She searched around for something to lever the lids off and spied a palette knife on the floor in the corner. The knife broke in two at the first attempt. She needed a tool – a chisel or the claw of a hammer.

No point asking Lizzie where the toolbox was. It had to be in the storeroom somewhere – wasn't that what storerooms were for?

The room was crammed to the rafters with boxes. *Why so many?* This was the first time Lizzie had let her in there. Her outburst the other day over *Porthchapel Cove. August 12, 2015* had won Rachel some leverage. Also, Lizzie was preoccupied and needed her to sort things for Piers – so she'd been allowed access to the Aladdin's Cave. But sadly, there was no genie to 'open sesame' the boxes.

There was a tower of six wooden boxes against one wall, positioned well away from the mess of paint pots and old brushes in mugs of turps. Hidden behind a giant roll of white paper was the tip of a step ladder. Rachel edged it out and set it up so she could feel around on the high shelf that ran along one side of the room. The first thing her hand touched was Lizzie's old sewing box – covered in dust and dirt, it didn't look like it had been used for decades. Next, she knocked against what felt like a pair of pliers and heard the tinkling of nails skittering on metal. *Getting warmer.* Picking up the pliers, she continued her search. Nothing.

'What are you doing up there?'

Rachel turned to see Lizzie in the doorway. 'Looking for a tool so I can open these boxes.'

'There are rather a lot of them.'

'You didn't know, Mum?'

'Meghan is such a madam. She asked if she could store a few things here – and she's taken over the room. Made it into a warehouse. I should charge her storage!'

'What's in the damn boxes?'

'I don't bloody know. I'm not a bloody detective! Meghan's been a treasure, helping me with Larry's paintings. I was returning a favour. There's a hammer under my bed, I'll get it.'

Lizzie was back with the hammer in minutes – looked as keen as Rachel to get the boxes open.

'Hurry, Rachel. Piers will be here soon.'

Rachel used the hammer claw on the box nearest to the

door. The nails were in tight, but with a bit of wiggling she managed to tug one out, which made the others easier to pull. She grabbed a piece of old curtain material on the floor and wrapped it round her left hand, which she used to steady the lid as she levered it off with the hammer claw in her right.

Lizzie clucked her approval. 'When did you become so handy?'

'It's a creeping condition – a symptom of severe poverty.' Rachel shook off the material and dipped her hand into a sea of shredded paper and foam chips.

'And?' Lizzie was by her side, peering in.

'Canvases.'

'No surprise there, then. No severed head?'

Rachel ignored her and reached down to pull one out. It was swaddled in multiple layers of bubble wrap and secured with duct tape.

'They've gone to an awful lot of trouble to protect these.'

'I'm not surprised,' Rachel said, peeling back the wrapping.

'Rachel! That looks very much like a Degas.'

'It can't be. Must be a reproduction.'

Lizzie pulled the wrapping right down to the floor to reveal a painting of two young ballerinas. 'If it is, it's a bloody good one. What else is in there?'

Rachel put the 'Degas' to one side and pulled out another canvas. Lizzie was on it in seconds.

'Sweetheart, get my sewing box down from the top shelf. There'll be scissors in there.'

Rachel scurried back up the steps. Lizzie was tearing the bubble wrap off with her hands before she'd got back down with the scissors.

'So exciting, Rachel!'

'We'll have to put all these back, though.'

'But not yet, eh, darling. Let's see what else is in there.'

Rachel cut into the covering of the second canvas. 'It looks like a Picasso Dove?'

'Boring!' Lizzie said, thrusting her hand in the box for the third canvas. 'Pablo churned those out – as common as gulls. He was practically his own forger! This one's smaller. What little gem do we have here? Give me the scissors, darling.'

Lizzie started to cut away at the plastic with care and precision. 'It's an old face.'

'Don't tell me – the Mona Lisa?'

Lizzie hooted with laughter. 'Rachel! Although it could be her daughter.'

'With a Pearl Earring?'

Lizzie hooted again. 'Oh, this is fun – it's like Christmas Day at the Tate. Open the next box.'

'What mischief are my lovely ladies up to today?'

Lizzie spun round. 'Piers! Darling – you're early. Naughty man.'

'I would say my timing is impeccable. What have you here?'

Rachel turned to face him. He was a little portlier, the flashy suit exchanged for pink chinos and khaki shirt, his hair a gossamer of snowy white. But he hadn't lost it. As debonair as ever.

'Piers. Lovely to see you.'

'And you, my dear. As ravishing as always – you look more like your lovely mother every day.'

'You'll make us blush, naughty Piers. Come here.' Lizzie flung open her arms and Piers pirouetted into them.

He turned to Rachel. 'I would swing you around the room, as I did when you were little. But …' He spread open his arms and looked around. 'No room to swing a cat. Oh my – what have you here? An annexe of the Guggenheim? I thought I was coming to authenticate Larry's work – not an entire wing of masterpieces?'

'It's a complete mystery to us too,' Lizzie said, pursing her lips and shaking her head. 'The Lawrence Matthews are in the studio.'

Piers' eyes were on the paintings in the room. 'Oh, I looked at those on the way in. Of course, they are his. They are unmistakeably Lawrence Matthews.'

'Told you.' Lizzie gave Rachel a triumphant look.

Can we have that in writing? Rachel kept the thought to herself. Didn't want to spoil the moment. Piers slipped on a pair of cotton gloves and descended on the ballerinas.

'This is quite a copy. It's remarkably good. Do you mind if I move it into the light?'

Lizzie nodded and Piers lifted it carefully, placing it on one of the unopened boxes by the door where it basked in a spotlight of winter sun.

'Incredible. This is a carbon copy of *Dancers With Yellow Dresses*. Even the signature. Let me see the others.'

He went through the three of them. 'If they weren't all so good, I would say these had to be forgeries. But the styles are so different – and each one so like the original. The colours, tone, materials, the aging. These are either the work of a master forger, or the work of a master thief. Where, may I ask, did you ladies get them?'

'Meghan,' Lizzie blurted out. 'She delivered them a few days back – asked me to look after them for a short while.'

'Interesting.'

'We didn't know what was in the box until ten minutes ago. We've only opened one.'

Piers rubbed his hands together. 'May I suggest we open another?'

By the time they'd gone through the third box it had become obvious what was inside the others.

'Well?' Rachel said as she watched Piers stroke the side of his nose and appraise what looked like a Chagall.

'Well, indeed. I think Miss Bacall has some explaining to do. Much as it pains me to say it, this looks very much like a haul of stolen art. I did hear some works disappeared off a yacht in St Tropez last month. A Degas and Picasso among them. And there have been rumours of items going missing in Le Freeport – the arts storage house in Luxembourg.'

Lizzie shook her head. 'But Meghan? There must be some mistake.'

Piers looked at Rachel. 'I'm just saying what it looks like.'

'And she's storing them here?' Lizzie was shaking. 'Rachel, phone her. Make her explain. Make her get that bloke of hers round here to pick them up.'

'Ed? He's in custody.'

Lizzie gave a strangled yelp. 'I need to sit down. Can we just leave this for now? Open that bottle chilling in the fridge. If I see one more famous portrait peep out from a box, I will scream.'

She looked frightened. 'Am I going mad, Rachel? Am I going mad? Is this real?'

Rachel sighed. 'This madness is real. What looked like forgeries now look like real masters. It's crazy. But it's real crazy.' She put an arm around her mother, leading her out of the storeroom and back to the house.

'What I don't understand,' Piers said, pouring them all a glass of champagne in the kitchen. 'Is why Meghan would store these paintings here? And in a garden shed. So unprofessional.'

'Desperate measures,' Rachel said, refusing the champagne.

She remembered the boxes Ed had been offloading in the harbour and the canvases in the St Malo warehouse, behind Benedict. 'Look, why don't you sit and enjoy your drinks and let me see if Meghan has an explanation?'

Piers raised an eyebrow. 'She was just looking after them for the Beckhams while they renovated their new Cornish home?'

'They could be forgeries, Piers. With all respect – some forgers are very good,' Rachel countered.

Lizzie spluttered into her glass.

Rachel got out her phone and tapped Meghan's number.

'She's not picking up her mobile.' She scrolled down for her landline. The call went straight to answer machine. 'She's not answering the gallery landline either,' Rachel said, turning to Lizzie. 'Odd. But it's been a tough time for her … with Ed in custody. I'll drop in at Newlyn Wave.'

'What's he in for?' Piers put down his glass, watching Rachel closely.

'Murder,' Rachel said as she went to leave.

'I think I'll just have that other glass of champagne,' Piers said, reaching for it and taking a gulp. 'Be careful, Rachel.'

'Call Brandon, darling.' Lizzie had got up and placed a hand on her arm. 'This isn't something you need to get involved in.'

'I did text him and put a call through to the station. He can't be disturbed. He's interviewing.'

'Well … don't get into any arguments with Meghan. She'll get the better of you.'

'Ye of little faith, Mum.'

'Take my hammer.'

'Mum!'

Piers guffawed. 'We don't want another murder in

Penzance, Lizzie.'

'It's not a laughing matter, Piers. This is my daughter – and she is putting herself in peril.'

'This is Meghan, Mum. Not some crazed psycho.' She regarded Lizzie, who was bristling with anger and fear. 'But I will be careful.'

As she went to leave, Lizzie picked up a stainless-steel cake slice from the kitchen work surface, ran a finger along its cutting edge, and slipped it in Rachel's rucksack. 'It's just a cake slice,' she said. 'And only use it if need be.'

58

Rachel

Meghan was locking up the gallery when Rachel drew up in her car.

Rachel rolled down the window. 'Closing early?'

'Yes. I can't concentrate at the moment. Too much on with all this business. Were you just passing?'

'I came to see you. Have you got a moment?'

Meghan folded her arms and considered. 'Why don't you park your car and come in? I'll put the kettle on.'

There were two mugs of coffee on the till desk when Rachel opened the door five minutes later. Meghan gestured for Rachel to sit at a chair on the other side of the desk.

'Is milk, no sugar okay for you?' She edged the mug towards Rachel.

'Fine. But I've just had one, thank you.'

'Are you sure?' She dimmed her full-beam smile, just enough to blow into her own coffee.

Rachel took the mug but didn't drink from it. She didn't expect to be in the gallery long – it wouldn't be rude to leave it on the table after a few minutes.

Meghan got to her feet. 'I forgot the biscuits.' She smiled at Rachel over her shoulder as she went to the storeroom.

Rachel picked up the mug and poured half of its contents into the pot plant by her chair. There was something of the Poison Ivy about Meghan today.

Meghan came back into the room with a big tin of biscuits, a plate balancing on the top with some hobnobs on it. Rachel waved the plate away as Meghan tried to push it on her.

'My, but you're disciplined today,' Meghan said, picking one up and putting it by her mug.

'Meghan, why have you stored six boxes of masterpiece reproductions at Lizzie's? I take it they are reproductions?'

Meghan's face fell, and then her smile cranked back into place. 'No room here, as you can see.'

'Where did you get them from?'

'Why do you want to know?'

'Because Piers Jardine thinks they are stolen masterpieces and you're storing them at my mum's.'

Meghan snorted a small laugh. 'And you believe that two-bit *expert*?'

Rachel looked at her, admired her bluff and nerve. 'You provided this *expert*.'

Meghan stared her straight in the eye. 'At great potential cost to my own reputation. Who else would authenticate Lizzie's forgeries?'

'What? Are you accusing my mother of forging her own husband's works?'

Meghan rolled her eyes. 'I caught her at it. When I went to collect the only *authentic* Lawrence Matthews you have – at least I assume it's authentic – for The Arthouse opening, I came across Lizzie putting the finishing touches to *Browned Off.*'

'I don't believe you.'

Meghan glanced down at her manicured red nails. 'I could pick up the phone now and call in any number of experts to back up my claim. Now, if there isn't anything else I can help you with?'

Meghan was on her feet as Rachel's phone started to ring. It was Brandon.

'Yes,' Rachel said, looking at Meghan, before turning away.

'Rachel, where are you?'

'I'm at NewlynWave with Meghan.'

'Okay. Keep her talking. Keep things light. I'll bring the car now. Don't worry. But be very careful – Jo called round there earlier. Tripped her up on a story Ed had fabricated about what was in those boxes he was offloading at the harbour.'

Rachel let out a small gasp. She could feel Meghan's eyes on her back.

'Rachel?' He sounded concerned.

She forced a smile into the phone. 'Lovely to hear from you. You want to meet up? Yep – sounds good. There's this brilliant crime box set we could see. It's at Lizzie's right now.'

'Okay,' he said. 'I understand. Just keep her happy for now – we'll be over asap. Take care.'

'Was that your boyfriend?' The colour was draining from Meghan's face, a fine sheen of sweat creating a pallor, smooth as alabaster.

'It was, as a matter of a fact.' Rachel's lips twitched into a semblance of what she hoped was a wistful smile. Meghan wasn't smiling.

'Things have been moving so fast. You know what's it's like. And so … we've moved onto takeaway suppers and box sets. We're practically a boring stay-at-home, doze on the sofa couple.' She was rambling. Her voice shaking.

Meghan sighed, a small spot of red appearing at her temple. 'How nice for you,' she said, trailing her fingertips along the edge of the biscuit tin lid. Curling them below its rim she pulled the lid off, letting it slide from the table and crash to the floor.

Rachel went to pick it up.

'Leave it.' Meghan's hands were gripping the tin.

Rachel edged forward on her chair. 'I will have a biscuit after all. What have you got in there for me?'

'This.' Meghan plunged her hand into the tin and pulled out a small handgun, aiming it directly at Rachel's chest.

Rachel rocked back on her chair. 'You are joking?' Her heart was pounding.

'No, Rachel. I'm not joking.'

'The police will be here in minutes. I don't think it will do you any favours if they see that in your hands. Put it away, Meghan.' She sounded calm. But her reflection in the glass cabinet opposite told a different story.

Meghan's expression looked sinister in its new alabaster cast. 'So, the police – your boyfriend – are on their way.'

She leapt up, knocking her chair backwards against the wall.

'Get up.' She was at Rachel's side, gun at her head, her other hand deftly jerking the door open. 'We're going to Seabird Cottage.'

59

Brandon

Brandon pulled up, just out of sight of the gallery. No need to alert Meghan. He felt the taser in his holster – just a precaution. Surely it wouldn't come to that? But he'd learnt early on to be prepared for all eventualities.

He nodded to Jo to stay put as he walked the few metres to the gallery. It looked empty. He expected the door to be locked, but it opened with a jerk of the handle. She hadn't locked up. Must have left in a hurry.

'Anyone there?' Brandon said, walking into the room and looking around. He pushed open the storeroom door. Empty.

'Hello?' Jo had followed him.

'They've gone.' Brandon ran a hand through his hair.

'Can't have gone far. She doesn't have a car. We've got the keys to Ed's.'

'The Fiat,' Brandon said, looking past Jo to the street beyond. 'Rachel would have driven here. Jo, put out an alert – white Fiat 500, Reg OV58 CHF or something like that. See what you can find.'

Jo got out her mobile. 'I'll call MCIT at Newquay. Use their database. But where do you think they've gone? Any ideas?'

Brandon brushed a hand across his mouth. 'Lizzie's? Maybe not. Too obvious. Although … Phillips might know something. It wouldn't do him any harm to share with us.'

Phillips, under investigation for his role in Benedict and Sam's ops, was being held at Newquay nick. Brandon gave Jo a pained look as they waited, impatiently, for their calls to be directed to the relevant Newquay departments.

It took a while for Phillips to get to the phone. Brandon could hear him lumbering towards the landline they kept in the Newquay investigations room. A rattle and clunk indicated the cuffs were being removed.

'Morning, Boss.'

'Meghan's gone AWOL. Where'd you think she's gone, Phil?' Brandon was rapping his fingers on the gallery cash counter, his head down, teeth gritted, willing him to come up with something.

'Eh, let me think.'

Brandon could hear him blowing out, could imagine his face billowing.

'Come on, Phil. Where would Meghan go? What contacts would she use? Transport – does she have access to another car? Anything at all? Come on. Think. Hard.'

There was just the sound of him breathing down the phone.

And then. 'The airport. Newquay. Sometimes they mixed things up a bit. Dunno why. Maybe a different operator, or they just wanted to make the shipments harder to trace. Anyway, they used an Aviat Husky, usually for smaller loads.'

Brandon threw back his head. 'That it?'

'Well, yes, Brandon. You've got the keys to Ed's car and the boat. Don't remember them having a copter.'

'Okay. Thanks, Phil. If anything else occurs, call me.'

Jo was on him in seconds. 'Rachel's Fiat – Reg OV58 CFH – I've put out an alert to the A30 and surrounds and Newquay Airport.'

'Brilliant. Thanks, Jo.'

Brandon was rushing to the door, feeling for his car keys.

'Where we going, Boss?'

'Seabird Cottage – just a hunch. And then onto Newquay Airport.'

60

Rachel

Rachel had walked up the path of Seabird Cottage many times in the past two and a half months, but never with a gun at her back. Although there'd occasionally been a metaphorical one to her head. She'd heard sirens as they'd driven out of Newlyn and onto New Road. They were minutes too late. Would Brandon guess where they'd gone? Surely, he would send someone to Seabird Cottage? If only to protect the artwork.

It was as if Meghan had read her mind. She pushed her hard with one hand, the other holding the gun to her neck. 'Move it.'

'Rachel, is that you?' Lizzie had appeared at the door with a glass of champagne as Meghan was frog marching Rachel round to the shed.

'Get back inside.' Meghan turned her frosty stare on Lizzie. 'Both of you,' she added as Piers came into view.

She shoved Rachel hard enough to knock her to the floor of the porch.

'Get up.' She grabbed hold of the cow bell rope hanging by the door and thrust it at Rachel. 'Use this to tie them up. Make it quick.' Her eyes were flitting around, and she jumped at the sound of a car passing at the end of the lane.

'Leave that!' Lizzie went to grab the rope, but Meghan moved forward – a warship forcing a small vessel back to port.

Lizzie was whimpering by the sofa as Rachel approached her with the rope. Meghan moved around her, poked her head in the kitchen and then in the living room, her eyes settling on the massive metal wood burner.

'Tie them face to face around the burner,' Meghan said. 'And, if you don't shut up, Lizzie, I'll light the wood.'

The wood burner was probably the only substantial thing in the house. *So good call, Meghan.*

'Meghan, be reasonable. Just take the paintings and go. We won't say a word. How long have you known me?' Piers was charm-bombing her.

'Long enough to know you're a self-serving snake.'

'Outrageous!' screeched Lizzie, lunging at her.

Piers pulled her back. 'Let her have her fun, darling. We can stand a few hours in each other's company, can't we?' He smiled nervously at Lizzie, who looked at Rachel.

'For God's sake, Mum, just do as she says.'

Lizzie was using her eyes to indicate where the hammer was resting behind the sofa. Rachel gave a quick, small nod, as much to calm her as anything. She'd take her time tying them up – it shouldn't be too long, surely, before the cavalry arrived. Rachel's mind was racing – Brandon would be working out right now where they'd gone. Meghan looked like she was making similar assumptions. She was getting increasingly agitated, the colour returning to her face.

'Hurry up. Hurry the fuck up.' She waved the gun at Rachel, her eyes roaming the room.

'What the fuck?' She stood back, her lips parted, noticing, for the first time, the masterpieces that Lizzie and Piers had propped up around the place. A fractured Picasso head peered down at them from the mantelpiece. Next to it a sobbing Lichtenstein blonde summed up their predicament.

'Looks like you were having some fun in here,' Meghan said, a ghost of a smile on her lips.

'*Were* is the operative word!' hissed Lizzie. 'Careful,' she added, as Rachel circled the rope around her wrists, linked it to Piers and tied them to the wood burner.

Meghan came over to check. 'Tighter.'

'If you tie us any tighter we'll have our faces slammed up against the steel; we won't be able to breathe.' Piers's face was scarlet.

'Best save your breath, then.' Meghan cocked the gun and pointed it at him.

'Excuse me?'

She pulled the trigger, letting rip a bullet, which caught the side of Pier's ear before tearing a hole in the Picasso head behind him. Piers screamed, his teeth smashing against the burner. Lizzie jolted, her own lips hitting the steel.

Rachel gasped, her hand involuntarily reaching out to Piers, as blood spurted from his ear, and streamed down the side of his face.

Meghan tutted and pushed the gun into Rachel's back. 'I said tighter. This isn't a game of *peek-a-boo*.'

Rachel pulled at the rope. Pulled so hard it cut into Lizzie's thin wrists, making her yelp. Piers, eyes closed, chin up, was biting into his top lip, the blood running from his wound.

'Can I just get something for him? To stem the blood?' Rachel said, looking over her shoulder at Meghan, as she finished tying Piers to the burner.

'No.' Meghan picked up some discarded duct tape from the floor and threw it at Rachel. 'Gag them.'

Rachel tore at the tape with her teeth and quickly gagged the two of them, putting a bit on Pier's wound. It was a botched job, but Meghan, her attention wavering, didn't notice.

She poked Rachel between the shoulder blades with the

gun. 'To the storeroom.'

'If you want me to open another box, I'll need a hammer,' Rachel said, as Meghan shoved her towards the front door.

'Nice try, Rachel. But I'll shoot the lid off if need be.'

There was just one box left unopened. Lizzie and Piers had clearly tried to open it as the lid was partially off. Meghan studied it and then leant down and took off one stilettoed kitten heel. 'Use this, but don't break it. Don't fucking break it.'

'Hurry!' Meghan had the gun pointed at her head.

Sweat poured down Rachel's neck. It was like trying to defuse a ticking bomb. Meghan was breathing heavily, pacing back and forth behind her.

'Come on,' she said. 'Come on. Then we're out of here.'

To where, thought Rachel, as she put down the shoe and started using her bare hands to wrench the lid off.

'For pity's sake,' Meghan said, cocking the gun and aiming it at the nails clinging stubbornly to the lid.

'I've got this. Don't fire!'

Rachel swung round to see Meghan taking aim like a punter shooting ducks at the fairground. One, two, three bullets ricocheted off the nails.

It did the trick. The shots loosened the nails and Rachel tugged off the lid.

Meghan pushed her aside, shoving a hand into the box as if it was a lucky dip.

'Take these,' she said, thrusting three average-size, bubble-wrapped canvases at her. She tucked another two under her arm.

'Don't you want to see what they are?' Rachel asked, as Meghan prodded her in the neck with the gun.

'No. They're just paper money – big, fat cheques. And if you want to survive, Rachel, you don't want to know what they are either. Why do you think I didn't just grab the Degas by the sofa? Get them in the car.'

Where were the police? Where was Brandon?

'Here's the keys, then. Take the car,' Rachel said after they'd packed the canvases in the boot and back of the Fiat.

Meghan leaned back, hands on hips. 'Do you think I'm stupid? Get in and drive.'

Rachel's heart lurched at the sound of a car at the bottom of the lane – and then the engine noise tailed off.

'Where to?' *When is this nightmare going to end?*

'Newquay.'

'Why?' She was playing for time now.

'Just get me on the A30.'

Meghan got in beside her, the gun trained on her heart. She was fussing around with the seat belt with her other hand. 'Does this work?'

'No.'

'For Chrissake!'

'I'm an impoverished artist. I have an old car.'

'So, you're an artist again now?' Meghan gave her a long cold stare. 'But this seat belt – it's illegal.'

And art theft isn't?

Rachel spun the little car around and headed off down the lane. Still no sign of Brandon. She didn't have her phone – Meghan had made her drop it in a bin. How would they track her down without her phone?

'Get a bloody move on.' Meghan was getting agitated again. Then her phone rang. 'Thank God! You're there already? Yes, I have them. Not all, but enough. I'll text you when we're ten minutes off. Make sure you're ready for take-off.'

Rachel gave her a side eye. Meghan's telephone smile froze. 'What are you staring at?'

'Nothing,' Rachel said, although she had caught something in her peripheral vision. A dot on the horizon, a man on a motorbike. *The Euan in Black?*

'Get a fucking move on.' Meghan shoved the barrel into her ribs, making Rachel jerk and jump a red light. 'Don't draw attention to us!'

In the mirror she could see the biker held at the lights; she took her foot off the accelerator slightly. There was traffic leading onto the A30 and Euan, if it was him, should be able to weave through it and catch them up.

As she took the third exit on the roundabout to the A30 she could see him approaching it. Just keep your head, thought Rachel, her heart racing.

Meghan was sitting forward on the passenger seat, rocking gently, the gun not visible to fellow travellers.

The biker was gaining ground, not getting too close, but she could now see it was Euan on his Triumph. Black helmet, black bike with chrome gas tank. He was tracking her.

Her hands were sweating, slipping on the steering wheel. She was going to have to do something. What if Euan pulled them over? Did something reckless? Meghan would kill him.

'How far to the A3059?'

I'm not a frigging SatNav. 'I think the turning is soon,' Rachel lied. As she spoke, she saw Euan pass on the bike. Except it wasn't Euan. It wasn't even a Triumph. *Shit!* She was going to end up in the clutches of some violent criminal. They'd never let her live. Maybe Meghan would make her drive the car into the sea at Newquay to hide the evidence. Or just shoot her, take off the handbrake, and push the car in. Once they'd got the paintings out, of course. She had to do something. Pick her time. Surely Meghan couldn't stay focused for the next twenty or so minutes it would take to get to Newquay?

'Why are you moving into the slow lane? Get back over!' Meghan missed nothing.

'Just getting in lane for the next roundabout.'

Meghan grunted and gave her a nudge with the gun barrel, her eyes tearing into her. Rachel moved into the inside lane as they approached the next roundabout – hoped she wouldn't notice they were going straight on.

'Thought we were taking the first exit?'

'Sorry, next one.'

Those heavily made-up eyes were still trained on her. As was the gun. Otherwise, she would have noticed the Skoda that had been following them for a few minutes. A blue light wasn't spinning, the car wasn't speeding – just cruising in the slow lane – but Rachel felt a surge of hope. It looked like Brandon's unmarked police car.

Rachel jacked up the speed to 80 miles an hour, all the while watching the Skoda. It moved to the fast lane, keeping pace. It was him. It had to be Brandon. Rachel took a deep breath and moved back into the slow lane. The car followed suit.

Meghan's eyes were on her.

Rachel made a stab at deflecting her suspicions. 'Nearly in Newquay. Where do you want to be dropped?'

Meghan said nothing for a beat. 'Airport.'

'Okay. I noticed a sign a short while back. We need to take the next exit. Should be there in around ten minutes.'

Meghan nodded and fumbled for something. Rachel figured it would be her phone. She'd want to text the person she was meeting at the airport.

The Skoda, still following in the slow lane, was gaining on them. Now was the time. She waited until the traffic thinned and dropped down to 40 miles an hour. Meghan's eyes flitted up before returning to her phone.

The Skoda slowed behind. Rachel took a breath and tugged the steering wheel down hard to the left, spinning them onto a layby. Slamming on the brakes, she sent Meghan crashing into the glove compartment.

Yanking up the handbrake, Rachel leapt on Meghan, her hand reaching for the gun that had been tossed to the floor.

'What are you doing!' Meghan yelled. She was dazed but still dangerous, her arms flailing, her free hand desperate to get the gun which had slid just out of reach. Rachel couldn't get to it either, but remembered the cake slice Lizzie had put in her rucksack. She clambered over Meghan to reach the bag on the back seat, pressing one knee into her groin. Grabbing the bag's strap, she yanked it over the seat and shoved it in Meghan's face.

'Shut the hell up!' Rachel pulled out the slicer and pushed it up under Meghan's chin.

She was breathing hard, adrenaline pumping through her, every muscle tense.

And then she felt Meghan go limp beneath her. *Shit! I've killed her?*

'Put the weapons down and get out of the car. Slowly. Hands above your head.'

Rachel looked over her shoulder, one hand gripping the slicer, the other pinning Meghan down. She wasn't ready to relinquish this advantage yet.

'I'll take over now, Rachel. It's okay. It's done.'

'Brandon, there's a gun on the floor. In the corner. I'm not giving up this cake slice until you have it.'

He opened the passenger door and picked up the gun. 'I've got it, Rachel. Does she have any other weapons on her?'

'You're going to have to pat me down and find out for yourself, Detective Inspector.' Meghan was reverting to type – bouncing back like an inflatable doll as Rachel moved off her.

Rachel edged over to the driver's seat. Jo was standing by the door, taser in hand.

Rachel turned back to Brandon. 'I'll leave this *charming* lady in your capable hands.' She couldn't smile. She could barely speak; her lips were trembling, her whole body shaking.

Brandon reached over and stroked her hair. 'Go and sit in the car with Jo, honey. I'll finish up here.'

61

Brandon

Brandon was sitting in the back of the Skoda with Meghan, Stew at the wheel. He'd packed Rachel off home with Jo. She was all in. She'd broken all the rules in the book, pulling Meghan in. But, hey, who was Brandon to notice. He could be mighty unobservant at times. All the same, he'd insisted Jo drive the Fiat and Rachel sit in the back, with the one other seat belt that worked.

Since he'd read Meghan her rights her face had been like thunder. It had taken both himself and Stew to cuff her and get her in the Skoda. He thought she was going to make a dash across the dual carriageway at one point. They sat in silence, Meghan's face turned to the window.

He wondered what plans she was hatching. She didn't have a lot of options.

'Brandon,' she said at last. 'Tell me how I can help. I've been a fool. I've let men manipulate me all my life … and look where it's got me?'

Brandon shuffled round to face her. 'You can start by telling me the name of this manipulating cad you're meeting at Newquay Airport. We'll be there in five minutes. I'd like to know who we'll be arresting.'

'Henri Chabrol.'

'Aha, and what does Monsieur Chabrol do, apart from traffic stolen artwork?'

'Well,' Meghan said, lifting her handcuffed hands and then letting them fall back into her lap. 'He's an art dealer. The…

transference of artworks of high value is a side-line.'

'A lucrative one. How did you meet Chabrol?'

Meghan turned to face him, a triumphant smile on her lips. 'Benedict. I'm surprised he hadn't mentioned him to you.'

Brandon glanced down at her feet – noticed the kitten heels. 'We weren't *that* close. Clearly, there were a lot of things he didn't tell me. And Trenowden? Did Sam know Chabrol too?'

'Yes, it was their gig, I was on the margins. They used me – and the gallery – to offload the goods.'

'Oh yeah? Who to?'

'Shady guys. Never the collectors or the tax evaders the paintings were going to. I didn't ask too many questions. It was best not to.'

'Where did they get the paintings?'

Meghan paused before continuing. 'Shouldn't you be torturing me to get all this information, Brandon?'

He smiled. 'Leave the silent treatment to Ed. You're a much smarter cookie, Meghan. If you make my job easier, then your life will be easier. I'm not going to lie to you, you will do time for this. But your cooperation now will influence how much, and under what conditions. Charm me, Meghan.'

'I'll do my best.'

'Did Ed kill Sam and Benedict?'

An ambulance flashed past in the fast lane, sirens blaring.

'Yes,' he thought he heard Meghan say.

'Did you just say "yes"?' Brandon knew he would have to get this in a formal recorded statement, but it was a crucial development.

'Yes.' Meghan was looking out of the window again.

'Why?'

She sighed. 'So many reasons. They were being greedy, using us and the gallery to launder money. Ed and Pat were shipping the canvases in from St Malo – were nearly intercepted a few times. We were taking huge risks for small margins. And Benedict was getting reckless, moving into drugs, dragging us into serious danger. He'd been played by some Mr Big in Marseille. Someone who wanted a mule to take the heat off his own ops. And.' She turned to look at Brandon. 'I knew the arts business better than him for all his *qualifications and breeding*. And I'd gotten to know his contacts. They preferred me. They could see Benedict was losing it.'

'Henri Chabrol?'

'Of course … and others.'

They were nearing the airport. 'Were you and Benedict lovers?'

Meghan scoffed. 'Some people might have called us that.'

'Did he take you on trips to meet these contacts?'

'Yes – the fool. It was his undoing. That and the sex, drugs, and alcohol.'

Stew was indicating right – they were about to arrive at Newquay Airport.

'Did Ed know? Did Ed approve of this relationship?'

Meghan sucked in her bottom lip. 'Yes, Ed knew and no. No, he didn't approve.'

'Did you ask Ed to kill Benedict?'

Meghan turned to him, her eyes filling with tears. 'No. Ed was insane with jealousy. And disgust. He couldn't understand how I could tolerate Benedict. Thought I should just side-line him. Dump him. But I couldn't. Benedict was being sticky. Wouldn't budge. Thought he was still the main man.' She wiped her eyes, careful not to smudge her mascara. 'I think I've told you enough for now, don't you?'

Brandon fell back in his seat. 'For now.'

He gathered his thoughts before continuing. Stew was

steering the Skoda into the small airport carpark. Brandon noticed there were quite a few parked cars. Looked like police.

He leant forward, his arms on his thighs. 'Meghan, you've always been a great salesperson. You've got some valuable information here on what looks like a multi-million-euro operation. We'll see how much it's worth to Interpol. Now, I'm going to undo your handcuffs. Don't make a run for it. The airport is on red alert and will swarm with cops if you make a wrong move. Just be your own sweet self – engage Chabrol and we'll do the rest.'

'Brandon, thank you.'

'There's nothing to thank me for, Meghan. Let's just make this as easy as possible, eh?' He gave her a carrier bag with two of the canvases as a prop.

Brandon watched from the car as Meghan strode over the tarmac to meet Henri Chabrol. After the first flurry of kisses, Meghan slipped her arm under his, glancing over her shoulder as they walked towards the small, light aircraft. Six undercover cops were on them in seconds, pinning Chabrol to the ground and cuffing Meghan. His next conversation with her would have to wait a while longer.

62

Rachel

Rachel asked Jo to go to the bin outside Warrens bakery before dropping her off at Lizzie's. Her phone was still there – but Rachel's arm was elbow deep in rubbish before she found it.

'Thanks, Jo,' Rachel said when she'd dropped her off at Seabird Cottage. That metaphorical gun was at her head as she walked up the garden path. What sort of state would Lizzie be in? She could barely cope herself.

The cow bell ringer was gone, so Rachel walked round the back – it was usually open. She'd have to have a word with Lizzie. In fact, she'd had words with her about this. They just didn't sink in.

'Mum?'

'Rachel?' Lizzie was on the sofa holding the hand of a policewoman with the pleasant face of a counsellor.

'This is PC Fredericks. Emily, I believe. She has been …' Lizzie started to cry. 'So, kind.'

'Thank you, PC Fredericks,' Rachel said, shaking her hand as she got up from the sofa. 'Is Mr Jardine, okay?'

'He's at the hospital, darling,' Lizzie said. 'Nothing too serious. Loss of blood and shock. He wanted to stay until you returned. But I shooed him off. I'm fine now. As soon as Brandon called and told me you were okay and said that awful woman had been … apprehended … I was fine.'

'Well, that makes the one of us, then.' Rachel sunk into the sofa.

'Would you like me to stay?' PC Fredericks looked concerned.

'No. I'll be okay – just need some time to process this. The adrenaline slump has left me shattered.'

'I'll get you a cup of tea.' Lizzie was smiling at her. 'Thank you, Emily,' she said, showing her to the door.

It was dark when Rachel woke up on the sofa, a blanket half over her, a scented candle burning in the corner by the window. She checked her phone – for the time and to see if she'd missed anything. There was a slew of messages – several from Euan, three from Julia and one from Brandon.

She clicked on his first. 'Lizzie said you're taking a nap. You deserve it. I'm so proud of you. It's a wrap, you know. All over. Speak soon. Bxx.'

'Where are you? So worried!' Rachel deleted Julia's. They'd stopped coming through four hours ago. Someone must have tipped her off.

'I need to see you,' read Euan's.

'Where are you? Call me. Ex.' He hadn't put his usual full stop between his initial and kiss. *Was this significant?* Rachel keyed a reply.

* * * * *

She heard his motorbike pull up outside the cottage around ten minutes later. She couldn't leave Lizzie tonight. She was sleeping peacefully in her bedroom – unusual for her. Maybe she'd taken a sedative? Or maybe she felt safer with Rachel there.

'Hi,' Euan said as she opened the front door. 'Is Lizzie asleep?'

'Yes, best be quiet.'

Euan followed her into the main room – stood there looking uncertain.

'Everything okay?' Rachel pulled him down on the sofa beside her.

'Compared to your day, I'd say yes.'

Rachel rolled her eyes. 'I'm over it already. It's just great to get some sort of closure. This has been dragging on as long as Brexit.'

Euan smiled. 'Well, I may have to disagree with you there.'

'What's new? Everyone disagrees on Brexit.' Rachel drew her legs up onto the sofa. 'Well, this has been going on longer than it took you to create Brexitannia.'

'Three weeks and four days – that's when I pitched up for the Montol. But funny you should mention Brexitannia.' He took her hands.

'Hmm?'

'I've brought a bottle of *Screaming Eagle* with me – from The Hall cellar. Julia insisted. She said you'd need a drink after a day like today.'

'Bless her. Although that nap has done me the power of good.' Rachel pulled her knees up to her chest as she watched Euan open the bottle. 'I'll get some glasses,' she said, snapping into action and going into the kitchen.

'So, *funny you mentioned Brexitannia?*' Rachel placed two glasses on the retro coffee table and poured the wine. 'Are you running off and leaving me for Julia?'

Euan laughed and picked up his glass. 'No.'

'Just checking.' She snuggled up to him and he drew her close.

Euan took a drink of wine before breaking the silence. 'I got a call this afternoon from Bridget Sargent of Shoreditch Studios. She's asked me to join her Neo-Constructivism project. Wants me to be part of the studios – maybe even work on something for the Trafalgar Square Fourth Plinth.'

'Gosh!' *Bloody hell.*

Rachel turned to face him. 'That really is something, Euan. Bridget Sargent is legend and so precious about her artists. You would be joining a national – international – artists' elite.'

She gave him a searching look.

Euan looked straight ahead, his eyes on the space where the Lawrence Matthews painting had been. 'If I join.'

Rachel gently nudged his face towards her. 'There is no if. You've got to join, Euan. This is the opportunity of a lifetime.'

He took her hands and looked her in the eye. 'Will you come with me?'

'I don't think my work will appeal to the Neo-Constructivism movement.'

'You know what I mean. Will you come with me – we could find a place with a studio. You could work there too. You've already started to paint again.'

Rachel squeezed his hands. 'I can't, can I? Lizzie needs me. Julia needs me. I've only just got used to the idea of living around here again – painting again. I can't go back to London right now.'

'Well, I –'

Rachel interrupted him. 'Don't you even dare say you won't go. You must. This is so important – for you, for art.'

Euan looked down and gave a short laugh. 'I think art will manage without me, somehow.'

'Go. If you don't you will regret it for the rest of your life.'

'But if I leave, I will regret it straightaway.'

Rachel moved closer, resting her legs against his. 'I'll still be here – and I'll visit. Just try and stop me.'

'Rachel.' He took her in his arms and kissed her. 'What we

had, have, is so special.'

'Yes. But it's not going to disappear if you go to London for a time. Moments of Love last forever. Remember?'

'I'll never forget.' He smiled and brushed a strand of hair from her forehead.

'And we'll talk often. Skype. None of that "should have, would have" stuff.' She paused before saying, almost whispering: 'When will you go?'

'They want me to start as soon as possible. Next week.' Euan tilted her chin so he could look into her eyes.

'Okay.' She felt a shift in the atmosphere, as if a cloud had edged into view.

'The irony is, that wretched manhunt – which made the nationals – is what caught their attention.'

'They say all publicity is good publicity. And you did say you were going to be the next *enfant terrible*.' Her remark was flippant, but she didn't feel it.

'Be careful what you wish for,' Euan said, drawing away.

'But this must be a dream come true for you, surely? Fame. Or at least the promise of it.' Rachel paused. 'What you told the reporter ... about the montages being an opportunity to package the past. That you'd spent too long observing. That it was time to ... live. Surely you don't want to go back to photographing weddings and bar mitzvahs?'

Euan sighed. 'Of course, I'm happy with how things have turned out for me. But Rachel, I want you to be a part of this. I thought, possibly, we could be ... a family. I know how hard it's been for you. For me too. But we're still young, we could start again. Try again.' He turned to her; the insouciant guard he often wore gone.

Rachel got up from the sofa and started to pace. 'No, Euan. Not now. Can't you see this would be the worse time? I feel

I've only just got my feet back on firm ground. I can't think about … having a baby. I'm not sure if I could ever think about more children.'

Euan sprang to his feet, grabbed her by the shoulders to stop her pacing. 'Why not? Why must you always pull away? You did it in Falmouth. You're doing it now. We've been so happy – why ruin it? What are you scared of?'

Rachel drew away, catching the irony in her action. 'Scared? Sure, I'm scared. I'm scared of being a bad parent. I'm scared of losing another child.'

'You were a good parent.'

'But I still lost a child, so it doesn't matter does it. I can't live with that fear. I've just learnt to live with the loss. You must understand that?'

He gave a slight shake of the head. 'Yes. I understand. But I don't understand how you can live with the loss of … us.'

Rachel turned to him. 'How can you say that? Do you really understand?'

He looked down and then jerked his head back up to face her. 'I'm not looking to replace Oliver. I was just trying to … Oh, what's the point.' He dropped the arm reaching out to her but kept eye contact. 'Trying too hard? Isn't that what you say when I just try to please you? Trying too fucking hard. Well, have it your way. Beat yourself up. Punish yourself – you have a talent for it.'

Rachel slumped back down on the sofa. 'This isn't going anywhere. We're both tired. I can't think about this now.'

'Okay, but when would be a good time? Will there ever be a good time? He was my son too, Rachel. I feel the loss as well.'

Rachel picked up her glass. 'I'm sorry.'

'Sorry for my loss?' He stared down at her. 'I don't need

platitudes.'

'Well, that's all I can give you. Right now, that's all I have.'

Euan moved to the window; the candle casting shadows on his turned back.

'Look,' she said after a while. 'We're going to create a space at The Arthouse called the Oliver Matthews Gallery. It will feature work by young artists – have links with Falmouth. Julia and I will run workshops for kids.'

He was staring through the crack in the curtains into the dark. 'Well, that will keep you busy. Give you solace. Was it Lizzie's idea?'

Rachel shook her head. There was no getting through to him.

'I'm not ready for all this.'

'Ready?' He turned round and stepped out of the shadows.

'Do you think I'm ready? Do you think I was ready to be hunted for crimes I didn't commit? And then hurled into the limelight by some perverse quirk of celebrity? The same quirk which could toss me back onto the scrap heap? But I – we – have an opportunity here. A messy one. It didn't come wrapped in fancy packaging with user instructions – it landed at our feet. And you're going to walk away because you're not ready?' He was speaking loudly. Rachel could hear Lizzie stirring upstairs.

'Euan.'

'It's okay. I'll go now. We've both said enough.'

'Where are you going?'

'Does it matter?' He moved to the door and stooped to pick up his helmet.

'It matters.' Rachel rose from the sofa, and they stood facing each other.

'Gulval and then, well, you know where to find me,' he

said, opening the door and closing it quietly behind him.

She walked to the window, watched him heave his bike off its stand and start to wheel it down the lane, before riding into the night.

63

Brandon

One day later, Meghan was sitting cross-legged on a chair in the interview room looking up at Brandon through thick, mascaraed eyelashes. She looked a cross between Princess Di in *that* interview and Sharon Stone in *that* film.

This should be fun.

'So, where shall we start, Ms Bacall,' Brandon said.

Meghan re-crossed her legs, and he couldn't help but glance. She noticed and smiled at him.

'Where do you want to start, Detective Inspector?'

He sat down, the table separating them. 'When did you decide to kill Sam Trenowden and then Benedict Arscott-Rowe?'

He was watching her closely – apart from lowering her eyes and trailing a finger across the tabletop, she betrayed nothing.

'I didn't decide to kill either Sam or Benedict. That was Ed's idea. He'd had enough of them. He could see I needed to use them to establish the contacts and my credentials. But Ed is a … passionate man. He's besotted with me.' She looked up at Brandon. 'He wanted them out of the way for both business and personal reasons.'

'And you didn't?'

Meghan gave a clipped laugh. 'No. I could handle them all. We were rubbing along wonderfully. If anything, Ed was the difficult one.'

Brandon stretched his forearms across the table. 'Ed sure is difficult, I don't disagree. Didn't say a word to me for days. And now, here's the thing, he won't shut up. He keeps on talking. And do you know who he keeps talking about?'

Meghan stretched out her own arms, her fingertips barely a centimetre from his own.

'Who?'

'You. He says you were behind the whole scheme. That he never wanted to get involved in the first place. He was happy working as an electrician – pays quite well, he said, with all the new money coming into town. But you got greedy. Sam first – he touted the idea of money laundering and then you got Ed involved with the shipments ... getting the canvases through the port at night and into the gallery. And then Benedict. He couldn't understand why you had to make a play for him. But I do.'

Meghan gave a little false laugh. 'Well, I wouldn't have credited Ed with such a vivid imagination. But tell me, DI Hammett, why do you think I made a play for your band member? The "Wildman of Penwith"?' She leant back, grazing his fingers with her nails as she did so.

'Because he was the main man. Sam was secondary; his gopher – calling in those shady guys that you spoke about. The mules who delivered the paintings to the collectors, the discreet galleries in London, and abroad. That's what I think.'

'But why would I kill ... have him killed? I had him where I wanted him?'

'I think you answered that question yesterday, Ms Bacall, in the car. You said he was getting reckless, wrecking a good business, one that you were ready to take over.'

'I said no such thing. And, Detective Inspector, I'm not so sure it is professional, or legal, to question suspects in a car.'

'I made myself clear at the time and we had a third party with us. So, everything above board, Ms Bacall.'

Brandon looked appealingly at Meghan's brief, Jemima

Rattison, an ardent defender of her sex.

'Morally and professionally this crosses a line. But it is ...' She paused for greater effect, exhaling through her long nose like a show pony. 'Legal. That isn't to say that any incriminating information *gained* via a casual conversation is admissible in court.'

Brandon gave a small nod of appreciation, which failed to penetrate Jemina's stony visage. He wasn't looking forward to meeting up with her in court.

'As you say, Ed is difficult. And he's proving that right now for you.' Brandon returned gratefully to the comparative warmth of Meghan.

She brushed aside an imaginary hair from her breast and looked Brandon in the eye. 'Ed is a jealous, passionate man. The woman he adores was having affairs with two of his business associates. Two men who were ripping him off – financially and emotionally. He had every motive to kill them. And not only that, but his DNA was also on their bodies. He's as guilty as hell.' She went to get up.

'Sit back down if you please.' Brandon rose to his feet as she settled back into her seat. 'Your dress and shoes were found at Benedict Arscott-Rowe's place. It's only a matter of time before we find your DNA on him too.'

Meghan smiled. 'We were lovers. I've admitted that. I'm sure you will find my DNA on some part of Benedict's poor, decaying body or his chipped objets d'art.'

Brandon smashed his fists down on the table. 'He was your lover, your friend. Have some respect.'.

Meghan looked pleased with his response, and it riled him even more. She treated him to her full beam smile. 'Jemina, I think we've finished our interview. If you need to ask me any further questions, then you know where to find me.'

There was a knock at the door. 'Boss, can I have a word?' Jo was looking like the proverbial cat that got the cream.

'Meeting adjourned, 10.50 am,' Brandon said, heading for the door.

'This came in ten minutes ago,' Jo said once they were outside. She handed Brandon an evidence bag with a mobile in it. 'It was found in a crack between rocks at Sennen Cove. I took the liberty of charging it and checking the number. It's Sam Trenowden's mobile.'

Brandon inhaled deeply before replying. 'Who brought it in?'

'A wild swimmer. She'd been looking for a hidey hole for her own mobile and purse and came across it. The pass code is 020485 – Julia gave me the number. It's his birthday.'

Brandon felt in his pockets for some plastic gloves. He pulled them on and tapped in the numbers. He went straight to Sam's messages. There were a couple to Julia, one to Nick and then a slew of WhatsApp messages with video attachments to Meghan.

'Woah,' Brandon said, his eyes widening.

'Can I have a look,' Jo was craning over his shoulder.

'Perhaps not,' Brandon said, giving her a quick glance. 'Sex tapes. Looks like Sam was threatening to release them online. Send them to H's wife. "Unless she got the fuck off his back and business".'

'A smoking gun?'

'A smoking something.' Brandon brushed a hand across his mouth. 'Don't recognise her mate. Not Benedict, or Sam. Could be one of her European conquests – H? Henri Chabrol?'

'This could be useful as more evidence that things weren't going well in her relationships with the two murder victims,'

346

Jo said.

Brandon nodded. 'Looks like they – and certainly, Sam – wanted her out of the way.' He paused. 'Benedict had suggested things weren't right with a 'woman', the last time Rachel saw him. The day before he died. Let's see what Meghan has to say about the videos and her less than happy message responses.'

Jo went to the door and called over the solicitor. 'An interesting item for disclosure,' she said, handing Rattison the mobile phone, with a still of the video on the screen and a threatening caption. Rattison's face flushed, but she regained her cool, and handed the phone back. 'Give me a few minutes to discuss this with my client,' she said, looking at Brandon, who nodded and held the door open for them.

'What!' they heard Meghan scream from inside the room.

She looked mighty cheesed off when they came back in.

'What kept you?'

'This,' Brandon said, placing the phone on the table just out of her reach. 'Sam Trenowden's mobile. It has some videos of you on it which he sent to you. Videos that you weren't especially happy with. He threatened to post them online if you didn't back off and "know your place". Send them to H's wife.'

Meghan lunged across the table. 'Give me the fucking phone.'

Brandon passed it to Jo. 'I take it that H is Henri Chabrol? Who shot the film?'

'Well, it wasn't his uncle Claude. Work it out!' Meghan was squirming in her chair.

Jemina Rattison also looked agitated. Meghan evidently hadn't told her about the videos. Probably thought she didn't need to.

'Sam was blackmailing you. And, possibly, so was Benedict. Did he take the footage on one of your business trips – was this the real reason you got rid of them? You got rid of them, before they could get rid of you?'

'Bullshit!' Meghan snarled. 'Empty threats. Henri's wife knew about us, anyway. And who cares about another sex tape on the web?'

'You did, Ms Bacall. It would have ruined you professionally. Both in your bone fide business and your art theft sideline. Just when things were going so well for you. Too well, obviously, for Sam and Benedict. They wanted you gone.'

'Your theory. That's all, Columbo.'

'I can check, of course, with Madam Chabrol whether she was as relaxed as you claim about your liaisons with her husband.'

Meghan's eyes flashed. 'The woman's a fool. Good luck getting a word of sense out of her.'

Brandon looked her in the eye. 'I'll leave that to our colleagues across the channel.'

'I suggest we adjourn now in light of this new ... development,' Jemina said, picking up her handbag and giving a small nod in Meghan's direction.

Meghan rose from her chair.

'No further questions this morning, Ms Rattison. But, Ms Bacall, if you feel it in your – *heart* – to make a confession at any time, you know where to find me. In the meantime, you are charged with carjacking, abduction, GBH and unlawful imprisonment, the unlawful possession of a firearm, and suspicion of aiding and abetting a murderer, laundering money, international art theft and being a party to drugs smuggling.'

Meghan swayed on her kitten heels as the full force of the charges hit her.

Yet she punched back. 'Would you like to take into consideration travelling without a seat belt? And assisting an elderly, demented art forger?'

Woah. She was some broad, but she wasn't going to get away with this. 'I have no idea what you're talking about. If you're ready, DC Bland here will escort you back down to the cells. Interview terminated. 11.12 am.'

He watched her sashay out of the room, Stew admiring the view from a few steps behind.

The list of charges and allegations he'd read out to her were damning, but he didn't expect her to admit them without a fight. As far as giving the orders to take out Sam and Benedict? To be fair, it was Ed's word against hers. There could well have been an element of *crime passionnel*. But, of course, their deaths were mighty convenient for Meghan. You might say crucial for a ruthless operator, given the new evidence. Maybe, one day, when those kitten heels clicked the cobbled streets of Penzance again, she would take the time to look him up and confess. Maybe not.

'Happy?' Jo said, as he joined her outside the room.

'Ninety-five per cent. But that's happy enough for me.'

'I guess she didn't confess to her part in Trenowden's and Arscott-Rowe's murders?'

'She was never going to do that. And I'm not sure it matters. Meghan is twice the person Ed is, so if he gets life for doing her dirty work, well, more fool him. And he wasn't very nice, was he?'

'Do you have a soft spot for our femme fatale?'

'No, but can't help having a sneaking admiration.' He looked away.

Jo took her cue to change the subject. 'Looks like today is one of those days for solving crimes, Boss. Ed's admitted tampering with the glitter ball to frighten Benedict – put pressure on him to drop the drugs business. He tried to match the lettering in his note with the hate mail Conor Robson had been sending him. Those letters you found at Benedict's.'

'It's nice to know we're doing our jobs!'

'I've got some other news on Euan Tremayne.'

Brandon's face fell. 'Do you want to spoil my day?'

Jo laughed. 'The opposite, Brandon.'

'What's he up to now?'

'He's off to London. Joining a new, *on trend* arts movement: Neo Something.'

Brandon took a step towards her, his head cocked. 'Neo Nothing?'

Jo laughed. 'Neo Con ... Neo Constructivism – if I have to be precise!'

'It's your job to be precise,' Brandon said, smiling softly. 'And you usually do a damn fine job of it.'

Jo reddened. 'Any way, he's been invited to work on a project at Shoreditch Studios – run by Bridget Sergeant. Have you heard of her?'

Brandon rubbed his chin. 'Of course. But ... why? How do you know all this?'

Jo adjusted the strap on her bag. 'I was just following up a few things with Tremayne, ticking the paperwork boxes, getting addresses, etc, and it came out. He didn't volunteer it, but I am a DS.'

'Indeed.' Brandon's smile widened. 'Well, well.'

'I believe he's bequeathing his two sculptures – Brexitannia and The Average-Size Merperson – to the town, to be displayed at The Arthouse.'

'There's always a downside.'

'Brandon!'

'This is turning out to be some day, eh, Jo?'

'Did anyone admit to planting that canvas at The Hall on the day of Sam Trenowden's murder, by the way?' Jo said, looking directly at him.

'That remains a mystery. Maybe the ghost of Lawrence Matthews?' Brandon turned his gaze to the station door. 'Or maybe it was a calling card for Rachel?'

'But from whom?' Jo was still looking at him. Looking at him as if he had all the answers.

'That's the million-dollar question, Jo.' He tapped her shoulder, signalling an end to the subject.

'We should go for a drink. Celebrate our success?' Jo said, adding quickly, 'If you've got time?'

He treated her to a long, thoughtful gaze. 'Good idea. I'd like that.'

'Great,' Jo said, glancing down and starting to open her bag.

He turned his attention back to the blank canvas – remembered how it had triggered the art lessons at his place. Put things in motion. Canvases popping up all over the place. Brandon thought of what Meghan had said about Lizzie and the forgeries and decided some cases were best left unsolved.

64

Rachel

'Are you absolutely sure you want to move in with Lizzie?' Julia's brow was furrowed, her hands clasped between her legs.

'Julia, please don't twist my arm.' Rachel was sitting on the opposite side of the kitchen table, mirroring her. 'She took quite a hit from the She Wolf.'

'And so did you!'

'But she was fragile beforehand.'

'And so were you.'

'And she's seventy-five.'

'And like aged beef, gets better by the day.'

'Thanks, Julia. I don't want to leave your lovely home. But I must.'

Julia stretched out a hand and Rachel took it. 'Now, don't make me cry. Seriously, it won't be so bad. She has what the Americans call "pleasant dementia" ... I think. She isn't harming anyone, but she forgets stuff. Forgets to eat, forgets to lock up, forgets to clean.'

'We could find a good care home for her?'

'I couldn't do that. It would destroy her. She is too much her own person to kowtow to a regime and its enforcers.'

Julia narrowed her eyes. 'Yes, I can see that. You Matthews are a determined bunch! You'll still come here to paint?' Julia let go of her hand and picked up the cafetiere.

'Maybe, sometimes. But I have Seabird Cottage and ...'

'And?'

'Brandon said a while back that I could use his attic as a studio. It's got great light and space.'

Julia smiled. 'Snog, marry or paint in an attic?'

Rachel burst out laughing. 'Possibly!'

'Which one?'

Rachel looked up through her fringe. 'Do I have to choose?'

'That's my girl.'

'I could ask Brandon to pose naked for me.' Rachel had a mischievous look on her face.

'Rachel!' Julia rested her chin on her hands and studied her. 'So, not missing Euan then?'

Rachel looked down, brushed aside some crumbs left from lunch. 'He hasn't gone yet. But I think he will be in London before Sam and Benedict's funerals.'

'All three leaving at the same time. Something else has gone too, hasn't it?' She met Rachel's eye.

'You're right. Something else has gone. That day when Euan met me at Porthchapel Cove, there was an imperceptible shift – from passion, to grief, to acceptance. I'm not sure if we can ever regain the passion.'

'Does he feel the same?'

Rachel looked away and shrunk back in her chair. 'We had a bit of a lover's tiff yesterday.' She paused and then fell forward, head bowed, arms on the table. 'I'm not a mind-reader, but I sense he might, although he may not be willing to admit it to himself.'

'That sounds a bit deep?'

'Certainly, we need some space. Bridget Sargent may have come along at exactly the right time.'

'She's bound to fancy him – she's notorious.'

'So what?' Rachel looked up sharply.

'You mean that?' Julia was watching her closely.

'Euan is going to Shoreditch Studios, not a monastery.'

'So, a complete break.'

Rachel sighed. 'I think so. He doesn't need any ties right now.'

'And nor do you?'

Rachel scraped up the crumbs and got up to empty them in the bin. Sitting back down, she said: 'He asked me to go with him. Suggested – no more than suggested – that we start a family. It just didn't occur to him that this wasn't the right time. After all that has happened. But more than that – how could I, we, ever replace Oliver?'

Julia leaned in. 'Did you see this coming?'

'Not really. Certainly not now. But, I suppose, the Shoreditch invitation triggered it. A bit like soldiers marrying or declaring their love before going off to war.'

'Bridget's not that bad!' Julia laughed. 'But, yes, I can see he was being a touch insensitive – maybe he couldn't help himself.'

'Maybe.'

Rachel looked at her phone as it beeped a text. 'Sorry. E.x.' She put it aside. 'So much has happened in so short a time – some truly awful things, but so much good, too. We've survived. I've got some sort of life back. I'm just not ready to … re-enter the battlefield.' She looked away.

'That makes the two of us.' Julia pushed her hair behind her ears. 'It may be selfish of me to say this, but I'm glad you're not going back to London.'

Rachel studied the dregs in her mug, as if reading the leaves. 'Euan said that I was pulling away from him and a great opportunity. The fulfilment of a dream. But maybe I don't share his fairy tale view of life. Maybe I'm not running away – this is where I want to be. Where I belong?'

The companionable silence which followed was broken by a flock of seagulls squawking like they were having a domestic.

'Where is that bottle of *Screaming Eagle* when you need it?' Julia said, smiling.

'It has been a voice of reason throughout all this.' Rachel gave a wry smile and swirled the remnants in her mug. 'I've got Lizzie, The Arthouse, my painting. I've got a lot to keep me busy ... and happy in Penzance.'

'And you've got me. Don't forget me.'

'How could I ever. Or Nick.' She could hear him on his Xbox upstairs, laughing every now and again with an online friend, probably Jack.

'He'll be calling down asking what's for supper in a minute,' Julia said, wiping away a tear.

'Stroganoff?' Rachel said, and they both smiled.

65

Rachel

'You're coming to live here?' Lizzie put down her paint brush and turned to Rachel.

'Well, if you'll have me for a short while.' Rachel placed a small holdall on the studio floor.

'What, has Julia slung you out because you nicked her boyfriend?'

'No, Mum. I just thought you might like me around a bit, to sort the house and Dad's paintings … now that Meghan's gone.'

'That witch! That scarlet woman! Terrorist!'

'Perhaps not a terrorist – she may need to work on that routine.'

'You know what I mean, Rachel. Scared me and Piers out of our wits. She should hang for this. I'd strangle her with my bare hands – hang her with my cow bell strap! She's ruined that for me now …' Lizzie began to sniffle, and Rachel put an arm around her.

'They've already got the *To Let* signs up at NewlynWave, she won't be back for a very long time.'

'Humph. Do you know?'

'What?' Rachel had spied a new portrait on the easel in the corner.

'She had the cheek to accuse me of forging Larry's paintings.'

She'd regained Rachel's attention.

'Well, Piers isn't having any of it. He's taken the new paintings to London to an even more established Lawrence Matthews expert – and a good friend of his. He is confident we should have accreditation and provenance within days.'

Lizzie was looking at her with serious intent. 'They're worth a lot of money, Rachel.'

'I can imagine.'

'We could use it to do this place up – restore the studio. Maybe extend? We might need to if you're coming to live here.'

'The spare room will do for now, Mum. But it would be good to get some work done here.'

'I'd paint the place myself,' Lizzie said. Rachel remembered them all painting the walls when they'd first moved in; Rachel barely five, but already using a roller and cutting in around the skirting boards. 'But I have so much real art I want to do right now.'

And so have I, thought Rachel.

'I wanted to show you something, darling,' Lizzie said, her tone softening. She was looking at the painting in the corner, the one that had been waiting patiently for its introduction since Rachel arrived.

Lizzie walked over and stood before it, her arms folded, exuding quiet pleasure and pride. 'I've been working on it for some time. Since the night of the storm when … when it got damaged.'

'I can see,' Rachel said. Her portrait had been transformed; the red gash gone. The face was her face but prettier, more assured. Rachel's features had emerged through the abstract; the jagged edges smoothed, the harsh rings and lines softened, the dark bruising blended to subtle shade. The gold sunburst she'd used in Oliver's painting was here too, creating a radiant light, highlighting the eyes, the cheekbones, the lips.

'What do you think, Rachel?'

'I don't think you've caught my likeness, but possibly my *joie de vivre*!'

'Rachel! You like it?'

'Of course. It's terrifically flattering. I'll buy it.'

'It's a gift. It's taken me a long time to create this. I wanted to make it special. Abstract isn't really you.'

'No – at least not anymore. You know, it has the same ethereal, dreamlike quality as the portrait you did of Oliver – the twinning of two styles, two worlds. I must bring that back from The Hall.'

Lizzie gave her a candid look; one she hadn't seen for years. 'I painted it as a companion piece. I hoped you'd like it.'

'It's beautiful. Thank you, Mum.'

'He calls to me across dreams, you know.'

Rachel felt a surge of empathy and recognition. 'Me too. He calls to me too. But the sad yearning has gone. It's like he's just saying hi, from time to time.'

'Yes. Maybe even "goodbye"?'

They looked at each other, sharing a moment of complete understanding.

'Shall I make up your bed in the spare room?' Lizzie asked.

'That would be good. I'm just leaving my things here for now. I need to go and see someone.'

Lizzie gave her a knowing, mother look. 'That copper friend of yours? The one with the wild daughter?'

Rachel smiled. 'Chelsea's not wild – she's just a teen testing the water.'

'Just teasing, darling. And weren't we all a little wild in our youth?'

And second youth.

'Brandon was so good to me the other day. Piers adores him. Send him my love.'

'Will do, Mum. Will certainly do.'

66

Brandon

Chelsea opened the door just as Brandon was putting his key in the lock. She had a cheeky grin on her face.

'What are you looking so chirpy about?'

'We've got a visitor.' Chelsea nodded at the stairs.

'Upstairs?'

Chelsea tugged his arm. 'Yes. Right at the top of the stairs!'

'Can I just take off my coat, young lady?'

'No!'

Chelsea got behind him and started to push him towards the stairs.

'Alright, already,' Brandon said, foot on the first step, ready to climb.

When he reached the top, he stood before the attic door, hesitant to open it.

'There's not a lion in there – at least not one with a fur coat.' Chelsea looped her arm around his back and opened the door, pushing it wide.

Rachel stood in a beam of light by the velux window, her back to an easel.

He didn't know what to say. 'You're here. I, well … and painting?'

Did that sound rude? Cold?

Rachel had a paintbrush in her hand, which she held in front of her like a microphone. 'I've been showing Chelsea some techniques.'

'Some techniques,' he echoed, a small smile beginning to form.

'Yes.'

Chelsea was in the middle of the two of them, twisting around from one to the other. 'I told Rachel.'

'Miss Matthews,' corrected Brandon.

'Rachel,' continued Chelsea, 'About that tool, Peter Burton. He was the dork who sent those photos to the head – the ones with Damien!'

'What?'

First, I've heard of this.

'He was snooping around spying on Damien and took the photos of him and Rachel at the Morrab Library. Got her the sack! So, I can call Miss Matthews Rachel now. She's no longer a teacher. Duh!'

Chelsea's eyes flamed with indignation. 'Peter's had it in for Rachel, ever since she dissed him about the seal. Thinks he's a private eye now.'

Rachel pulled an incredulous face and shrugged.

'Chelsea, I think we've heard enough.'

'I know when I'm not wanted,' Chelsea said, flicking her nose with her finger and affecting a mock haughty walk out of the door.

Brandon moved towards the centre of the room, took off his coat and flung it on the leather armchair. 'So, not only have you been driving recklessly, with broken seatbelts, and violently apprehending a felon, you've been sacked from your job?'

'Yes.' Rachel was smiling broadly.

'I can see you have no remorse, Miss Matthews.'

'Very little. And you can call me Rachel now that I'm a civilian again.'

'And how did you get into my attic. Breaking and entering?'

'I had an accomplice. She let me in. And I didn't think you'd mind.'

'And why's that?' He was in front of her now, could see the blush forming on her cheeks.

'I had a feeling.' She looked down. 'And, you did say – about a hundred years ago – that I could come here and paint when I was ready.'

She turned round to the canvas Chelsea had been working on.

'I did say that. And I meant it.'

He picked up one of the brushes in the jug of water on the side table.

'Here,' he said, dipping his brush into a pot of red paint, his arm circling her. 'I don't think you've got this brush stroke quite right. Let me show you.' He dabbed at the painting unconvincingly. She didn't move as his body glanced hers.

Rachel turned to face him and took the brush from his hand. 'I think you'd make a lousy teacher, Detective Inspector. And an even worse painter.'

'Maybe not as lousy as you would make a copper.'

They looked at each other for what seemed a very long time.

'You'll make a great painter, though,' he said eventually. 'With a little support and the right studio. One with a great sea view.'

'How is that sea doing?' Rachel said, looking over at the window.

'Splashing around – doing its usual thing. No mystery there.' Brandon was grinning at her. 'Let's go investigate,' he said, resting his hand on the small of her back, and steering her back into the light.

The End

Acknowledgements

I must go back in time to give credit to all the people and places which have contributed to *Dark Arts* – the prequel to *Fairest Creatures*. Many of the characters in this book appear in Fairest Creatures, which was the first to be published in my DI Brandon Hammett series.

A year after my sister Yvonne and I bought a place together in Penzance I started an MA in Creative Writing (Crime Fiction) at the University of East Anglia. It was Yvonne who tipped me off about a Crime Fiction evening hosted by *The Times* in London in 2017 and where Henry Sutton, the director of the course, gave a presentation. I applied and was delighted to be accepted into what turned out to be an extremely talented and collaborative cohort. Their input, together with Henry's fellow professors Tom Benn, Nathan Ashman and William Ryan, helped me craft this book.

It has been redrafted several times since I graduated in 2019, but the story is essentially the same: a close-knit arts community in the historic seaside town of Penzance, struggling with their own demons, while under attack from dark and dangerous players. Special thanks to Antony Dunford, my fellow UEA cohort student, who read one of the recent drafts and gave much constructive criticism, focusing on police procedural. My detective Brandon Hammett doesn't always follow the rules religiously. I have taken him to task ... but please forgive his maverick moments.

I'd also like to thank my many friends in Penzance – the artists, especially Janine Wing, who creates the cover artwork, the writers, poets, musicians, librarians, booksellers and the local community, who have inspired and encouraged me. Penzance is a veritable character too and won my heart the day I drove into town and was welcomed by the majestic sweep of Mount Bay.

I hope you enjoy Dark Arts. It won't be so long before the third in the series is published. It's written, and waiting in the wings, like the phantom of The Acorn Theatre ...